Tales of Sin & Fury

Troublemakers

By the same author:
Tales of Sin & Fury Part 1: The Beach, publ. Matador 2013

Each novel in the *Tales of Sin & Fury* saga stands alone and also forms part of a web of events which links the characters.

For help and advice on the long and arduous journey bringing this text to publication, the author thanks AD and all the members of her writing group; also friends JG, SJ, DS, MW and TW who read earlier versions and gave valuable feedback. For initiation into the difficult art of fiction-writing, she is very grateful to YG and SP; also to SF and RWC for years of patiently listening to fragments, giving wise comments and crucial encouragement. For stoically re-reading versions of the whole text and generously giving frank and perceptive responses she is deeply indebted to her friend HJA. Finally, she thanks her dear family who will never read it but who put up with her preoccupation and papers everywhere; they know who they are.

Acknowledgements
Excerpt from 'Put it on the Ground' from *The Little Red Songbook*, publ. Industrial Workers of the World, Philadelphia 2005 (first publ. 1909), pp. 24-25; with thanks.

Tales of Sin & Fury

Troublemakers

SONIA PAIGE

Published in Great Britain by
Just Press
www.justpress.co.uk

ISBN: 978-1-907352-08-9

British Library Cataloguing in Publication Data
A catalogue record for this book is available from the British Library

Just Press offers books, DVDs, art works and
lectures/exhibitions that provide a platform for exchange
between different generations and interests. In areas
including history, religion, theature, health, politics,
art, poetry and fiction, we honour unsung aspects of
human experience and celebrate the unorthodox.

Printed and bound by Advantage Digital Print, Dorchester
sales@advantagedigitalprint.com

Page design and typesetting by Catherine Weld
www.catherineweld.com

To the people whose lives inspired these stories

'It is not only what is likely which happens'
Jasper Griffin, *The Odyssey*

Contents

Prologue

Thursday 3rd May 1979 10.30pm

'He moves in mysterious ways,' said Ren.

'Is that with a capital 'H'?' asked Alex. She drained her beer and banged it down on the pub table where the six of them were sitting.

'If Thatcher gets in tonight,' said Taffy, 'it could be He's lost the plot altogether. Maybe letting the other guy take over.' He laughed at his own joke with the careless enthusiasm of someone who has followed two spliffs with three pints of real ale, the speciality of the Hackney pub. Election night seemed a good time to drown any potential sorrows in advance. His laugh ended with some heavy coughing.

'Let's bloody hope not,' said Alex. 'The milk-snatcher. She's shown her colours already. She could make short work of the welfare state and anything else half good that we've been struggling to defend.'

'Time, gentlemen, please!' the barman's voice sang out over the sea of chatter, and he tapped a glass several times with a spoon.

'Couldna' be all bad. She might make people finally sit up and fight back,' Duncan said.

'In your dreams,' said Alex. 'It never works like that. People just get more ground down, and look for someone to blame – usually in the wrong places.'

1

A shout came from the bar: 'You pushing in?'

They turned round.

'This gentleman was here first,' said the barman.

'"This gentleman"? He's a fucking wog!' The speaker standing at the bar was a burly white guy in a fine-checked shirt and a zip-up cardigan with horizontal stripes.

'Watch your tongue, brother.' The youngish black man a few feet away turned with a weary expression and dusted off the sleeve of his jacket.

'You gonna make me?' the man's speech was slurred. 'I've got a couple of mates over there, wanna take us on? We don't want your sort here.'

'And *we* don't want *your* sort!' Alex's voice cut in.

'Take it easy, mate,' the barman told the man.

There was a scraping of chairs and muttering as the friends got up from their table and headed for the bar. Taffy at the front was the loudest: 'Shut your face, racist git!' He stumbled towards the man, who fended him off. A copy of *National Front News* fell from the counter to the ground.

'Who spoke to you, you big girl's blouse?' the man snarled as he aimed a blow at Taffy, who swerved and then fell forward. His weight unbalanced the man who went over, cracking his head on the bar. Taffy landed on top of him. The barman rang the police.

'Thanks for your trouble,' said the black man, Frank, who had joined Duncan and Ren at the table. 'But you shouldn't have bothered, right? It happens all the time. And *they* won't take no notice, they never do.' He jerked his head towards the police who were at the door preparing to take Taffy away. Brenda in her Afghan coat could be seen gesticulating at them, with Ute beside her.

'If Reuben were here,' said Ren, looking at the door, 'he would be singing that song. David Bowie. About the' – she sang – '"lawman beating up the wrong guy…"'

Duncan's heavy features fell into a scowl. 'Never knew what Reuben saw in him.'

Alex came back to the table: 'I got names of two people who'll come forward as witnesses. Someone called Anthea Moor, that fat chick with frizzy red hair sitting with that lot by the wall. And a wishy-washy blonde woman in the back…' she consulted the piece of paper in her hand, '… Corinne Jenkins, she's called. Seems a bit out to lunch, but they're both prepared to testify that Taffy didn't hit the bloke. I've got their phone contacts.'

'And there's no' anyone else brave enough to step up?' Duncan's face registered disgust.

'The kindness of strangers,' said Ren.

The white man was sitting at the bar with a fresh drink. He ostentatiously held a handkerchief to the side of his head while he enjoyed the spectacle of Taffy's arrest.

'That'll learn him to stick his nose in,' he jeered towards the friends at the table.

Alex didn't look at him, but pronounced the word 'Nazi!' in a loud voice directed to the pub at large.

'Lefty scum,' the man responded. 'We'll soon be rid of the likes of you. You and the niggers and pakis bringing the country down. Tories get in tonight, they'll sort you out. Where are you lot gonna be in ten years' time?'

'It's a good question,' said Ren, as Ute came back to the table now that the police had gone.

'We got the coppers' numbers,' said Brenda, sitting down next to her. 'He'll be up in court tomorrow.'

'He'll get out on bail,' said Ren. 'But if this is the way things are going, it's a good question: where will we all be in ten years' time?'

1

Chapter One

Wednesday 19th December 1990 11am

I'm not going to mess this up. I'm not going to mess this up.

I always say that and what good does it do?

We're only leafletting after all. It's like old times. Even if it's a weird leaflet.

Huddling with the others on the pavement I can see lights and human shapes through the frosted glass windows of the pub doors. I can hear ragged sounds of voices chattering in pre-Christmas festivities. The occasional braying of drink-fuelled laughter. A waft of tobacco smoke.

My housemate Vivienne calls to me, 'Ant, ready to go?'

I nod. She gets out a piece of paper and starts reading aloud:

'In this pub the barman bites the barmaids' buttocks.' This is the text of our A5 leaflet. I can just hear her above the late morning traffic going up Stoke Newington High Street. It's pinching cold, but she has no hat over her green hair, which she dyed with Crazy Colour a few weeks ago. Wish I could dye mine. I was born with it ginger and frizzy. There's nothing I can do about it.

I put my hand into my coat pocket and feel the tiny fragment of human bone. The little bone I brought back from Crete. Most of it is smooth, with one jagged end. It's come a long way from that ancient tomb where I found it.

But it feels happy to be here. I'm always nervous at this point, and it reassures me.

Vivienne raises her voice and carries on reading the leaflet: *'Women working here have been sexually harassed by management. One young woman when she was hired was told by the manager, "If you break three glasses, I'll bite your bum." She thought it was an attempt at a joke, but four weeks later after she had broken two wine glasses and a beer glass, she was standing on a stool refilling one of the high bottles when he came up and bit her on the buttock…'*

Like I said, it's not a normal leaflet.

That really happened. The barmaid involved is standing at the back of the group, a stripey bobble cap pulled down over her eyes to hide her face. She's a friend of Vivienne's. The rest of us are here to support her. We all live locally. There's a teacher in her late thirties, a cleaner, a student and a younger barmaid from another pub. Vivienne and me are the oldest. Hitting our forties but none the wiser.

So here we are on another demo. My pulse is racing like it always did with direct actions. That hasn't changed. Part of me wants to sink into the ground, to escape all those eyes that will turn on us once we get inside.

The mist of Vivienne's breath hangs in the air as she reads the rest: *'…bit her on the buttock, hard enough to hurt. When she complained he threatened to fire her. DO YOU WANT TO SUPPORT A PLACE LIKE THIS? TAKE YOUR CUSTOM ELSEWHERE!'* Vivienne stops reading. 'Before we go in, is everyone OK with that?'

We mumble agreement, and turn when we hear a slow handclap. A young man sitting in a sleeping bag on the pavement outside the next-door shop window evidently likes our leaflet too. Just then a man in a worn overcoat shuffles out of the door coughing, and while it is open we troop in, taking off our gloves. I stuff mine in my coat pockets. Vivienne gives us a small pile of leaflets each.

Now, quick. We need to get the leaflets distributed among the customers before that manager stops us and throws us out. Spread out. I follow Vivienne straight down inside the pub, where she goes up to a woman with sharp features and dark curly hair sitting at a table with a black guy in a woolly hat. They take a leaflet each and the woman starts to read it aloud: '"*In this pub the barman bites the barmaids' buttocks…*"' Vivienne gives some to a group of white lads at the next door table. They start laughing. As I walk past, they call out, 'Here, Ginge, I'll bite yours if you like.'

Ginger. That's me. I've got called that since I was a kid. At least they didn't call me fatty. I half turn towards them. They've got hard eyes and they're taunting me with their guffaws. One of them, in a Gap T-shirt, balances on the back legs of his chair in a parody of confidence.

Mercifully I think of a reply: 'That could be hard with your mouth up your arse.' But as I turn away to sweep proudly on into the back of the pub, I catch my foot on something. Fuck. It's the stool of the guy with the woolly hat on the next table. Too late, my weight goes over.

Crash. I fall towards the lads' table, try to grab it and down it comes. Ash tray skids, glasses fall and break, peanuts scatter. The table hits the guy leaning back in his chair. Crash he goes over backwards. My leaflets go flying.

Now the lads have suddenly gone quiet. In fact everything's gone quiet. And I have a close-up view of the tiled floor with debris scattered all around.

So much for not messing this up. Wherever I go I seem to create a scene.

Then the noise starts again. Somewhere I can hear the lads mouthing off: 'Clumsy cow', 'Have a good trip?', 'Gobby bitch'.

Things are a blur as someone helps me up. It's the woman with the dark curly hair. 'Good shot!' she says. I'm vaguely aware that the others are still leafletting around the pub as she and her friend lead me outside. I must have created a diversion. The woman asks me, 'You all right?'

I stand on the pavement and try to shake beer and cigarette ash off my coat. 'This always has to happen to me,' I say. My hands and lower arms hurt, they hit the ground first. I dust them off and pull out my gloves. Check the bone's still there. Good. It's so hard it's like a fossil.

'Break a few glasses, serve them right,' says the woman. 'At least you shut those blokes up.'

I notice some people coming out of the pub holding our leaflet, as the guy in the woolly hat turns to her and kisses her on the cheek. 'You know, I appreciate meeting you,' he says.

Then a strange thing happens. He turns to me and says, 'What you did in there saved my life. You are an angel sent by God.' And he turns and walks off with a jaunty step up Stoke Newington High Street and round the corner into Church Street.

What's that about? I raise my eyebrows and look at the woman with the pointy nose and the curly hair. Perhaps she can explain. She just shrugs. 'It's a long story.' She gives me a kind of perfunctory smile and crosses the road through a gap in the traffic.

I just stand there, wondering. We move through mysteries.

He called me an angel. After I fell flat on my face.

I feel the bone. Some archaeologist I am. An imperfect archaeologist. We're meant to be interested in bones. But my friends tell me that my interest is more like a preoccupation. Or an obsession.

Wednesday 18th December 1990 11pm
Things are quiet at this time on a Wednesday night in Cazenove Road. Not many drunks wandering home from

the pubs. And they're closed, those makeshift places of prayer – a synagogue and a mosque – that have carved out space for themselves by taking over houses in this run-down street. Early on a Friday evening you see people streaming down the pavements: Moslem men in their long white robes, Hasidic Jews in their black coats and wide fur-rimmed hats. They cross paths, heading in different directions, each to their own version of the divine. As far as I know, there's never been a fight between them, or any kind of incident. Unlike the bloody theatre of conflict staged by the West in the Middle East. Wars seem to be started by governments, not people.

It looks like a certain George H.W. Bush is about to start another.

I can hear a police siren in the distance. Luckily we're too far north for the clubs, the drugs and shootings and knifings that happen down near Amhurst Road. A day later we'll be walking past the police cordons, and reading about them in the *Hackney Gazette*. Our part of Stoke Newington, up towards Stamford Hill, is less intense. When it's not flooded with worshippers, or children going to one of the schools, the tall houses rest quietly with their memories of better days. Sitting back from the road, they look aloof and anonymous.

Cazenove Road. Apparently Cazenove is the name of a bank founded in Victorian times with the employees owning 95% of the shares. I don't know if that's what our road's named after. The drivers that speed along it under the trees to cut from Stoke Newington High Street to Clapton probably don't even know what it's called.

Morton is reading aloud to me from a lecture he's writing. In his accent, his childhood in New York City is overlaid by years of living in London. '... *I can only refer in passing to the long global history of the portmanteau story – inset or nested yarns – multiple tales of many hues harnessed together to pull one creative chariot.'* He stops and looks at me.

Horses pulling a chariot, I like that. I can see it in my mind's eye: different-coloured horses kicking up the turf and tossing their manes as they canter along, pulling together to carry a racy narrative. Then before I can do anything, they morph into the horsemen of the apocalypse: war, famine, disease and death. Skulls grinning at the horrors inflicted by a government that doesn't care about human beings, as *Spitting Image* portrayed it a few years ago – their comment on the Thatcher years. Now over, but so recently over that we are still reeling. A decade of attacks by government on the services, institutions and rights that make a society human. And though she has gone, the Tories are still in power. We are living in dark days.

I try to put her out of my mind, and look at the fragment of bone resting in my open palm as I sit cross-legged on our bedroom floor. I put it down and stare at it. It blends into the cream-painted floorboards. It's hard like ceramic but its texture is organic – with irregularities, fibres, and a jagged end. Like something alive that got frozen at a moment in time. A messenger from another age. If only it could reassure me that I'm hearing it right. All archaeologists try to read ancient remains, but I'm trying to hear as well.

And what I hear is bothering me. Ever since I picked up the little fragments at that tomb in Crete, I feel that the bones want to warn me. This one in particular. I hold it, shut my eyes, and I get a picture of a Greek hillside covered with huge boulders. And a sense of danger. As if it's telling me not to go back.

I keep getting scary dreams.

It's my own fault. I insisted on bringing the bones home.

Dr. Scheiner from the Archaeology Department thinks I'm too concerned with the bones. My friends think I'm going crazy. But they can't hear what I can hear.

Morton is sitting at the small table on the other side of

the bedroom with his nose in his papers. The lecture he's preparing is on Homer and story-telling, and his neat italics are flowing evenly across the page. He's smiling, oblivious to the mess around him – my books and clothes strewn over the floor.

He stops to scratch his arm. So much for that flea treatment Bert put on the dog.

Over his shoulder he asks, 'Can I read you some more?'

I put the bone in my pyjama pocket and pick my way over to the table: 'How about coming to bed?'

'One second, Anthea, my angel. Let me just finish this paragraph.'

He always calls me 'angel' when he wants to fob me off. And he calls me 'Anthea', when he's put out. Otherwise it's 'Ant', like everyone calls me. His face, which is usually smooth and boyish, has a little frown of concentration.

I keep trying: 'How's it going?'

'Not bad.' He finishes a sentence, pauses, then puts the cap on his pen and looks up. 'OK. So would you like to hear a bit more?'

I wriggle under the duvet, hands and lower arms and knees still sore from falling in the pub this morning. He brings his pen and papers over to sit on the side of the bed: 'This is from near the beginning too.'

I close my hand around the little bone and try to assemble my brain as he reads out loud: *'In a long tradition of multiple stories nested together, the best known example in the West is of course the* 1001 Nights, *or* Arabian Nights. *Another monumental example is* Monkey, *popularized in the 1970s by a cult* TV *series made in Hong Kong.'*

I interrupt: 'Some of the audience may have seen the *Monkey* programmes.'

'Yes?'

'You could mention that. Help them link what you're saying to their own experience.'

'OK.' Morton makes some notes. 'OK…'. He starts his sentence again: *'Another monumental example is* Monkey, *popularized in the 1970s by a cult* TV *series made in Hong Kong – which some of you may have seen. It is a collection of stories about a monkey and other magical creatures who go on a quest and have adventures. Its origin lies further east, but – like the* 1001 Nights *– this cycle of fantastic legends reached its present form during the first millennium* AD. *Drawing together folklore, social satire, allegory, history, religion and poetry, it combines the sublime with the ridiculous. What might seem a monolithic narrative is in fact a melding of many different parts. This parallels a view of community or society as a collective weaving together of diverse human beings rather than their subservience to a monochrome centralized authority. '*

He looks up and twiddles his Parker pen between his skinny fingers. 'What d'you think?'

I like it. 'But you can't push the parallel between literature and society too far, can you?'

'Author. Authority,' he replies. 'It's the same word. The same vision of a world of centralized power and individualism rather than a diffuse and multivocal creativity.'

I can't argue with him. He always has an answer.

He smiles: 'OK, that's Homer put to bed for the night, now to put us to bed.'

He places his pen and papers back neatly on the table, then takes off his jeans and climbs under the duvet. He nuzzles into my hair and kisses me on the ear. As he puts his arm round me, he feels for my hand, and finds it tightly clasped around the bone.

'Let it go, hon,' he says. 'It's bedtime. You might need two hands for what I had in mind.'

I open my fist; he takes the bone in his fingers and holds it up. 'Hello, bone,' he says. 'What seems to be the problem?' He puts it to his ear. 'See, I can hear it too! It says it's actually complaining about the weather.' He perches the tiny thing in his hand and does a high-pitched ventriloquist voice: 'It's too cold. She should never have brought us here. I blame that hashcake hangover. We don't like this snow. Bone go home...'

He's trying to make light of things. He means well, but it doesn't help. I tell him there is snow in Crete, on the mountaintops, so it's got nothing to complain about. He just laughs. He tells me to put the bone back in its box with the others and forget about it.

I put it down next to my bedside. I don't want it too far away.

Morton's writing has left him in lovey-dovey mood. We cuddle and my pyjamas come off and we make love. We lie there afterwards, like butter and flour melted into one smooth sweet paste, with slow breaths and foolish smiles.

And then I want more. It's like with food, once I get going I have a big appetite.

There's a story in one of the first fragments of Greek literature about the prophet Teiresias. He watches some snakes mating and then Zeus and his wife Hera ask him to settle an argument as to whether men or women enjoy sex more. He replies: 'Of ten parts a man enjoys only one, but a woman's senses enjoy all ten.' As a punishment Hera strikes him blind, but Zeus makes him a prophet and he becomes the blind seer of later Greek literature.

I've often wondered, why did Hera do that? You'd think she'd take what Teiresias said as a compliment. You'd think women getting more out of sex would be something for her to celebrate.

Anyway, perhaps his pronouncement about sex was true. Women can be multi-orgasmic and men can't always come back so many times for more. It's not a problem with me and Morton. When he's had enough he uses his finger. Or his thumb. To pleasure me. That's a nice word. Pleasure.

That's what it's all about.

Tonight he uses his thumb. I'm very slow getting there sometimes on the third and fourth times. A delicious meandering journey. He's getting bored and he starts teasing me about how long I'm taking. He starts pulling faces, rolling his eyes, pretending to yawn. I start giggling at the same time as the excitement is catching my breath. He's pretending to whistle to while away the time while his thumb is turning inside me. I can't stop laughing. I can feel the orgasm coming, like a tidal wave gathering in my body, rolling through the night over the dark surface of an empty sea, building power as it travels. And at the same time I'm creasing up at the faces he's pulling. He mimes stifling a yawn with the hand that isn't occupied. I'm still shaking with laughter as the wave breaks and the tide sweeps through; the orgasm and the laughter kind of break on the beach all at once, and I'm chucked over and over and tossed around in glorious chaos like a surfer who's fallen off the board and gets hurled onto the sand in disarray.

Morton disentangles himself and is asleep in seconds. I lie there and find it impossible to sleep with my body so expanded and unfurled. I look at the window, the brown curtain with some whispers of light from the sleeping city creeping round its edges. I try to understand what's happening about Greece and the bones and why I'm so scared. I try to look at everything that has happened from the beginning. I drift asleep with it on my mind.

The next thing I know, I wake sharply bringing up a dream with me. That nightmare again. It isn't so much a dream, more of an image. A picture. There's a wall. And behind it a building. I can see into it like in cross-section. I can see myself trapped in a room, walled in. I am dying. In another room Dr. Scheiner from the Archaeology Department is hurling his huge body against the wall. Trying to break through it. Trying again and again to free me. I wake frozen with terror. I think I'm going to die. I'm sure of it. The room is quiet apart from Morton breathing softly in his sleep beside me. I can make out the shadowy shapes of the furniture in our bedroom still there around us. But the dream is with me as vividly as anything that happens in daytime Hackney. I can't sleep now. I lie there for what seems hours with my eyes open, staring into the darkness.

Friday 21st December 1990 12 midday

If only I hadn't been born with red hair. Perhaps then things would have been all right.

I'm still feeling a bit bruised as I stand here in my back garden. That fall in the pub scraped my knees, and my lower arms have come up purple. And there was the knock my head took last night. Morton said it was concussion, insisted on wrapping wet tea towels round my head. Why do I keep having these accidents? It's as if the ground is trying to pull me in. And the universe is rapping me on the head, telling me to pay attention.

But I have to get this grave dug. It's warmer today, but the ground is frozen deep after all the bad weather, and it's hard to get the spade in. There's bits of snow left in corners of what used to be the flower beds. I have to make the hole big enough. And deep enough so the dog won't dig it up.

My mother always told the story about when she was pregnant with me. 'I don't care what it is,' she told everyone, 'as long as it isn't a little girl with red hair. I can't stand little girls with red hair.'

'Don't worry', the neighbour said, 'when it comes, you'll love it whatever it is. It's a law of nature.'

But she didn't. Nature didn't count for much with my mother. I think her face fell when she first saw me, just out of the womb. Things went downhill from then on. There was never enough room in that council house for both of us.

The earth doesn't seem to be awake. The sky is overcast, ready to weep. At last the blade sinks into the dark soil. I manage to loose a spadeful, and find a little grub in a watertight case. Spending the winter building up to its moment of glory as a butterfly or crawling insect when the days are warmer. I have disturbed its miniscule studious preparation.

I stop to rest a moment on the spade. I can hear the sounds from the street: there's no such thing as silence in Hackney. But if I look up I can see the branches of the big poplar tree from several gardens down, stretching out against the December sky. And I can hear someone practising the saxophone in one of the houses that backs onto ours. Rich, luxurious sounds that you can hear down to your toes. And there's a stillness in the air that feels very ancient, and patient with the comings and goings of humanity. There may not be silence, but there is majesty.

I look into the Safeways carrier bag and apologize to the small things nestling inside. You will get a decent burial. I love the gentle touch of the drizzle stroking my cheeks.

It's cold. I feel a sneeze coming on, and there it goes! The anticipation is bitter-sweet, the release electrifying. Some of our bodily functions seem to have been made gratuitously ecstatic, an act of generosity by evolution.

'Bless you!' says Freddie, one of my housemates, as he comes out of the kitchen door. Now he's someone who did something drastic with his hair. The matted dreadlocks, unusual on a white boy. I should say white 'man'. He's around my age, pushing forty. But did he ever grow up?

Who am I to talk?

Did any of us?

They always try to make out that rebelliousness against the status quo is a juvenile disorder. So how come we've reached this age and we're still misfits?

He's standing looking, I don't know what at. He and I have lived as tenants in the same house for years but I still don't know what goes on in the corners of his mind. Our housemate Vivienne says there was a woman in his life once.

I start digging again. Pushing my weight onto the spade. My considerable weight. At least it's good for something. I dug a makeshift grave last night, before I banged my head on the underneath of the kitchen table and totally passed out. Another accident. Long story. I'm still feeling strange. But this will be a proper deep hole.

Freddie's face always looks half-way between surprised and weary. It breathes the calm of someone who gave up hoping years ago. Nothing left to yearn for. He lets the small pleasures of life fill his horizon. I wish I could survive on such a sparse diet. I'm still hungry for everything.

His dreadlocks fall over his face as he bends over a millipede scuttling away, watching it as intensely as if it were the first and last creature on earth. 'It's an incredible feat of coordination,' he says, 'for such a small creature. Not to get his legs tangled up.'

I look over while I'm digging. 'It might be a she,' I say.

'It might be. We'll never know.'

I look back and see that I've sliced a worm in half with the sharp edge of the spade. There are two halves wriggling. Writhing. In agony, I imagine. Remorse is a bad taste in my mouth. Freddie looks at it and looks up at me.

'"The cut worm forgives the plough,"' I say hopefully.

'How do you know?' he asks. Freddie asks questions you don't expect.

'That's William Blake,' I say.

'How does he know?'

Now he's asking. 'Visions,' I say. 'He just knows things.' I can see justice in there being forgiveness for an act committed without intention or malice. Even if it inadevertently causes pain.

Freddie scratches his head. 'Where does he live, that Blake guy? There's a few things I'd like to know about.'

I say, 'He died in 1827.'

'People have to be dead a few hundred years before you listen to them, eh?'

'Perhaps he talked to worms.'

Freddie smiles and nods as if he's considering that possibility. 'Is the grave finished?' he asks. 'Only Morton sent me to tell you that lunch is ready.' Morton is punctual. When it's his turn to cook, we often eat before we're hungry and wash up before we've finished eating. Freddie's keen to get me inside: 'Shall we do a quick funeral for those casserole bones?'

My son Bert appears at the kitchen door with his dog. 'Don't let her off yet!' I yell. My ginger frizz falls over my face as I put the bones from last night's supper into the pit. My hair's always in the way: standing up, sticking out, flopping over – and it won't take no for an answer. I shovel the earth back on top of the bones. Then I stand up and look around. Our garden looks desolate in winter, and my digging hasn't helped.

I bury the bones from all our meals. It was the little fragments from Crete that made me realize how precious bones are. Both of humans and of animals. And we need to take care of things that are precious. The garden has lots of filled-in holes, with only a hebe bush and a laburnum tree standing at the far end.

The laburnum tree drops its leaves into the garden of my next-door neighbour. Her garden is concreted over and she's very house proud. Her mother probably trained her strictly back in the Caribbean. She sweeps the leaves up in an aggrieved way, as if she thinks the tree should clear up after itself.

'That's still not deep enough, Mum,' says Bert, coming over with his big brown mongrel straining at her lead. 'Dusty'll have that up in no time.' He looks at me with that sweet untidy face under the brown curls, so like his dad. His hands on the dog's lead have the same broad fingers too. The dad he never knew.

'Not with this on, she won't.' I drop the spade and fetch a small paving stone from the side of the garden. I lay the stone over the filled-in hole and stroke a few crumbs of earth off the top of it. I say, 'Rest in peace.'

Bert protests, 'Mum, they're dead.'

'So?'

'And anyway, pork chops don't understand English.'

'They'll get the message.'

'Mum, you never used to bury bones.'

'I never realized that they need to be treated respectfully. They were part of a living animal once.'

Bert lets Dusty off her lead and she sniffs around the paving slab, squealing and winding her tail in circles.

'You reap what you sow,' says Freddie. He looks at the slab and shakes his dreadlocks. 'What are you expecting here, Dr. Anthea, a crop of piglets in the spring?'

He's teasing me. I'm not a doctor, not till I finish my PhD. *If* I finish my PhD.

I do a pig snort at Freddie and use the shovel to tidy the earth around the slab and stamp it down. My housemates like their jokes at my expense.

'Mum, do all archaeologists talk to bones?' He's only nine, how could he understand?

'No,' I admit, 'But in lots of cultures they treat bones differently from us. And animals. More respect. Alive or dead. Think, love. If Dusty died, we'd bury her so carefully. Just because these are the remains of a pig we've eaten, why would we chuck them in the bin like rubbish? It was a living animal too.'

18

The kitchen door opens again and Morton sticks his head out. 'Lunch is ready!' he calls in his mid-Atlantic lilt. 'Leave the bones, honey.' He comes out, puts his thin arm round me, and leads me into the kitchen. 'You're still recovering from that concussion.' He's right, I need to eat. My legs are wobbly and I can feel the glimmer of a migraine coming on.

The table is neatly laid with four plates, four knives and forks and glasses: Vivienne and our other housemate Pete are at work. There's a large flat dish in the middle, and a bowl of freshly-washed tomatoes, a plate of raw peeled carrots and one of houmous.

'Wash your hands, Bert,' I say. When you're a mother, you say things like that automatically, like scratching an itch.

The old television's on in the corner of the kitchen. There's a glamorous middle-aged woman chopping dried apricots. She's demonstrating a recipe for turkey stuffing. Her kitchen is a million miles different from ours. Hers is all bare stainless steel and shining surfaces. Tastefully decorated with glittering silver Christmas stars and spheres. They must have set her back a few bob.

In ours you can hardly see a clear surface. Morton likes things neat and minimal, and to make space for lunch he's created an island of order. He's cleared everything off the kitchen table onto the dresser, including books, a torch, some sheet music, fruit, Bert's school bag, a tin of dog food and a cardboard box of Christmas decorations we haven't managed to put up yet. One nudge would have the lot on the floor.

There's coats hanging all over the kitchen door. On top there's Freddie's Father Christmas costume and his red windcheater. The walls are covered with posters about the Poll Tax and we still have that one showing Reagan carrying a smiling Thatcher to the ends of the earth with a nuclear explosion in the background. It's getting tatty round the edges. The draining board is piled high with breakfast dishes. On the floor next to the table are three shopping bags and my big handbag. Leaning against the fridge are the remains of an expensive bicycle – its frame twisted, its front wheel crumpled and the front light smashed. Thereby hangs a tale. Next to it on the floor are Dusty's two dishes with dog paw decoration.

Despite it all, Morton is his usual cool self as he scoops the fried eggs out of the pan and arranges them on the neat squares of toast on each plate, as carefully as if he were arranging his thoughts on some early Greek poem to teach his students.

'Help yourselves if you want more,' he says. He puts more squares of toast on the large central dish and adds a sprig of parsley saying, 'Presentation is everything, according to the Goddess in the Kitchen holding forth there.' He glances at the elegant woman on the telly.

As I munch through my egg, I take a good look at her and it rings a bell. The Goddess in the Kitchen she calls herself, also known as Mimi Divine. There's self-promotion for you. But I don't think she's that bad. I remember years ago when I was at college, she came down to give a talk about ancient Greek herbs or something. She was already a TV personality, but afterwards I plucked up courage and went and spoke to her, and we made a connection. She was friendly, not as posh as she looks on the box. 'She's been doing that a long time,' I say.

'And she still looks as fresh as one she made earlier,' says Morton.

It's true, her russet-blond hair hardly moves and there is no sag of sadness round her eyes.

Freddie's gone quiet.

'Perhaps it's the make-up,' says Morton. He's a fast eater. He's finished his egg and dips a piece of toast neatly into the houmous. 'I read a thing in a mag at the dentist's. Said she's done thirty years in show business. They had early pictures of her presenting the show with her little daughter in tow.'

Freddie starts tugging at the earring in his right ear. He does that when he's agitated.

Morton doesn't notice. 'Lucky that eggs don't have bones,' he says as he takes another square of toast.

'Every sensate creature deserves a decent burial.' I keep trying to explain it to them. 'North American Indians used to thank the Spirit for their animal food.'

'We never used to have these problems,' said Freddie. 'Maybe you lot should all turn vegetarian like Ant and me.'

'Maybe we'd understand better if the bones talked to us too,' Morton winks at Freddie and dips the toast with a flick of his fingers.

That again. He can't resist having a go at me about the bones I have upstairs. The human ones from the Cretan tomb. In particular he's bothered about the one I carry with me. He thinks I'm losing my marbles. He thinks it's ruining my chances of getting a PhD. I open my mouth to defend myself, 'Bones are the core of our being...' but Bert interrupts.

'Mum, do you have to keep going on about bones? It's putting me off.' He takes two more tomatoes out of the bowl.

I close my mouth.

But Morton doesn't let it go. 'Did last night's pork chops have any comments?' he asks. 'Like, lay off the apple sauce?'

I can feel myself flushing. 'I know you all find it funny. I know it's not rational. But perhaps rational isn't everything.' I look at Morton across the table. 'Perhaps the rational covers only a small part of life.'

There's a moment of silence and our attention drifts back to the telly where the long varnished fingernails of the 'Goddess in the Kitchen' are chopping walnuts: 'Christmas is a time for families,' she's saying, 'and this stuffing will appeal to young and old…'

There's nothing like television for sucking the emotion out of a room and focusing it into a plastic box full of wires.

I ask, 'Are we eating this meal in front of us, or vicariously consuming the one on TV?' I take another piece of toast and dip it into the bowl of houmous, to show my loyalty to the here and now. On the way back with the toast, I drop some houmous on the tablecloth. I can never be as neat as Morton. And I'm always hungry for that little bit more.

'That is indeed the dilemma of the denizens of the Gaze,' says Morton.

'What are denizens?' asks Bert. 'What's the gaze?' How can Morton expect Bert to understand him when he talks that academic gobbledegook? It's hard enough for me coming back to the academic world after years of teaching little ones.

I try to explain. 'People say our culture is all about looking at things, love. Looking, gazing, instead of living.' I can see Bert's trying to work that one out.

'Sorry about having the box on over lunch, guys,' says Morton, 'but I want to use that apricot and walnut stuffing in our turkey.'

I can't get over how well preserved she is. 'She's been sweating over a hot stove for years,' I say.

'People like her don't sweat,' said Morton. 'I'm surprised she was mortal enough to give birth.'

Freddie tugs at his earring.

'So who was the dad, then?' I ask, 'of the little daughter?'

'Big secret, apparently,' said Morton. 'She's never told anyone. Maybe some showbiz king, top notch celebrity, hush hush.'

Bert's looking out of the kitchen window. 'Mum, Dusty's digging round that stone.'

It's my turn to wash up, but I go with Bert out into the

garden to protect the buried bones.

Friday 21st December 1990 1.30pm
They all think I'm going crazy. That's why I've started having sessions with Ren. Unusual name. She's hard to describe. She's not really a normal psychotherapist. Her advertisement in the local paper said 'Crisis Counselling', but also something about spiritual problems. And I know she does massage, too, because there's a portable massage table folded up in her treatment room. She's fortyish, not beautiful but pale and soothing.

My session's at 2.30 pm. It's not far to go, but I've lost my purse. She doesn't charge much because I'm a student, but I've got to give her something.

I had the purse this morning, I can't remember where.

In our bedroom I find Morton sitting at the little table working on his public lecture. He never seems to have any difficulty concentrating. He's happily oblivious to me coming in and starting a frantic search of the room.

I look in my chest of drawers. Underclothes mixed with sunglasses and scissors and sellotape, and oh joy! I find my bedside clock that I've been missing for a while. Time does strange things unless you keep an eye on it. But no purse. Eventually I ask Morton:

'Have you seen my purse?'

I have to say it a few times to attract his attention.

'Can I read you this bit?' he replies.

'I've lost my purse and I've got a session at 2.30pm.'

'Why don't you ask the bones? They might know where it is.'

'Ha ha.'

'Listen to this bit, then I'll help you find it. You've got masses of time.'

'OK. If it's short.'

Morton lifts his papers and clears his throat: *'While we are on the subject of weaving yarns, I'd like to mention the name given in Greek culture to the singers of Homer's epics. The ones who performed the poems, singing to the lyre, in the smoky halls and meeting-places of early Greece. They were called "rhapsodes." That's made up of "odes", as in songs or poems (our word "ode" comes from the Greek), and "rhaps-", the stem of the Greek word to "sew" or "string together". In other words, the bards sewed poems together. They were "song-stitchers". This reflects the process of oral literature, where various stories known by heart are linked together impromptu in live performance. The singers who repeated motifs and scenes from memory, developing and embellishing them, and joining them up with other scenes, were like needle-workers who have at their disposal a number of pieces that can be sewn together in various formations. Rather like the squares of a patchwork quilt. Every square is part of the totality, but their disposition can vary. The audience, familiar with the material after listening to the stories since childhood, would have a sense of the whole in which all the elements are ultimately suspended simultaneously in a timeless continuum rather than following a chronological sequence.'*

Morton scrutinizes what he's written. 'What do you think?'

I try to take my focus off my lost purse and apply myself instead to Morton's talk. But my mind's like a horse loose in a field, who doesn't want to be caught. Eventually I manage a few words:

'I like the metaphor of the patchwork quilt. But there was a sentence in there – about developing and embellishing? – that was a bit long. I lost track of the grammar.'

He nods as if he hasn't really heard me and scribbles a few notes.

'OK,' I say. 'Now will you help me search?'

He puts down his pen and papers and starts to tidy the room, looking underneath everything for my purse. He's very systematic, folding clothes, putting books in piles. He can't resist the odd comment: 'What's this you're reading about reincarnation? You know that stuff's not sensible, honey.'

'Nothing.' I haven't told him very much about the weird things that have been happening to me. Strange experiences, like visions, flashes of being in ancient Greece, that have made me question a lot of what people think are 'sensible' ideas about life and death. He'd only laugh.

'When did you last have the purse?' he asks.

'I can't remember.'

'Expensive business, those bones. Now you're having to pay for therapy.'

'She gives me a special rate.'

He's started on the big pile of precious things by my bedside that he calls 'clutter'.

'I did tell you to leave them be,' he's saying. 'Those poor bones. They spent thousands of years on that Cretan hillside. In a nice cosy tomb with their friends and family. They were too old to be getting on an aeroplane to London.'

I'm waiting for the next bit.

'And you said so yourself, Ant, it's illegal to take away any antiquities from archaeological sites.'

Don't I know it. I took a risk hiding them in my bag. But I had such a feeling of kinship when I held those bones in my hands. And they're only tiny fragments. I wanted to look after them. I try to defend myself, 'They were on the spoil heap, the excavators had thrown them away.'

'Tell that to the archaeological thought police. And now they're driving you crazy.'

'They're trying to warn me. Especially that particular one. It's trying to help me.' When I hold it, it burns in the palm of my hand and I have the feeling it's trying to tell me something. Something bad that'll happen if I go back to Greece.

'Huh! Warn you? Help you? Like it did last night?' I knew Morton would bring up last night. He shakes his head, 'I'm going to look under the bed. Perhaps that's where you've mislaid your sanity.' He shoots me a despairing glance, 'My girlfriend who listens to bones.'

'I'm not the only one.'

I look under my pillow and find a small piece of paper with childlike writing on it. It says *'WHO IS MY DAD?'* Oh dear. It's coming up for Christmas and Bert's started that again. He's fond of Morton, but hasn't known him that long. He's still curious about his biological dad.

I put it back and bend down to peer under the other side of the bed. Its base is made of two wooden palettes nailed together so there's lots of spaces underneath where spiders have made their homes. I'm on my knees and sticky with their webs, not the most dignified position for defending myself, but I have to do it. 'Bones are the part of the body that lasts longest,' I say. 'And some people believe they are the home of the soul. They say the inner essence, the life force, of any living being is guarded in the marrow of the bones. Bones are strong and secret. Lots of people in the past have told the future from bones. What about the Chinese oracle bones? There is undisputed archaeological evidence for them. I just thought there might be a link with divination in Greece too. I wanted to try handling the bones, to get familiar with the material. Experiment, investigate. That's the scientific method, the academic method, isn't it? I wanted to get to know them. I had no idea what that experience would actually be like. Or what effect it would have on me.'

Morton stands up on the other side of the bed. Like me, he's got a few spiders' webs on him.

'Nor did I,' he says, dusting himself off. 'When was the last time anyone cleaned under there?'

'And what about the oracle of Trophonios?' I say.

'What about it?'

'He was dead. His tomb was in north Greece, it was an oracle. People slept in it overnight to get answers to their problems.'

'Creepy.'

I've got the bit between my teeth now. 'And you get it in the Bible. What about that passage in Ezekiel, "And the Lord said unto me, 'Prophesy upon these bones…'"?'

Morton is looking at me with his head on one side.

'Ezekiel Chapter 37,' I add for good measure.

'Very good, Anthea. Get your sources right. That's how you'll get your PhD.'

Now he's taking the piss.

'Iatromantic practices, that's what my PhD's about,' I can hear my voice rising. '"Iatro," i.e. doctor, plus "mantic," i.e. prophetic. Diagnosis of medical and social problems via divination. That's how they did it in those days. I can't write my thesis without delving into it.'

He's looking at me blankly again from the other side of the bed. 'I keep thinking I've seen it somewhere. Your purse. Did you have any reason to put it in the airing cupboard?'

The rain is still spitting down when I set off for my session. I've taken to walking through the Abney Park Cemetery. Outside its gate there is the usual group of meths drinkers sitting on a low wall. They're laughing amongst themselves as they swig, but their faces are drawn and their clothes are grubby. Putting a brave face on the social wreckage of Thatcher's Britain. I think they sleep inside the graveyard, even at this time of year. Bitter, and scary. Some of the graves date back to the nineteenth century, and the paths lead between Gothic monuments ten feet high that loom above you. Stone carvings of huge urns draped with cloth, and giant winged figures clutching Celtic crosses.

The trees and bushes are overgrown; the ivy climbing on the graves makes them part of the place's wildness. While their bones lie there patiently waiting, the aspirations and self-importance of the human dead are drawn back into nature, absorbed into the foliage as the memory of their existence ebbs away. There are too many of us for everyone to be remembered.

Some graves are more recent: there is one in particular that I always visit, just inside the gateway on the right. The tombstone is small and heart-shaped, and it commemorates a three-month-old baby who died only a few years ago. The inscription reads: *'Our beautiful brave Bethy – We will always love you'*. As I walk down the gravel avenue between the trees and the sepulchral statues, I picture the baby's parents looking at her in her cot with their hearts torn open.

A grey squirrel runs into the path, stops and looks at me. Doesn't it know that they are meant to run away from humans?

I'm dreading my session with Ren today. The decision I made last night, I'm afraid she'll think it's wrong. I'm not sure how to break it to her.

When I come out of the cemetery into Stoke Newington Church Street, I stop to pick up a newspaper. The Pentagon has warned Saddam Hussein. It does look like the country's going to be at war very soon. A war in the Gulf. My madness seems pretty small compared with theirs.

Ren says my experiences and thoughts about the bones are unusual; she avoids using the word 'mad'. She's not someone who judges. She's very quiet and I think she's bald, because she always wears a scarf on her head and she has no eyebrows. Morton says it must be alopecia – people who have no hair. She sits in her treatment room in Stoke Newington, with plants and purple things and a kind of clear light around her. She smiles thoughtfully and asks questions and listens. Inscrutable like a Buddha.

Perhaps she just seems that way because I don't give her a chance to get a word in edgeways. I've only had a few sessions so far and there's so much bursting to come out. Experiences that are bubbling away inside, coming up for air, revisiting me like food that's not properly digested.

I get through the entry phone, up the stairs, knock on her door, then…

I feel like I'm breaking the spell of the calm in her room as I burst in and try not to crash into her potted plant. I've hardly got in and put my bags down before I splurge it out like everything else in my life.

'I've made a decision.' I wonder every time whether her wicker chair will take my weight as I sink into it and take my shoes off. I have a feeling of being too much in every direction. I need to rein myself in. But no, I'm already launched into it full tilt. I'm staring at my socked feet on the ground and I'm gabbling.

'I've made a decision. I'm not going to Greece in February. I don't care about finishing my fieldwork. Or my PhD. I feel something bad will happen to me if I go. Forebodings. Something weird happened to me last night. Last night at home, after supper. In the kitchen. It's like an omen.'

There. I've said it. Now she'll think I've completely gone over the edge. I look up at her. But she doesn't look phased. She even looks interested.

'Oh?' she says, and she looks at me with clear eyes as she asks: 'What is the fear?'

I hesitate for a moment. How much detail should I go into about last night? I have a blurred memory of how it all happened. Bert went to bed. Everybody else went out and then Morton and I made love under the kitchen table. I'll leave that bit out. She doesn't need to hear that. But then how to explain how the bone hit me on the head? On the temple, of all places… Why else would I be under the table when the dog knocked over my bag and the bones flew out of it? And then sitting up sharply and cracking my head on the underneath of the table? And passing out… Perhaps Morton's right and I'm just concussed. He says it can make you confused and emotional. But this stuff has been in my mind for a while and now I feel as if I'm seeing things clearer than ever.

'It's about the bone,' I start. When I think about it, despair hits me. I should never have brought those bones back from Crete. As I start to get agitated I can feel myself shifting my weight around, and the wicker chair creaks. Ever since I picked them up on that hillside… I put my head in my hands. It's a disaster. One mistake after the other.

Ren sits still facing me over the low table. 'Anthea, I'm hearing that something happened last night with the bones that's troubling you?'

'I insisted,' I tell her. 'I insisted on bringing them home. It's my own fault.'

When I hold my hands to my head, all the frizz of my hair gets squashed and I can feel my skull, hard and solid and reassuring. My eye is caught by the tape recorder sitting on her table next to a purple candle, a small clock and a box of tissues. All very neat, and the tape goes relentlessly round and round.

I can't stop myself: 'I still haven't got used to that thing recording. I keep reminding myself it's for training and it's confidential, like you said. But it still makes me nervous. Because I know I must sound crazy. All the strange stuff that's been happening to me, it's built up and up till… . I used to see the world so rationally. But now… No wonder my friends think I'm going off my rocker.'

I look down at my feet, planted on the purple-striped rug, surrounded by my bags. I'm in mid-flow. I can't stop the storm of words. 'And then last night after the bone hit me on the head and I sat up suddenly and cracked my head on the table and I passed out, I saw it. The hill. And the stones. But it wasn't just that. This time they were moving. And I was too. Falling… Like in the dreams I told you about but so much clearer. I was dying.'

I'm glad I've got that out. I look at her and in my mind I'm daring her to laugh or dismiss it all. She just keeps on looking at me, open-eyed. So I carry on.

'So last night I decided not to go to Greece in February. I'm cancelling our field trip.' I look round the small room, daring anything in it to disagree with me, and then I slump back into the chair. 'That's it.'

Ren raises her bare eyebrows, 'I see.'

'It means cancelling everything.' I'm trying not to face this. 'All the visits to tombs I had to make. The flight's booked and I won't get the money back. It will delay finishing my PhD. But life and death's more important, isn't it? And it feels like that's what's at stake.'

I keep expecting her to object, but all she says is: 'I see.'

So I carry on. 'Morton thinks it's funny. He sits in bed doing ventriloquism with the bone, he says it's actually complaining about the weather. I tell him it wanted to come. He just laughs. He tells me to put the bone back in its box with the others and forget about it.'

Ren doesn't say anything.

Eventually I ask, 'Do you think I'm going mad, as well?'

She hesitates, then she speaks slowly. 'No, Anthea, I don't. Having ideas that are unusual for our culture doesn't make you mad, not in my book. I feel that some of the "normal" ideas in our culture are pretty crazy.'

'So I've made the right decision?'

'I can't tell you that. It's not my place to interfere with your decisions about your life. They may be based on thoughts and experiences that are unknown to me. But take care. Sometimes our intuitions or gut feelings are sound, sometimes they miss the mark. Imagination can help us or lead us astray. It's always useful to do a reality check.'

I want to tell her how these sessions over the last week have helped. Going through what's been happening… I feel less alone with the fears. I'm coping better. I tell her, 'You're the only person who hasn't laughed at me.' I know she hasn't necessarily agreed, but she's said, that's your experience, let's see what it means for you.

There's a silence.

Then Ren says, 'We all have more resources than we think we have.'

'I remember that Evan used to say that.' Evan, the one who opened my eyes to how the world works and who helped me at a crucial time. I try to explain to Ren, 'I might have gone under years ago if it wasn't for him.'

'So Evan is a person in your past?' Her eyes open wide in question.

'A friend, not a boyfriend. It was about twenty years ago, when I left home.'

'You left home permanently?'

'At the end of my first year at university.' I've hardly seen my mother since.

Ren's missing eyebrows meet in a frown. 'That must have been hard.'

'It was.' But not as hard as staying. OK, I might as well give her the whole story.

'Things were always difficult with my mum,' I tell her, 'but when I came back from my first year at university, they got worse. I'd been back briefly at Christmas and Easter, but in the long summer holidays the tensions really started to show. The house was small, and we couldn't avoid rubbing up against each other the wrong way.

'I was overweight – well, I've always been overweight – and I'd got into the hippy thing. It must have been the summer of 1972, it was all happening. So I suppose those loose flowing batique dresses made me look even bigger. And my hair... When I let it grow, it sticks out into one gigantic frizz. She never liked my hair. Perhaps it reminded her of my dad. Maybe it was that. I don't know.

'Anyway, one night things came to a head. I'd just got in from work. I was doing barmaid at a local pub to help with the bills. She was always struggling over money.

'She takes one look at me and says, "What do you think you're wearing?"

'"It's a dress, mum. People wear dresses like this these days."

'"Not round here they don't. Fancy student ways. I suppose you think you're too good to help around the house now."

'She was in the middle of washing up, so I picked up a drying-up cloth.

'"Don't bother with that. You'll only put things away in the wrong places."

'I couldn't do anything right. I ignored her comment and leant past her to clear a saucepan off the draining board. She snorted, "Ugh, you smell like the inside of a church. What have you put on yourself?"

'She elbowed me away from her. I felt I was taking up too much space. Too big all ways.

'I carried on drying up anyway. She started again, "You'd do better if you tidied up your room. Have you seen the state of it? Maybe they don't mind at 'university'..." She said the last word as if it was something the dog brought in. Not that we had a dog. I always wanted one.

'She was right. My bedroom was a tip. I've always been messy.

'"Sorry, mum. I'll have a go at clearing it up."

'She was getting the bit between her teeth. "And letting your hair grow like that. Anyone would think you were proud of it. Can't you afford a hair cut? You get a grant, don't you? Money for nothing. All right for some."

'She never earned much all her life. She had no qualifications. So she never got work that used her intelligence. Playground assistant at the local junior school. You don't get much. I think she resented that. Poor mum.

'She kept going on. "All that hippy nonsense. Just an excuse to show off if you ask me. Parading around the town in that. It looks like a dressing gown. Aren't you ashamed? I have to live here, you know."

'I don't know what it was that tipped me over. Suddenly I felt angry. And I found myself using new-found confidence from my months away from home. And new-learnt vocabulary from my friends at college. I slammed a pyrex dish down on the table and yelled: "Leave me alone! Fuck off!"

'I stormed up to my room and collapsed on the bed in tears.

'I kept out of her way for the rest of the evening and went to bed early.

'But I had difficulty getting to sleep. My childhood bedroom didn't feel comfortable any more. She'd moved most of my old things out, and it felt unfriendly. Eventually I dropped off.

'I didn't know what woke me, but when I opened my eyes my bedside clock said 2.30am. Then I looked up and saw a dark shape beside my bed, leaning over me.

'It was a shock to my bones.

'I sat up and switched on the bedside lamp. It was her. As my eyes adjusted to the light I saw that she was holding a pair of scissors.'

'A pair of scissors?' Ren sounds startled. 'Are you sure?'

I nod. 'My first thought was that she was going to kill me. Then I realized that was stupid. She wouldn't do that. She was going to cut my hair.'

'Cut your hair?' says Ren.

'She could never stand it.'

'How did you feel?'

'Scary. I felt invaded. Hated. I don't know, I was young at the time. All I knew was that I couldn't stay in that house another day. I lay awake for the rest of the night, and as soon as I heard her leave for work in the morning I packed everything I could into my big student rucksack and left. I took a train from Maidstone to London. Where to go from there? The only place I knew at all was Camden Town. There was a bookshop called Compendium that I'd visited. It had loads of interesting books. I spent the afternoon moving from section to section, and reading what I could. There were psychology books but I couldn't find any answers about how to sort things out with my mum.

'The shop closed late but when the time came I was still tucked into a corner in the basement, wondering where I could go and hoping nobody would find me.

'But somebody did. One of the staff. I'd seen him there before.

'He told me, "I'm afraid it's time to go home."

'I shook my head. Eventually I managed to say, "Not possible".

'He must have taken pity on me, because we got talking and he asked me what was the matter and I told him. I don't know whether he believed me. But he listened and eventually he said, "It's dark outside. You can't go off wandering around the streets of London." He told me there was a spare room in the flat where he lived. He seemed genuine and I went with him.'

Ren opens her eyes wide. 'You took a big risk.'

'I was desperate. But it was OK,' I reassure her. 'He was as good as his word. We travelled to a flat in east London. It was a bit spartan, but clean and nice. He made up a bed for me in the spare room. I woke in the night a few times, but apart from that I slept well.

'The next day the full weight of what had happened sank into me. When Evan got back from work I was sitting weeping.

'"OK?" he asked.

"Shattered. I'm so sorry to land on you like this. With all my problems. You don't even know me." I could feel a migraine coming on.

'He made us both a cup of strong tea and put some music on. The Modern Jazz Quartet, he told me. The sounds were melancholy, silky and soothing, like a hand stroking you.'

Now I remember why I'm telling Ren all this.

'He sat down with his tea and said, "Life sucks. Sometimes. Other times it glows. You have to be prepared to wait for the good bits. You're a great girl. Don't give up. Sit tight and things will get better. We all have more resources than we think we have."

'I nearly burst into tears again, but I didn't want to disturb the neatness and order of his flat with my distress. My mum could never stand me crying. And I didn't want him to think I was throwing myself at him. I could see he was out of my league. He was a bit older, and knew so much more than me. And I'd realized that he was also ever so slightly posh, it slipped out in his accent every so often. He wouldn't be interested in a fat council house girl like me. Not that he ever said anything like that. He always treated me as if I mattered. Very polite and considerate. That evening he said that if I liked I could stay for a few days. It turned into a few weeks until I went back to college.'

Ren nods. 'He really helped you.'

'He made me feel better about myself.' I remember that there's more: 'And it wasn't just a lucky landing at a point of crisis in my life when I really needed it. It was also a turning-point. The man was an activist. He told me about class. I never realized that I was working-class. I just thought we had less money than some because my dad wasn't there. Evan told me that the wealth in society is monopolized by the upper classes. That they hold all the important jobs in government and the professions. Mostly male and white. That women are treated unequally from the day they're born. I'd never seen things that way. Things I'd thought were my fault were more to do with divisions in the world.'

Ren's eyes sparkle. 'A conversion?'

I think for a moment that she's teasing me. 'It wasn't brain-washing, if that's what you mean. He never sat me down and lectured me. But he was doing stuff around me and I asked questions. His answers made sense of things I'd never understood before. When we saw demonstrations on the telly, my mum always said these were troublemakers. And when people protested about their situation, she said they were bleating and should put up or shut up. With what Evan said I began to realize why my mum's life had been so hard and how she'd got so bitter and how sad it was she'd never been able to do anything about it.

'Evan wasn't actually there much. Outside work hours he was always writing leaflets and pamphlets and going to meetings. One evening he took me to see an old Marx Brothers film with a friend of his, but on the whole he was very serious, very dedicated. At first I thought it strange that he was upper class. His motivation didn't come from self-interest. He seemed to genuinely want a fairer world.

'I hadn't met anyone like him. I admired him. And his description of the world started to make sense to me. He gave me books to read. Simone de Beauvoir, *The Second Sex*. It was like a veil lifting from my eyes. That summer there were building workers' strikes going on; I remember helping him make placards, and we went on a huge demonstration in the middle of London. I'd never seen so many people. By the beginning of September, I was helping him type leaflets.'

'You became attached to him?' asks Ren.

'I suppose so. He was actually quite nice-looking. Small, with a well-ordered face and dark hair. I think I was still in love with my first boyfriend Terry, but I hadn't seen him or heard of him for over a year and I could have got involved with Evan. But I never expected him to be interested in me. And he wasn't. He never touched me or made any approach of that sort. I think perhaps there had been a girlfriend. Perhaps she'd had that room before. Evan never spoke about her.'

'The kindness of strangers.'

'Yes. He helped me big time. When I went back to college I joined a women's group and the Socialist Society and those ideas have been part of my life ever since. Not that I'm a very good activist these days. Any more than I'm a good archaeologist.

'Especially since the bones started telling me things.

'A little while ago, I would have laughed myself at someone who listens to bones. Now everyone thinks I'm losing my mind. Some people at college turn their backs on me. That's happened quite a lot since the trouble started with Dr. Scheiner.'

Ren picks up the name. 'Dr. Scheiner? You haven't mentioned him before.'

There's a good reason I haven't.

I look out of the window. There's light rain still falling on the rooftops. Oh well, I've let his name out now. I have to tell her about him some time. I try to explain my hesitation: 'I think because I'm embarrassed. He's a lecturer in the Archaeology Department.'

She sits in silence. It's not a cold silence. It's a kind of welcoming silence. But she's obviously not going to say anything. It's up to me to fill the space with something. And that something has to be the sorry saga of my behaviour towards Dr. Scheiner. So here goes.

'I first met him on a trip to Crete. Bert had gone away to camp, it was summer. Morton and I were staying at the archaeologists' hostel. It's a kind of outpost of Empire from before the First World War, balmy evenings sitting under the cypress trees at a long wooden table sipping wine. Dr. Scheiner seemed different from the other archaeologists. More human. At those mealtimes that were so English – mean and competitive – he didn't seem to fit in. He's not English, for a start. Austrian, originally. If you asked him a question he'd give you a long, full answer. He was generous with his knowledge. And he didn't put people down.

'If you said, "I'm not sure that the tomb's antechamber has been correctly dated," he might say: "Well, Bloggs thinks the floor is continuous from the inside of the tomb. But he might have been wrong about the pottery, he had very little to go by. We all make mistakes sometimes." That would be a kind reply.

'And kindness like that was unusual in archaeological circles. That was what made me respond. It wasn't a sexual thing or anything. In fact, I'd always thought that he was rather repulsive physically. Ginger hair, standing on end, and spectacles. A great tall man. He used to sit in the back row in seminars, glowering, as I used to imagine. But when I met him I was surprised at the softness I found. An academic with some gaps in his armour. A rawness somewhere. I felt I could almost reach him. After that visit to Crete, the memory of our conversations lingered with me.'

'You were attracted to him?'

'Yes, but not in that way. Nothing romantic, more like he was a long-lost friend. When we got back to London I wanted to talk to him some more. I used the bones as an excuse. I wrote him a letter. Typed and formal. *"Dear Dr. Scheiner, I wonder whether it might be possible to meet briefly to* discuss a question relating to Aegean human skeletal remains? We could perhaps talk over tea at the library, or if it were more convenient for you I could come to your office. Yours sincerely, etc.... ", that type of thing.

'In the event we met at the library, in the same oak-panelled tea room where Morton first propositioned me. Heinrich, or rather I should call him Dr. Scheiner, had a black coffee. I tucked into a rock cake to keep myself steady. My excuse for consulting him was that some of the bones I was studying at college for my PhD were from a tomb that he'd dug. I asked him lots of questions about how they'd been handled after burial, after the flesh had decayed. My theory was that people attributed meaning to the bones, perhaps using them for rituals. I asked him whether he would agree that some of the cut marks were not just butchery marks – from stripping the flesh off the bones – but made for some other reason. He was perfectly pleasant. Several times he ran his hand through his wiry hair. He heard me out, and advised me to tread carefully with my theory:

'"In structuring your thesis I recommend that you put your evidence all together at the beginning, then put your speculations separately at the end. Don't mix it." His English is practically perfect, with an almost undetectable accent. Then he stood up to his full height. A big hulk of a man. "Sorry, but I must dash away now. There is a student waiting for a tutorial. Good luck with the work!" And he was gone.

'It wasn't anything very much really, but he left an impression on me, like a taste that lingers. The thought of him would crop up at strange times. When I saw him at seminars at first glance he looked like an old friend, and I had to remind myself that I hardly knew him. I always found myself greeting him warmly. In response he was restrained.

'I couldn't really understand my reaction to him.'

There are lots of things I'm not understanding. Like the visions – or were they hallucinations…? Like the night at the Knossos hostel when the hash cake blasted my mind wide open and I thought I was back in ancient Greece being attacked by an angry crowd.'

I look at Ren. 'When I don't understand something, my friend Crystal always says, "Ask for a dream to explain it." Hippy nonsense, I always think, typical of her. I'm the rational academic, I don't do things like that.

'But if you've got questions on your mind late at night, maybe that makes dreams happen.

Like the dream I keep having about Dr. Scheiner. It's embarrassing, I've never spoken to anyone about it. But since we started these sessions, you've listened to lots of my stuff, maybe you could hear this too.'

I tell her about the dream where I'm trapped in a stone building and Dr. Scheiner is trying to free me. And that I had it again last night: 'When I woke in the morning, the sunshine was leaking round the curtains and I had a strong feeling of gratitude towards Dr. Scheiner. As if he'd saved my life. Or tried to. I always have that feeling after the dream.

'Morton came in with a cup of tea for me. The dog came in with him and jumped on the bed. She's not really allowed, but she was carrying one of Freddie's knitted hats and we laughed about it.

'I try to put the whole thing out of my mind. But Dr. Scheiner keeps cropping up. I see him at the photocopy machine. I think about him when I'm just falling asleep. Then I wake up with that dream first thing in the morning.'

At this point Ren looks at the clock and says, 'I'm sorry to stop you here, but I'm afraid it's the end of our session. If you like we could talk more about this next time. Tomorrow.'

I stand up. This is my cue to tidy myself out of here. The end always seems to come at the worst possible time. 'Thank you. And thank you again for seeing me at a reduced rate.' I start fumbling in my handbag for my money, but I can't resist adding: 'Dr. Scheiner seemed to understand. He seemed to realize that something was wrong. He told me, "You should seek help."'

Chapter Two

Friday 21st December 1990 11.30am

Rain drizzled on Corinne's straggling fair hair and she shivered in her blue cardigan. Her breath settled on the outside of the café window as she leant against it with her black plastic bag, looking in. She couldn't hear their words, but she watched two women sit down at a table with a copy of *The Sun* lying on it.

'My Derek's had enough of that place,' said Edie, taking off her plastic mac. She lit a cigarette and discarded the match into a metal ashtray.

'You mean up there?' asked Vera, sitting down opposite. She poured some tea from her saucer back into the cup, spilling some on to *The Sun*.

Edie gave a tight nod. 'That Detox Unit's the worst. You want to know what happened yesterday? There was a woman in the cell. Lying on the floor having a fit. You know, epileptic, when they foam at the mouth. I tell you, they only ask my Derek to go in and put her in the right position so she don't swallow her tongue.'

'Why's that?' Vera moved the wet newspaper onto the next table as Corinne came into the café and sat down there.

'They die, you know', said Edie, 'if they lie on their back and swallow their tongue,' She drew on her cigarette and tapped it over the ash tray although there was no ash to fall. 'So he's meant to go in and turn her onto her face. On his own, with her on the floor shaking and gnashing her teeth. Like a wild thing. He could have got bitten. God alone knows what diseases they got. He said one came in last week covered with fleas.'

'So what'd he do?'

'He refused, didn't he? He says to them, "I'm not going in there, with *that*." And you know what? He got a reprimand. I ask you. Ten years he's been a prison officer. He's supposed to risk hisself for that scum?' She rearranged the chiffon scarf at her neck.

'So what happened?' Vera asked.

'I told you, he got a reprimand.'

'No, I mean, what happened to the woman?'

'Oh, she didn't have no problem. They all watched through the window in the door. She coughed and spluttered, made a big thing of gasping and that, but she survived. That sort always do. If she didn't, I'd say good riddance. Drug addicts, most of them.' She looked around as if the café might be full of them and moved her Woolworths carrier bag closer to her feet as if someone might steal it. Corinne averted her eyes.

Vera drained her cup. 'So is he leaving the job, then, Derek?'

'Not that easy. If he leaves, we lose the house. Out on our ear. Where can we go? Everything's laid on for people like them, but decent folks like us, no. You see them let out of there in the morning, carrying their black plastic bags. That's for their things. You see them coming out, bold as brass. They'll have a drink can in their hand before they get to the bus stop. You can't help some people.' She crushed the remains of her cigarette in the ash tray.

Corinne stretched out a foot wearing a Doc Martens boot with multicoloured laces to slide her black plastic bag further under the table.

'Two Cornish pasties?' a young girl carrying a tray looked hopefully up and down the café.

'Over here, love,' said Vera. 'And another tea please.'

The girl turned to Corinne: 'Have you ordered?'

Corinne reached into the plastic bag and pulled out a striped shoulder bag. She opened her purse and counted the money in it. She watched the two women eating pasties at their table. She looked at a photograph of a footballer on the back of *The Sun*, and the container of ketchup in the middle of the table. She looked out through the window misty with condensation. A bus roared past on the road outside.

She closed her purse, gathered her things and walked out of the café. The two women stared after her and Edie tutted: 'See what I mean? Doesn't know the day of the week.'

Outside, the snow of two days earlier had melted and there were puddles on the pavement.

At a Turkish supermarket further down the road, Corinne stopped and went in. She looked at the mangoes and the large red apples. She looked at the fresh pitta bread, hot on the shelves. She looked at the cans of olive oil. She looked at the tins of *dolmades*. She went further into the shop and chose two bottles of wine in bulbous, rounded bottles. Vinho Verde and Rosé d'Anjou. On her way out she picked up a stray banana lying alone in a fruit crate.

She joined the queue to check out, and bumped into a woman wearing a purple scarf around her head. Her supermarket basket held onions, sweet potatoes, parsnips and green bunches of coriander.

Corinne started. 'Ren!' she said, and smiled. Then immediately she looked away.

'Hello,' said Ren, her pale face opening with surprise. 'You're out.' Ren kept her eyes on Corinne until she looked back.

'I didn't think you'd recognize me,' said Corinne. 'I

was in your massage session on Tuesday, yeah? Up there. Inside. People look different outside. I've just been to court. I got bail.'

'I noticed you weren't in the session this morning. Got somewhere to go?'

Corinne looked at the bottles of wine in her basket. 'Sort of… But I was going to try to stay off it.'

'Anywhere else to go?'

Corinne shrugged.

Friday 21st December 1990 12.30pm

'You must be breaking a few rules here,' said Corinne as Ren unrolled a foam mattress along the beige carpet of her living room. On it she spread a soft sheet of white linen like a layer of snow. The walls of the room were light green. On them hung line drawings of human bodies, male and female, all ages and shapes, framed in plain wood. The curtains were dark green velvet, and a grey light came in through the tall windows. The room was on the first floor overlooking the street. At the far end was an old-fashioned fireplace blocked off with a flowery screen, and in front of it a large sheepskin rug. In the corner a bay tree in a pot.

Corinne looked around. 'Nice house.'

'I rent just the top two floors,' said Ren.

'Do you do massage in here?'

'Not any more,' Ren said. 'I like having somewhere else to work.'

'Did you do those drawings?'

'A friend did.'

'Are you sure this is OK? All the way here on the bus I was wondering if you really wanted me to come.'

Ren dropped two blankets on to the mattress and looked at her. 'I wouldn't have asked you otherwise. Rules were meant to be broken. Well, some rules. The trick is knowing which ones. I'm sure about this one.'

'Coincidence, meeting in the shop,' said Corinne.

'Maybe. Things happen.'

'Do you do this often for escaped jailbirds?'

A smile flickered across Ren's face. 'It's never happened before.'

'Don't you wonder what I did to end up in prison?'

Ren shrugged. 'Not especially. You'll tell me when you want to. If you want to. Most people are in there for victim-less crimes. Unlike many people walking free committing crimes that aren't illegal.'

Corinne hesitated. 'My crime had a victim.'

Ren lifted her brows. 'I'll take a chance.' She finished putting a pillow in a white pillowcase decorated with a green leaf pattern. 'Is there anyone you'd like to contact, let them know you're here?'

'I've got a mother I don't want to see. And a lover who doesn't want to see me; not after what I did.'

'So is there anything else you need?' Ren asked.

'I need to get clean from the booze. I need to be able to write again, that would make life worth living. And I need to get a grip of things. It's too much to expect you to help me with any of those.'

'Maybe,' Ren smiled. 'Perhaps I should say, is there anything else you need this morning?'

'No, thank you.' Corinne looked at her. 'Thank you for this.'

Ren plumped up the pillow and smoothed it off. 'I'll be cooking later, in case you want to eat anything with your wine.'

Corinne put the two bottles behind the bay tree in the corner. 'I'm not going to touch it.'

As soon as Ren left the room, Corinne sank onto the mattress. She lay and studied the leaves of the bay tree. She looked at the pattern of the raindrops on the outside of the windows. She fiddled with the silver ring on the little finger of her right hand and looked at the scar underneath it.

She heard the front door shut and went to the window to see Ren walking out and turning right along Cazenove Road towards the high street. She looked at the row of shops opposite. One was a run-down greengrocers with mostly empty boxes displayed in the window. Two doors down there was a brightly-lit stationery shop. A tall figure hooded in a Father Christmas costume walked past on the pavement. She turned to fetch the wine bottles from the corner, and put them beside the bed. She stroked their rounded contours. She pulled a book out of her black plastic bag. On the front cover it said '*An Angel at my Table* by Janet Frame'. She read a few pages.

In the kitchen next door the phone rang and the answer machine responded: 'This is Ren's phone. Thank you for calling. If you would like to make an appointment for massage treatment or counselling, please leave your name and number clearly. Thank you.' Then the pips.

A voice said: 'This is Alex. Hi. Just to say, the Christmas cake recipe worked out fine, thanks for that. And yeah, I'd love to come round after the worst of the festivities are over. Maybe Boxing Day? Take care.'

The answer machine peeped, stopped and rewound.

Corinne faced away from the bottles and shut her eyes. She slept for fifteen minutes. She dreamt she threw a teacup into the bushes at the edge of a garden. She looked and saw it had fallen onto a pile of rubbish: rotting apples, dead slugs, autumn leaves, cardboard Macdonalds cartons and one lifeless human finger. On the lawn people were drinking tea and chatting politely about supermarket queues. Then the man who was speaking stopped mid-sentence as if he heard something. There was no sound, but a few seconds later a cuckoo called and in the depths of the bushes the finger twitched. Corinne woke with a start. She sat up and looked around her. She checked her fingers and shook her hands.

She found she could reach the small TV set from the mattress, and flicked between channels. A business programme discussing the economic downturn; a black-and-white movie; a cartoon; then a cookery programme where an elegant older woman was demonstrating how to make an apricot and walnut stuffing for turkey. Abruptly she switched the TV off.

She reached for the Vinho Verde, and tried to push the cork into it. She struggled for a while using her fingers without success. She rummaged inside her striped shoulder bag and eventually produced a comb with a long handle. She pushed the handle onto the cork, gently at first and then with increasing desperation. Eventually it moved a little and then suddenly shot down into the bottle, splashing her hand with wine. She licked her hand. She licked the handle of the comb. She sniffed at the neck of the bottle. She put it down again and picked up her book. She wasn't reading. She got out the banana and stared at it. She didn't eat it. She picked up the book again.

She put down the book, reached for the Vinho Verde, held the cork down with the handle of her comb and took a sip. Then another. She threw the book across the room and drank a full draught. She held the bottle out to see how much she had emptied, then gulped some more. She put the bottle down beside the bed. 'Oh, fuck,' she said out loud. She rolled over onto her other side and slept.

Friday 21st December 1990 1.30pm
On the Essex Road drizzle was falling on a slim figure in a Father Christmas suit. He was walking down the pavement with his left arm in a blood-stained sling; the other carried a placard saying 'REPENT.' He stopped outside a restaurant

smartly painted in dark green with its name 'Mon Repas' picked out in white. Inside, a few customers could be seen having lunch over spotless white tablecloths. He took his left arm out of its sling, pulled the white-trimmed Father Christmas hood up over his light brown dreadlocks, and then put his arm back in the sling.

'Fred! Como está? How's tricks?' A young man came across the road carrying a camera. 'You choose this weather to make your point?' He smoothed the rain off his straight jet-black hair. 'Why?'

Freddie turned round. The other side of the placard read 'All I want for Xmas is a bicycle.' His face lightened: 'Vicente! What's a little rain between friends?'

At that moment the door of the restaurant opened and a tall woman in a tailored trouser suit strode out onto the pavement. 'This has to stop!' her gold bracelets rattled as she shook her finger at Freddie. 'This is against the law. I shall call the police again…'

'I'm allowed to walk up and down, like anyone else,' said Freddie. He tugged on his earring. 'I have to walk; you know what happened to my bike.'

There was a flash as Vicente took a photograph of the exchange. Freddie broke away and started walking up and down again as the woman turned on Vicente. 'And what do you think you're doing?'

'This maybe interest the local newspaper,' Vicente brandished the camera.

'This is outrageous!' She tossed her fashionable greying bob. 'I'm going to telephone the police now. And as for you, little man,' she turned on Vicente, 'wherever you come from, I suggest you go back there!'

Vicente stared after her as she stormed inside. The door closed more sedately behind her as its spring hinge released.

Friday 21st December 1990 4pm

When Corinne woke, the light in the room had faded. She lay very still and stared at the empty window. Then she crawled off the foam mattress and tidied the bedclothes away. She tucked the half-drunk bottle out of sight. She sat under the bay tree and shut her eyes. She opened her eyes, adjusted her position, and shut them again. After a few minutes, she started fidgeting.

She got up and started looking for pencil and paper. Rummaging in her bag, she found a pencil. She paced about the room looking on all the surfaces for paper. She pulled a piece of tissue out of the wastepaper basket, but it tore when she started to write on it. She paced some more, then retrieved her book. She sat down and opened it at the empty fly pages at the beginning. She started doodling, drawing spiders' webs around the edges of the first blank page. Then she wrote:

'I never recovered from 1971.'

After a pause she crossed it out and wrote: *'I never recovered from my mother.'*

She looked round the room, then started writing more.

'Why do memories of her persecute me? The more I try to put her out of my mind and out of my life. I shut my eyes and I hear that voice calling me: Corinne! Corinne! At least I'm writing this down. That's a break-through after all those years with a wall of silence between me and the page. I'm writing! But what I'm writing is a memory I'd rather forget.

'I'm in the apple tree when she calls me in. Corinne! There's always a touch of reproof in her voice. Only calling my name, but I always felt she was telling me off. She used to ask me why I wasted so much time in the garden. Day-dreaming, she called it. What she meant was that I'd never be successful like her. She called me as if I should be somewhere else, doing something else. Do some pruning instead of talking to the plants. I didn't talk to them, I listened. Trees have a low hum, not one you can hear

with your ears, more like a whisper you can sense in your sinews. My limbs were stretched along the branch of the apple tree, I could feel it breathing. There aren't many places in London where you don't hear traffic noise. The tree was moving, imperceptibly. Many people don't realize that trees dance. Even when the wind is still. It's a slow dance. The late afternoon sunlight was dappled through the leaves. Sharp points of light slid into shadow as the branches trembled. I always tried not to disturb them as I climbed the tree. I was thin, like I am now. When I heard my name, I slithered down without shaking the blossoms.

'I walked barefoot across the lawn, carrying my sandals. She had stopped calling. The house was quiet again. When I came in to the kitchen, there was my tea. A little tart and a piece of fruit and a triangular sandwich and a glass of juice, all laid out neatly like one of her cookery photo-shoots. But she wasn't there. She was upstairs putting on her lipstick ready to go out. Why call me if you don't want me? I didn't eat it. I left my leaf-covered sandals in the middle of the spotless kitchen floor. Just so she would know: I am here. You wish I wasn't, but I am. My sandals are evidence. And where are you?

'Her dressing table was like a shrine to herself. She had a powder puff in a small engraved wooden tub. The powder was like magic dust to me. Leaves nestled outside her bedroom window, stroking the glass. She was perfecting the edge of her lipstick with an intense interest I never saw her direct at me. Her make-up was like an untouchable armour. I was porous, transparent, I didn't exist. She sat like a queen in her throne, and outside blackbirds rattled their cry of warning of some possible intruder in the fading summer light. Her face was taut like a stretched elastic band. I never knew what it was holding in. I feared if I got too close it would snap. I stood watching her, my whole being wrapped in the scent of her perfume. It was a kind of hug. It was the closest I got to a hug.'

There was no more blank space on the pages at the beginning of the novel. Corinne shivered and turned to the back of the book, then gave up and dropped it on the floor. She heard Ren come in the front door and up the stairs. She picked up the novel again and read some pages. Ren knocked and came in to bring her a cup of tea, then slipped out again. Corinne drank it and then lay face down on the floor, cheek pressed against the beige carpet.

The bay tree became a silhouette.

Ren called her for supper. She took with her the book and the unopened bottle of Rosé d'Anjou.

Ren's kitchen was neat, with a big wooden table and red-painted wooden chairs. Ren was turning something under the grill. Corinne clutched the wine and book, and looked around. Herbs and onions hung by the window. On the wall beside the sink was pinned an A5 flyer headed *'We exist…'* Corinne read the first sentence: *'Queen Victoria didn't believe that lesbians could exist. Maybe she didn't know because we have always been forced to hide, to keep quiet about our lesbianism for fear of losing our jobs, our homes, our children, our friends…'* Beside it on the wall was a yellowing Steve Bell cartoon cut out from *The Guardian*. A US colonel was telling congressman 'Wimp Lilyliver' what he believes in: *'Apple pie, Santa Claus, the Tooth Fairy, God, the American way… John Wayne, Bambi and Toadal Freedom from Bodily Odours…'* In the last frame, below a scene of native people lying dead on a battlefield, the Colonel concludes *'But I don't believe in Ghosts. No way do I believe in Ghosts.'*

'Do you believe in ghosts?' Corinne asked Ren.

Ren put a dish on the table. 'I don't not believe in ghosts.'

The supper was lamb chops with mint sauce and roast parsnips. Ren took the lid off the parsnips with a flourish, 'You've got something to celebrate. Bail is a chance to breathe.'

Corinne pushed her food around her plate. 'I'm wondering why I thought you would be a vegetarian.'

'I should be, on what I earn.'

'You know, animal loving and that.'

'I love plants too,' said Ren. 'Whatever I eat, I have to kill something. We are destructive creatures, human beings.'

'Kind, too.'

'Sometimes. Full of contradictions. We can ask the lamb to forgive us. Nobody's perfect.'

'Thank you, lamb,' said Corinne, and tucked in.

They ate in silence. As she put the last piece of parsnip in her mouth, Corinne asked 'Don't you want to open the wine?' She gave a long look to the bottle standing on the draining board.

'Not especially,' said Ren. She poured them both some apple juice and asked 'What did you do all day?'

'I watched the shadows move around your sitting room.'

'The shadows and the light move together,' said Ren. 'Do you like tinned pears and custard? It's a favourite from my childhood. Some people find it disgusting.' She put the plates in the sink.

'I'll try anything. Let me help.'

While Ren stirred the custard, Corinne tried to open the tin of pears, but the opener jammed. She tried again, with no results. She let it drop on the table. 'I feel my life's out of control. I'm coasting downhill on a bicycle with no brakes. I don't know what I'm going to hit at the bottom. And now I can't even open a can of pears.'

Ren put the custard on the table. 'Don't worry. I've had that tin-opener for years, it has always given grief. If you knew its story you'd understand why.'

'This tin-opener has a story?'

'Yes, a sad one,' said Ren. 'It concerns a friend of mine. It started with that tin-opener and it ended with his relationship wrecked.'

'A tin-opener wrecked a relationship?'

Ren nodded.

Corinne examined it. 'It looks inoffensive enough. What

is the story?'

'You want to hear?'

'It might distract me from the wreckage of my own life.'

'He wouldn't mind. He's a great guy. He told me about it at the time. It was one of his great strengths that he loved telling stories at his own expense. It was nearly twenty years ago. 1971. He was living in a squat.'

'Near here?'

'Not far. See, it can work…' Ren opened the tin, divided up the pears and poured the custard over.

'Eat up,' she said, 'and I'll tell you.

'My friend Reuben always went to the football. That was a bad day. After Arsenal lost, it started to drizzle. It was one of those Saturday afternoons when everything goes the wrong way like rain down the back of your neck.

'When he got back to the squat there was no one at home. He said he felt as if the world was having a party somewhere without him. It was a long time since breakfast. They weren't very organized in that house. In the makeshift kitchen he found an old packet of Mother's Pride, just a few slices. He thought they'd be OK toasted up. A packet of cocoa. An empty bottle of HP sauce. A brand new jar of thyme, not much good on its own. And a tin of baked beans. Communal housekeeping had reached an all-time low.

'He took out the money he had in his trouser pocket and put it on the table. Not even enough for chips. He'd thought that Ute – that was his girlfriend – would be at home for him to borrow from. Getting out of bed that morning she'd said "See you tonight" with her neat German accent and her tentative smile.

'He rolled a joint to clear his head and as the fumes slid through his veins he realized with a shining sense of revelation that the best hope to fend off starvation was the tin of beans. When you feel demoralized, fantasy runs amok but the brain works slowly. He was feasting in his mind's eye on a steaming plate of beans long before he remembered that the kitchen didn't have a tin-opener yet. They'd only recently squatted the house.

'He said the lights of the corner shop looked bright through the evening rain. Dodging puddles, Reuben made his plan. It was only a small object. He couldn't ask for credit. Laws were for straight people. That's the way they used to think at that time. The plan was, liberate it now. Bring the money in tomorrow. Like that Dylan song: "To live outside the law you must be honest." It was a radical squat, full of activists. They had their own honesty; they thought the legal system was only there to protect the rich.'

'Activists?'

'Politically active people. Not politics like at Westminster, but in the community.

'The shopkeeper looked pre-occupied, as if the long hours perched at the till under the flicker of fluorescent lights had set his mind vibrating in a private film show. He was miles away, perhaps in the fields of his village in Donegal, or at home sitting with his wife in front of *The Black and White Minstrel Show*, while his children were all tucked in bed. He barely acknowledged Reuben's usual mumbled good evening.

'So far, so good. Reuben didn't attract the shopkeeper's attention by launching into one of his furious attacks on the misleading headlines in the day's newspapers, or a diatribe about Apartheid or the Industrial Relations Bill, or re-starting their long-running debate about Irish politics. He kept unusually quiet as he went in. Reuben was a big burly youth, with thick black hair, but he tried to make himself inconspicuous as he shuffled into the back of the shop.

'The tin-opener hung on a rack, blocked from the till by food shelves. It slipped unseen into the left pocket of Reuben's donkey jacket. He would have got away with it except for the hole in the pocket. The tin-opener was heavy enough to work its way through the frayed threads. It was more loyal to gravity than to its new owner, and it landed with a rattle at Reuben's feet just as he passed the counter on his way out.

'The shopkeeper's eyes startled from his reverie into focus. "Would it be a tin-opener you were after, sir?"

'Reuben told me that for a minute he tried to improvise an expression of surprise; then he hung his head. "What would you say if I told you that this little object could be the key to a man's happiness for an evening?"

'"I'd say there's no accounting for tastes," said the shopkeeper.

'"There's a tin of baked beans at home" Reuben told him. "They look good on the label. Juicy. But I can't get to touch them. It's like making love using a condom."

'"I wouldn't know about that, sir. I'm a Catholic. But I do know that tin-opener costs 2/11d."

'Reuben picked it up off the floor and put it on the counter between them. "I'm skint. The bastards owe me money and they've all gone out."

'"Well, that's a problem, now, isn't it? A problem for me and a problem for you."

'There was a pause. Then Reuben's face lit up. "If you were a restaurant, I could wash up."

'"You know, I appreciate the offer."

'"I was going to bring in the money tomorrow anyway. I'm not into nicking things from small shops. It's not like Sainsbury's, is it?"

'"I appreciate your consideration." The shopkeeper was eyeing him thoughtfully. "Perhaps there *is* something you could do for me."

'By the time Reuben got back to the squat his shoes were wet and his clothes smelt of rotten vegetables. Clearing all the rubbish out of the shop's back yard and putting it in plastic bags had been a messy job. Then taking it down the road.

'Still, he had the tin-opener safely in his right-hand pocket. The pocket without a hole. And there was an extra bonus. The storekeeper had given him a couple of over-ripe tomatoes which were due to be chucked out. The damp from the donkey jacket was seeping through his T-shirt onto his shoulders when he turned the key to get in the house. The front door was covered with patches of wood nailed over the damage from when they broke in.

'Immediately he was struck by a strong smell. Bacon cooking. In the kitchen a young woman was standing with her back to him, turning rashers in a frying-pan. On the next ring, baked beans were bubbling in a saucepan. The figure was too tall to be Ute. It was one of the others living in the house, I won't tell you her name. On the table was a superior new tin-opener that she had bought. "Hello," she said, glancing over her shoulder. "Do you fancy some bacon?"

'I will draw a veil over what happened in the rest of the evening, but it is a tale of temptation and betrayal.'

'Sounds quite biblical,' said Corinne.

'Something about Reuben's stature was quite biblical,' said Ren. 'That evening I think he was demoralized by his struggle over the tin-opener, and he didn't do himself credit. He yielded to temptation and erred on an epic scale. Remember, there was an ideology of free love in left-wing circles in those days. And our mutual friend cooking the bacon was a very determined and seductive woman. But it was a first big hurt to his girlfriend Ute. It contributed to Reuben losing her, who I think he loved more than anyone in the world. Apart from his mother.

'In his room he had a mattress on the floor, and he said that after it was all over he rolled naked off the edge of the mattress on to his donkey jacket which was lying there. He felt a prod in his back. Discomfort nudged into his sleep. He was already snoring, but he had to wake up and move to avoid something sharp sticking into him from his jacket pocket. That was when he realized what he had done. It was the handle of the tin-opener.

'This tin-opener.' Ren held it up.

'Serve him right,' said Corinne. 'The nudge of conscience.'

'Reuben blamed the tin-opener for getting him into it in the first place.'

'Only himself to blame,' said Corinne. 'I hope he lay awake all night. It would be funny if it wasn't tragic. I feel sorry for Ute. Did she find out? Did she forgive him?'

'You can ask her yourself if you want. She's coming on Christmas Day. She always does. I think you'll like her.'

'You're still friends?'

'Experiences like being in that squat can bind you together for a lifetime.'

'I've never learnt how to keep friends. People and things seem to drift on past me. And the political beliefs that you say you all had? Have they survived too?'

'Judge for yourself. Ute might laugh about the tin-opener herself now. But she's always said it was the beginning of the end for her relationship with Reuben.'

'And you kept the tin-opener all this time?'

'I have to believe there's always a chance of redemption. Even for a tin-opener.'

Friday 21st December 1990 7.30pm
It had stopped raining and the street lights of Essex Road picked out Freddie's locks flying free as he sped down the wide pavement on his unicycle. The trousers of his Father Christmas costume were tucked up, and he followed a jerky trajectory like a moth bouncing off a hot light bulb. As he zig-zagged round passing pedestrians, they turned

to stare and read the placard that was tied to his back: 'THE OTHER HALF OF MY BIKE GOT SMASHED.' The waiters preparing tables at the 'Mon Repas' restaurant moved towards the window to watch as he slowed down and started circling round and round on the pavement outside.

A few minutes passed before the door of the restaurant opened and the owner came out wearing a steely expression: 'Riding that contraption on a busy pavement is a public danger. I've rung the police.'

Saturday 22nd December 1990 10am

The next morning as Ren was having her breakfast, Corinne appeared shivering in the kitchen. She poured herself a glass of wine from the half-empty bottle of Vinho Verde which she'd put in the fridge the night before.

'Hi,' said Ren, looking up from a plate of cornflakes. 'Having a good start to the day?' Her eyes twinkled under a turquoise headscarf.

'Horrible dream,' mumbled Corinne, and she took several gulps from the glass.

'Do you want to unload it?'

'You'll be late for work.'

'I'm offering.'

Corinne looked closely at her glass. 'There was a house. Lots of people around. And a pond of dirty water outside it. I was wearing a lovely white fluffy coat, like one I used to have as a teenager. From C&A in Oxford Street. My first grown-up coat. I loved it. My mother bought it for me. That was before I realized that every gift she gave me was a poisoned chalice.

'In the dream I was walking beside the pond and there was a bush hanging across the path, its branches were covered in oil. I tried to move it aside but I got oil on the front of my coat. A dark stain across the white fluffy fabric.

Then on the ground I saw a present I had wrapped up earlier, but the level of the pond was rising and lifting it off the bank. It was getting wet and muddy.'

'How did you feel when you woke up?' asked Ren.

'Like everything in my life was spoilt.'

'Upsetting?'

Corinne put her glass down and sank into a chair. 'Desperate.'

Ren looked at her and nodded.

Corinne looked up. 'I can't believe you don't want to know what I did to end up in there. I feel ashamed.'

'It wouldn't make any difference,' said Ren, and spooned up the last cornflakes from her bowl.

'What if I murdered someone?'

'I'll bet you didn't,' Ren was washing up her bowl. 'Anyway, you wouldn't be out on bail.'

'It was a mindless attempt at revenge gone wrong.'

'Revenge?'

'I was suffering. From what you could call emotional GBH. That's not defined as a crime, is it? All's fair in love and war and that. Love triangles. Power for the course. The other woman, his ex, she smiled as she turned the knife in the wound. Emotionally. But when my revenge back-fired I find I've committed a crime. Next thing I know I'm in a police station.'

'Scary.'

'Not that I actually knew much about it. I was totally plastered. Didn't come round till I woke up in the Detox Unit at Her Majesty's Pleasure. That'll teach me to try to get my own back. Best to do what I usually do. Roll over and get fucked.'

Ren had her eyes on Corinne. 'There's laws against abuse, and mental cruelty,' she said. 'But you're right, most emotional crimes are outside the law. Emotional fraud. Emotional robbery. No laws about crimes against the human heart.'

'And they're often the ones that hurt most,' said Corinne. She drained her glass and refilled it, emptying the bottle. 'Emotional GBH. If it was in the statute books, then self-defence against it would be treated with leniency. That bitch, his ex, she reappeared from his past like a spectre and moved straight in so close I could see her breath on his glasses. She didn't even want him, but she took him anyway. Destroyed my world. They call it charm, don't they, people who get away with things like that. I've got a better word for it.'

'Pain in the arse,' said Ren.

'I'd had a few drinks. It always helped me through before. How stupid could I be? I feel so ashamed.'

Ren sat back down at the table. 'I read a thing in the paper last year. A woman stabbed her mother. The mother was eighty-four and had nagged her for years. Criticizing all the time, telling lies. The woman who did it was a deputy head teacher. She told the police, "She was horrible to me". Everyone who knew her signed a petition. To support her.'

'What happened?'

'She got let off. Three years' probation.'

Corinne looked up from her wine. 'Are you saying that to cheer me up?'

'I really did read it.' said Ren.

'Being "horrible," what does that mean?' Corinne turned the word over. 'Mmm. And what about being manipulative? Invading other people's lives? Emotional imperialism? His ex was an expert at that. I'm not defending what I did. But I felt under attack. It felt like a physical attack. I felt her spinning a web round him. Throwing a lasso around him and hauling him in.'

Ren stood up. 'There are ropes and threads between human beings, they're very strong. It's just that usually we can't see them. Perhaps that's why we get surprised by things people do and by our reactions.'

'Is this the kind of thing you discuss with your clients?'

'Maybe. Once I've found found the energy to get there this morning. Christmas is a hard time for them. They experience so much pressure to be happy, it makes it even more painful to be unhappy.'

'Do you have far to go?'

'Less than a mile. I could walk through the cemetery but I like stopping for tea at the Turkish restaurant on the way. Do you have any plans for this morning?'

Corinne shrugged. 'I need to go home for some clothes.'

'There's a front door key hanging above the draining board. So you can get back in.'

'I don't know what will happen if I go round there. I don't want to run into him. Or her. The ex. She's probably moved in already.'

'So she didn't suffer from your attempt at revenge?'

'She thrived on it. One of the last things I remember through a drunken haze is her triumphant smile. When they took me away. That and the water everywhere.'

'Had you been drinking a lot?'

'I'm afraid so. But not for that long. I don't think I'm actually an alcoholic.' She paused. 'But they all say that, don't they?' She looked at the empty bottle of Vinho Verde. 'I'm definitely going to come off it.'

Ren smiled. 'It's a tough one. You'll need to take very good care of yourself, treat yourself kindly. Eat well. Do you want anything else for breakfast, apart from the Vinho?' She set a bowl and spoon on the table alongside the packets of cereal.

She left Corinne staring dully into a bowl of cornflakes while the radio played *Bohemian Rhapsody*, 'Our Christmas Number One, it's there again: Queen with the late, great, Mercury, king of understatement, a voice from the grave,' and light rain whispered at the window.

Saturday 22nd December 1990 10am

In South End Green the shop windows threw trails of light on the wet pavements. Ute stood in the doorway of 'Threads' to watch Christmas shoppers passing in the drizzle. She looked at her own window display. At one end were curtain fabrics in rainbow colours draped in rolls. In the middle of the window were two rolls of wallpaper, a little unrolled, with a bucket and a wide paint brush between them, as if inviting passers-by to come in and paste them up. On the other end of the window there was a display with a patchwork quilt made of different-coloured knitted squares. Above the window silver lettering read: 'Threads: for all your interior design needs'.

The phone rang on the counter inside the shop and Ute went to answer it.

'Hello?… Hello, Mr. Goforth!… Yes, your curtain material has come in…' She re-opened a large brown paper packet on the end of the counter and ran her hand over the fabric inside, which featured cave painting designs against a grey background. 'I'm afraid that I cannot guarantee a delivery on Monday because it is Christmas Eve. But I can post it on Monday and the fabric will reach you soon after Christmas……. Yes, it is very fine, exactly the same colours as the sample… You could almost believe you are living in a cave… Yes, I will do that… '. She smiled, 'Happy Hunting to you, too, Mr. Goforth. Goodbye.'

She put the phone down and watched as two customers examined some small wood-carved ornaments at the front of the shop.

She sat and pulled some knitting out of a bag under the counter. It was a small square in green wool. She worked a couple of rows in plain stitch and matched it for size with another knitted square in pale pink.

When the shop was empty again, Ute stopped knitting

and wandered around, stroking the fabrics, picking up small items and setting them down again. The place was draped with furnishing materials in designs ranging from William Morris to deckchair-type stripes, seas of poppies and starry skies. On a table at the side she picked up a handmade velvet pincushion shaped like a heart, and took it to the counter. She wrapped it in emerald green tissue paper. With a pair of scissors she cut out a small label and wrote on it, 'For Ren HAPPY CHRISTMAS Love from Ute.' She tied the label onto the present with green thread.

Looking round the shop again, she found a miniature travel sewing kit in a pouch of maroon linen. She wrapped that too, and wrote a label: 'For Vicente, in case a button falls off when you are on assignment! Happy Christmas from Ute.' She found a small sponge bag she had handmade from a zebra fabric, which she wrapped and labelled: 'For Brenda, still wild at heart... Seasons Greetings, love Ute'.

A tall man came in to the shop. His long hair was soaked from the rain and hanging in rat's tails. He had no coat on. His face was handsome in an untidy way, but it did not look happy. He put a pair of rimless glasses into his shirt's breast pocket, and Ute could see that his eyes were red.

He lurched onto the counter. 'Good morning, Ute. How are they selling?'

She looked at him with concern: 'Good morning, Terry. You do look wet, you must take care not to catch cold. The little wooden sculptures, they are doing well. I have sold two of the badgers, so I would like to order two more of those if that is possible.'

'OK,' the man said. 'OK, OK, OK.' He pulled himself up off the counter.

Ute's eyes followed him. 'But something it seems perhaps is not OK?'

'Nothing... Everything... is not OK. I'm sorry, I don't

mean to trouble you. The badgers, yes, the badgers…' He turned to walk out of the shop. 'At least I know *they're* not going to disappear…'

3

Chapter Three

Saturday 22nd December 1990 12 midday

Casenove Road is busy this morning. On the way to my session with Ren I can't resist popping in to the junk shop at the end of the road near the corner of the high street. It's always crammed full of clothing on rails, and smells musty as if the contents of the shop were as old as the gentleman who runs it. He sits at the back, peering over an old-fashioned till. His English is broken and his smile is rusty; I have never asked him where he is from, in case that is a painful question. I look at a red cardigan; it's my colour, but I don't like the buttons. Anyway, I probably wouldn't fit into it. In the back there is a floor-to-ceiling shelf unit full of shoes. It was here I bought Bert's first pair of boots.

Poor Bert. This morning I found another note from him on the kitchen table: *'WHERE IS MY DAD?'* Every year it's the same. And every year I don't know what to tell him.

I try on some pink high heels with a tiny bow. Good condition and they're very beautiful, but no good for me. Too showy. And too wobbly. I have enough trouble keeping my balance in ordinary shoes. I thank the old man and leave.

On the way through the Abney cemetery I can't help stopping to read some of the gravestones and wonder about the lives of the people underneath. What made them happy and sad? Did they find comfort at the moment of their death? Did religion sustain them, or did they face the void with an atheist's blind courage? I read somewhere that the cemetery was built on the land of a man who had attended the Stoke Newington Dissenters Academy, and therefore it attracted a lot of dissenters. It was a non-denominational garden cemetery. So even then Stokey was a place for people who diverged from the norm.

I've got myself late so I have to speed along to catch up. I'm out of breath by the time I'm sitting again in Ren's wicker chair and she's sitting facing me looking paler than ever. The tape recorder is slowly, slowly, turning and I'm wondering how I managed to end up in this crisis. With past, present and future all tangled up and a head full of ideas that don't make sense to anyone else. She's sitting there waiting for me to speak and I can't get the question out of my head, so in the end I say it:

'How did I manage to end up in this mess?'

'I wouldn't call it a mess, but do you have a sense of how this train of events began?'

I wish I knew. I try to thread my thoughts together. 'It all started as a rational process. From the work on my PhD. You know my topic. "Iatromantic Practices in Ancient Greece". That includes treatment of the sick through incubation and divination. And consulting the dead. I've been trying to understand and analyze these practices, I began to think they had beliefs about an afterlife, or some sort of rebirth for the dead. It was a rational hypothesis based on the evidence.

'But the other archaeologists didn't react rationally. They don't like those kind of ideas. Either they're Christians, in which case they're wanting to find some kind of religion with personified deities, or else they're secular thinkers, in which case they're not interested in thinking about unusual spiritual practices. To them it's all just mumbo jumbo, and they have no time for it. They're more interested in studying technology and social hierarchy. So nobody liked the ideas I was coming up with.'

'Was that hard for you?'

I'm nodding. I'm thinking about all the times I put in ideas or questions at seminars, and there's a silence after I finish speaking. As if I had committed some *faux pas* so terrible that no one was even going to tell me what it was. I can feel my stomach tightening. I remember the times I'd go home and go to bed with a migraine. I decide to come clean with her about what happened on Tuesday. 'I went to a seminar this week,' I say. 'What happened really upset me.'

Ren lifts where one eyebrow would be. It's an invitation to continue.

I don't want to remember. I've tried to put it out of my mind. The honest fact is, I don't want to talk about it. But this whole therapy or counselling business seems to be exactly that – talking about things you don't want to talk about. It's supposed to make you feel better. That's meant to be why I'm here. So I tell her.

'The seminar was on ancient Greek beliefs about death and attitudes to the dead. At the end I asked a question about whether they talked to bones. One of the other PhD students made fun of me. He said "Is that a serious question?" and they all laughed. It was unfair because we know they had well-established oracles of the dead in classical times. But it was humiliating. I felt myself going bright red. Only the speaker came to my help. Dr. Chrysostomos, he's on the staff there. I know him a little.

'Afterwards when we all went for refreshments, I found that no one came near me. Dr. Chrysostomos was busy with some students, and none of the others wanted to speak to me. They left a space around me, as if there was a contagion zone and they would catch something if they came close. I felt like a leper.'

'Were they really avoiding you, or could it have been coincidence?'

'Not one single person spoke to me.'

'What were they really afraid of catching if they came close?'

'Infectious ideas. Bad ideas. Mad ideas. Or just new unauthorized ideas. Terminal for any academic who wants to keep a spotless reputation for good sense. The old guys have a vested interest in the theories they've developed. The young ones are scared to step out of line. Their standing would suffer if they were seen talking to me.'

'Sounds difficult.'

'It was dreadful. They were acting as if I wasn't there. That *does* make me feel crazy. Because of the stuff that happened with Dr. Scheiner, I think word has got around and some of the other lecturers are ostracizing me too, blanking me in the corridor, let alone anything I say in a seminar.'

'So you have had more encounters with Dr. Scheiner?'

'I'm afraid so. Anyway, after this seminar on Tuesday I went home with a migraine, and a neck ache.' I can feel it again now and I turn my head on my shoulders.

'I suggest you do that a little more,' says Ren. 'Take it slowly, gently, and take some full breaths with a long exhale. Let your neck move and relax.'

I clutch my neck, a handful of my hair with it, and I make some stroking movements. Then I let my head fall right back, it's a relief and I let out a sigh. What a weight it is. Then I slowly start rotating it. I remember how things were when I first started on my PhD work, and I say, 'The rational Anthea researching for her doctorate seems so far away from this other Anthea who everyone thinks is going bonkers.'

'Do you want to talk about this other Anthea?'

'It's her thoughts. Not just about the bones and Dr. Scheiner. But also thinking this connects with the reason I've always been interested in Greece. Even from reading Greek myths when I was still in primary school. I always longed to go there. I've never believed in reincarnation – I've always regarded it as nonsense – but now I find myself wondering whether I'm finishing some business from another life thousands of years ago. Thinking that perhaps the daydreams or imaginary scenes I've been witnessing are not visions but memories.'

'Memories?'

'Perhaps a past I had forgotten in my conscious mind seeping through unconsciously.'

I remember the time in 1971 when I was at a stone circle in Dorset, and hearing the words that were meant to be prophetic because it was midsummer and they were heard by chance. An ancient Greek custom, Kledonas. You ask a question, and then it's the first words you hear, spoken by a passing stranger. Two walkers went past in the rain. They seemed to be having some kind of a row. Strange. What are the chances of that happening? I heard just the four words: 'talking to the dead'. Those four words stuck with me. I saw myself following that path by studying the ancient world, by doing academic research into the lives of people who lived thousands of years ago. Then over time it changed and I thought, maybe those words meant something different. Maybe it meant that dead people could literally speak to me. And that's where the bones come in.

I look at Ren. 'I'm afraid I've been acting strangely too. Mostly around this Dr. Scheiner. Part of me is sure these things are true. And that he's involved.'

'Dr. Scheiner again.'

'After I had the dream where he was trying to save me, he was constantly on my mind. The dream was – what's that expression? – burning a hole in my pocket. I kept wondering if he had any dreams similar to mine. Or thoughts. That dream was so strong, I couldn't believe he wasn't part of it.'

'So, you did something…?'

'In the end I plucked up my courage and approached him after a seminar. He was talking to a professor from Birmingham and I hovered on the edge of their conversation for a few minutes. I didn't know if they had noticed me standing there. Sometimes, if you're not important, academics act as if they can't see you. But eventually Dr. Scheiner turned to me: "Hello, Anthea."

'I said, "I'm sorry to trouble you, but I wondered if it would be possible to have another word with you?"

'He said, "This isn't a good time, I'm afraid. Drop me a note and we'll fix something up."

'So I sent another note. "I appreciate you are very busy, but I would be most grateful if this might be possible… " etc.

'I didn't hear back for several weeks. I was going down every morning to check the post, falling over Freddie's bike in the hall. Our house is a bit of a mess…' I stop. The thought of the chaos in the house is infectious, I feel as if it has spread to my brain and paralysed it. 'Where was I…?'

Ren prompts me: 'You had written another letter.'

'Well, in the end I got back a rather terse typed note. "How about 3.30pm on 4th November in my office?" then he signed his name "Heinrich" with "Dr. Scheiner" typed below.

'When I got there on the day, his secretary showed me in to his office, lined wall to wall with books like they usually are. He was sitting at a large desk with two neat piles of papers in front of him.

'"Well, what can I do for you?" He sounded a bit brusque.

'"I wanted your advice, really," I started cautiously. "It's about the bones."

'"Oh, the bones again," he said.

'"Yes, except this time looking not just at your site but at those bones in the context of the other tombs. I would value your opinion. My thought is that the cut marks on the bones might be the only surviving evidence of an ongoing dialogue between the living and the dead. Perhaps involving divination."

'"You're determined to find significance in those bones, aren't you?" he said.

'"Yes. Well, no. I'm not determined to find anything particular. I'm trying to find hypotheses which would explain these phenomena associated with the bones."

'"Speculation. I'm afraid it's all speculation."

'I stuck to my guns: "There are many ethnographic parallels for such uses of bones."

'He agreed, "It's generally accepted that in prehistoric religion the ancestors played a role, but as for the specifics…"

'I continued: "Many cultures believe in the return of the dead. Reincarnation, summoning of spirits, oracular dreams … There's the Witch of Endor in the Bible… Western culture is unusual in not subscribing to such ideas."

'He was uncomfortable now. "I am aware of this…"

'He glanced around his study and seemed to be losing patience so I took the plunge. "Have you ever had any direct experience of any such thing?"

'There, I'd asked it. He looked up at me sharply. "I beg your pardon?"

'I tried again: "I wondered whether you had ever experienced anything like that? I mean, not just theoretically?"

'His voice was unusually slow and sarcastic. "Have I conversed with the dead? Had oracular dreams? No, I can safely say that I don't regard that as a necessary part of my researches. I am not sure what you're trying to say. I have a lot of things to get on with this afternoon."

'So I got a total blank. I tried to make a joke of it: "It would be useful, though, wouldn't it? One could ask the Minoans a few leading questions...."

'A flicker of amusement passed over his face and he took off his spectacles to clean them. "Yes, I daresay it would be. Now, if we've finished our business..."

'I made one last ditch effort: "I wondered if you remember any dream at all ... anything..."

'He stared me full in the face. For a flash of a moment I was sure he knew exactly what I was talking about. The wall. His desperate efforts. My terror. Our terror. He had been there with me. I was sure of it. Then his face clouded over. He stood up and suddenly left his office. I followed him. He walked straight down the corridor without looking back. I wanted to call after him but I couldn't. He bolted like a rabbit and disappeared through a pair of double doors at the end.

'The departmental secretary came out of the office next door and looked down the corridor after him. She seemed surprised too. She looked at her watch, shrugged, and went back in again. Apparently he had another appointment in five minutes and she wasn't expecting him to go anywhere.

'I went home. I wolfed down the rice left from supper the night before and went to bed with a migraine. I had meant to thank him and I did it all wrong. I blew it. Nothing Morton could do all evening could cheer me up.'

I stop and look around Ren's room. I look at the candle burning on the table, the rug on the floor, the large potted plant like the ones the Victorians were so fond of, the view out of the window onto the nearby houses. The tape going round and round in the machine recording the session.

I persuade myself that I don't need to tell Ren any more about Dr. Scheiner. About how after that I wrote again. And again. Trying to arrange to see him, without getting any response. So I turned up outside his office and waited. I was only trying to see him to apologize. And thank him. I never thought he would call Security. I don't need to tell her all that.

'So do you think I'm mad?' I ask her eventually.

'That question again.' Ren shook her head. 'I'm not sure what you mean by that word, but there's nothing you've told me that would make me think your functioning was impaired. Or that you were any less of a human being. Your experiences of dreaming, and seeing things, might seem unusual to some people, but they are no less valid for that. It can be problematic to share them with people who are on a different wavelength, like Dr. Scheiner. But they're your experiences. Such experiences are more common than our culture acknowledges. I'm glad you're able to talk to me about them. Bringing them into the daylight, as it were, is a first step towards appraising them and understanding where they're coming from. And how much weight they should be given. We need to find a way to help you deal with them, because they're evidently troubling you.'

I keep returning in my mind to that flash of connection at the end of my conversation with Dr. Scheiner. I say, 'For that moment it didn't feel as if he was on a different wavelength. I felt in total communication with him.'

'We have to ask whether he felt that too. Or indeed whether he could be capable of such a feeling.'

I bury my head in my hands. 'I've messed everything up, haven't I? I don't know what's the matter with me. I used to be so together. Morton's right, I've lost it…'

'I certainly wouldn't say that you have lost it, Anthea. You're here, you're talking, you're trying to grapple with the issues.' Ren looks at the clock on the low table. 'You can talk more about this in your next session if you want, but I'm afraid our time is up for today.'

Saturday 22nd December 1990 5pm

That evening Corinne was grating cheese when Ren walked into the kitchen and sank onto one of the red chairs.

Corinne asked 'Would you like a cup of tea?'

'Please. It's on the shelf.'

'Hard day?'

Ren nodded.

Corinne reached up to the shelf and took down a Chinese-decorated tea caddy with a dragon on the side. She peered inside. 'Is this ordinary tea? Is this a dragon I can chase safely? Nothing looks or smells normal any more. But at least my sense of smell has come back.'

'Your body's cleaned out some of the alcohol?'

'Guess so. I didn't buy any booze today.' Corinne put a spoonful in the pot. 'You're a masseur, right? How does that work? Do you hoover up people's problems with your hands? Is that why you look knackered? Is that why they feel better afterwards?'

Ren watched her put the kettle on. 'Not quite. You're trained to act as a channel. Allow them to receive what they need. Take away what they don't. It doesn't come from me, it just passes through.'

Corinne stared at the shelf. 'Does it matter which cups I use?'

'Any you like.'

'I feel like blue.' She took two pale blue cups from their pegs. 'Can you do that? Channel stuff?'

Ren smiled. 'If I focus. You have to pay a lot of attention to keep the channel clear. Not let your own worries and stupid thoughts get in the way.'

The kettle boiled and Corinne's hand shook slightly as she filled the pot. 'Sounds tricky. Channels, pipes, drains… Stuff could get caught in the U-bend?' She sniffed the top of the milk bottle. 'Is this the right milk?'

'The other bottle's fresher. Sometimes I don't massage.

People just talk.'

'And you get weighed down with their words?' Corinne poured milk from the other bottle and added tea. 'This tea looks really weak. Sometimes the simplest task seems insuperable.' She slumped onto one of the kitchen chairs. 'I'm sorry.'

'The tea's fine.' Ren smacked her lips playfully to prove her point. 'Give yourself a break. You're in recovery. And no, I don't get weighed down. It's mostly just listening. Paying attention. Not enough attention gets paid in this world. People often know the answers themselves if you listen carefully. People have incredible stories.'

'True stories?'

'They're the most incredible.'

Ren sipped her tea. Corinne stared at her hands, 'We told each other stories in the prison.'

'The stories I hear in the sessions can never be repeated,' said Ren. 'Client confidentiality.'

'We spilled our hearts out in the nick,' said Corinne. 'I distracted my cell mates with an episode from my mis-spent youth. Aeons ago. In 1971 I had a love affair that shook my bones and when it broke up I self-harmed. Eventually I got to Greece… On the beach there I met two blond boys living in tents on the sand. Sun-bound and vacant. 1970s dopeheads. They were Dutch, from Nijmegen. I'll leave the rest to your imagination.' She turned the silver ring on the little finger of her right hand.

'Nijmegen? That's an important place. It was the first Dutch city to fall to the Germans in World War II. Then in 1944 the USA bombed the city. By mistake. 750 people died.'

'That's weird. How come you know this stuff?'

'A mis-spent middle age. Trying to catch up on the education I never had. The roots of people's behaviour often lie in the past.'

Corinne played with her teaspoon. 'I never thought

about why those boys were so cut off. I never asked them stuff like that. I was pretty blank myself at the time.'

'Did your friends in the prison like your story?'

'They listened. Time drags in detox. It was a bit revealing. I don't know why I told them.'

'Or perhaps you do?'

'Perhaps... To make a connection? To get their attention? There's nothing like sex to get people interested.'

'Were they interested?'

'Seemed to be. There's so much more texture to sex than is usually spoken about. In films you usually get glamorous close-ups then fade to black. But there are as many different ways to have sex as to have a conversation. It can be interesting, dull, kind, ecstatic, abusive...'

'That's very true.'

'Magnificent, embarassing, catastrophic... None of that gets talked about. It's meant to be wonderful or nothing, full stop.'

Ren looked at her. 'Do you regret talking about it in the prison?'

Corinne pursed her lips. 'By the end I felt exposed. I'm embarrassed about what happened on the beach. But I don't really regret telling it. As Mandy said...'

'Mandy?'

'She was one of the women. She was only twenty-seven, but she'd lived through enough pain to last a lifetime. Another woman, Debs, was younger; she was sharp as nails. And Beverly, an older black woman. They were all clucking–going through withdrawal. We shared a lot. But as Mandy said, I'll probably never see any of them again.'

'That made it easier to talk?'

'In some way. And telling them about that summer in Greece helped process it. I'd never talked about that stuff, and they listened. When I went to Greece that time I was in crisis – like now. On that beach I recovered a bit then. And re-telling it in the prison helped me recover now. A little. Making a story of something helps you find some grace and meaning in it. It helped me.'

'Like therapy?'

'I guess so. That time on the beach was when I hit rock bottom and bounced back up.' Corinne screwed her face up and shrugged. 'What is it turns our life around? Is it other people? Chance…? Or personal resolve? Or situations…? The climate of a time?'

'Or all the above? Someone said, "We do not change. We only stand more revealed."' Ren shook her head. 'I can't remember who it was.'

'Do you believe it?' asked Corinne.

Ren poured herself another cup of tea. 'My friend Ute believes that in certain years there is a coming together of influences that make drastic changes, or perhaps revelations, in people's lives. She always says 1971 was a turning point for her: after her time in the squat, she says she was never the same.'

Corinne said, '1971? That's weird, it was for me too. That was the year I fell in love, self-harmed, watched the sky fall in on me, changed, started the whole cycle of events that ended up on the beach in Greece in 1972. I came back and tried to pick up the pieces, but they've never gone back together the same way since.' She paused. 'Does your friend Ute have ideas about what makes some years do that?'

'She talks about things that were happening socially. Politically. And personally for her, caught up in it. Other people might say it was planetary energies.' Ren stood up, took two large potatoes from the vegetable rack and washed them.

'I had a friend who used to blame everything on Saturn's return,' said Corinne. 'But you were all activists. I don't expect you rated astrology.'

Ren shook her head. 'But some years there's something

in the air that pushes all of us a little further towards our destiny.'

'Do you believe in destiny?'

'Only as a figure of speech. To mean something whose seeds will grow – something that has the potential to unfold.'

'There's another thing about 1971,' Corinne said. 'Being in the prison reminded me that I used to write stories. Fiction. When I was very young. And then again in 1971.' Corinne lifted her mug of tea, then put it back down on the table. 'Telling that story in the prison brought it all back. I realized what a loss it's been. If only I could write again…' Corinne watched Ren removing the bad bits from the potatoes. 'Can I help you with that?'

'It's OK. Do you like baked spuds?'

'I do. Thank you. Thank you for giving me the front door key. I went out today. Out into the big bad world.'

'Was it very big and bad?'

'It was OK at first. I wandered up and down your road. It's got two schools, that knocked me back a bit. I started thinking about my childhood. I got sent away to boarding school. The uniform was a dress with a thin purple stripe, and we wore white socks and brown sandals. I remember being bullied and I felt sad. The past is no good for me, I have to look to the future like a ship in a storm looks for dry land.'

'Land ahoy…' Ren laughed.

'And the other depressing thing about schools,' said Corinne, 'is that they have to start again with each generation of children. To teach them. And then those children, they grow old and die. And the teaching has to start again. It's thankless, on and on. Exhausting to think about.'

'I suppose so…' said Ren. 'But you could look at it another way: with every generation you get a fresh chance to begin again with a clean slate. A chance to do things better, to make things better from scratch.'

Corinne sat in silence. Then she spoke slowly: 'I went back to my home. The first time since I was arrested. It's hardly been more than a week, but it feels like a lifetime ago.'

'You went home?'

'I knew he wouldn't be there, I knew he'd be out at two o'clock on a Saturday. But I didn't see any signs of her there either. No stuff moved in. It was weird. It looked just the same. As if I was still living there. The kettle was warm from him making a cup of tea. His socks were on the floor. I looked at his woodcarvings, he was still working on the same ones. I was tempted to take one of the badgers, but I didn't. Best I try to forget all about him.

'No sign of her. I don't know where she was. I picked up some stuff. My coat. Cheque book, so now I can help pay for food. Address book. Change of clothes. What I could carry. Tattered remnants of my life.

'And while I was there, I fished in my underclothes drawer and pulled my story out. One I wrote all that time ago, in 1971. I haven't written anything since. After all that storytelling when I was in the prison, I wanted to have it with me. It's a seaside story. I wanted to look at it again.

'Then while I was still in the house the phone rang, and I bottled and legged it. But I brought the story with me.'

'A seaside story?'

'Kind of. I lost the top copy when I lost the diary I wrote in 1971. It was folded in the diary. But I've always had the carbon copy.'

'I'd love to hear it.'

'It's not really ready for… anyone to hear.'

'Don't worry about that. Or is it that you're shy?'

'Maybe,' Corinne hesitated, then pulled some closely-typed foolscap pages out of her stripey shoulder bag. The paper was almost transparent, the carbon type dark and blurred round the edges. 'I'll read you the first bit. Just to give you a taste.' She played with one of the rusty staples which held the pages together. 'I was in a weird state when I wrote it.'

Ren said: 'You don't need to apologize.'

Corinne started to read.

The air was thickening along the dusky esplanade. A torn awning flapped over the front of a boarded-up newsagents. Gulls screeched and scratched the sky as the green bus stopped by the pier to drop its last load of passengers before returning to the depot. The engine whirred while passengers clambered off, clutching hats and billowing plastic macs. "Goodnight" muttered the driver. The next day was Sunday, his day off. No one needed a bus on Sunday. No one came or went in the sleepy sea-resort on the Lord's day of rest. It was a place that people retired to, where they sat in small boarding houses spinning out their fragile lives like crochet, waiting to die. Many of them were too old to go to church. On Sunday they hid behind lace curtains close to the fire, holding china cups in trembling hands and talking about past years. And sometimes a cold finger of wind pierced in through the lattice; cup and saucer drooped, and the thin thread of life snapped.

'There was a funeral passing the end of the esplanade now. As the bus pulled away the small group of passengers dispersed across the twilight streets. Agnes Reynolds pulled her shabby brown overcoat around her and set out along the sea-front. In one hand her ringed fingers clutched a leather handbag, in the other a light travelling grip. Her bright bird-like eyes looked out across the sea from a face already lined with what she had missed...'

Corinne sighed and put the pages down on the table. 'And so it goes on.'

Ren lit the oven with a match and put the potatoes inside on the top shelf. 'It sounds interesting. Have you ever tried to get anything published?'

Corinne put her hands round her cup of undrunk tea as if she were trying to warm them. 'Never. Hundreds of people you don't know seeing into your soul. Scary.'

Saturday 22nd December 1990 6pm
Alex sat in her South London council flat composing an article.

Her typewriter was on a desk looking down from the fourth floor onto a treeless panorama of traffic and tower blocks. Her fingers moved restlessly over the keys:

'A heavy drug user walks down the street and attacks an elderly woman. He grabs her handbag and takes her purse to feed his addiction to heroin. Public response would be to arrest and punish him.

'But consider a parallel scenario. An obese dollar-swollen superstate, over-dependent on petrol-guzzling cars, luxuries, unnecessary gadgets and TV, undertakes a war in the Middle East and attacks Iraq to feed its addiction to oil. As a result homes are destroyed, thousands of innocent civilians are killed and the poorest in that country suffer most.

'Can anyone explain why the lone individual is called a junkie and a criminal, while the gorged superstate inflicting its addiction on a global scale claims the moral high ground as part of the "free world" involved in a "justified war"? That is what the USA is doing now as it stands on the brink of involvement in a Gulf war.'

Alex hesitated and frowned. She scrunched up her black curly hair then let it go. As it bounced back into its original shape, she started typing again.

'One way to tackle this dilemma is...'

Her phone rang and she left her seat to answer it. 'Hello? Oh, hi, that's a surprise... Yeah, tonight's fine... I think Attila the Stockbroker is on at Shepherds Bush... Yes... No, come to think of it, it's not him, it's one of the other ranters... Great, I'll meet you outside...'

She put down the receiver and picked up an unopened envelope lying next to it. Inside was a Christmas card. She made a face, sat down at her typewriter, pulled the previous page out and put in a clean sheet of paper. After a moment's pause, she started typing furiously:

'Christmas Greetings to all and please forgive me writing a Round Robin to send my news. I started writing individual letters and cards but it turned out to be far too much trouble so I tore them up. I couldn't think how to make them different from each other and I don't expect anyone's that interested anyway. I hate receiving long letters, it takes ages to read them and I haven't got time especially round Christmas when there's stress and madness going on everywhere. As if I really care whose children have had how many grandchildren. I can never remember their names and they all look the same in those mawkish baby snaps people insist on sending me. It's all unbelievably tedious: so-and-so has been ill, we moved house… (why bother? Why tell me about it?). It would be great if people could just get on with their own lives and leave me to lead mine. With lashings of Christmas spirit (the liquid variety), Alex.'

She pulled the page out of the typewriter and read it with satisfaction.

Saturday 22nd December 1990 9.30pm

Alex waited half-an-hour outside the pub in the rain. When Duane arrived he had the wide lapels of his faded overcoat turned up and his woolly hat well pulled down. He swaggered up and kissed her on the cheek with no apology. Inside it was crowded. He bought two lagers and they found seats at the back. Alex took off her coat and flapped her low-cut T-shirt to help the air circulate around her breasts. She leant towards Duane: 'Aren't you hot?'

'No, I'm coool,' his lips mouthed with a smile. He sat quite still in his long oatmeal-coloured overcoat, and didn't take off the brown woolly hat which hid his dreadlocks.

On the stage in front, through the smoke and darkness

of the audience squeezed together round tables or fetching drinks, a spotlight shone on the second variety act of the evening as it ended amid applause. Then the compère came on, an older man in a trilby, wearing a waistcoat with a large tattoo visible on his bare arm. Brandishing a glass of beer, he announced:

'Ladies and gentlemen, now we've got a treat for you. Here's the guy to put the ass into Christmass, one of our regulars. We like him here, his act's so excoriating (look it up, guys!) he cleans the cobwebs off the ceiling. If you're not careful he takes the paint off the walls, too. Put your hands together for Haranguing Henry!!'

The performer was a young man in jeans and T-shirt weating dark glasses. His high, rasping voice slashed through the hum of the audience:

'Up for work and don't be late
Eat your tedium off the plate
Drink a cup of bland and boring
The papers say 'Ain't it appalling?
Celebrity marriage is in tatters
They never say what really matters
Wages falling prices rising
Pump him with more advertising
Consumer garbage sell it fast
To keep him sitting on his arse
No sod is gonna start a riot
Hooked onto the media diet.
Shock and horror, 'Ain't it awful?'
But the worst crimes they've made them lawful:
Fleecing the poor while the rich get bloated
Think you've got power because you voted?
They're the same whatever stripe they come
From grocer's daughters to Oxbridge scum…'

Alex kicked off her high-heeled shoes and wriggled her toes, stretching out her long thin legs in front of her in their skin-tight trousers.

The performer raised his voice to a yell:

'Trivialized homogenised toxic pap
You sit at home and lap it up…'

Alex wrapped her legs around each other like a corkscrew, and looked at Duane.

'…The straightjacket of your day's routine
It's all happening beyond the screen
The spectacle, glamour and the Queen
Watch and yearn, know what I mean?
Goggle the box with a beer or two
Don't catch on what they're doing to you
Aneasthetised to a thousand cuts
Paralysed in your little rut
They robbed your dignity, bled you dry,
You think happiness comes from what you buy?
You never ask the question "Why?"
The world's like they tell you
You want what they sell you
Even though your job's precarious
And all your pleasures are vicarious…'

Haranguing Henry curled his lips into a snarl and spat his last two lines into the audience:

'…You like to teach the world to sing
"It's fucking brilliant, everything"…'

Duane leant over and whispered in Alex's ear: 'This guy not happy, you know what I'm saying?'

Back in Alex's flat Duane kept his woolly hat on as they made love slowly and carefully. Afterwards she nestled against the smooth dark skin of his shoulder and said, 'I wasn't expecting to see you again. I thought last week was a one-off.'

'I know a good thing, right?'

'So what do you think of sex south of the river?'

'It's beautiful, yeah. You got a nice place here.' His brown eyes flicked around the small neat bedroom. They landed on a print of Van Gogh's Sunflowers hanging on the white wall in a plain wood frame. 'Them flowers are lively, you know what I'm saying? Like they're actually like breathing... I suppose since you are a cultured lady you love art and paintings and things.'

'Yes. And things.'

'Painting windows like what I do is not the same.'

'That can be a work of art too.'

'Sometimes it is and sometimes it isn't, know what I mean?'

Alex asked, 'Did you get back OK on Wednesday morning?'

'You could say there was only moments to spare. That fat lady that fell over, she saved my life. If she hadn't of got me out of the pub like right then, when I got home my chick could of been gone. She was, like, on the edge of walking out with the kids. Over Christmas. She acts strange sometimes.' He shook his head. 'Thank you, fat lady. Her fate to fall over, saved Christmas. Or perhaps it was the finger of God.'

Alex rolled her eyes but said nothing.

They lay for some moments in silence. There were footsteps in the flat above.

Duane stroked Alex's nipple and said, 'My chick sometimes cries afterwards.' He stared at the ceiling and then added, 'Maybe she has good reason.'

'It sounds like she has. You told me you make a habit of playing away.''

'No, it's not that. It's just ...' he took a breath and shut his eyes. 'You're the kind of person that listens good, and you know things, right? Perhaps you can answer me something. Why it is easier with someone you don't know so well.'

'How do you mean?'

'Put it this way. With my chick, right, it is not always easy. Not to spoil it, you know. All over too soon. And she's still waiting. When you've known someone a long time. You know what I'm saying. It's different with someone you don't know so well.' He didn't open his eyes and he didn't move.

'That sounds hard.' She stroked his chest.

'That is not a good feeling, you know what I mean? To disappoint someone you care about.'

'I'm sorry.' Alex looked at his face. She pulled the bedclothes over them both. 'Your chick, as you call her, your partner, must love you a lot.'

He started and opened his eyes. 'When you say that, it feels like a trap. Someone wants something from you, more than what you can be able to give.'

She carried on stroking his chest. Gradually his breathing slowed.

After a while, Alex said, 'Perhaps, with someone you don't know so well, the stakes are not so high. Not so scary.'

A mumbled reply, 'Uh huh.'

She paused. 'What d'you think?'

A faint 'Uh huh…'

She looked at his face and saw he was asleep.

She switched off the bedside light and settled under the bedclothes.

Sunday 23rd December 1990 11.30am

In 'Mon Repas' restaurant on the Essex Road, Mimi was sitting over a cold coffee. Outside the window a figure on the pavement caught her eye. Under a murky sky, a figure in a Father Christmas costume was limping past on two large crutches. Out of the red hood with its white fur trim, light brown dreadlocks struggled to escape. The figure turned and walked back again along the pavement outside the restaurant window. On his back he had a placard which read, 'LEGLESS SANTA GETS THE SACK'.

The restaurant owner swept out of the kitchen, strode to the door and onto the pavement. 'Go away!' she screamed, 'Go away! Go away! How dare you! You are insane!!…' At that point the restaurant door closed itself and her words could no longer be heard from inside. The Father Christmas figure looked the picture of sanity and seasonal goodwill, waving to her politely as he continued on his crippled path patrolling from one side to the other in front of the restaurant. The waiters tried not to attract attention as they edged towards the window to see their boss's outburst continuing in dumb show.

Then they made themselves scarce as she burst back in through the door and stormed towards the kitchen at the back. She made a token gesture of restrained exasperation in Mimi's direction before she disappeared.

For a while Mimi watched the Father Christmas figure hobbling to and fro without further disturbance, then she took a sip of her coffee and turned back to her reading. In her hand she held a hard-backed diary which had been decorated front and back with an exuberant collage of images including a sun, lips, a tree, waves, an eye, and clouds; the pictures were faded and had started peeling off. She opened the book where she had been saving a place with her thumb, and studied one page. Then she took from it some typed sheets of foolscap paper and opened them out. She read:

'The air was thickening along the dusky esplanade. A torn awning flapped over the front of a boarded-up newsagents. Gulls screeched and scratched the sky as the green bus stopped by the pier to drop its last load of passengers before returning to the depot. The engine whirred while passengers clambered off, clutching hats and billowing plastic macs. "Goodnight" muttered

the driver. The next day was Sunday, his day off. No one needed a bus on Sunday. No one came or went in the sleepy sea-resort on the Lord's day of rest. It was a place that people retired to, where they sat in small boarding houses spinning out their fragile lives like crochet, waiting to die...'

Sunday 23rd December 1990 3pm

Ren sat in her bedroom in a low chair with her hands resting palms upwards on her knees. Her white face and her smooth hairless scalp reflected the wintry light from outside. The wind was throwing rain at the window-panes, but her every muscle was relaxed. Her breathing was soft. Her tape player turned slowly and the sound of a single flute circled her seated body.

The melody wandered down the stairs and into the sitting room, where Corinne was sitting writing inside a late Christmas card to her school friend Carole:

'Greetings from the homeland, where a kind person has rescued me temporarily from the wreckage of my relationship, from legal problems, and most importantly from myself. I narrowly escaped spending Xmas in prison. (Long story, don't ask.) This woman is the most...'

Corinne heard the music, and broke off writing to listen. She started to draw spiders' webs round the edge of the card. After a few minutes, she dropped the card on the floor and started to dance.

Sunday 23rd December 1990 4pm

Sitting at the work desk which dominated his small sitting room, Sang was typing on his portable typewriter:

'Dear Anthea,

Thank you for the invitation to Christmas lunch with you and Morton and your housemates. Unfortunately I cannot accept as I am having some problems here. When I leave the house and come back, things are not always as I left them and this is disturbing. For this reason I prefer not to leave the house at the moment for any long periods. You know that since 1981 undertakings that are easy for other people present some difficulties for me. I like your friends very much but standards of hygiene are rarely high in shared accommodation and so I think I will be more comfortable at home. I hope to see you soon and take this opportunity to send you seasonal greetings,

Sang'

He stopped, blinked three times, glanced round the room to make sure nothing had moved, and then added another paragraph:

'P.S. Thank you for lending me the Odyssey *translation by T.E. Lawrence under his pseudonym as Private Shaw. As the Introduction notes, the reader may journey with two heroes of the Mediterranean simultaneously: Odysseus of Ithaca and Lawrence of Arabia. I am returning the book under separate cover. He was indeed a polymath. In this, as in other regards, T.E. Lawrence – as we should call him – was above all the quintessential Englishman. During World War I when, in his flowing white robes, he led an Arab army to take Akkaba, the world first became aware of his courage and endurance, in addition to his stoicism, intelligence, asceticism and determination. In the years following WWI, when he sought to hide his celebrated identity and re-entered the armed forces with an attempt at anonymity under a changed name, what became apparent was his modesty and self-deprecation. We see here the cover of ordinariness under which all great Englishmen from Shakespeare onwards have sought to hide their colours and deceive the unperceptive. I shall deliver this letter by hand. S.'*

Sang went upstairs to fetch his scarf. In the front bedroom he stopped in front of a small formica table which stood against the wall opposite the window. On it stood an old-fashioned gramophone, three model camels, a mirror, a small replica Hittite sculpture bought at the British Museum, and some photographs of T.E. Lawrence. He bowed twice to the photographs, blinked, and glanced momentarily in the mirror. His fingers touched the millimetre of black Chinese hair showing at the roots of his brown-dyed short-back-and-sides. Then he took his scarf from a drawer, closed it, opened it and closed it again twice, went downstairs to put on his overcoat, picked up the letter and left the house.

Sunday 23rd December 1990 7pm

Ren and Corinne were preparing sprouts. They removed the discoloured outer leaves and cut a neat cross into the bottom. The end result went into a colander to be washed.

'How many people are you expecting for the Christmas meal?' Corinne asked.

'There's you and me. Ute and her partner Emilio, and their two children. And Emilio's friend Vicente. That's seven.'

'Do they eat a lot of sprouts?'

'I think the Brazilians regard sprouts as a kind of inedible English eccentricity. But they'll eat a few.' Ren took off her headscarf and rubbed her bare scalp with her free hand. 'You don't mind, do you?' she said to Corinne. 'It gets itchy sometimes.'

Corinne asked, 'How did you…? Have you always… '

'No, I haven't always been bald. I lost my hair in my teens.'

'Is it…'

'It was hard at first, but I've got used to it. We all have crosses to bear. I think if hair grew back on my head now I wouldn't know what to do with it… How about you? How are you feeling?'

'Better. Gradually. Thank you. Being here is helping me get off the vino.' She rummaged in the brown paper bag for the next sprout. 'Since we talked about it, I've been thinking about 1971. What changes our lives and how.'

'It seems that year has a lot to answer for.'

'Like I said, that was the year I fell in love. Perhaps love is not the right word. It was more like bleeding from a fatal wound. I felt like I'd been turned inside out and all the need was on the outside. When your breath hangs on someone else's slightest move. In the years afterwards I thought I'd recovered from that love affair. But it's like there was a pit dug then and since things went badly wrong again I've fallen down into the same pit again twenty years later – as if time was cyclical. As if we only move forward in loops and keep revisiting the same places on a different level. Can I get out of the loop? Or am I doomed forever to return to hell?'

Ren thought for a moment. 'It depends how you look at it. Whether what you see is the doomed-to-return bit, or the fact that it's at a different level. That it's never quite the same the second and the third time around.'

Corinne dropped the last sprout into the colander. 'If you show me what you want done, I could put up the decorations in the sitting room.'

Ren stood up and pulled a battered cardboard box out of the kitchen cupboard. 'I'm afraid my Christmas decorations always return, but not necessarily on a better level.'

4

Chapter Four

Monday 24th December 1990 9am

'I'm still not going to Crete.' We've just woken up and I'm sitting in bed beside Morton.

'You know you're being irrational, Ant.' With a thin finger Morton steers a bunch of my frizzy red curls off my forehead, and kisses my eyebrow.

'Perhaps it's you who's trapped in your rationality,' I say.

Or perhaps he's right and I am going crazy, I don't know any more.

'Will you talk to your counsellor lady about it some more?' His pale green eyes are peering into my face.

I look down. 'Probably.'

'She might make you see sense.'

'She doesn't make me do anything.'

He looks up at the ceiling as if patience might descend onto him from there. Then he rallies: 'Can I read you another bit of my lecture?'

'More?' I'm trying to sound enthusiastic.

'It's nearly finished. This is a bit near the start, that I've been tidying up.'

'Go on, then.'

He disentangles himself from me and reaches down beside the bed for a piece of paper.

'Ready? OK.' He puts on a clear, lecture-reading voice:

'*Theories about stories – or perhaps I should say the stories we tell about stories – have changed dramatically since the 1970s, and Pasolini's idea of the multiplicity of truth has come into its own. Post-modernism, challenging the "grand narratives" of our society, has drawn our attention instead to the many chopped up, varied accounts of reality which emerge from diverse viewpoints, all expressing different subjectivities, and lacking the omnipotent authority of a voice-of-God narration.*'

I interrupt him. 'That's what I've got!'

'What?'

'A – what did you call it? – a diverse viewpoint. How come it's OK in your lecture but not in your girlfriend?'

'Touché. So what do you think of that paragraph? Is it clear?'

'It's OK. A complicated topic, but a good summary. Now can I read you something?' I can see he was hoping to read more, but I rarely get a chance and I'm seizing it. From the clutter of books at my bedside, I fish out a copy of the *Homeric Hymns*.

Inside it I find another handwritten note from Bert: 'Is my dad COOL?'. Oh dear. I tuck it into the back of the book. Now I have Morton's attention I carry on:

'I want to try out a theory on you, right? A theory about the origins of divination in the Aegean. I want to read you a bit from one of the *Homeric Hymns*. Apollo the god of prophecy is speaking, right? He says: "*Whoever comes to me guided by the cries and flight of birds of sure omen, that person will benefit from my words, and I will not deceive them.*" He's referring to divination from birds, OK? Then he goes on to say: "*There are three holy virgins, born sisters, gifted with wings... they live under a ridge of Mount Parnassus, and they are teachers of prophecy... From their home they fly here and there, feeding on honeycomb and making things happen.*" What do you think of that?'

'It's from the *Hymn to Hermes*, yeah?'

'Yeah. Now, listen up to my theory. What can it be based on, this myth about three winged sisters who tell the future feeding on honeycomb?'

'What can it be based on? Ho, hum… I give up.' He's humouring me now.

'They did divination from the flight of birds, right.? That's clear in Homer. And the best explanation of this passage is that they also did divination from the flight of bees. Who else has wings and honeycombs? I think it was part of daily life to learn and try to understand things by watching nature. Various aspects of nature. I think bees as well as birds. Then as society developed, when religion got more organized and started to involve people running rituals and taking power into human hands, they substituted priestesses.'

I look at him to check he's still listening. His eyes are wandering back to the draft of his lecture, but he snaps back to attention and I carry on with my hypothesis:

'We know some of the early oracular priestesses were called Doves. And some were called Bees. These three sisters mentioned in this passage were like bees and ate honeycomb and had wings, perhaps some sort of costume. The point is that people shifted from using the natural world for guidance to making it part of human social processes.'

'Sounds plausible.' That's high praise from him. 'But birds and bees aren't bones, what you're obsessed with. Bones aren't part of the natural world.'

'Not to us. But to them, the bones of the ancestors may have been seen in a similar light. And all these elements could have been embedded in rituals carried out by specialized people, perhaps in costume. Performances.'

He nods, 'Sure, sure'. I've caught his interest now. 'Before the days of books, radio, TV, and now the new Worldwide Web, it's hard for us to imagine how much important stuff was done person to person, in live action and performance…

Just like the Homeric bards. Just imagine it, performances of the poems were live; they were fluid. The bards used bits they'd learned and bits they created on the spot, all stitched together on the spur of the moment. And that spirit was captured centuries later when they were finally written down. George Chapman said: "Homer's poems were writ from a free furie, an absolute and full soule".'

'A creative patchwork, like you said.' I put my book down. 'I had a patchwork quilt myself when I was little.'

'Did you make it?'

'No. I loved it, but the moths got it and my mother chucked it out. I never learnt to knit.'

'Never mind, you have other talents.' He undoes the top button of my pink pyjamas. Then he puts the draft of his paper down and wraps his arms around me. We slide down under the duvet.

'I ate too much last night,' I tell him. 'I feel like a hippopotamus in the arms of a hyena. I'm surprised you can reach round me.'

'We hyenas have long arms.' He makes a loud laugh like a violin bow skeetering on the edge of a saw.

From the kitchen below comes an answering bark.

'Now you've woken Dusty,' I say.

'She knows a good hyena impression when she hears one.'

We are both giggling under the covers while we make love.

Afterwards we sit and look at the rain on the window.

'Happy Christmas Eve, Ant.' He turns to me, 'What would you like for Christmas to make you happy, honey?'

I pause a moment and then pluck up courage: 'It would feel a happier Christmas if I wasn't stuck with my PhD. I have a block about finishing it. Perhaps I should give up.'

'You've already done a bunch of work on it.'

I take a deep breath: 'How can I make the case for the

academics to re-think their ideas about ancient divination? Everyone knows the Greeks believed in oracles. They believed there were gods who were prescient and kind so they gave humans fair warning of things to come. People sacrificed animals and looked at the entrails to tell the future. But the evidence points to them also finding wisdom in living things. Listening to the chattering of birds and watching their flight. Listening to the rustling of the leaves on the trees. I believe also watching how bees moved, where they swarmed. And they learnt stuff from stones, there was a big one at the oracle of Delphi that they said was the centre of the world. And the bones. I think they consulted bones to tell them about the future and the past. Like I am now with the bones that I picked up in Crete. They believed the dead knew about life and death…'

'Slow down, love,' says Morton, 'I'm trying to keep up.'

I stop for a second and that's when I see a flea crawling up my arm. I freeze. It'll be a dog-flea, one of Dusty's. My eyes are fixed on it. Fleas move fast, even when they're not jumping. Morton realizes and picks it off with one fell swoop.

'They're difficult to kill,' he says, 'because they have a hard outside. You have to crush them between your nails.' He demonstrates.

I think perhaps it's time to get up.

That flea on my arm has galvanized me into action. Once I get downstairs I put the kettle on the ring and start sweeping the kitchen floor. It's covered in junk. A chewed-up red rubber ball left by the dog. Bert's football boots, they may be too small for him by next term. I pick up a big bit of white cotton wool that must have come from Freddie's Father Christmas outfit. Vivienne and Peter, our other two housemates, work pretty much full-time, but even they have made their mark. She's left a bag of shopping and he's left a pair of wet socks that he must have taken off after walking back from the pub yesterday. And there's an umbrella Vivienne left open on the floor to dry. My mother used to say that was bad luck. But then, everything was bad luck to her. When I try to fold up the brolly, I see the wire bits inside are broken and my finger gets caught. Ouch. That was definitely bad luck.

The kettle suddenly starts to screech and next minute it's brimming over with scalding water onto the stove like a miniature volcano. I filled it too full. The hot surface spits back. I can't stop the kettle screaming because the spring lever to open the nozzle isn't working and the cap itself is too hot to touch. Its wailing echoes my inner sense of imminent catastrophe, and when my fingers get scalded trying to pull it off, I hardly feel it.

By the time the kettle crisis is over, I see that Freddie has come down and is sitting playing the Jew's harp at the kitchen table.

Freddie hardly ever says that he needs anything. Usually when he's troubled he just tugs on his earring and says nothing. Or plays his Jew's harp. I know he hasn't had much musician work recently. So I'm reading the signs.

'Did that come with the cornflakes?' asks Morton as he comes down the stairs and goes out the door to get a newspaper.

Freddie doesn't reply. Something's eating at him. You don't see Freddie making any effort, but sometimes you get the sense that just being alive is difficult.

'What's the matter, Freddie?' I ask.

No reply. He just carries on with the mournful twanging.

Wait, Ant. Give him time. I make myself a slice of toast and can't resist another. The way the butter slides over the crisp porous texture, and the sharp fruity edge of the marmalade cuts through the bland comforting munchiness of the bread. A bit like life: comfort shot through with fear. I shouldn't have any more if I want to lose weight. But how much do I want to lose weight compared with the thrill of toast and marmalade in my mouth? I'm just putting the third slice under the grill when the sound of the Jew's harp stops. I turn around. Try again.

'Are you OK, Freddie?' No reply.

Eventually I hear a mumble, 'What's the point?'

He slips through your fingers. I give up.

Then he speaks: 'D'you fancy going to Epping Forest this morning? You and Morton and all?'

'Why not? You want to go on an outing?'

'The company of trees. The company of people.'

He looks bereft sitting there at the kitchen table, in his baggy jumper with holes at the elbows. When he's depressed, his dreadlocks droop in a hangdog way. Bereft of what? I don't know. He never says.

As I put the third slice of toast on my plate, I feel Dusty's wet nose scavenging into the palm of my other hand. Her tail is wagging, How does she know she's going for a big walk?

The woods are dank. I can feel the little bone in my pocket. It's warmer today, but the melted snow left a chill that has sunk into the ground and risen up through the tree trunks. The rain doesn't stop dripping through onto the forest floor. Twigs crunch to pieces under our feet. None of us want to walk on the path, so instead we make our way through wild patches and thickets. I get caught on brambles and sink into boggy places that appear without warning. My Wellington boots make a sucking sound as I pull them out. It's like the earth wants to draw me in, claim me.

After a while, we come to a green-carpeted glade. There is a huge tree, its moss-covered roots can be traced running just under the ground, like veins in the skin. I rest the palm of my hand on its bark, it's rough and crinkled and I can feel it is alive, though in a different way from me.

'Is it talking to you?' Morton likes to tease.

I tilt my head at him. 'Look, don't mock my ideas. After all, what is the scientific approach? Not to be limited by received opinion, and to devise and record your own experiments. That's exactly what I'm doing. For my thesis I could produce something conventional. I know what they want. I could write something full of jargon and nit-picking. But I have no appetite for that.'

I can feel the tree throbbing against my hand.

'Or?' he asks.

'Or I could write something that says what this tree's telling me. What trees might have told the early Greeks. When they tuned in to the natural world. The line we draw between rational and irrational is arbitrary. The Greeks thought the natural world gave them signs about the future and what path to take. It helped them make decisions, and heal the sick. Dancing, touching leaves, listening to the rustling...'

There's a moment of silence. We can hear a creaking of trees adjusting their weight. Some bird makes a guttural sound in another part of the wood.

'What's that?' Bert asks in a whisper.

I notice we are all standing rooted. As if we're waiting for something. Even Dusty is still.

I say, 'In Greek traditions, the sites of the big oracles were picked out by animals. Do you believe in power of place? That some places have a certain quality to make things happen?'

The silence and the stillness hold us in thrall. As if we're all wondering if this is one of those places. All I can hear is the quiet fingertips of the rain touching my hood.

Then I take my hand away from the tree.

Morton breaks the moment by sniffing the air. 'This is one of the things I love about your country,' he says. 'How many different kinds of damp? Heavy damp and light damp, cold damp, warm damp, damp that burns into your bones. What other country has so many varieties?'

'57 varieties,' says Freddie. 'Or is it 58? You old academics like to get everything precisely right…'

'Less of the "old",' cries Morton. He picks up a piece of wood with twisted branches like a cross-bow and pretends to fire an arrow at Freddie.

Bert turns round and laughs and steps backwards into the open mouth of a badger hole.

'Watch out for badgers!' cries Freddie. 'And for madmen with cross-bows!' He starts singing 'Hit me with your rhythm stick' and backs away from Morton.

I help Bert get himself out of the hole.

As we walk, I take the fragment of bone out to hold it in my hand. It's friendly, a talisman. A companion. My hand wraps itself around it and I'm not alone. I read that every cell in the body holds the genetic code for the whole body. So a small bit of bone holds the key to the whole person, a person who once lived. Ages ago. When there was flesh on the bone. I'm walking. Did that person walk? In trees? Could they see the sea? Were they hot? Did they want to swim? What did they think about? How did they feel? Hopeful or sad? There must have been a lot of death to live with. Was he or she tending animals, biblical style?

We come across the half-hearted remains of a fence. Just a post on its side with a scrap of barbed wire attached to it.

'Mind out, Bert!' I call as he follows me over it.

'I'm not blind, Mum,' he replies.

It's a ritual: I fuss, he rejects what I say. A dance between mother and child. It goes with the territory. I need you, I need you not. But he steps carefully over the barbed wire all the same.

We come to another clearing. Above us, a bird of prey is hovering, ready to pounce on some unwary vole or rabbit. Poor thing. But the birds of prey have to eat too. Can we only survive at the expense of others' suffering?

I glance at Morton to check whether he's going to suggest lighting a fire. He loves using his survival training. Hopefully he thinks it's too wet.

As we walk on Bert runs from tree to tree, grabbing branches he can reach and greeting them with a handshake. 'How do you do, Mr. Tree?' 'Hello, Mrs. Tree, sorry about your leaves. Never mind, they'll come back in the spring.' 'Hello, I'm Bert, what's your name? Sorry, I didn't catch that...' When he finds one he doesn't like, he's forthright: 'Hello. No need to be unfriendly. I'm only walking by. No skin off your bark, no need to look at me like that... Spooky Fingers!' and he makes a claw-like gesture.

I'm starting to feel cold, and I notice Bert give a shiver. This part of the wood is darker, like the forest where Red Riding Hood meets the wolf. Leaves cushion our feet. A heavy silence drapes itself over us. Freddie looks around as if he had seen something out of the corner of his eye. He starts to whistle the tune of 'Scarborough Fair', but he lets the melody fade away.

I don't know what it is that makes me fall, perhaps it's the root of a tree. One minute I'm walking along and the next minute I'm on my stomach and I have a close up of the forest floor right in front of my eyes. The ground has come up to meet me again. Dozens of leaves in different shades of russet and brown. Unnaturally magnified. I feel as if I've had the breath knocked out of me and from faraway I can hear voices saying 'Are you all right?' There's a lot of me, and I fall heavy. I'm winded. But I gradually pick myself up. Morton's there, he's good on first aid. I dust the mud off my coat and it's only after a few minutes that I realize I've dropped the bone. I can see it at the foot of a bush a few feet ahead. Before I can bend down to pick up the little fragment, Dusty has rushed up and run off with it in her mouth. I call after her but she takes no notice. I try to run after her but she has disappeared into the trees and I don't know in which direction. She's never been good at 'Fetch' and 'Bring'. Far worse than the shock of the fall is the chill of the realization that I have lost the bone.

Monday 24th December 1990 3pm

I'm on Stoke Newington High Street clutching a shopping list. Everything is a frantic, pre-Christmas panic: traffic is hooting, people are pushing, and Freddie is being unusually vocal.

'Seriously, Ant, you're asking a vegetarian to pick up the turkey?' He's not happy. 'I get all the breaks.'

'I've still got presents to buy. And I've got to get to my session.' I'm trying to read the list as I walk along and so I keep bumping into other pedestrians.

He doesn't give up. 'It will be white and clammy and goose-pimply and there will be a tiny bit of feather attached somewhere to remind me it was once a living creature walking the earth.'

'I brought a strong bag specially.' I hold it out to him.

'One bird corpse bag.' He looks at it in a dispirited way. 'If we have to have one, why not from Safeways all wrapped up in cellophane?'

'Morton likes the shop. Organic. Or he knows the man. Some reason. You just don't want to fetch it. I'll get it myself. I'm not crazy about the idea either.'

'Only teasing.' He takes the bag and crosses the road to the butcher's shop. I'm looking after him and walk into an elderly lady with one of those shopping bags on wheels.

'Mind yourself, dear. You could have a nasty accident.'

How right she is. And not just in Hackney, according to

those wise bones. Take more care, Anthea.

Monday 24th December 1990 4pm

I've lost the bone. I've lost the bone. I've lost the bone. But I'm not going to tell Ren. What would she think of me?

The first thing I say to her as I come in the door is 'Thank you very much for seeing me on Christmas Eve.'

'That's OK,' she smiles.

'It's finally stopped raining,' I say, and I shake my hair which is still wet.

I pause and wonder where to start.

'You were talking in the last session about a Dr. Scheiner,' she says. 'We came to the end of our time and I was sorry I had to stop you in the middle.'

But I have something else to talk about. Something else has come up. These notes from Bert, the question he always starts asking at this time of year. I wonder how to broach this topic.

As usual, I end up just blurting it out: 'Bert has started asking me again about who his father is. He wants information, a full account, a phone number if possible. I always struggle about what I should tell him.'

Ren accepts this change of direction without a flicker. 'What could you tell him?'

'At a pinch, the truth, but I'm reluctant.'

She's looking at me quizzically now. I suppose I would need to tell her about Bert's parentage sooner or later. It would be a relief to tell someone. I never have. Even Morton doesn't know. I'm the only person who knows.

'Terry,' I say. 'Tel. I mentioned him to you already as my first love. In 1971. When I was working at the bank, just after I left school. Meeting Tel there was a really big thing for me. It wasn't just that he was tall and good-looking with his brown curly hair and friendly smile. He was also very kind. I knew all along that he was living in the same bedsit with his ex-girlfriend Francine…'

Ren looks up at me, 'Yes, I remember you mentioned Francine.'

'At first I thought everything was over between them. Like he said it was. By the time I realized it wasn't quite over, I had already fallen for him hook, line and sinker. But he wasn't available. We never made love. I was a virgin at the time, and that's how it stayed. Francine made sure of that. A few kisses was all we had.

'Then there was a mystery. When he disappeared suddenly in early August that year, I was devastated. I never saw him to say goodbye. He just vanished. One Friday afternoon he was ill at work: he had a temperature and he went home. Then he never came back to the bank again. Monday morning, no Terry. I became obsessed with his disappearance. I found he'd left his bed-sitting room. Gone without trace. And in September I went off to university. I thought that was it. I carried a flame for him for many years afterwards.

'It was one day in 1981 we met again. By chance. Thanks to British Rail Inter-City. I can't remember why I was travelling back from York. I was still single then. It was long before I met Morton. I was sitting on the train and suddenly I realized he was sitting opposite me. Brown leather jacket, nice jumper. Workman's hands, his broad fingers scarred and swollen, I noticed them first as I unpacked my handbag and took out my book. Then I looked up at him. He was heavier-built, and his face had aged over the ten years since I saw him. He still had that slightly troubled look he always had, only not so marked. At first I didn't recognize him but he recognized me.

'"Ant?"

'I closed my archaeology book and stared at him. "Terry!"

'"Good to see you."

'"How are you?" I felt pathetic. All I could think of was platitudes.

'"Better than I have been".

'"Are you still doing wood-carvings?"

'He nodded with a grin. "More than ever. But I earn my living on building sites. Mostly as a chippy, but not always. You can tell," he looked down at his mangled hands.

'"No more working in banks?"

'He shook his head. "I blew that, didn't I?" He paused, then asked:

'"How about you? Are you still interested in stone circles and mummies and smashed up Greek vases?"

'"That kind of thing. Since I last saw you I got a degree in archaeology."

'"Good for you!" He smiled and launched into a version of the Monty Python song: "I'm an archaeologist and I'm OK/I sleep all night and I dig all day..."

'I told him I was teaching, but wanted to get back to archaeology. I was trying to avoid asking him the big question, but I couldn't: "So what happened to you? All those years ago, in 1971? One day you were working at the bank, the next you disappeared off the face of the earth."

'"It's a long story."

'"Are you going all the way to London? It's a long journey, you've got time."

'"Not long enough. I went through the wringer. I did some bad things – I didn't mean to. I went to prison, Ant. For a year. I don't want to talk about all that. Even now. But things are a lot better at the moment. I've got my life back together again. From rock bottom I've crawled up the ladder rung by rung. With a little help from some good people."

'I asked him what he meant by rock bottom.

'"When I first got out of prison, that was tough. I had nowhere to go, I didn't even have a coat. But a guy befriended me. A gay guy. He was a BBC Producer!" Terry smiled at the unlikeliness of this. "I didn't know him. I just turned up one evening outside his house in Twickenham. It must have been August 1972. I was thinking of sleeping in his garden. But he took me in. He gave me his coat. Fed me. We got close. I was there a couple of months, licking my wounds. Until we bloody went and had a row. Stupid, what it was about. About some posh restaurant he didn't want to be seen in with me. I took it personal. I went into one and I stormed out. Trust me. I think that was the worst moment. The rock bottom."

'"So what happened?" I asked him.

'"You want to hear what happened?"

'I nodded.

'"Well, like I said, we had a row. I slammed Don's front door behind me. That was his name. I set off down the street in a fury. Muttering to myself. Leafy Twickenham, home of snobs. That he was ashamed of me, that made my blood boil. He could keep his bloody Twickers.

'"When I got as far as the street corner I stopped. I realized I was homeless. All I had were the few bits I'd hurled into my rucksack in the heat of the moment. No money either. My mum always said my temper would be the end of me. 'Our Terry,' she goes, 'Acts like butter wouldn't melt in his mouth. But don't you believe it, next minute he'll be having one of his temper tantrums.' I wasn't going back to her, either. Sitting in her council flat passing judgment on the world. Not that she'd let me back after I'd been in prison.

'"I walked down to the main road and started hitching. I had to go somewhere, anywhere. After a while a red MG stopped. The driver was a young man my age but all neat and tidy, in a suit – everything I wasn't. He said he was going to Worthing. OK, I thought, I'll go to the seaside. It doesn't cost any bread to sleep on the beach.

'"What am I saying, 'bread'? That's how she used to talk.

Francine. Cause of all my troubles. That's her hippy talk. Look where it got me. You remember her, Anthea?"

'I nodded. I remembered Francine only too well.

'Terry went on: "The driver tried to make small talk, but I wasn't in the mood. In the end he put the radio on. They played that song, 'It might as well rain until September'. I remember thinking, it never stops raining anyway. Stupid. Everything felt stupid, especially me. It started to drizzle. I closed my eyes. I wanted to shut out the world. With the heater on and the windscreen wipers going, I gradually dropped off.

'"Next thing I knew, he was shaking my shoulder: 'Destination Worthing!' He had stopped on the seafront, near the pier. I stood there shivering on the pavement as he drove off. It didn't seem as if it was going to clear up. The clouds were thick, I felt the sky was going to fall in on me. I wandered onto the beach. There wasn't a soul there. It looked like someone had pulled the plug out: the sea was far away, with seagulls bobbing on it. In between were miles of flat grey sand covered in puddles of water.

'"I found a place under the pier, avoiding the bird shit. It was cold for October and I didn't have a sleeping bag. I didn't even have the coat my friend Don gave me when I first met him, that night after I just got out of jail. I'd left that behind too. Then I noticed a pile of cardboard boxes by one of the pier supports, and I went over.

'"I gave a tug on a flap of cardboard but it didn't come away. The whole thing started heaving around and this woman put her head out. She was oldish, with long greasy white hair and wind-beaten skin like she'd been sleeping outside for years.

'"'Knock, knock, knock,' She smelt a bit, but she seemed friendly. 'Who's there, i' the name of Beelzebub?' Her voice was posh.

'"'Sorry,' I stepped back, 'Didn't realize you were inside.'

I couldn't understand why she was talking in that old-fashioned way.

'"What do you want?' she asked. 'Here's a knocking indeed! If a man were porter of hell-gate, he should have old turning the key.' She pulled off the outer layer of the cardboard boxes around her. 'But you probably don't know Macbeth. They don't teach Shakespeare like they used to.'

'"So that was why she was talking strange. 'We did King Lear,' I said.

'"She looked me up and down. 'I don't like Lear. He was unbalanced. What do you want?'

'"Trying to keep warm. I'm sleeping down there.'

'"Away from the hurly burly. You made a good choice.'

'"I wasn't sure how to explain that I didn't exactly choose to sleep on the beach.

'"Fresh air,' she went on as she clambered out of her nest. She was wearing a strange collection of mismatching clothes all piled on top of each other. 'But better move further up. You'll get wet there when the tide comes in. Take some of these boxes.'

'"Don't you need them?'

'"There are plenty more where they came from. I'm a valued customer at Sainsbury's.'

'"She started dismantling the next layer of her home. Her hands were clean in between the bits that were ingrained with dirt.

'"Do you sleep here all the time?,' I asked.

'"She nodded, 'In all weathers.' She walked a few yards, found a spot and started assembling a shelter for me. 'The problem's not the weather, it's the people.'

'"Holiday makers?'

'"She threw up her arms. 'They gawp. Teenagers come down here sometimes drunk and kick my things around. But the worst are the social workers.'

'"Can't they help you find housing?'

'"She stopped, stood up and looked at me. 'Don't talk to me about housing. Curtained sleep. Crushed between walls. Trapped in brick prisons. I've been trying to explain to them ever since the first time I put my bed out on the pavement. I need fresh air. All they say is, Go back to your house.'

'"'You mean you've got a house?' I thought she was making this up.

'"'So they keep reminding me: Sylvie, you've got a perfectly nice two-bedroomed home in Windermere Crescent. You can't put your bed on the street. That's all they go on about. That's why I came down here. There's nothing like fresh air and a sea view.'

'"I couldn't get it. 'You mean you like it here?'

'"'Inside that house I dwindle, peak and pine. Here I can stretch as far as France.' She put the finishing touches to my box house and looked out to sea. 'There's husbandry in heaven.' She wandered back to her nest with a strange rolling gait. She started muttering about 'Sleep, sleep...' then turned to me and asked, 'Do you like knitting?' and she disappeared into her cardboard contraption."

'Tel paused and looked at me across the railway carriage.

'"It takes all sorts," I said.

'He said, "As it turned out, she was a very kind sort. The next day she showed me her empty house. It was furnished n'all. When she realized I hadn't slept a wink on the beach, she told me to stay there till I got back on my feet. I found a job in a café and after a few weeks I'd saved enough to start again. I set off for London.

'"The first thing I did was go to the house of my friend Don in Twickenham. He wasn't there. I tried several times. He was never there. I went to his workplace at the BBC. He wasn't there either. Then I found out that he was dead."

'Tel's eyes went red and he fell silent. I felt bad that I'd asked him to talk about a time in his life that was so distressing. I wondered if I should open my book and pretend to read until he felt better.

'In the end, he blew his nose and said, "Anyhow, that's the past. Many years ago. 1972. Let's not dwell on that. We're here now, this is a happy accident to meet an old friend. Tell me more about your Greek mumbo jumbo.'

'And so we chatted on. Like I said, he was the first love of my life, and from listening to his story my heart had melted all over again. It seemed tragic that we'd lost touch. If you believed in fate you'd think that it had conspired to place an obstacle between us. Such a sense of waste, of what might have been. I had the feeling he was married now. He didn't wear a ring but I didn't ask. I didn't want to know. I just felt that we had unfinished business. We'd never had a chance to get close, to spend time together, to be sexual. We had things to catch up on. He seemed to feel the same.

'At one point there was a silence and then he said rather shyly, "I don't know if it is cheeky of me to say this, but you are looking as attractive as ever."

'I held out a hand towards him.

'Our palms lingered together.

'We decided to go to the buffet car for a drink. I followed him as he moved with familiar big strides. His body was wider now. The train was rattling along and swaying. I got thrown to one side and he caught me, accidentally brushing my breast. He jumped back off in embarrassment. I wanted to reassure him, to give him something. Settle a score with history. I felt we had both been cheated. It seemed a long way to the buffet car. I realized I didn't want to go there.

'We were passing one of the train toilets. It said vacant. On impulse I opened the door, took his hand, and pulled him in. He looked surprised. I said "Can I lock the door?"

'He said, "What did you have in mind?"

'I said "This," and I gave him a kiss. He tasted like a stranger. He responded by wrapping his arms around me and rubbing his cheek against mine.

'I said, "We missed our chance before. Now we're both older. And wiser. Too wise to let it slip by us again?"

'This time *he* kissed *me*. It was a dry, polite kiss.

'He whispered in my ear, "My life is complicated. I shouldn't be doing this." We swayed, holding each other awkwardly. He whispered again, "And then again perhaps I should."

'Next time we kissed, he opened his mouth. From years ago I recognized the taste, it brought memories of Old Spice after-shave and panting in the back seats of the cinema in Maidstone. And the French kisses, that long tongue reaching for my throat, rehearsing a different penetration that had never happened.'

At this point I stop. Telling this story is getting embarrassing. My eyes hang on Ren's. The tape recorder keeps on turning between us, impervious. I say to her, 'I'm sorry you're having to listen to all this personal stuff, but everything seems to come out all tangled up together. I've never talked about any of this before. I suppose it's your job and you're used to it…?'

Ren says: 'I'm not sure if that's a question. If so, the answer is that it's fine for you to talk about anything you need to. Nothing you're talking about offends me.'

That's a relief. I say, 'Thank you'. I smile and bite my lip.

So where was I? Do I really have to retell this fugitive memory? Of a journey that changed my life? I feel no pressure from Ren. She's just sitting there, available to listen. It's me who's driven to put into words how it happened. An experience that until now has been hidden in my body. Here goes. I tell her:

'The train braked and it threw us towards the lavatory seat. He put the lid down. It wasn't the most romantic of places. There were bits of paper and an empty coke bottle on the floor which rattled to and fro with each lurch of the train. But he couldn't have been more tender if we had been in the honeymoon suite at the Ritz.

'We undressed each other carefully. We were in no hurry, we were only at Doncaster. We danced close like we had never been able to. We kissed greedily like teenagers hiding from our parents. His tongue reached into every corner of my mouth till I felt I had no secrets. Our courtship telescoped: weeks of slowly gathering momentum became five minutes and he reached for my bra. I remembered how he had fumbled with it ten years before. This time he knew where it unfastened. This time around I didn't push his hand away and my breasts fell out. He stroked and encroached insistently, and this time I let him. I didn't want to stop him. I couldn't stop myself. He draped my blouse over the paper towel dispenser. He hung my bra on the hook on the back of the door and my skirt on top of it. He dropped his trousers on top of the wastepaper bin. We laughed at the sordid surroundings. They didn't matter. What mattered was a longing for each other that had survived all those years.

'He was naked, his body skinny but muscley with little bits of hair on his torso. It gleamed white in the light through the opaque window. Lucky it wasn't cold. I was naked, wrapping my arms around myself to cover up my size. We clung to each other as we lurched from side to side with the train. Eventually he sat on top of the toilet lid and I slowly sank onto him. We rocked with the train, and sounds stopped for a split second as we met inside.

'We were luxurious. As if we had all the time in the world. The train leapt forward across the countryside but we were lazy. We twisted and stretched and turned and squirmed. Every so often the train stopped at a station. The tannoy blared. We heard passengers struggling past outside, their luggage banging on the door, indistinct voices, the guard's whistle. We waited. Then the train set off again and so did we. Despite age and wear and tear, he was man enough for the job. He ploughed on bravely, disseminating joy from Newark to Huntingdon.

'My climaxes rose and fell. We stared at each other insatiably. We had ten years of lost lovemaking to catch up on. Sometimes we whispered in each other's ears : "Do you remember when…?" "What if we'd done this in the back seats in *Patton*? …". We laughed. Neither of us mentioned Francine.

'Once a passenger decided that we had been in there too long. She started banging on the door and shouting. Terry made the "V" sign and mouthed "Fuck off!" and then shut his eyes and put his fingers in his ears. He could manage fine with no hands. He could manage exquisitely with no hands.

'I have never been so dismayed to hear that I was in Stevenage. Only twenty minutes to King's Cross. Our bodies slowly drew apart and we started to get dressed. Hello, and goodbye again so soon. We both knew that we would not meet again. That he was not free, only on loan for an hour or so. We patched ourselves up, tried to look like train passengers. I felt everyone in the carriage would see what we had been doing. Our pores were open. Our faces hung loose, our eyes watery and our cheeks still breathless. We tried to tighten the strings, to put back on a mask of normality.

'We peeped out like children who have been hiding. The coast was clear. He came back in, and his tongue searched inside my mouth for the last time. Then he left. After a discreet interval I followed him back into the carriage. Outside the windows the railway tracks widened and there was a procession of tower blocks, old factories, bridges, brick walls covered with creepers and graffiti. We sat facing each other and exchanged small glances. As the train slid in to Kings Cross through a sea of sidings, gas canisters, and cranes I tried to pull back into myself.

'"You always did like history," he said. "Well, today you found yourself a bit of history on the train."

'"Living history," I replied.

'"Living...? Well, just about..." he laughed and looked down at his battered hands with those broad fingers I remembered so well.

I let him get off the train first. In case he was being met. Before he left he gave me a peck on the side of my cheek. As if we had been married for twenty years. Then he got his rucksack down from the rack and followed the queue slowly filing off the train. I watched the battered brown leather jacket disappear into the crowd. I was still sitting there when the cleaners came in to pick up the newspapers and empty bottles and half-eaten bits of slab cake. I had to drag myself off the train. I didn't want to leave the scene of our reunion. I had a last look at the closed toilet door as I left.

'And that was how Bert was conceived.'

5

Chapter Five

Tuesday 25th December 1990 8pm

The green curtains of Ren's sitting room were draped with tinsel. The old fireplace at the end of the room had a real fire burning in the grate and, over the mantelpiece, some branches of holly tied with silver ribbon. Every so often a gust of wind blew down the chimney. The cushions which were usually spread around the room were piled at the other end, and Corinne's foam mattress was rolled up and tucked away in a corner. The ceiling was festooned with handmade paper chains in various pastel shades, and there was a spray of mistletoe hanging near the door. The wooden table from the kitchen had been set up in the middle of the room, its flaps pulled out at both ends. Around it Ren and her friends sat on the red kitchen chairs which had been supplemented by a tall wooden stool, a small box on legs from the bathroom and a folding garden chair. The purple tablecloth was strewn with the remains of Christmas lunch and cracker halves whose gunpowder smell still lingered.

Ren was at the end of the table with a half-eaten Christmas pudding on a serving plate in front of her. Beside her Corinne's face was flushed, with a blue paper hat at a rakish angle on her faded blonde hair. She was looking across the table at Ute. 'Did I ever meet you before?'

Ute smiled, 'Not that I remember. Not in this life.' She

117

had only a trace of a German accent.

Corinne drained her glass of red wine and said 'You look familiar in some way.'

Ute said, 'Me, people often do not recognize me. They say my face is like a blank sheet of paper. It changes with what is written on it. And as for this…' she pulled a handful of straight mousy hair away from her head. 'There is nothing special to remember. It is all dull, ordinary!'

'Apart from those green eyes!' said Ren. 'Anyway, you can't judge a book by its cover.'

Ute's five-year-old daughter Rosa emerged from under the table holding a small piece of paper with a cracker riddle on it. 'Mutti, when do pigs lie?'

'When they have wings and eff off,' said Corinne.

'That's when they fly,' Ren explained to the little girl, 'with the 'f' off.'

Corinne tried again: 'When they want a nap.'

Ute's face screwed up into an exaggeration of thinking, then let go. 'I give up.'

'When they tell porkies,' Ute's eight-year-old son read over his sister's shoulder.

'I think my answers were better,' said Corinne.

Ute said, 'One more riddle, Rosa, then it will be time to go home with your Dad.'

'I want more ice cream,' the little girl jumped up and down.

'Say please,' Ute reminded her.

'Please, please.'

'What flavour?' asked Ren.

'Blood frogs,' said the boy.

'Ants legs,' said the girl.

'I'm afraid we're all out of those,' said Ren, 'We've only got vanilla or strawberry.'

The ice cream cartons sat on the table amidst sprigs of holly and dishes of left-over vegetables. There were still a few crispy roast potatoes, one burnt parsnip, and enough brussel sprouts to feed seven people all over again. Three empty bottles of wine, paper streamers, an ash tray, a purple candle.

Ute's husband came in from the kitchen with an orange paper hat resting on his tangled mass of dark brown hair, which showed only a few strands of grey. He was carrying a tea towel between finger and thumb as if he was not sure what it was. 'Ren, you want I dry the things?'

'Don't worry, Emilio.'

He leant close over Ute's shoulder. 'I go soon, yes? The children are tired. It is an early start for me tomorrow.'

'Going on a job?' asked Ren.

He nodded. 'To photograph what kind of Christmas they have, the homeless people. Vicente started on the project yesterday. He wants to do an exposé. The conditions in the hostels. He pass himself off as homeless. Stay the night. Sleep with all the others. Photos when he get the chance. In secret.'

Vicente came in from the kitchen with the back of his pullover pulled up over his short black hair so his face was hardly visible. 'Tomorrow,' he whispered, 'I will sleep at Highward Hill House.'

Ren raised her brows. 'That's strictly for people in mental distress. People have to be certified to get in. You haven't been sectioned.'

'Not yet!' Vicente rolled his brown eyes and swung his lower arms from the elbows.

The little girl was studying another cracker motto. 'Sherlock Bones' she read with effort and looked around the table.

The boy looked over her shoulder. 'That's the answer.'

'Now we have to guess the question,' said Corinne.

Vicente knocked ash from his cigarette into the ashtray. 'I have a plan.'

'He drive himself crazy to get in there,' said Emilio. 'Expose how those people have to sleep. Like cattle.'

'He might end up having to stay there,' said Corinne. 'Like the man in *Shock Corridor*.'

'*Shock Corridor*? What is that?' Ute had her daughter on her lap.

'A Sam Fuller film,' said Corinne. 'A journalist gets himself checked into a mental hospital to find the culprit in an unsolved murder. He cracks it and he wins the Pulitzer prize. But he never comes out again. Those places can drive you mad if you aren't already.'

'You know this for a fact?' said Vicente, lifting the sweater off his head.

Corinne filled up her glass and looked at him without a smile. 'I know this for a fact,' she said, 'So you'd better watch yourself.' Then she smiled, 'Let's face it, none of us have very far to fall.'

Ren said, 'We all balance on the edge of madness.'

Corinne laughed. 'Some of us trampoline on it.'

'Mutti, what do you get if you cross a kangaroo with a mohair sweater?'

'I don't know, what do you get if you cross a kangaroo with a mohair sweater?'

'More strawberry ice cream,' said the little boy.

'No more ice cream now.'

'Please, coats on, both of you,' said their father. 'It will be a cold walk home.'

'I know that one,' said Corinne.

'When are you coming back, Mutti?' asked the little boy.

'Later,' said Ute. 'Behave nicely for your father please.'

'Why aren't you coming?'

'I stay to talk a little bit with my friend.'

'A woolly jumper,' the girl read slowly.

Corinne groaned. 'That's terrible.'

'Take some Christmas pudding back with you,' said Ren,

giving Emilio a chunk wrapped in a serviette decorated with holly berries. 'I've got another one for tomorrow. And Thursday. Maureen will be here then.'

'She's coming from New York?' asked Ute.

'Yes, isn't it great?' Ren's face beamed under her purple scarf.

'Ciao, ciao. Come kids,' said Emilio. 'Put on your coats. Say thank you. Great party!'

'Happy Christmas.'

Outside, the boy looked around the empty street. 'Why are we walking?'

'Your Mum will come in the car later. It's not far. We take a short cut through Clapton.'

They walked for a while in silence and then under his breath Emilio started to sing, *'Eu fui à terra do bravo, Bravo meu bem para ver se embravecia, Cada vez fiquei mas manço, Bravo meu bem para a tua companhia...'*

'What's that song about, Dad? I can't follow all the words.'

'It's about a man who travels to a dangerous place to get braver. But instead he comes back more gentle.'

The boy tried to sing, *'Eu fui à terra do bravo...'*

The girl said, 'You can't sing like Dad.'

'I can too.'

'It's cold,' said the girl.

Emilio said, 'Tie your scarf warm. Hold my hand, querida.'

'Dad, he kicked me.'

'She said I couldn't sing.'

'I know you both tired, but behave, you two!'

'She kicked me.'

'He kicked me first. Ooooouuuww... ' The little girl ran round to the other side of her father.

'Stop the shouting. *Que barulho!*'

'I never did kick her first.'

'Ooooouuuww…'

'Dad, tell her to shut up. Rosa, if you yell like that, you'll wake the Ghost of Christmas.'

'Shut up yourself,' she replied. 'There isn't a Ghost of Christmas.'

'There is too,' said the boy. 'He's got a pale white face and yellow eyes and he pops out when you aren't expecting him. He comes to get little girls. Tell her, Dad.'

'Stop scaring her. There is no such things.' Emilio was sauntering slowly, his hands in his pockets, gazing upwards. 'There is only houses full of English people recovering after the turkey, and a sky so clear you can see the Milky Way.'

'Dad, why did they call it after a chocolate bar?'

'I think that the stars came before the chocolate. A few million years before…'

'Na, na, na na na, little Rosa! Ghost of Christmas'll get you!'

'Dad, make him shut up.'

Emilio and the children were passing a row of houses when one of the front doors opened and a figure emerged dressed in white flowing robes. Its face was shaded by draped headgear as it swept across the front garden towards them. The children screamed and fled up the street, with their father running after them.

Tuesday 25th December 1990 8.45pm

Vicente was taking a mini-cab home. He looked across the table at Corinne. 'I think the rain has stopped. I can give you a ride to anywhere?' he asked. 'To Camden Town? To happiness? In a taxi named Desire? To certified insanity?'

Corinne smiled. 'Thank you, I can get there all by myself. At least the last place.' Her paper hat had slipped down over her head and lolled like a necklace round her neck. 'Thanks for the offer, but I'm staying the night here at Ren's.'

When the front door had shut downstairs, she turned to Ute.

'Would you tell me about 1971?' she asked.

'1971?'

'Ren said you thought there was something about it.'

'That was the year for me,' said Ute. 'It was only a few months we were living in that creaking house, but it changed the course of my life.'

'Do you think it was something they put in the water?'

Ute laughed. 'Not quite. But it was something in the air. A peculiar joining of circumstances. And I happened to be on the place, on the spot. Like parking your car on a water hydrant that bursts. I didn't know what hit me.'

'That was a big year for me too, I went into meltdown and never quite recovered. What was it about 1971?'

Ute looked at her watch. 'It's a long story. And it is, I think, nearly nine o'clock.'

'That's a good time to start a story,' said Corinne. 'The nights are long and the year is ending. It's a time to look back and forward. I've been on a downward spiral and I need to pull myself up by my own bootlaces or whatever it is you can pull yourself up by. I'm not sure any more.'

Ute smiled. 'What is the phrase I read recently, to be hoist on your own petard?'

'No, no,' said Corinne, 'I've been through that one. I need a different phrase or saying.'

Ren looked at Ute across the festive clutter on the purple tablecloth, 'Can you face talking about it?'

'I can. In fact I wish, that I could talk more to express what is inside me. I think of it often. Those few months in 1971 taught me a lot. Painfully. But still I am grateful.'

'What did you learn about?' Corinne asked.

Ute thought for a moment. 'That more things were

possible than my mother taught me. That my being can stretch to imagine more and try things out, to learn who I am, to fight for what I and others need. I learned to stand up for myself.'

'I need to learn about that,' said Corinne.

'Why don't you tell Corinne about it, Ute? Tell her about the house. If you like, tell her what happened to you. It may ring some bells with her own life.'

'You are interested?' Ute asked Corinne.

Corinne nodded.

'And it's Christmas,' said Ren. 'And you're a free woman for the evening. And we so rarely have the chance to get together.'

'I don't know how much I remember…'

'You have a memory like an elephant.'

'OK,' said Ute. 'You must remind me if I forget some bits. It all started with meeting Reuben, when I first came from Germany in January 1971.'

'I'll put the kettle on, ' said Ren. 'It's definitely time for a cup of tea.'

When she came back, Ute began her story. 'I was grateful to Reuben for providing me with a home in London, even though I nearly got arrested moving in. A squat. "Courtesy of some rich bastard," he told me. "We're going in next week. 'Des res' with plenty of room. Any friend of Erich's is a friend of mine." My English was not so good at the time. I didn't know what a 'des res' was, and I didn't know it was a joke.'

'Your English is brilliant now,' said Corinne.

'It always was,' said Ren. 'She's being typically modest.'

'So,' Ute went on, 'It was a dark brick house in a terrace of three-storey houses, with five steps up to the front door. He told me they decided to move in during the daytime so they look less suspicious. But they didn't know before how hard it will be to break down the front door. So I was standing on the doorstep keeping the look-out while Reuben and Geoff were attacking it, so, with a crowbar and a hammer. I was shivering with cold. The others were trying to make an entrance through the back. "Once you're in, you're protected by the law," said Reuben. They thought the traffic on the road would hide the noise. But the door, it was very solid. It was ages they were putting a lever at the lock and trying to smash the panels in the door. Then suddenly the first floor window next door opens and a man in a T-shirt he leans out.

'He asked us "What do you think you're playing at? I'm trying to sleep."

'"We're trying to squat the house," said Reuben.

'"I'm on night shift. Why don't you try another house?"

'Then the policeman. In that funny hat, so different from the German police. At first he was just strolling up the road. I whispered to the other two. Geoff turned to see him, and suddenly he gives the crowbar to Reuben.

'"I've got to see my aunt."

'"What?" said Reuben.

'"She's ill" said Geoff, and the next minute he was down the steps and running up the road towards the other way. His flared trousers flapping, his straight blond hair flying. Reuben turned round slowly and looked at the policeman, who was now making advance towards us as if he had a purpose. I watched Geoff's desert boots getting smaller up the road, then a big van came round the corner and wiped him from my sight.

'"Rubber soles," said Reuben. He put a sweaty hand through his black hair, thick like tufts of grass.

'I had read things about English prisons. The policeman stopped at the bottom of the steps and took out a notebook. You know how they talk, in policeman language.

'"Are you aware that you are committing an offence? Do you have any previous?"

'He sounded like someone reciting lines of a play that he had learned. I felt that I was caught in the middle of a strange piece of theatre.

'"Look officer," said Reuben, holding out his hands as if he was helpless, "We need somewhere to live."

'The policeman was writing on his notepad and reciting to himself. "Breaking and entry. Criminal damage."

'"Criminal!" Reuben gestured like a wild man, you remember how he was. "The criminal is the owner of this house. To leave it standing empty."

'At this moment I noticed that the door panel by the lock had, what you call it, a crack, a split. Enough to see through a little. Enough for a small woman's hand to reach through. I could do it, the knob inside turned, the door opened. At that same moment we heard a sound like whooping from inside of the house. The others, the reserve team at the back, had succeeded to get in too. Reuben used his dirty wrist to wipe the sweat from his brow, he picked up the other tools, and he followed me inside with a weary step. He turned to the policeman and he shrugged: "You'll have to come and visit us sometime. In your civvies, of course." And he shut the door behind us.'

Ren's phone rang, interrupting Ute's story.

Ren went into the kitchen and came back with the phone on the end of a lead. She held the receiver out to Ute, 'It's for you.' She went back into the kitchen and returned carrying a tray with teapot, milk and some mugs. Ute was laughing as she put the phone down. 'They got back OK, and the children are asleep,' she said. 'After it seems that they raised the Ghost of Christmas…'

Ren poured the teas.

Ute took a sip and picked up where she had left off. 'I'll always remember that first night in the kitchen after we squatted the house. Were you there, Ren? I don't think you were.'

'No, Geoff didn't invite me to the house till he had his room ready. He always liked to create an impression.'

Ute smiled. 'In that kitchen it was like a magic atmosphere. There were candles, they gave a little warmth against the chill. They were balanced, so, on the dirty plates and they made a ragged flickering pool of light, all around the remains of the sausages and mashed potatoes on the table. It was like a quiet celebration, a jubilation, the first supper, and all around us was the darkness of the unknown kitchen and the unknown house beyond.

'Geoff was telling everyone how things were.'

'Sounds familiar,' said Ren.

'He was waving a can of beer and telling us, "They can't touch you once you're in. Not without a lot of paperwork. Squatter's rights."

'Reuben turned onto him "Who asked you to speak? You come crawling back now. Where were you when we needed you? The disappearing man."

'Geoff says, "I had to go".

'"How's your aunty?" Reuben asks him.

'"Not well," he replies.

'"Oh dear," says Reuben, very sarcastic, "But then I'd have been not well if the Old Bill had felt my collar. There I was standing on the doorstep with the crowbar in my hand, and up he comes: 'Have you got any previous?'"

'"He never really said that," Geoff objected.

'"His very words," said Reuben.

'"He'd been watching too much Z *Cars*," said Alex, dismissing him with a wave of her hand. She had always poise. And always smart in her clothes, even in that messy kitchen.

'"Or *Dixon of Dock Green*," said Reuben. "Anyway, there I was…"

'Geoff waved him off. "Yeah, we've heard three times already. About your heroics. I had to go. It was urgent."

'Reuben said "Rubber soles." That was from the soles of his boots, yes, that we could see as he ran up the road? Rubber Soles, was it also a record? Anyway, the name stuck to Geoff.

'The table was a small one they found in the basement, and they had pulled out flaps at the ends. It wobbled as Reuben lent on it to roll a cigarette, manipulating, so, the tiny cigarette paper and the shreds of strong-smelling tobacco in his big hands. I always was surprised he could do it so fast. There were some old chairs they had found somewhere in the house, and a couple of wooden boxes. The sausages had been a bit burnt, but it was a surprise the old gas stove worked at all. No electricity.

'"I'll get us wired up in the morning," said Duncan. He was Scottish, I cannot copy the accent well. "It's no' a problem. That's unless any of you other wankers know how." His sharp eyes looked around the table. I used to find his accent hard to understand. He had strong features and he was serious, as if his nose and his thoughts were too heavy for his body. I don't think I ever saw him smile.

'Alex said, "We should speak to the neighbours. The house on that side's empty." She took Reuben's tobacco pouch from him without asking and started to roll a cigarette for herself with her elegant fingers and long fingernails. She wore leather boots up to her knees, and a mini-skirt that showed her long thin legs. To me she seemed fierce. I think that, she said she was a feminist, but she did not always behave so at first impressions. I used to admire it, the courage she had to take other people's things. That was in the beginning. Later as things turned out I didn't like it so much.

'"If next door on that side is empty, that'll be another house to squat," said Duncan. "We'll need to keep someone on the premises all day tomorrow. Until we can get a new lock organized. Geoff?"

'"I'm teaching all day," Geoff was stroking his neat beard, "Won't be back till six."

'"Anyhow, we wouldn't want to leave you here," said Reuben. "You might remember another aunty." He was sitting next to me and I could feel his thigh touching mine. I feel shy to talk about these things now. But this is how it was. In that kitchen meal, his thigh against mine, it is probably the thing I remember most.

'I said, "I can be at the house tomorrow." But I don't think they heard me. Alex's quick brain had already jumped forwards to another topic: "We need to look at the plumbing."

'"Reuben gets ground floor front room," said Duncan, "since he's friendly with the local law."

'"I've put my stuff in the first floor front," said Geoff. That was the best room, but the others, they did not seem to mind. Duncan, he agreed to take the room at the front on the second floor. To me the ways of decision-making seemed as chaotic and shadowy as that room. Compared to the scrubbed table and shining wooden floors of our kitchen in Frankfurt. The meetings of our commune there had an agenda, a procedure. That was where they decided that I should come here: "Make contact with our comrades in the Car Group organizing the workforce in the Fords factory at Dagenham in East London. Send information for our workers in Fords in Cologne. Make a contribution to international solidarity." Even Ingrid, my best friend in the commune there, she said I should go. At those days, I was always eager to do the right thing. So I had bought a three-month return ticket at the train station and I prepared to leave. I felt I had a job of work to do. My commune's decision had been unanimous. Things were clear.

'But there in that kitchen in the squatted house, it seemed to be each person for themselves. I said I could take the small room at the back on the second floor, I thought no one else would want it. Alex wanted the first floor back room, she said it would be "Cosy."

'"That leaves the basement for Taff and Brenda," Reuben said. "They won't like it."

'A moment later we all froze. There was a loud noise at the back door, and footsteps. Duncan stood up and grabbed a broom Alex had bought. Then there was a knock at the kitchen door. From the other side we heard a loud voice:

'"All right, we know you're in there. Open up!"

'Then the door flew open and Taff and Brenda burst into the room. They were kind of wrapped around each other and giggling crazy as if someone was tickling them. "You daft sods, the back door's open," said Brenda.

'"The local's not bad," said Taffy, "we've been researching background on our property investment."

'"Getting pissed, you mean," Brenda's face was glowing and she pulled Taff's halo of corkscrew curls into the furry collar of her Afghan coat.

'He said, "Apart from next door on one side, almost the whole row of houses is empty. They've been clearing tenants out for refurbishment."

'"For selling off at a profit more like."

'"We could get some more people in."

'"Did we miss supper?"

'"Give us a roll-up, man."

'"You two are in the basement, OK?" said Reuben. "So we'll all be spared listening to your raucous love-making."

'"How many mattresses did we manage to bring in?"

'"For those who need such luxuries," Duncan snorted.

'"So you're volunteering to sleep on the floor?" said Geoff.

'"We bring nothing into this life," Duncan replied, "and we take nothing out of it. Anything we gather in between weighs us down. Eliminate the unnecessary, that's my motto. Focus on essentials."

'Reuben was making a loud yawn, with his hand like this. "Hark to the sayings of Chairman Duncan."

'"You can mock. We'd all be a lot better off, instead of being caught in this consumerist capitalist shite-trap."

'"So we'll be needing to join the Party too?" Brenda used to find all this very funny.

'"Too right. It's just my luck to end up with a houseful of flabby-gut ultra-leftist libertarians who think they can change the world by having fun." Duncan was in the Socialist Labour League. The others in the house called it "the Party that doesn't party" and they would accuse him that he was a Stalinist. If they wanted to annoy him they called him Uncle Joe.'

Ute paused in her story. Her green eyes shone and she giggled as she looked around the table. Corinne took the opportunity to ask: 'Sorry, but I'm trying to understand. So did you all know each other before you squatted the house?'

'Some people did, a bit,' said Ute. 'Not me. I was sent. Go away to England, broaden your experience of life, they said to me at the last meeting in my commune in Germany. I wondered if this was what they had in mind, as I climbed under Reuben's blankets that night in the empty front room of the squat. He had no sheets. Go to London, they said. Your relationship with Erich is oppressive for everyone here in the commune. It is privatised, bourgeois. The couple relationship is too exclusive. Get away from this dependency on him.

'I'm doing my best, I thought, as Reuben's sweet sweaty smell surrounded me. One candle still burned on a plate on the floor beside his mattress. Cars passing on the road outside made the shutters rattle. The January night was chilly and I cuddled close to him.'

'So had you been with Reuben long?' asked Corinne. 'If it's OK to ask.'

'Not long,' said Ute. 'There had been a first kiss the week before. Awkward, you know, a fumble… I had noticed that he tasted of something I had always known. So after that, the barriers to the international solidarity they crumbled. Like Aladdin, I had been sent down into the cave. Banished on a perilous journey to England. A quest. Down into this world of warmth under the blankets. Like Aladdin, I had found treasure.'

'Treasure? That's a strong word,' said Ren.

'It was,' said Ute. 'I am embarrassed to speak of it now. It is personal. But that is me being silly perhaps. What happened in that bed is an important part of the story. It is a long time ago now. I shall try not to be coy.

'Reuben was not so considerate a lover as Erich. He did not bother with technique. A quick rub and then he climbed on top. His weight was reassuring. His manner was friendly, but you know it was not so personal. I did not feel crowded. I did not feel judged. He just concentrated on the matter in hand. "Call me George Job," he always said when there was a task of any kind in front of him, as for example if he had to write something. "If you want a job done, no frills, I'm your man." That was his attitude in bed, and he did a good job under the blankets too. Enthusiastic. During the day he could sometimes be moody or bitchy, but that fell off him with his clothes, and his big hairy body, the benevolence of his body took over. Kindness perspired from every pore of his flesh. His sweat, his smell, his weight, everything poured out good will. At the end of the love-making, you know, at the climax, it felt like a moment of truth, a blessing. It was a gift, a visiting by an essence of goodness.

'Then he threw himself off with a sigh, with satisfaction, saying, "And to think it's free."

'He did not bother to look at me afterwards like Erich always did, so curiously. Erich's interest in me sometimes was like a burden. But Reuben, he looked at the ceiling. He took his pouch, rolled a cigarette and lit up. He took it for sure that all was right with the world. His love was more generalized: you could say, not so specific.

'Afterwards was when the laughing started.

'"Good evening, madam," Reuben says, "Thank you for calling the Star of David Escort Agency. Yes, we have many fine upstanding Jewish boys on our register. And when I say upstanding… Does Madam prefer hairy, very hairy, or extremely hairy?"

'"To which category do you belong?" I ask.

'"Very hairy, madam. You might think there are no other places on the human body where hair could be provided, but believe me, you would be wrong."

'"I do not wish to be personal, but I wonder if you could show me where?"

'"My pleasure, madam,' says Reuben. 'And I use that word advisedly. I do not mean to be personal either, but if you could slide your hand further down, I think you might find what you're looking for. Thank you. A little further and I think we may have another surprise for you."'

Ute covered her face. 'They were silly times. But I felt like I had not laughed for years. Perhaps never. It was strange that I found myself without any aspiration beyond this ballet, this inelegant ballet, under the blankets. Me who had always thought the most important thing in life was to work as hard as you can. At the commune in Frankfurt perhaps most of all. It was such a big struggle we faced, to find a new way to live, to shed the values of our parents. Ways of living that were reactionary. We needed to dig them out. In all parts of our lives. Such hard work to make those changes.

'Like that time with my plant. You know that type, I think they call it the Mexican Breadfruit? Many middle class people have it in their homes? I had one in my room.

I had it some years. The commune discussed it at a house meeting and decided that because it was linked with the bourgeoisie it was not acceptable politically. It was removed from the house to the back yard. From my bedroom window I watched while it slowly gave way to the winter weather. The leaves, they wilted. I wanted so much to go down to rescue it. But I fought against that wish. They would call that a revisionist wish, yes? My plant died. You know, I felt I had to stay by the collective decision. I could not let Erich down. He was very serious about such things. But it was painful.

'That first night in the squat I asked Reuben if he would like a plant for his room. But he said, "I'd probably forget to water it."

'I asked him, "Will you decorate the room?"

'He said "I think Duncan's getting some paints. He thinks he can get us all organized. Personally I don't give a toss. He'll get us all on a washing-up rota soon."

'I told him, "We had such a rota in Frankfurt."

'"I'm not surprised. Your Erich, he likes to keep everything under control. They don't realize that everything went wrong in 1924."

'"1924?"

'Reuben sat up in bed, took his pouch of Golden Virginia tobacco and started to roll another cigarette. "When Trotsky sent the troops in on the Kronstadt sailors. Crushed their autonomous uprising. Suppressed people's power. It was downhill all the way after that, right down to Uncle Joe."

'"Stalin." I realized very soon that it was not wise to try to put more than one word in edgeways once Reuben had got started. I used to let his words wash over me. I found it invigorating, his passion for the history of people wanting justice.

'He went on: "Stalin's show trials, purges and mass executions were a travesty of the ideals of the Russian revolution. You should read a great book, *From Lenin to Stalin* by Victor Serge. He shows how it all went wrong. Went from an original movement to share wealth and power more equally – I mean, no-one can disagree with that, can they? – to state capitalism wielding a reign of terror. Disgraced the name of socialism."

'I turned the word on my tongue, "Sozialismus."

'"It sounds better in German. A sorry word, tarnished by misuse." He brandished his cigarette.

'I told him, "My mother has relatives in East Germany."

'That started a fresh stream of ideas from Reuben: "Eastern Europe. They've felt the iron hand. From Poland and Hungary in '56 to Czechoslovakia in '68, all part of the systematic suppression of the autonomy of the people in the USSR. You know what they had in Hungary? Council communism, people running their own workplaces. There you're talking." He put out his cigarette on the plate on the floor, and slid down under the bedclothes.

'I rested my head on his chest that was like a rug and said: "Erich told me you were an anarchist."

'"Anarcho-syndicalist." He stroked my hair with a big hand. "There's a difference. I'll explain it to you."

'"Liberty, is it possible really?"

'Reuben tutted: "The Teutonic urge for generalization."

'"Erich wanted, that I should have more liberty."

'"Liberty. Another word that you have to ask, where has it been? Liberty, Equality, Fraternity. Where have they been? If you do anything because of an ideology then you're bound to get fucked up. When one person's freedom reduces another person's freedom, what can we call it? Erich is a dangerous idealist. What did he really want?"

'I wasn't sure how to reply. "Erich wanted me to be more independent from him."

'"Did his master plan involve you having fun along the way?"

'When Reuben said things like that it made me uncomfortable. Suddenly the blankets felt prickly. I sat up and tried to make him understand: "Erich's mind was fixed that I should come over here."

'Reuben snorted. "His mind is jammed up with 'oughts'. Not the old 'oughts', but the new 'oughts'. Turning change into a duty. He shouldn't believe everything his mind is fixed on. Neither should you."

'I told him that Erich was a man with a strong morality.

'"Sure, I know the guy. We travelled round Italy together, remember? He's got principles. But do you think his principles will help him when he finds out that I have got to know you in the biblical sense?"

'Suddenly I didn't know any more whether I was doing the right thing according to the political ideology. Or whether I should feel guilty to be there in bed with Reuben. I said, "I need to have some sleep. There is the meeting tomorrow about the Ford Motor Company. I must do the work I was sent to do." I pulled up the bedclothes, turned away, and put a pillow over my head.'

Ute stopped in her narrative and looked into her cup to see if it still held any tea.

'This Reuben sounds quite a character,' said Corinne.

'He was a true libertarian,' said Ren as she squeezed another round of teas out of the pot. 'Politics in bed. The horizontal path to socialism.'

'Not only horizontal,' said Ute. 'The next day he took me to show me Clissold Park. There was a children's playground. Trees. A big area of mown grass where boys were playing football. Further down we walked by the ponds in the winter sunshine and he came back to the topic of Hungary. "I believe in what they had there," he said. "The uprising against Russia was started by students and professionals, but it soon got taken over by the workers. They occupied public buildings and set up revolutionary councils. Collective control at a local level, taking it away from the Party and the state. That's the way. In October '56 Nagy set up a democratic government including peasants' and farmers' parties. Some of the Hungarian army defected to their side." He waved his hands as he walked. A group of ducks scattered, skimming along the surface of the pond.

'"But it didn't last," I said.

'"Street fighting," he said. An elderly lady walking past looked up in alarm. He didn't notice, he was in full flow: "The rebels seized guns from the arms factories and the police. But the Russians sent in tanks. They couldn't risk sending in foot soldiers in case they got talked over to the rebels' side. You can't beat tanks with rifles and petrol bombs. Two weeks of pitched battle. You have to hand it to the Hungarians for courage. Thousands died. It took the Russians a year to get rid of all the local councils. And yet another chance for freedom from dictatorship was destroyed."

'At the edge of the park we found a van selling snacks and he bought me two ice-creams as if to make up for the historical tragedy. "Eat, Ute, eat. We must enjoy the freedoms that we have."' Ute smiled and fell silent. 'They were the good times,' she said.

She drank her tea slowly and then she resumed her narrative:

'Being on my own in the house was harder. Later that day I went to the Car Group meeting. Reuben and Duncan were there, and I met the other activists, and the Ford workers who were in the group organizing from inside the factory. I felt awkward because I was the only woman. But they were all friendly, and they gave me piles of papers to read: minutes of previous meetings, leaflets and analyses of the current situation in Fords.'

Ren nodded. 'I remember the papers that lined every surface in that house. The radical ideas drew a trail of pages after them like a bride's train stretching back down the aisle. Minutes, manifestos, discussion documents. What was wrong with the world. What a better world could be like. How we could make it better.'

'I went back to my room,' said Ute, 'and read until the light faded. Duncan had not yet succeeded to connect the electricity.'

Ute paused and Ren turned to Corinne: 'I still have some of those documents. They're in that chest over there beside the fire. Do you want to see? When we moved out of the squat, I somehow got left with them and I've never wanted to throw them away. In these days of defeat and despair on the Left, since Thatcher trampled on our hopes, they make strange reading. But those ideas, I always thought their time might come again. Have a look, Corinne, if you want to. They might give you some entertainment.'

They were both looking at Corinne. She started, 'OK'. She pulled her paper hat up from around her neck and put it back on top of her head. 'No time like the present. Over here?' She went to the chest and lifted the lid. It was wedged full of papers, neatly stacked. 'Oh my God,' she said, 'you produced all this?' She rummaged around inside among yellowing news cuttings, duplicated leaflets and pages typed on old-fashioned typewriters. She glanced at some passages, flicked through documents and eventually settled on a stapled set of pages with the heading '*Autonomy in Everyday Life. March 1971.*' The pages were typed, with the dark print of carbon copies, lines close together and lots of crossings out.

'Word power,' said Ren. 'Some of the group were very into word power. Mostly the men, but Alex kept her end up for the women.'

'Did she write this?' asked Corinne, holding up the document.

'What's it say?' asked Ren.

Corinne giggled. 'Shall I read it?'

'Please,' said Ute. 'You will remind us of our youthful folly. And I will be happy to hear someone else's voice for a change.'

Corinne came back to her chair carrying the document, took a sip of cold tea, and read:

'"*After World War II the working class was militant from the struggles of the 1930s and the war years. Soldiers coming home wanted to know they hadn't fought for nothing. In the post-war boom, capitalism tried to defuse this militancy by getting the working class to buy into the system: using the wage as a motor to increase production; improving welfare benefits to stabilize society; promising upwards social mobility via rising wages and mass education; introducing a new immigrant work force for lower grade jobs. Also through building up the nuclear family as the unit for domestic bliss; promising better living conditions in the post-war housing schemes; and offering more consumer goodies, as credit became available. It looked as if every man could have his home, his family, his car and his television – 'You've never had it so good.'"*'

She stopped reading and rifled through the remaining pages of the document. 'There's lots more,' she said. 'It's heavy stuff. It's history. I was never very good at that. It's like a foreign language to me. Shall I read more?'

'No, that's enough, thank you!' said Ren. She and Ute were laughing. 'After all, it is Christmas!'

'Alex, she was very good at writing like that,' said Ute. 'I laugh because it is sad to remember how much intelligence and optimism we gave to our project. And who listened? I laugh, because otherwise I cry.'

Ren nodded.

Corinne put the pages down on the table.

'But on that day in early 1971,' said Ute, 'when I read the documents then, they gave me hope. It really seemed as if changes in society might be possible. That things could get better for the people who are poor and suffer.

'About my room I was not so hopeful. After I read the Fords papers, I set to work on it. It was small and depressive. There was a pipe sticking out of the brickwork outside above the window and it was dripping water onto the sill. Drip, drip, drip... without stopping. It made the wall damp inside too. I had bought a thin mattress of sponge in a second hand shop. Its cover had a flowery pattern, and it brightened up one corner. The floor was faded brown carpet. In another corner there was a fitted cupboard with a door hanging open. I wondered who had lived in this room before, what had happened here. I fetched a bowl of cold water, and – as best as possible with cold water – I gave it all a clean, a very good clean. My mother believed in the importance of hygiene and order, and I was still my mother's girl in some way in those days.

'Then I spread out my sleeping bag on the bed and started to unpack my giant rucksack, putting the things in rows. I had not brought much with me to England. A big sponge bag full of soaps and creams; I would need to do a lot of washing in that place. There was the knitting I was doing for Erich's birthday, a striped pullover with balls of wool in different colours.

'It was very quiet in my room. The traffic noise didn't seem to travel from the front. I unpacked a green cardigan I had knitted for myself when I still lived at home. It had buttons I had covered so carefully in embroidered fabric, always the hard-working little girl I was then. I had a pair of smart shoes and a suit my mother saved up money to buy for me when I got my first job in Germany. I was thinking, that I would need to work in England. I had a smart blouse in emerald green. A spare pair of trousers. Some plastic bags, a notepad and some other little things. There were some scraps of material I had brought because I liked the patterns, thinking perhaps I will sew something. Socks and underclothes. Another skirt. That was all.

'I sat on the mattress and looked at it. Now what?

'I picked up my knitting needles. A new blue stripe for Erich's jumper. I was only three weeks in England and I missed him so much. And no reply to my letters. I didn't know why he did not write to me. My best friend Ingrid, she had not written either. Ten rows of knitting and the light from the window had faded even more. In the dusk the colours in the pullover looked wrong – the new blue jarred with the red next to it. I felt *etwas* cold, but I needed some air.

'I got up and walked to the window. It was stiff to open. I leant out and the air was even more cold. It was January and you could smell the evening coming. The sky had clouds over it, grey like a heavy cushion. Right outside, close to the house, there were the dry branches of a tree. They reached up to me, I could see small buds on the twigs, waiting to throw out leaves when the spring came. I wondered what kind of tree it was. Later I found that it was a sycamore. Beyond I had a narrow view past that back part of the house, the back extension, to a slice of the garden beyond. It stretched down some metres to a brick wall at the end. There was some overgrown untidy lawn, some nettles and some ragged shrubs. And the ruins of an old wheelbarrow. On each side a high brick wall separated our garden from the ones next door. Later I put a desk by that window so I could look into that view of the garden.

'As I turned back into the room, my eye fell on the green cardigan I had brought with me from Germany, and suddenly I was full with hatred. I was so hard-working when I was knitting it. Neat little rows. Being the good girl. What a waste of time. How foolish it looked. Every stitch smelt of my silly hopes. People didn't wear things like that here. Certainly not in green. I was disgusted. I wished it gone. I took a carrier bag out of my rucksack, and I put the green cardigan inside. I tied the top and put it in the bottom of the cupboard, then I closed the door. Out of sight. Good. I looked around the room. It needed some posters, and a table and chair. Curtains, perhaps a bedside lamp. All in time. I picked up Erich's pullover and with difficulty to see, I knitted two more rows. Nothing felt right.'

Ren was puzzled. 'So what did the green cardigan ever do to you to end up in that bag?'

'I called it the banishment bag. My *Verbannungssack*. It was for things I wanted to banish. Things I couldn't face,' said Ute. 'Later I took that green cardigan to an Oxfam shop.'

'I first met you in the house at about that time,' said Ren. 'When I came to see Geoff. You were very quiet.'

'So were you.'

'It was the men who held court,' Ren told Corinne. 'Especially Reuben. He had a relish for life. When he was in a good mood, he radiated warmth like the sun, and we all bathed in it.'

'But even then,' said Ute, 'There were small shadows of what was to come.'

6

Chapter Six

Tuesday 25th December 1990 11pm

'It is late, now,' said Ute. 'Surely, Corinna, you have listened long enough about our crazy life in 1971?'

'Please go on,' said Corinne. 'I want to hear what happened in the end.'

'It is a sad story, overall. But with many good times along the way. In fact, you could find many endings, some of them were happy. Is that not so, Ren?'

Ren nodded. 'After all, we survived.'

Ute smiled. 'The seeds of the downfall were there to see from the early days. I remember one afternoon I came back to the house. I had found a job as a secretary. It must have been in February some time. I walked up to the front door and put my key into the new lock. The door itself was still scarred from the crowbar attack on the first day. I stepped from the daylight into the dark passageway and I could hear voices in Reuben's room. I knocked, no reply. I looked round the door. Reuben was sitting on what he called his armchair, it was really an old car seat covered with a blanket. He was wearing nothing except a green towel wrapped around his lower half. Perhaps he had been brave enough to try the plumbing in the bathroom; it was uncertain to work or not. I thought he must be cold but he seemed to glow. He had a small book in his hands. The others were spread around the room, sitting on his bed and on the floor, listening as he read:

> *"I am sitting in Mike's Place trying to figure out*
> *what's going to happen*
> *without Fidel Castro*
> *Among the salami sandwiches and spittoons*
> *I see no solution*
> *It's going to be a tragedy…"*

'Reuben's voice was rich and soft, and he let it trail away at the end of the lines, suggesting a shared memory of good times past. I love that poem. I heard him read these poems so often that I still know parts of them by heart. They always recreate for me a picture of Beat poets hanging out, very cool, on the streets of San Francisco in the 1950s and 60s.

'"Ferlinghetti wrote that in the early '60s," Reuben explained, "Soon after coming back from Cuba, just after Castro took power. Prophetic."

'"He didn't foresee the Cuban missile crisis," said Duncan who was reading a newspaper under the window.

'I put my bag on the floor and sat down near him.

'"A short tragedy was averted then," Reuben agreed, "but there could still be a long tragedy. Cuba is a thorn in America's side and it's still vulnerable."

'"What's the use of poetry written ten years ago?" Taffy was at the foot of the bed rolling a joint, sprinkling the fragments of dried green leaves onto the tobacco and twisting the Rizla papers like a master craftsman.

'"Never mock history," Reuben replied, "it's always with us, most of all when we deny it. We're all still living in the shadow of World War II, just like the Beat poets. They were one of the first manifestations of post-war alternative culture. We won the war, but for what? They were among the first to reject the post-war nicey-nicey, meat and two veg, 2.4 kids, TV-fixated, your dinner's in the oven honey, Spock-fed, happy families fantasy."

'Duncan looked up from his paper: "Spock. The one with the ears."

'Alex groaned "Doesn't anyone north of the border read?"

'"What's this then ?" Duncan held up his copy of the *Workers Press*.

'"That doesn't count" said Reuben, "a Trotskyist comic full of answers and no questions. For people who don't want to think for themselves."

'"Too much small print for the likes of you," said Duncan, "not enough sex and drugs and touchie-feelies."

'On the bed Alex's boyfriend Evan, who was lying flat on his front, he started, he made a half-sound, turned his head the other way and went back to sleep. Alex patted his shoulder. "He was up most of the night getting the *Muck-Raker* ready for the printers."

'Reuben was turning pages, "The past has demons which have to be laid. Allen Ginsberg was the same generation, the Beats. His mother Naomi had a series of breakdowns throughout his childhood. Here's a bit about her:

'"*The telephone rang at 2AM – Emergency – she'd gone mad – Naomi hiding under the bed screaming bugs of Mussolini – Help! Louis! Buba! Fascists! Death – the landlady frightened...* ' Ginsberg was only a schoolboy at the time. The shadow of the concentration camps reached across the Atlantic."

'He read some more.

'"*Her big leg crouched to her breast, hand outstretched Keep Away, wool dress on her thighs, fur coat dragged under the bed – she barricaded herself under bedspring with suitcases.*'"

'Reuben stopped reading and looked around. "Ginsberg had a lot of trouble with his mum."

'"Don't we all?" said Brenda.

'"His was heavy duty," said Reuben. "She was away for years on end, in hospitals and so on. He wrote this poem after she died. It starts:

145

'"'Strange now to think of you, gone without corsets and eyes, while I walk on the sunny pavement of Greenwich village. Life goes on.'"

'Reuben's reading rose and fell like music, and it seemed that it had mesmerized everyone. After he finished there was a long silence. I remember I wondered then why he had chosen that piece to read. I found out later. Taffy took two long pulls on the joint and passed it to Reuben. Then a knock at the front door broke the atmosphere.

'Duncan peered out of the window: "Young laddie on the steps. Rather smartly dressed. But he's never an instrument of the state, too innocent-looking. I'll go." Reuben passed the joint to me and I drew deep. The sensation of the dreamsmoke filling my lungs had become familiar to me in the weeks since we moved in.

'A voice in the hall: "I want to give it to Reuben himself." Taffy started packing the tobacco things away. I held the joint carefully inside my hand so it could not be seen.

'Then came Duncan's reply, "He's no' dressed for visitors."

'The door opened and a young man came in. He was tall, with a nice face and curly hair. It was much shorter than the hair of the other men. He hesitated and held out an envelope: "For Reuben. I have to give it personally." He looked around the room as if he was lost, until he saw Reuben. "Do you remember me?" he asked. "I'm Franny's friend."

Reuben closed the book of poems on his lap and put it on the floor. "Franny doesn't have friends. She has victims," he said as he took the envelope. "She sent you with this. Why? What do I have that she could possibly want?"

The young man looked full of doubt and stepped from one foot to the other. "I don't know. She's upset. She thinks she's in danger."

"Believe me, my friend," said Reuben, "you are the one

who is in danger. Are you stopping?"

"No."

'After the front door closed again, the mood had changed and people started to leave Reuben's room. Alex shook Evan until he woke up. "You can sleep upstairs in my room. Come." Duncan picked up some teacups saying, "Which one of you lazy bastards is washing up? Poetry class is over. Some of us have got work to do." He disappeared into the kitchen.

'The last few bodies drifted out and when we were alone I asked Reuben, "Who's Franny?"

'"You don't want to know."

'"Please do not patronize me," I said to him. "I do want to know."

'"Keep clear of her. A nice girl like you."

'"Who is she?"

'"Just baggage from the past. We all have baggage. You have Erich. Did you think I was a virgin when you met me? Come here." He pulled me onto his lap and carefully unbuttoned the smart blouse I had put on for work. Underneath I was wearing a low-cut black brassiere which I had bought in Germany in the hope that Erich would find it sexy. Reuben had a way of getting inside a brassiere without undoing it. "Forget her. I try to." His hands tunnelled into my skirt and his towel fell off. Soon I was riding on his lap, with the dope dragging my eyelids down into a private world. A world I had not known, where my senses sang to his movements inside.

'Afterwards, with different garments wrapped awkward around my neck, my waist and my ankles, I stumbled over to lie on the bed with him and very soon he was snoring. His face looked harder and sadder when he was asleep. On the floorboards by the chair I could see his book of poems, the green towel, and the letter unopened.'

Ute paused in her account. 'That letter.' She sighed.

'Excuse me for a minute, I have to go to the bathroom.'

'I think we need a fresh pot of tea,' said Ren, and went into the kitchen.

When Ute came back, Ren asked, 'Is this upsetting you?'

'No, really,' said Ute. 'It is so long ago. It is like a memory of a memory of a pain.'

'More tea all round?' asked Ren. As she poured she turned to Ute: 'Knowing what happened afterwards, do you wish you'd burnt that letter?'

'I don't know,' said Ute. 'Would that have prevented what happened? What can we do to change the future? Or the past? Anyway, I didn't. I couldn't. I did not even have that thought. I was so happy with that friendly giant of a man, in spite of the chaos and discomfort that spread all around him like ripples in a pond.

'Some days he drove me exasperated.

'One morning soon after that, he came into the kitchen loaded down with packages. I remember he was wearing that red T-shirt he had. It said "Sure, I'm a Marxist", with a picture of Groucho Marx and the other brothers. He liked them.

'"Busy with your smalls?" he asked. I was not sure what he meant. I had boiled a kettle and I was washing my underclothes with my hands in the kitchen sink. Not the low-cut black bra. I am embarrassed to tell you that I had felt it necessary to put that in the cupboard. In the banishment bag, the *Verbannungsack*. I needed somewhere to put my shame. There was still hope for my other underclothes if I washed them well enough. Still hope for me to be the good girl my mother wanted.

'Reuben dropped a pile of books and papers on the shaky kitchen table. It was still the only surface for work in the house apart from Geoff's desk, which was in his room. The door was locked, and nobody else could go in.

'Reuben said, "I've just been to Company House, getting

some gen for a piece on 'Who Owns the Borough?'. For the next *Muck-Raker*. Forget democracy, the whole area is controlled by big business."

'I scrubbed my underclothes very seriously. Reuben didn't seem to bother about washing his underclothes. None of them worried much about such things. I remember Geoff once found his sheets were so dirty that they smelt, so he threw them away and bought some new ones.'

'I remember that,' said Ren. 'That was after I stopped washing them for him.'

Ute took a sip of her tea and carried on. 'Reuben seemed that he couldn't understand what I was doing at the sink. "Isn't there a laundrette somewhere down the road?"

'"I'm not quite sure how that works, an English laundrette," I explained to him. Washing clothes was a long job, but this was the work for which I had been reared. My mother's daughter. Not for college and work in journalism, that was meant for my younger brother. That was their dream for him, not for me. My parents disapproved a little bit, if I speak the truth, about my work, as if I had stepped onto his preserved area. Certainly I had not been reared for living outside of marriage vows in communes; no-one in my family had ever been reared for that. And as for adventuring in England... That was right off the map for my life. So you see the least that I could do was to keep clean, talk polite and wash my underclothes thoroughly.

'Reuben talked aloud, half to himself, as he wrote by hand on papers spread out on the kitchen table. His writing was big and bold, like a child's writing. He explained it was for a supplement to the *Muck-Raker* called *Torpor Times:* "It's an apathy special. How the brain-numbing toxins of capitalism lull us into a life of platitudes. Sleep – Work – Consume – Sleep – Work – Consume. Dead from the neck up. Dead from the waist down. Wake, sleepers, remember you were once human!"

'I rinsed my clothes like a good girl while he read me some of his article. What he wrote was always fiery, wanting to sweep away banality. It would be like: *"They promised you happiness – they gave you boredom!"* It was all about how after the War the establishment promised people that social democracy and a growing economy would result with a happy classless society. Things like: *"These 'carrots' and consumer goodies could be held before everyone's eyes in their own sitting rooms. TV, along with mass education and growing newspaper readership, helped capitalism to wage its battle for the hearts and minds of the people. On always more subtle and intimate levels they persuade us that things are fine as they are: all we have to do is sit on our backsides"* – Reuben would say "arses" – *"and consume and let the banality wash over us."* That was the kind of thing. He said that these new forms of social control were like a replacement for religion.

'He made some improvements to his text while I went out to hang my washing on a string I had tied up in the garden. When I came back, he had packed his papers back into some plastic carrier bags.

'"Got to take this stuff to the printers. Evan up the road. He's going to show me how to work the machine too. Wanna come?"

'Outside it was cold but sunny. Some boys were kicking a football around. Reuben and I held hands as we walked through the council estate. I wondered if perhaps we looked like a real couple. "I won't contact you," Erich had said. "No phoney reassurance. A break that is total." But my best friend Ingrid who lived in the commune, she had not written either. Reuben walked fast, he always forgot that I had shorter legs and was attached to him.

'The printing press was in the ground floor of a half-ruin semi-detached house with a blue door. It was another squat. The front bay window was covered with brown paper on the inside. Reuben knocked and a few seconds later Evan opened the front door with a big welcome.

'"Hi. Do you want to start with one pound notes or five pound notes?"

'"Ten pound notes to save time," said Reuben.

'Evan shut the door and waved at the machinery spread out around what used to be the living room of someone's home. Two rooms connected, running from the front to the back. "The pen is mightier than the sword, but the duplicating machine is mightier than either of them. And as for the printing press, it has brought down governments," said Evan. He was a bit like a small greyhound dog, very tight and fast and energetic, always very hard-working for the revolutionary project. But as if it was through the gaps in his overalls, you could *manchmal* see a glimpse of something behind. You could catch a view of a certain charm, like a confidence that nothing can touch, typical of men who have been to the expensive English public schools. He sent a smile in my direction like an automatic routine, almost without him noticing.

'"I'd be happy just to bring down the local council," said Reuben. "I've got that piece for the next issue, shall I type it out?" He put a sheet of duplicating paper into an old typewriter.

'I quite quickly learned how to operate the duplicator, but I could not grasp the printing machine. It was partly difficulties with the technical language – a lot of new vocabulary – and partly that the process was complicated. Evan put emphasis on the importance of everyone being able to operate the press, that the skills should be reachable to all so there was equality. There should not be an elite operating the machine or getting others to operate it. But at the end of the day I still had no confidence that I would actually be able to print a leaflet if necessary. I was not sure that Reuben was following it better than me, though he looked cheerful and gave Evan a warm thank you and goodbye when we left: "I'll be back here next week to learn about doing the £20 notes."

'We walked back without talking. When we turned into our street, there was a black handbag lying open in the gutter. Reuben picked it up and inside he found a purse, which was empty, as well as some keys, a powder compact, a Kleenex tissue and a small booklet: *A Visitor's Guide to London*. "What's this doing here? It's not dropped, it's been nicked. No-one does tourism in this part of town." So we made a detour with the handbag to the police station, we filled in papers at a cold counter and Reuben discussed the local crime statistics with the policeman on duty. After all this, we did not set out for the house again until after ten o'clock. As we passed a fish and chip shop Reuben said he was starving and marched in. He bought himself a large piece of fish and a big bag of chips, and he ate them walking along the road, dropping bits of orange batter and white fish down the front of his donkey jacket.

'I had asked for a small helping and tried to concentrate on eating it without dropping any. I was surprised at the greasiness of the chips. There was an interesting article on the newspaper wrapping. A small boy had fallen from a third floor window and survived. I thought: perhaps then there is hope for me too.

'The house was in darkness when we arrived back, but lights came on obediently when we touched the switch, like a new invention. Duncan had fixed it. "They must all be in the pub," said Reuben as he slouched off to the toilet. His room looked much worse now it was lit up by electricity. The bare bulb gave a hard light, it picked out a pile of dirty clothes in one corner, boxes of books overflowing and dust on the floorboards all around the edge of the room.

'"Home sweet home." As Reuben came in, he took off only his shoes and trousers and got under the blankets as he was. I went to clean my teeth, and when I came back in my nightie he was already asleep. He was occupying most of the bed, he was too heavy to move, and he did not respond when I tried to wake him. Also, he smelt of fish. In the end I squeezed myself into the small space that was left, it was a thin strip of mattress on the outside edge. I had one arm and one leg spreading onto the floor, but I finally managed to doze off into sleep.

'Some time later I heard through the wall the sound of the front door banging loudly, very close to where our heads were resting. Waterfalls of laughter in the hall. The others had returned, I think they were drunk. Some hours later again Reuben woke. "Got to piss." I opened an eye. The small alarm clock said 3am. I shut my eye again. Soon he was back. He tripped over my leg, landed heavily on my arm, and pulled all the blankets over to his side. He still had no sheets. I screwed up my eyes, determined that I would get back to sleep. Then, while I think he was still half-conscious, he started to become amorous. There were sleepy grunting noises and he pulled at my nightie. I was only half-awake, but I managed to smack his hand:

'"*Nein, nein, nein, ich schlafe schon.*"

'"*Ach, mein Fräulein, du bist so hart. Ich liebe dich.*" He stretched out his great limbs all over the bed and in another two minutes he was asleep again.

'By now I was very awake and I was almost completely pushed off from the mattress. I lay with my eyes open for what seemed a long time. Long enough to feel the rough itchiness of the blankets. Long enough to remember my cosy clean bed and the nice turquoise coloured curtains in my room in Frankfurt. Long enough to remember how Erich always made you feel someone was in charge of things and was running them properly. Long enough to wonder whether England was really the place I most wanted to be.'

Ute paused in her narrative.

'But you stayed,' said Corinne.

'Yes, I stayed,' said Ute. 'And I have not yet ever regretted it. I started to send information back that helped the workers at Fords in Germany to fight for better conditions. There was more water passed under the bridge with Reuben. Troubled waters. But then we human beings, none of us are easy…'

'Life in that squat sounds challenging to say the least,' said Corinne, moving from a stool to one of the more comfortable chairs, and putting a cushion on it. 'I've never been in that close contact with so many people.'

'There were recompenses,' said Ren. 'There was a sense of purpose and belonging that lit up the horizon.'

'And that chaos, it did change,' said Ute. 'Life improved after I bought sheets for Reuben at the jumble sale. Do you remember that we went, Ren? With Alex and Duncan?'

Ren nodded. 'You'd never been to a jumble sale. That was the first time I got to know you at all.'

Ute smiled. 'You were introduced to me as Geoff's girlfriend. I remember that I said, "Ren? That is not a name I have heard," and you told me, "The first part of my name got worn out," and I tried to work out what that first part was. Before we set off you explained to me that I should not take it so personal if people elbowed me at the jumble sale. You told me, "That's how it's done. It's nature red in tooth and claw."'

'Even then I could see you were a gentle soul,' said Ren. 'I was afraid you might get hurt.' She took the lid off the teapot to see if there was anything left inside. 'That was the day of the incident of Alex and the coat.'

Corinne looked from Ren to Ute, 'Alex and the coat?'

'Are you going to tell it, Ute?'

'Yes, OK, I tell it from the beginning. When we got to the church hall for the jumble sale, there was already a long queue in the road outside it. Women with permed hair and shabby coats, large empty bags and needy faces. There was poverty then, real poverty like in Germany when I was growing up after the War. The women moved closer to the double doors, and at one minute before 2 o'clock they started to bang on them. When the doors opened at last there was like a wave of people, it swept me forward. I was carried to a table piled high with women's clothes which seemed to writhe and twist as the crowd pulled them this way and that. All around me people were arguing:

'"How much for this dress, dear?"

'"Excuse me, I've got that one, I was holding the arm before you even saw it."

'"Some people!"

'I was crushed against the edge of the table by the pushing of the crowd behind. There was no escape. Ren, you were not to be seen, but to my right I could see Alex grasping some flowery blouses. I picked up a pair of jeans from the top of the pile. They looked about the right size for me and I had never had a pair. "How much is this please?" They had just introduced the decimalized money, so I had difficulty to work out the coins. I handed over 10p then I turned and tried to slide back through the crowd to get out. My mother would have been shocked to see me buying second hand clothes. But that was the smallest thing of what she would be shocked by.'

Ute turned to Ren, 'I remember you standing at the household goods stall, saying "Don't they need a bigger kettle at the house?" I found the sheets for Reuben at the fabrics and curtains stall. They had faded stripes in pink, blue and green; they were clean, only a bit thin with a tear in one corner.

'When we got back to the squat we put the new, bigger kettle on the stove. Then we showed our purchases in a parade around the kitchen. Ren, you had bought a necklace of purple beads. I found that the jeans I had bought were skin tight with flares. Alex made some comment like

"Sex –y!! Reuben will like you in those!" I felt embarrassed.

'Alex tried on many pieces of clothing that she had bought; she walked round the kitchen and posed very slender and elegant like a model on a catwalk. The last one was a grey coat in a very good condition. "Only 15p!" she laughed as she spun round, stretching out her right arm and putting her left hand in the pocket. Then her face changed. "There's something in here!"

'It was a ladies' purse, with some pound notes folded in the wallet part at the back and some coins in the purse bit. "It must belong to someone." There was a small compartment with plastic in the front and you could see through it a slip of paper with a name, address and phone number. It was a road not so far away.

'Alex was giggling, "I suppose I could keep it anyway," but I'm sure she didn't mean that. We sent her off with some coins to make a phone call in the phone box down the road.

'She came back with a cross face. "I got through to the woman, but she didn't even thank me. She was just annoyed that I'd bought her coat for 15p. She kept saying 'It's almost new!' She was running the stall. It's not my fault if she got her own coat mixed in. She's coming round for it. I don't think I'm even going to get my 15p back."'

Ren picked up the story from Ute. 'Alex *didn't* get her 15p back,' she told Corinne. 'When the woman turned up, Alex sent Ute to the door with the coat, and Ute got an earful. That was a learning experience, that day.'

'Yes,' Ute sighed. 'There were many learning experiences. So many that I wondered sometimes whether the word "learning" was a substitute – what is the word – a euphemism for some other word.'

She paused. Then a crowd of Christmas revellers passed on the street outside Ren's window, with singing and shouting. Their merriment broke Ute's pensive mood, and she picked up her story in a brighter vein.

'But Reuben liked the sheets,' she said. 'I gave them to him two days later. First I washed them in the sink and hung them out to dry in the back garden. Then I put them on the bed when he was out. He didn't notice. Then later, when we went to bed, he didn't notice either. When he was writing he was always so absorbed in what he was doing, and with sex it was the same. It was only afterwards, as we were lying close, me with my head resting on that dear chest, that suddenly he said "Am I correct in thinking that there have been some domestic improvements at work here? Bourgeois bed linen! Duncan will be down to criticise us for our revisionist ways! Sheets! All the better to tumble you in, my dear!" and he did.'

Ute smiled as she sipped her cup, then grimaced when she found the drink was cold. 'Those were our glory days. I remember the afternoon when I asked him the question I had been burning to ask. We were walking back through the council estate after a meeting, it was getting dark. It suddenly came out of my mouth:

'"Do you hate me because I am German?"

'"No. Why should I?"

'"Because you are Jewish. Because of Hitler. Because of what my people did."

'He stopped on the concrete path next to a children's play area and looked me in the face. "Your people didn't do it. Your government did it. The government of the time. There is a difference."

'I couldn't meet his eyes. "You think so?"

'"You've got some strange ideas." He put down his plastic bag full of papers next to one of the children's swings, and sat on it. He patted the next swing. "Come and sit down and listen to a story."

'We both swung to and fro in the twilight, sometimes in unison, sometimes in different directions, and he started talking in the special sing-song voice he used when he was making his *Erklärungen*: "In 1933, on the night of the 27th February, the government building, the Reichstag, burnt down, right? The work of the Nazis, right, no one disputes that. But Hitler blamed it on a communist. Why do you think he did that? And why did people believe him and allow him to retaliate against the communists? Because the communists were strong. In '32 they had nearly 17% of the vote. Soon after the Reichstag fire they were banned.

'"Do you know how many communists were executed and sent to concentration camps? And how many ordinary people who opposed the Nazis? The Nazis never had a majority of the vote, by the way. A quarter of a million people served prison sentences for political opposition in the pre-war years. Altogether, including the war years, three million non-Jewish people were held in prison at different times or sent to concentration camps. Three million ordinary people. They were Germans too, and they were among the first victims of Hitler. Have you heard of the White Rose? Do you know how courageously some Germans carried on resistance even during the war itself?"

'I was feeling like a schoolgirl in an enjoyable detention. I started to swing higher. He joined in, and soon we were soaring as high as the top of the swing at the front, then at the back, almost keeping time with the each other, and the metal structure it was shaking with Reuben's weight. "That may be true," I called out on a sudden drop, out of breath, "But still so many people sat and did nothing." Above the black silhouettes of the blocks of flats, studded with the lights of people's suppers, and TV sets, and family arguments, I could see huge clouds moving across the sky. I remembered the rows with my parents in my teenage years, when I reproached them: "How could you? How could you? You knew what Hitler was, and yet you did not raise a hand to stop him!" My mother's face twisted with tears, my father turning away in dark shame and anger.

'"After the Reichstag incident," Reuben was swinging slowly now with sing-song again, "the Head of the Berlin Fire Department came forward. Gempp. He spoke out, he said Hitler's brownshirts had been at the scene and the brownshirts had stopped his own men from using all their fire engines. Also he said that he had found mountains of incendiary stuff in bits of the building that were not burnt. This showed a level of organization far beyond the resources of the communists. What happened as a result? He lost his job. In '37 he was arrested and two years later he was found strangled in his cell. The price of challenging Hitler was very high."

'"It was a price that people like my parents were too cowardly to pay."

'"You weren't there, you can't judge them. People were beheaded for offences like criticizing Hitler in a railway compartment, or putting up anti-Nazi graffiti in the toilet at work. Even listening to broadcasts by the BBC. Not everyone is made to be a martyr. If your parents had been, you wouldn't be here today, sitting on that swing."

'"Feeling cold. And hungry."

'"Let's go."'

Ute stopped her story. She shivered and looked around Ren's sitting room. 'I'm feeling a bit cold myself now. Rosa left her cardigan.' She picked it up from an empty chair, and wrapped it round her shoulders.

'I'll remind the central heating that we're still up,' said Ren, and disappeared into the kitchen.

'You are yawning, Corinna,' said Ute. 'It's late. Perhaps you are bored, perhaps you are tired of hearing about those days of struggle and sillinesses?'

'Please go on. I'm wondering what happened to these people.'

'They're all still around,' said Ren, returning from the kitchen with a bowl of fruit. 'Living their lives with the memory of that house lurking somewhere in their being.

'It affected us all,' Ren went on. 'The house was a dark tunnel leading to change. On the way were random pools of light where individuality lit up in an erratic way. The hallway, stairs and landings were murky. Wallpaper peeled, the spiders squatted too, and empty light sockets swayed in the draught. But these hallways opened onto islands of comfort or neglect, the rugs, posters, makeshift beds and tables inside people's bedrooms. Usually lit by light bulbs taken from the stairwells. Red flags, road signs picked up on drunken evenings, words of Bertold Brecht reminding us of our common humanity and the need for justice for the poor of the earth. And lots of dust. The road to revolution was paved with good intentions but they usually did not include housework.

'From the rooms came sounds. Arguments or love-making. In Alex's room Evan would sometimes be playing Duke Ellington. Or you might hear Reuben singing that Bowie song, "All the Madmen".

'In the basement Taff and Brenda had filled their room with bean bags and cushions wrapped in Indian fabrics. You couldn't walk: you had to crawl, roll or sink deep to disappear for an hour or two into the atmosphere of an exotic boudeoir. A poster on the wall said *"Be Here Now"*. A net curtain covered the small window and there was a permanent scent of hash smoke and incense. Reuben often went there to get his dope back from Taff: "You good-for-nothing layabout. You think the world owes you a living. I paid good money for that, it's best Thai grass."

'Taff was never happy to part with it: "Property is theft."

'"My property, your theft," Reuben would say.

'"But I do it with love," said Taffy.

'"Fuck off. Get a job," said Reuben.'

Ute said, 'I must confess, I found Taffy and Brenda's cushions uncomfortable. They gave way underneath me.

After a day's work I wanted something to support me. The lack of structure was disconcerting, the lack of a boundary between floor and cushion. When I took my shoes off I could never find them again.

'Taff and Brenda made love at any time of day or night, and the sounds often rose up through the bare floorboards to Reuben's room. His was a place of much creativity, it was intense and untidy. Here you could discuss anything, and from the cardboard boxes piled against the wall he could usually pull out a book about it: UFOs, trade union rights, poetry, football, Yiddish curses, working class history. His favourite book, *The Society of the Spectacle*, was usually near the top of the pile. It was here in his room that news sheets were created with bits of paper stuck down with Cow Gum in the early hours of the morning. Scalding text and drastic graphics on political themes, mixed with advice on places to go, music to hear, how to avoid bad trips, and how to eat cheaply. They gave a recipe for pigeon pie, starting with how to catch your pigeon. There was information on VD and discussion of the good and bad points of the different clinics in London for treating sexual diseases.

'Here on his good days Reuben was a human dynamo, so full of plans and ideas that the room didn't seem big enough for him. But there were bad days too. He was usually low when he came back from visiting his parents. I used to come in and find him sitting in his chair with a smell of despair around him. If I asked him what was the matter, he would shake his head, "You wouldn't understand." I asked, "How can I understand when I do not know your parents?" He wouldn't reply but stayed there sunk into the car seat, looking crushed, staring at the door.

'Taffy would try to coax him out of his mood with a spliff. And here on some hash-lit afternoons Taff and Reuben invented elaborate jokes, like the "Scroungers United Party", which produced an endless series of slogans written with red pens onto the wallpaper: "They exploit, we scrounge!" "Don't deplete the world's resources: scrounge!" "Fight for the right to scrounge!", *undsoweiter*.

'There would be discussions about all sorts of things – including teddy bears. Reuben and Taffy argued that after the revolution it should be a world full of free teddy bears. Duncan thought that in that world teddy bears should be banned: "They're a substitute. Remove the substitute, remove the pacifier, man, and then people will start to take notice of what's being done to them."

'Here too Reuben planned the lessons for the apprentices in his classes at the Further Education College. And Duncan came down to tell him he was doing it all wrong. Duncan argued for the advantages of a strict Scottish education; Reuben always said that he had to start from what his lads were interested in: "These apprentices, all they like is football. I'm meant to teach them Liberal Studies. OK, I'll teach them Liberal Studies. I'll teach them everything through football. Through football I can teach them geography – where the teams are from. Immigration – look at the names of the team members. Economics – which towns can afford to buy which players and why. Sociology – look at the supporters. Mass psychology of fascism – how people can behave in crowds. Issues further afield – there's the World Cup…"

'Geoff used Reuben's ideas for his own teaching as a supply teacher in secondary schools, but Duncan was scornful. "You're kidding yourself, man. Those lads need education. To better themselves. They need a chance to get out of the shite they were born into. Don't pander to them, you bloody liberal intellectual wanker."

'Reuben always responded to insults with good humour. "So what are you going to teach them? To join the Party? Is that the way forward for them? Mouthing the Party line? What about encouraging them to think for themselves?"

'"They're no' going to do that through football. It's a good way to destroy brain cells. Supporting your side, your town, your country. That's the narrow nationalism which created two World Wars."

'"I suppose Scottish nationalism is different?"

'If he was bothered by what Reuben said, Duncan never showed it, although his accent got stronger and his tone became more didactic: "Marx said history repeats itself, the first time as tragedy, the second time as farce. After the tragedy of World War II we have the farce of all those same countries fighting it out on the football field. Don't make me laugh."

'"Football is their culture. You tell me you're for the people but you despise their culture. Respecting our own culture is what helps us get up off our knees."

'"Look man, ban it! If I had my way they'd ban it. Then people might start to notice they're being robbed every day of the wealth they create by the labour of their hands."

'These arguments were never resolved, they would go round and round. I used to sit and listen. If I spoke, neither of them took any notice. It was a dance for two.

'From the hallway looking up the stairs, you could see a central pathway of wood that was a lighter colour, the ghost of a stair carpet which had once led people up in comfort to the first floor. On the first floor you were faced by the door to Geoff's room which was at the front overlooking the street. There was a Yale lock to prevent unauthorised visitors. Inside you entered alien territory, clean and tidy, and he had equipment and smart things. He had bought a big desk and paid two local youth to carry it up the stairs. He also had an anglepoise lamp, an in-tray, a swivel chair and a proper bed with black sheets. I remember I knew when he had shared it with you, Ren, because you always washed the dishes before you left for work in the morning.

'Sometimes, Geoff caused problems.'

Ute paused in her story. 'Ren, is it painful for you if I speak about Geoff and that student? You knew about it, yes?'

Ren said, 'That is water passed so, so far under the bridge that it is lost in the ocean. In a way he did me a favour. It helped me see what kind of man he was.'

'So, I'll tell you that tragic episode,' Ute said to Corinne. 'This was a bad day at the squat. One night when Ren wasn't there, Geoff brought a pupil of his home with him. He'd taken her out for drinks, I don't know how many. I saw the back of her going up the stairs with him, she was stumbling and unsure as if she didn't know where she was. From behind she looked as if she had dressed up specially for the occasion: a tartan mini-skirt and white plastic high-heeled shoes. I met her again the next morning on the way to the bathroom – she looked shaken up with her hair all over the place. I wondered what she had lost in the night.

'"You bastard!" Reuben confronted Geoff later that day, "Have you no morals?"

'Geoff was cooking himself some supper. He gave a thin smile. "That's rich, coming from you, you great hairy libertine."

'"At least I'm not a cradle snatcher. She can't be more than sixteen."

'"So speaks the champion of sexual freedom. Scratch the surface and you're as uptight as your parents."

'It was unusual for Reuben to raise his voice. "You leave my parents out of this. You don't know fuckall about my parents. Exploiting some kid who looks up to you, you call that freedom? That poor innocent girl."

'"Innocent my arse. Did you see her? She came on to me like it was Christmas."

'"You're her teacher," said Reuben. "That gives you responsibility. Not the right to give her education outside the curriculum. Makes you feel big, does it?"'

Ute turned to Ren. 'It was lucky for Geoff that Alex was away at that time. She would have lynched Geoff. I don't think anyone ever told her. I noticed that you were not around for a while after that. I missed you.'

'I was gutted at the time,' Ren replied. 'That was the beginning of the end for me and Geoff. I only got wind of it indirectly. But I had to ask myself: why am I with this guy? And why am I always with guys who behave like this? Do I have a choice? I should have known when I saw his black silk sheets and his neater than neat desk.'

Ute said, 'We always wondered what you saw in him.'

'I was young,' said Ren. 'People in my family didn't have degrees. I thought I had achieved something by going out with a man who was educated. I didn't know then that school teachers can behave worse than any working class man, only they do it politely.'

'Anyway,' said Corinne, picking up a tangerine and starting to peel it, 'Reuben wasn't exactly a saint, from what I've heard.' She aimed a piece of peel across the table at the wastepaper basket and it went in.

'Shot,' said Ren.

'I heard about Reuben and the tin opener,' said Corinne.

'That was the beginning of the end for him and me,' said Ute. 'That was hard. You want to hear? It feels strange, to talk like this about my life. As if it mattered. Telling it, I feel it again. But perhaps that is good for me. I will try to tell what happened.'

Ute screwed up her eyes. 'I can remember every detail of that Sunday morning. I had been out in the Saturday evening to a meeting, and when I got back to the house Reuben's light was off. I listened for a minute outside his door, but there was no sound and I didn't want to wake him.

'In the morning I got up about 10 o'clock. I had not slept well and I decided to bring Reuben a cup of coffee in bed.

He was usually very funny in the mornings when his wits were, you know, sharp. As I came down the stairs I noticed his door was a little bit open.

'In the kitchen Alex was sitting at the table rolling a cigarette. I put the kettle on and started to look for some clean mugs. You remember, it was never easy, and there was a hill of dirty plates from the night before. I noticed that it was Reuben's tobacco pouch that Alex was using, so I thought maybe he was up. There were no mugs clean. I moved some frying-pans and saucepans covered with remains of bacon and baked beans, so I could reach to the taps to wash up.

'I said to Alex, "I am making a coffee for Reuben, would you like one too?"

'"He's asleep," she said, in a voice with authority. "I think I wore him out." And she lit her cigarette. I did not understand. I looked at Alex and noticed that she was wearing one of Reuben's T-shirts, with bare legs. I couldn't make sense of what I was seeing and hearing. Or perhaps I did not want to make sense of it. Stupidly, I said "I am sorry?"

'Alex ignored my question. She replied, "The women all say there's nobody like Reuben for a good sexist fuck." She grinned at me and took a draw on her cigarette.

'I stood frozen like an idiot, half-turned away from the sink with a mug in one hand. I forgot what I was in the middle of doing. In my ears a sound like the rushing of water, and I seemed to be moving very slowly. Then the pain in my stomach started, as if somebody had kicked me.

'"It's true, isn't it?" Alex went on, still smiling. I looked at her as if I were seeing her for the first time. Those sharp features were pretty. Our eyes met and it was the closest contact we had ever had. Almost intimate. To me that smile suddenly seemed to be full of malice. Her eyes seemed to know everything as she looked into my suffering. Like a fisherman watches a fish flopping on the beach, gasping for breath. I think then I felt a pure hatred for her for doing this to me. I couldn't remember what she had said, so I said "What?"

'"About Reuben," Alex seemed to curl his name round her tongue as if she knew him very well, as if she owned him.

'I said "Reuben." I must have sounded so foolish. I looked down at my hand holding the mug and I saw it was shaking. I realized my legs were shaking too. I caught hold of the back of one of the chairs. The kettle started to boil.

'"Did you say coffee?" asked Alex.

'I couldn't think of anything to say. I put the cup down on its side on the table and walked out of the room as if I were hypnotized. Behind me I could hear the whistle of the kettle. I stopped outside Reuben's door. Some part of me still did not want to believe what Alex's words had told me. I tried to make my hand steady, and knocked on his door. No reply. I knocked again. "Reuben?" I pushed the door open a little more and put my head round.

'There, half out of bed, with his arms stretched out of the bedclothes, lay Reuben's familiar beloved body. That hairy back now suddenly looked a stranger to me. It belonged to someone else. It touched others, not me. On the floor beside the bed were crumpled clothes, among them was a bra and a woman's blouse. And, for some reason, a tin-opener. My stomach felt hollow. I closed the door and went upstairs.

'It was some days before Reuben seemed to notice that I was upset. He would give me a grin, so, when we saw each other across the kitchen. I tried to smile back. Alex did not seem to be around. A few days later I was trying to hurry past him in the hall, when he asked: "Are you avoiding me?"

'I couldn't find the words to reply. In the end I said, "Yes."

'"Don't you like me any more?" he asked.

'I answered, "That is not the question."

'"What then? Come and talk to me about it."

'When we went into his room, I saw it had been transformed. Some clothes were hanging up from a hook in the wall, and his chaos of books and papers had been piled up neatly together. It even looked as if the sheets had visited the laundrette, and the bed had been made. He had pinned some African fabric around the lower half of the bay window, and the old blankets nailed from the top had been taken down. I looked around, then I sank onto the car seat.

'"Did Alex do this?" I asked.

'"Alex? What's Alex got to do with anything?" Memory spread over his face. "Oh, that. What's that got to do with anything?"

'My body felt so heavy I could not move my mouth to speak. There was a long silence. Reuben started to pace around the room, "What did she tell you?" I swallowed and carefully remembered the words: "She said that all the women say you are good for a sexist fuck."

'Reuben paused. For a moment he looked unsure whether he should be insulted or flattered, then he waved an arm in a gesture to dismiss it. "They know I'm available." He turned to me and shrugged in a friendly way, "Anyone can have me."

'I stared at the floor, "And what about me?"

'"You're different," he replied. "But you weren't here." His voice raised a little bit. "You'd gone out," there was indignation. "And we're not married." He gradually started to sound angry. "And anyway, you've got Erich. How do you think that makes me feel, knowing that he could turn up at any moment to claim his prize? Do you want to keep both of us on a string? What kind of game are you playing?"

'I had to drag the words out of my throat to tell him my shameful secret, that Erich had not written to me since I came to England. That I did not know what he was feeling.

That I did not expect to see him.

'"Pull the other one," snarled Reuben, "I don't know who's going to turn up on the doorstep first, him or the bailiffs. I open the front door and – 'Good morning, I've come to take away your home.' Or – 'Guten Tag, I've come to take my woman back. And what is this I hear, that you have gotten to know her too well? Take that, you *Schwein!*' You'd like that, wouldn't you? Grown men fighting over you?"

'I looked at the floor. I couldn't understand how somehow I had ended up in the wrong. I couldn't say more. I was silenced.

'As it happened, it was the bailiffs who came first. A man in a suit knocked one morning when Reuben wasn't teaching, and when he opened the front door the man produced a document and asked Reuben his name. They needed to know who to evict. Reuben said "Mickey Mouse". He refused to give any more information and the man left muttering about court cases and eviction orders. The next week a typed legal document arrived reporting on the incident. It wrote that an official had visited the house and the door had been opened by a "tall swarthy man in his late thirties," and it stated that they were seeking to repossess the premises. "Tall swarthy man in his late thirties." They all laughed about that. Reuben was only in his twenties and he was indignant. The others never let him forget it. "I see a tall swarthy man is coming in for breakfast", "I hear music in the room of that swarthy man in his late thirties," and so on.

'After more days of avoiding Reuben, one day I found a bunch of daffodils on the floor of my room. It looked like he had actually bought them in a shop, that was a thing unheard of for Reuben. Next to them was a note. In his bold simple letters he invited me to go to the cinema with him to see a new film, *Dad's Army*. I agreed to go. I couldn't help laughing at the way the Germans and the British were characterized. During the film he took my hand, and our courtship started all over again.

'That evening we went to bed together. We went to my room, avoiding the scene of the crime. When he kissed me and started to undo my blouse, I started crying. When you make love, you have to forgive the other person everything. And forgive yourself. That means you must let go of everything, like a dam bursting. So much weeping came, I couldn't help it. It was slow at first, but the tears kept running until it was like a torrent pouring from my eyes and nose, and my chest was shuddering as if I could not catch my breath. Reuben fussed about and gave me a very dirty handkerchief. He dabbed at my face with it as if he was not sure what to do, saying, "Come on," and "You're making it worse." When he kissed me again he got wet with a lot of fresh tears but he kept on kissing, and unbuttoning with his big tender hands, and I let him. He still had that taste – of lust, maple syrup and autumn leaves. My body folded in to him. I carried on crying and opened my legs.'

Chapter Seven

Tuesday 26th December 1990 11.45pm
When Ute finished telling the story of Reuben and Alex, there was a silence around the table.

'You went through it,' said Ren.

'What a bastard,' said Corinne.

'You should understand,' said Ute, 'that they believed it was wrong to have privatized relationships. I knew that I had no right to be possessive about Reuben. It was correct to sleep with many people. But I must confess that, if it was correct or incorrect, it still hurt just the same.'

'And to come back to him after what happened,' said Corinne, 'that is something I have never learnt to do. If that was me, I would break down or run away, end everything. To believe that in spite of the hurt there can still be trust... to have so much trust. I have never had that.'

'It takes a lot,' said Ren. 'I don't know if the ideology helped. Conventional morality was seen as a form of social control.' She picked up the carbon-copied document that Corinne had read from, and scanned some paragraphs. 'See, here it is.' She read:

"The students' and women's movements which emerged in the late 1960s have opened up whole new areas of struggle because of the particular contradictions they experience. They have shown that the way capitalism seeks to control our conditioning,

consciousness and sexuality is as crucial to its survival as the other more obvious forms of control it exercises over our lives. The intensified struggle around sexuality and personal relations and against the oppression of the nuclear family has been manifested in women organizing against wife-battering and for abortion, teenagers in sexual rebellion…"'

Ute said, 'I think Alex saw it correctly, that the nuclear family was used to prop up capitalism. But finding alternatives was not easy, especially as we had all been brought up ourselves inside that system.'

Corinne paused, then asked 'So have you been able to forget and forgive Alex? If you don't mind my asking?'

Ute studied the remains of the Christmas meal. Then she said, 'I think it is like that story of "The Princess and the Pea". That betrayal is a small thing buried under layer after layer of years and experiences. But you can still feel it sometimes, just a little.'

Ren said, 'She's coming tomorrow, Boxing Day, as usual. You know you're welcome.'

Ute shook her head, 'No, thank you.'

Corinne asked, 'What did Alex do? Did she carry on sleeping with Reuben?'

'Never,' said Ute. 'For some reason she was away from the squat a lot after that. Staying with her boyfriend Evan in Forest Gate. It seemed that they were much closer.'

'Huh!' said Corinne. 'Maybe she used Reuben to make a point with Evan.'

'I don't know,' said Ute. 'All I know is, some time after that when she was in the house for a few days, she had a very big row with Reuben about him not doing the washing up. She could be very sharp like a knife. She accused him of all sorts of things: "You're a parasite, you know that? Off the labour of women. You champion the working class and then you behave as if you think you deserve servants. Did you never learn to wipe your own bum? Or do you need

172

your mum to do it for you? Why don't you bring your mum to live here as well?"

'When she said that, I knew she had gone too far. It was not usual for the good humour to go out of Reuben's face. He said, "I don't want to hear any words about my mother coming out of your mouth. I don't even want you in the same room." And he turned and walked out, his features cold like a wall. She continued being angry with him. I remember a bright-coloured knitted scarf she had, I think he borrowed it one night without asking to go to a meeting, and left it there. She was furious. And I don't think she succeeded in getting him to do more in the kitchen, because when we came back from the cinema one evening we found that she had left a bowlful of dirty washing up all over his bed – plates, mugs, knives and forks and saucepans. We went to sleep in my bed instead, but I think after that things between them were poisoned. It was almost as if they were both angry about that night they spent together.'

'Remorse?' said Corinne.

'Remorse?' said Ren. 'Maybe another way to see that is as the pain we feel when we have not been true to ourselves.'

'He was sensitive if anyone spoke about his family,' said Ute.

'I remember that,' said Ren.

'I couldn't understand it,' said Ute. 'At first he did not want me to meet them. I said to him, "You seem very close to your parents. I would like, to meet them." He would say, "Believe me, you wouldn't. You don't know what you're asking." I would say, "But why would I not like them? They are your parents. They must be like you in some way." He said, "Shockingly so," and went very quiet.'

'For such an open guy,' said Ren, 'he was very private about some things.'

Ute nodded. 'When we had got back together after Alex, in some strange way we trusted each other more. One day he finally said, "OK, you want to come and meet the folks? Don't say I didn't warn you." So we went.

'They lived in a brick terrace house with net curtains in the windows. It was even smaller than my parents' home. His mother opened the door, she looked as if she had been a handsome woman at one time, with iron grey hair and a strong jaw. She looked at Reuben: "What kind of time do you call this?"

'"Mum, I said three o'clock. It's only ten past."

'"Ten past three, half past three, four o'clock... What can I do? He is my son." She suddenly smiled, held out her arms and clutched him tight.

'"Mum, this is Ute."

'She held out a warm hand and looked me up and down, with intelligent, tired eyes. She was tall and thin, with a big, bony frame like a man's. "Reuben told me about you. Nothing serious, Mum, he says. Never anything serious with him. By the time he settles down I shall be too old to be a grandmother. I shall be dead."

'"Leave it out, Mum. Spare the violins," said Reuben.

'"He talks to me of violins. Come in, my dear. Never mind my son. He is a good boy at heart."

'We went into a dark passage which smelled of damp plaster and stale cigarette smoke. There was a big hat stand made of dark varnished wood, with a square bit at the bottom for umbrellas. The hooks at the top were empty, but at the bottom there was one black umbrella leaning onto an old tennis racquet. Ahead of us at the end of the passage was the sitting room; the door opened and we saw an open fire in the hearth. There was a bookcase with books piled on it, and a framed photograph of Lenin. On the wall there was a print of a Chagall painting, and one of Picasso's *Guernica*.

'In an armchair next to the fire, an old man was sitting bent over, so.

'"Heimi, we've got visitors," Reuben's mother called

out. The man turned a little towards us as if he was not sure it was worth moving.

'"Hello, Dad. It's your long-lost son."

'Reuben's mother moved a *Daily Mirror* out of the other armchair and gestured to me to sit down. "You drink coffee? You want coffee? Talk to him. He doesn't get much company."

'She went into the kitchen.

'The old man twinkled at Reuben. "Your mother misses you." He had a strong accent.

'"Dad, I've brought a friend: Ute."

'"Did you come a long way, Ute?" the old man asked without looking at me.

'I looked round to Reuben. Surely his father knew where he lived? I said "Hackney."

'"Yes, yes, today. But your journey before that?" he asked.

'"From Germany."

'"A long journey." He paused. Then he clutched the arm of his chair and looked up. "A long journey from 1918 and the ruins of your country's self-respect. Crippling Germany's economy at the Versailles Treaty. You know about that, Ute?'

'I nodded, but I didn't know what to say.

'"The Versailles Treaty," he went on. "That was a luxury the allies could not afford. A defeated enemy with nothing left to lose, that was soil ripe for fascism and Hitler. Despair needs scapegoats. Persecuting the Left. The assassination of all your radical thinkers. Dead. All dead. Like my uncle Solly. Poisoned air. They breathed poisoned air all across Germany."

'"It was gas killed Uncle Solly, Dad."

'"And your Aunt Hannah. It escaped from Austria, the poison. And it spread across Europe. They couldn't stop it, you understand me? All the trees died. People couldn't breathe. They choked to death and the clouds of smoke hung over all the fields. So no one could see the atrocities. They covered the truth."

'He started to cough and reached for a packet of Senior Service cigarettes from the table next to him.

'Reuben said, "My dad likes to look on the bright side of things."

'His father struck a match with a shaking hand and as he lit his cigarette he looked at me directly for the first time. "Did you come by bus, Ute?"

'I wasn't sure if he meant from Germany. He prompted me: "From Hackney?"

'I told him yes. He nodded as he shook the match out. "I used to cycle down there, when I was younger. We liked going to Victoria Park. Or sometimes Hyde Park. On a Sunday. Especially in the summer. Hire a deck-chair, watch the rich people going by on the horses. You know Hyde Park, Ute?" I nodded, and he went on, "All the people used to be out there, walking, after the War. Those, that still alive were. For a while the water in the Serpentine sucked the poison out of the air. But now they can't stop it." He coughed and tapped his cigarette into an ash tray which said it was "A present from Scarborough".

'Reuben's mother came in with a tray of coffees. There were some slices of *Kranzkuchen* too. "So how is it going with the teaching, son?" she asked.

'"It's good, Mum. The apprentices think they can better themselves. Some of them."

'"Good luck to them. You ask me, you're born poor, you stay poor."

'"We're campaigning with workers from Fords, Mum. The miners' strike in '69 was a turning point. People are waking up. Now manufacturing workers are at the forefront of the struggle. They could bring the economy to a halt. Some people think they could bring a revolution."

'"A revolution." She exchanged glances with the old man

and sighed. "We'll see even less of him then."

'The old man seemed to be looking past me. Staring at the top of the TV. I turned and looked at the painted stacking Russian dolls which were sitting there in a row. Then I realized he was looking at me. "You know how long it takes, Ute? Eight minutes."

'I wasn't sure what he was referring to.

'"To die," he went on, "in those chambers. The air was no good, you see. And now it's spreading here."

'Reuben's mother took his free hand. "Heimi, it's over now. We have Ute visiting." She patted his hand. "Well, Ute, do you like England?" I nodded and smiled.

'Reuben broke the silence. "So it looks like Heath is going to be crippling the trades unions, eh, Mum? That Industrial Relations Act is going through!" He put two slices of *Kranzkuchen* into his mouth one straight after the other.

'"Don't talk to me about our Prime Minister. He should stick to singing hymns and sailing yachts. You can't trust a man with that many teeth. Like that Geoff you knew at school. He's that type. That *mishugena*. Butter wouldn't melt in his mouth. But he used to cheat in his tests. He was no good, that one. Crossed eyes, crossed teeth, everything crossed."

'"Come on, Mum. Some people have crossed teeth and a heart of gold. Anyway, Geoff had his teeth fixed. He's got a perfect set now. The dentist rearranged his mouth."

'"Too bad they couldn't rearrange what comes out of it." Reuben's mother dismissed Geoff and turned to me. "Brilliant pupil, they said he was, this one. Your boy Reuben, they said, he could go far. Far, he says. As far as a squat in Hackney. At least here we pay rent. He left a house with a roof over his head for a squat where they could evict him any day. You call that an improvement?"

'"I've got a big room, Mum."

'"But can you breathe, son?" asked his father. "Do they

poison the air up there?"

'"No, Dad, there's a fresh breeze coming in from the Hackney Marshes. I can breathe easy. We've even got a tree in the back garden."

'His mother sighed. "We spent years struggling to get out of the East End. And how can you sleep at night with the bailiff at the door?" She pointed at a varnished wooden bust of Karl Marx sitting on the mantelpiece. "He didn't say anything about moving into empty houses that don't belong to you."

'"He would have done, Mum, if he'd thought of it. Changed times, changed strategies. Houses are standing empty. People are homeless." He took one of his father's cigarettes and lit up. His mother shrugged theatrically and the room fell silent.

'"Ute," she added after a few moments, "You're not eating any cakes. You don't like them? I made them specially."

'I took one. It was very good, chewy and rich with rum.

'With Reuben and his father puffing on their cigarettes, the room was getting smoky.

'"You want I open the window?" his mother asked. She did, and a blast of cold air came into the room. But Reuben's father muttered "Ach, Clara, you want to let them in?" and she closed it again. We sat in silence some more.

'In the end, Reuben and his father watched the football, while his mother and I discussed German food, about which she knew a lot although the family was from Poland. I was grateful for my mother's cookery training, so that I could speak back with her on that subject. Afterwards a programme was starting about Alexander the Great, which they wanted to watch, and Reuben's mum invited us to stay for supper: "Eat some proper food, better than the *drek* you'll be eating in that squat!" But Reuben made his apologies, and we left.

'As we walked down the road, I asked Reuben "What was your father's job, before… before…"

'He said "…before he lost his marbles? You can say it. My dad was a printer. He'd worked for the same firm for years. He was still working fine, but he started saying strange things. Like today. As soon as they noticed, they couldn't get him out of there fast enough. They used it as an excuse for no golden handshake, in fact no handshake of any kind, more like two fingers. No redundancy payment in spite of his track record, and he wasn't retirement age. They gave him the bum's rush. Suddenly he found himself on the scrap heap. In that armchair with no reason to get out of it. And the air outside getting more poisonous all the time. My mum tries, but he hasn't been out of the house since."'

Ute stopped speaking and there was silence round the Christmas table. Corinne took a sprout and ate it. After a while, Ute asked Ren, 'Did you ever meet Reuben's parents?'

'I never met them, no,' said Ren. 'But as I got to know him better, he did talk to me about them sometimes.'

Corinne said, 'His father being like that, it must have been hard for him.'

Ute said, 'He never hid his wounds. But he never made a show of them either.'

Corinne yawned. 'Please go on. I'm learning so much here about a different way of approaching life.'

Ute tilted her head to one side. 'I am not sure what you mean.'

'I'm not quite sure either,' said Corinne. 'It's something about resilience, about accepting imperfection and working with it rather than insisting on perfection or nothing. Which in my case usually means nothing. About fighting things through, going for what you need. Instead of giving up.' She sank her head into her hands. 'That's what I always do.'

Ren said, 'I think we've reached the point where only

179

coffee will do. I'll put the kettle on again.'

While she was out of the room, Ute turned to Corinne. 'You know, I learnt so many things from Reuben. Mostly things my mother would not have wanted me to learn. And I cannot imagine what his mother would have said if she knew.

'Like how to not pay in expensive restaurants. He showed me the secret: to move very slowly as you walk out. So you don't look suspicious. He felt no guilt about it. "They can afford it," he used to say, "The profits they make. Rip-off merchants. Stuffing the faces of moneyed *machers* with *haute cuisine*." There were other things I never expected to learn, like how to recognize scabies… remember, Ren?'

Ren groaned as she came back in with the coffee. 'The itching, terrible… '

Ute spread out her hands on the table, 'On the knuckles, lower arms…'

Ren said, 'We were all scratching like crazy people. In the War lots of soldiers got it, so they had conscientious objectors taking part in trials. Deliberately giving them scabies to find out how it's caught and treated. I should think some of them would have rather been on the front line. It spreads through physical contact. And there was plenty of that in the squat. As you've heard.'

'In the end,' said Ute, 'Geoff went to the doctor and had a diagnosis, and we all had to be treated. I remember going down to the public health clinic. I am sure that building was standing when your Queen Victoria was alive. Old red brick, and inside white tiles everywhere. All eight of us walked in with our heads low like naughty children, and they treated us very business-like and kept a safe distance away from us as if we had the plague. We had to take a bath and be scrubbed and then they painted that white stuff all over us, remember? It smelled so powerful nobody would sit near us on the bus going home. All our clothes had to be washed at a high temperature. We never discovered who brought the parasites into the house. But the men did try a bit harder with cleaning their rooms after that.

'Then there was all the excitement when the Brazilians moved into the other houses in the row. They were squatting too. Most of them were musicians, we used to hear Caetano Veloso songs till late at night. Then often at 5am we would get woken by the car picking up Reg from next door the other side to go to work at Fords.'

'That clapped-out Cortina,' said Ren. 'the exhaust needed fixing. There was always a screeching of brakes, loud revving of the engine, the opening and slamming of doors and then another screech as they carried Reg off to the day shift at Dagenham. Who could forget Reg? Ute, Tell Corinne the story about Reg and the rat.'

Ute said, 'I think, that Corinna is tired.'

Corinne stretched, yawned, and shook her head. 'Nothing that this coffee can't fix. Shall I pour?'

'I first met Reg soon after we moved in,' said Ute. 'One day I came home from work and went into the kitchen and he was sitting there with Reuben drinking a cup of tea. He jumped to his feet and shook my hand so energetically his black curls shook. "Hello, Ute! I hear you're the one who was with this load of layabouts when they disturbed my beauty sleep the other day. Didn't anyone never teach you how to smash down a door quietly?"

'I said, "I'm sorry."

'Some people shake your hand almost without touching you, but not Reggie. He was about my height, and after he slapped his hand flat onto mine, and gave a powerful shake, he held on tight. His palm was warm and dry.

'He grinned, "No problem. Nothing keeps you awake for long when you've been on the line all night. Settled in good, now are you?" It was strange for me at first to hear his cockney accent when he was so brown.'

'His mother was Egyptian,' Ren told Corinne.

'Then,' said Ute, 'before I could reply, Reuben said "Reggie's telling me about the rat."

'"Rat?" I looked nervously around the dirty kitchen.

'Reuben said, "No, the rat at Fords."

'Reg said, "Fords cars, you know, the ones that sell all over the world and made Henry Ford a multimillionaire? Pity it hasn't done the same for any of the poor bastards who work in his factories. Great cars, they are. We call them F – O – R – D: Fix Or Repair Daily."

'Reuben said, "Tell Ute about the rat."

'"More than one, mate," said Reg, and he carried on with his story.

'He told me that he was one of the shop stewards in the Engine Plant, and the men had been complaining about rats. I suppose they were attracted by the crumbs and bits from the men's sandwiches, I don't know. They couldn't smell the rats, too much oil and engine smell in there, but they had been seen running along the walls.

'Reg had been several times to complain at Personnel, a Mr. Griggs.

'"That Griggs is a mean type," said Reg, "he's got his tie on so tight he looks half strangled and he keeps smoothing his Barnet like he's got a nervous tick. Did he believe me? No way! He goes, I've made enquiries among the foremen and they say it's absolutely not true. Company hygiene can't be faulted on this. He thought I was pulling his leg. They just think we're looking for an excuse to belly-ache about something.

'"You know, it's war in there. You have to get permission to leave the line to take a leak. They put a spare man on to take your place. But if one of the lads takes too long the foreman comes down like a ton of bricks. What's he doing in there, Reg, he goes, having a piss or taking the piss? You'd better make up your mind, he says. Guy gets a verbal warning, and if it happens again he gets called in to the supervisor's office. Loses pay. They think we're a load of skyvers. That's rich, ay? Up there in Management, they take a two-hour lunch break, but that's not skyving. Henry Ford lives the life of Riley, but that's not skyving. We're the ones who do the hard graft all hours of the day and night, we get paid peanuts compared to them, but if we linger more than thirty seconds in the kasi, they think we're a load of workshy layabouts. Makes you wonder, dunnit?

'"Anyway, soon after, one of the men on the line saw a big bastard of a rat scuttling under a pile of palettes in the corner of the plant. A brown one. Clear as day. He starts shouting, but with the clanking of metal, it's like hell in there, it takes a while before we hear him and by then the rat has gone. I got one of the lads driving a forklift outside to bring it in and clear the palettes. It didn't take too long, and when it's cleared – there's a turn-up for the books – there's a great nest of them swarming about under there. The big ones scarper out of the building pronto and there's all these little babies left in a mess on the factory floor. Got their eyes shut, some of them. So I picked one of them up by the tail and put it in my overalls pocket. I went straight up to Grigg's office. I go in to his secretary and ask to see him. What's it about? she goes, looking down her nose like they do. I go, It's about the rats down in the plant. Grigg's door was open, he could hear all this, so he comes out smoothing his hair down like he's afraid it'll get unattached saying, I'm sorry, Reg, but about the rats there is absolutely no evidence that there is any bona fide cause for... I say, You want proof, do you? I had my hand in my pocket and I just pulled out the baby rat and laid it on the secretary's desk. It was kind of pink and curled up, but it squirmed a bit and opened an eye. What's this, then, I said, Scotch mist?

'"That put the cat among the pigeons. She started screaming and his face twisted like it was in an orange squeezer. He backed off with gritted teeth: Get that thing out of here!

'"I turned round and walked off.

'"After that they had to get the janitors to clear the nest off the factory floor."

'When he'd finished his story, Reg laughed out loud. Then he stood up and said he had to go. As he left he shook my hand again. "Nice to meet you, Ute." Keeping hold of my hand, he leant forward and whispered to me: "It's a pity, though, enit, that it's a bit harder to get rid of the real rats. The ones in suits." And he chuckled to himself as he left.

'He was a regular visitor after that. Reuben tried to introduce him to taking dope, but he refused: "Can't touch that stuff, mate. Makes me paranoid. Got enough of the bastards on my back as it is, without imagining more."

'The next time I saw him was when we were down there leafletting.'

Ren groaned. 'Those crack of dawn starts! The alarm going at 4am…'

Ute asked, 'Why is it you were always dragged in to help, but Geoff never came?'

'He always had some cast-iron excuse.'

Ute went on: 'They had put in a wage claim, and our Car Group were supporting the claim. Making links with other Ford workers in factories outside London. The first time I went to do leafletting, Reuben had borrowed a car from his friend Bob. Four of us set off in it to drive out to Dagenham. I was still half asleep. The streets were deserted. Traffic lights, asphalt and concrete stretching out flat for miles towards the east. Even the Bow flyover was empty. Reuben insisted on singing David Bowie songs as he drove. Duncan, who was sitting next to him, complained all the way about his driving and his singing. It was girls in the back, Ren and me kept quiet. Evan and Alex were in another car.

'When we got there the darkness was beginning to get thinner, but the factory lights were still on. We placed ourselves at the gates just as the first trickle of workers started to come out from the night shift. Soon it turned into a flood. Most of them were black. Some of them came out slowly with their heads hanging, they looked tired. Some of them seemed to wander as if they weren't sure where they were going. Some of them looked like they had been released by a starting pistol on a race to get home.

'There were a few who would not accept the leaflets. A couple of them looked over their shoulders at the factory as if they were being watched. Most of them took the leaflets and started reading with an interest. The headline said, "They can afFORD it!"'

Ren laughed. 'The slogans were Reuben's speciality,' she told Corinne. 'Some were quite good. There's copies of all this stuff in that same wooden chest over there. Have a look at them too if you fancy it.'

'Ren ended up with all the souvenirs,' said Ute. 'Somebody had to be the guardian.'

'Anyway, go on,' said Ren.

'So we were leafletting,' said Ute. 'One white man stopped and asked me "Who are you?"'

'I explained about the group and that we were there to support Ford workers organizing for better conditions. "Why?" he asked. I explained how we thought they set the pace for other workers in workplaces that were less organized and less well-paid, and they helped everybody move towards a better standard of living.

'He was quite angry. "We're well paid, are we, according to you? You know what shift work does to your family life? Anyway, you'll never get anything going in this place. Too many blacks. Wogs and Pakis. Like trying to organize a herd of monkeys." And he walked off with the leaflet.

'When we had finished the leafletting we went back to the car. Reuben had just got into the driver's seat and he switched on the engine and then two policemen suddenly appeared from nowhere. It was as if they had been waiting for us. "This your car, sir?"

'"No, I borrowed it from a friend," said Reuben.

'I saw the two policeman give a look to each other.

'"Got the documents, have you?" one of them asked.

'"No."

'They made him get out of the car. I noticed the one behind was holding a copy of our leaflet. The one in front asked "What's the registration number?"

'"Don't know. I can give you the name of the owner."

'"You don't know the registration number?"

'"Like I said, it's not my car. Ask the owner."

'"There'll be plenty of time to do that, sir, down at the station."

'The last we saw of Reuben was in the back of a police car driving away into the distance.

'They wouldn't tell us where they were taking him. Evan and Alex had left earlier, so we travelled back on the Tube and went to the house of his friend Bob who owned the car. Duncan had memorized the numbers of the police officers. We didn't know what to do, until Alex turned up and took charge of things. She spent hours on the phone ringing all the possible police stations to find out where he was. In the end we tracked him down to a station in West London. Alex told them on the phone that we were coming down with the documents and a solicitor. That was bluffing, but it seemed to have the effect we hoped.'

'Wait a minute,' Corinne interrupted. 'I thought you said that Alex and Reuben were at war with each other?'

Ute nodded. 'Over the washing-up, yes. But with an attack like this on one of the group, those personal things were forgotten. We all stood together to support each other.'

'That's impressive,' said Corinne. 'So it was Alex who got him out?'

Ute replied, 'Yes. When we got to the police station she gave them a slice of her tongue about civil rights and so on, and in the end they released him. It was about 4 o'clock by then and we were all exhausted, apart from Reuben. His time in captivity, it seemed that it made his wits sharper. They had been asking him a lot of questions about the group, and he refused to reply. After being silent for so many hours, he talked without stopping for the rest of the afternoon and all evening to make up for it.

'We realized the Ford company was worried about the leaflet. Otherwise why would they call the police to harass us?

'Reg started coming to the group meetings. When he was working days, he and Reuben sometimes went to the pub together, and came back singing "Yesterday," and "I wanna hold your hand." Reg wasn't keen on David Bowie, he said Bowie was "kinky"; but he liked the Beatles.

'Then one day I found him sitting in the kitchen with Reuben and he looked depressed. He was afraid he was going to lose his job. They had suspended him from work for being absent from the assembly line. He'd gone to a shop stewards' meeting, and according to the official rules, he was allowed to go. But the company made an exception and said the meeting was not properly authorised.

'"It's ever since I took that rat up there," Reg said. "They've been gunning for me, waiting their chance. Now they've stitched me up good and proper."

'After he was suspended, the workers in the plant had done a walk-out immediately, in protest, unofficial. We went down there the next morning to the picket to support them and let the other workers know what happened. Evan and Reuben were up most of the night duplicating the leaflet. Its headline said "Without your shop stewards you are F***ED! Walk out in support of Reg Burnley!" When we arrived at the factory there was a small crowd outside the gates in the morning light, some of them had placards. When Reg appeared, he got a cheer.

'Many of the workers arriving for their shift read the leaflet and stayed out on the picket line instead of going in to the factory. Some of them were Asians who arrived in groups, and they knew Reg. They hugged him and slapped him on the back. Among those going in, I saw the white man I had spoken to before, the one who complained about Pakis. I decided to go across to give him the leaflet. He stopped and looked at it and grunted. I was surprised when he took it.

'I said, "You'll read it?"

'He growled, "Yes. Gotta support Reg."

'That surprised me. "Even though he's what you called a Paki?"

'He looked at me with indignation. "He's one of our shop stewards, ain't he?" and he went to join the picket.'

Corinne rubbed her eyes and asked 'Did Reg get his job back?'

'Yes. But no thanks to the union. It was a wildcat picket, the union were not happy. But it forced them to take action and after a week he was back on the line.'

'So you did have victories?' asked Corinne.

'Yes, but you know,' said Ute, 'we felt that even a victory under capitalism is a contradiction. Reg went back to work saying to Reuben, "Back to wage slavery, thanks a lot, mate."'

Ute paused. She cut a slice off the remains of the Christmas pudding, and ate it in her fingers. 'This remembering 1971,' she said, 'I don't know why, but it makes me hungry.'

'You could say the road campaign was a victory,' said Ren. 'But then again that was what broke everything up in the end.'

'What road campaign?' asked Corinne.

'Are you up for telling it?' Ren asked Ute. 'Corinne, you look tired.'

'I'm fine,' said Corinne, rubbing her face. 'I love a good story.'

'OK,' said Ute. 'Keep it short. It was soon after the Fords picket that the group had a new challenge. We first knew about it when we heard cars' horns hooting first thing in the morning. It went on for half an hour, so we went out to see. Two streets away from us, the people living there had put a pile – a barrier... how do you say, a barricade? – across the street. The traffic was stopped in the streets all around. They had put supermarket trolleys filled with stones, piles of bricks, some branches, an old chest of drawers and a sofa, rubbish bags, broken chairs, all piled up in the middle of the street.

'The people told us that on the day before there had been an accident. A boy of five years old had been knocked and hurt badly by a supermarket lorry driving along the street.

'"We already asked the Council to make the road safer," one woman told us. "But did they listen? Nah! They done nothing. After what happened to that kid, looks like we're going to have to make them listen. So we all got up early and done this.' Some of the parents had home-made placards written on pieces of cardboard: "One child hurt – how many more before the council listens?" "What matters – supermarkets or people?"

'The mother of the boy who was hurt was there, she was crying. The drivers were furious, they were hooting. They were blocked in, front and back. A man got out of a blue van and started trying to take the blockade down. The residents shouted at him, and dragged the things back into the road. Some more drivers got out of their vehicles to join the argument, and fighting started. One of the rubbish bags got burst, and there were nappies and potato peelings and empty cereal packets spreading everywhere.'

'I missed that,' said Ren. 'I had left for work before then.'

'In the end,' said Ute, 'the police arrived. They calmed things down and directed the traffic out of the area. Then they talked to the residents. They were sympathetic about the accident, but they said the blockade had to go. An old officer told the parents: "You've made your point. If you want to take things further, you need to proceed through the proper channels. We can't do anything about the lorries coming through here, but the Council can. They're the people you need to go to. You can't take the law into your own hands." They said if the street was made clear within an hour they would not arrest anybody.

'So by lunchtime all that was left was a few big items at the side of the road, with old newspapers and crisp packets blowing around the pavements. One of the unemployed teenagers climbed over a fence and lit a bonfire in a patch of overgrown waste land on a corner of the street. The chest of drawers burnt well, but the sofa frame made a bad smell.

'"That land's going to waste," one of the mothers said. "If the kids could play in there they wouldn't have to be out on the road." That idea spread. By the evening the street looked back to normal, it was as if the protest never happened. But that was the beginning of the campaign to take over that patch of land for children to play. I think that it was perhaps a bomb site from the War. Someone told me that hundreds of bombs were dropped on Hackney in the War. That always made me to feel guilty.'

'Oh, Ute! ' Ren shook her head. 'For goodness sake!'

'Anyway,' Ute went on, 'It was the most fierce argument I ever heard in the group, when Alex suggested that they should support the campaign about the road and the play space.

'"The Left has always overlooked struggles going on in areas of life outside the factory," she told the group. "But capitalism's tentacles have spread into social life. The lorry driving through streets where people live. The TV adverts telling people to buy more. The profits made by the big shopping chains. These are a big part of the way the system screws us."

'We were all in Reuben's room and Duncan was sitting on the car seat like a throne, holding a pile of papers. He was totally against it: "It's no' but a waste of time. Marx wrote about the struggle between Labour and Capital at the point of production. In the factory."

'"That's a typical narrow Leftist view," Alex was sitting on the floor next to him and she replied with such passion that she seemed to rise up to his height: "When he gets home the worker is a consumer. He buys at the supermarket. He needs housing. His kids need schools."

'Duncan replied: "But it's in the factory he has the power to push for better pay and conditions, and ultimately to strike. That's the only way to bring down the system. We can think later about where the wee kiddies play."

'I could hear the anger in Alex's voice: "But what about the women? Are you saying their needs and struggles aren't important? If you don't listen to them now, what kind of kind of world are you going to end up with after your revolution? Not one that I'd like to live in, that's for sure." She drew on her cigarette and blew out fiercely.

'Duncan was trying to get a word in, but she was hard to stop when she got going: "We have to develop a wider view of the struggle against capitalism," she told him. "I'm talking about struggles around housing, education, prices, consciousness, sexuality, the media, the law, healthcare, welfare rights, leisure, culture, transport, childcare, racial and sexual prejudice... And the rest. These aren't just secondary issues." She stopped speaking and started writing furiously in a notepad on her lap.

'Duncan was fixed in his opinion: "Och ay, I know there's

some not too far from this room who think that having sex is going to bring down capitalism, but I think we have other priorities..."

'I heard Alex muttering something about "Prurient jibes..." and "None so obsessed with sex as those who aren't getting any," but that was under her breath, and it was Reuben who took up the argument. He got up from sitting on the mattress and stretched his limbs, then he wandered to the window and looked out.

'"Where's your imagination, man?" he asked Duncan. "You're thinking in straight lines. You're not open to looking at what's around you. Look out in the street. We need to learn from working class people what's important to them and how they are organizing autonomously to fight back." He held out a big hand to include the world outside, "It's not up to us to dictate to people how they should be organising. Nor to follow dogma based on what happened in Russia fifty years ago. You have to start from where people are at, and right now there's a lot of people down the road who are angry and on the move. I say we should do all we can to support them."

'Geoff didn't say anything, he just kept looking at his watch. There was a man Clive with a beard who'd come all the way from Broadway Market to attend the meeting; he didn't say anything, but he had a heavy silence about him which made me feel scared to speak. He and Alex seemed to go out of their way to ignore each other. Evan backed Alex up.

'Reg didn't say much, but when they asked him his opinion he shrugged and said "You needed a home and you took this house, see. They need somewhere safe for their kids to play and they want to take a bit of land, OK? So what's the difference? What's the harm in that? If you can pull it off. It's like at the factory. On one side it's the property owners, on the other it's the poor bleeders who ain't got any. Getting together gives you strength whether you're on the shop floor or the street. People learn about how the system works and they won't never see things the same after that."

'In the end it was Reuben and Alex and Reg who won the day. Duncan was too disciplined to go against the majority decision of the group, although he made it clear that he was humouring us in a futile diversion from the true struggle. The split in the politics in the house was more clear than ever before. And there were other cracks starting to show. Soon after that the break up between me and Reuben really began.'

Corinne had her head resting on her arms and her eyes shut.

'I never understood how that all happened,' said Ren, 'and I've never talked to you about it. I'd love to hear. Can you face talking about it now?'

'I can,' said Ute. 'In fact, it helps to revisit that time from the distance of so many years. My break-up with Reuben was gradual at first. Perhaps if I had recognized the signs I would have acted differently.

'One evening I got home to the squat late after my bus from work had broken down. I found Reuben sitting at the kitchen table and he was very involved in talking to a woman who I did not know. When I came in, she had her back to me and all I could see was like a waterfall of long black curly hair. The room was full of smoke. They didn't realize I had come in. It seemed difficult for them to take their eyes off each other, as if they were connected by some invisible wire.

'When at last he did look up and notice me, Reuben cried "Ute!", as if I was the last person he expected to see. Then there came a pause as if he was waiting for me to go out again.'

Ute sighed.

'Oh, Reuben!' said Ren.

Corinne stirred in her sleep and turned her head the other way.

Ute continued, 'The woman with the black hair turned round with a charming smile. "Oh, you're Ute! You're not at all how I imagined you." She stared at me through thick locks of hair which hung over her face.

'I wondered if there was something wrong with the way I was. And I couldn't understand why she should be imagining me at all. I didn't know her. She was wearing a white blouse, one of those in a peasant style with embroidery, the material was almost transparent and she had no bra. Her face was pretty, but somehow hard to pin down. It seemed to change as you looked at it. She went on talking, "I know how much you mean to Reuben. He's always been the susceptible type."

'She looked at Reuben. "You remember that girl in Rome? Spanish, wasn't she?" Then she turned to me, "We were hitching in a group and we got separated. Our lot arrived only two days behind him and already he was sharing his bed with some sultry beauty. There's no stopping him. Insatiable." She took Reuben's hand across the table and gazed into his eyes. "Come on, Rubes, you know I'm right. Famous for always being shacked up with some attractive female. I should know, I know you better than anyone." She stroked his hair as if he was a child, her child. "How many years is it?" Then she glanced over her shoulder at me and pulled a funny face, "He doesn't want to admit it."

'I was wondering how many years it was.

'She took the joint out of Reuben's hand and drew on it. Turning back to me, she added, "They're not all as nice as you, believe me." I was wondering how many others there were. And how she knew whether I was nice or not, since she had not even met me before. As if she was replying, the woman went on:

"He's told me all about you. You must come and visit."
She had turned back to Reuben and I was not sure whether
the invitation included me. I looked out of the window at
the sunshine on the brick wall between our house and the
next one. I could feel my handbag heavy on my shoulder
and I wanted to take my shoes off.

'The woman tossed her hair back off her shoulders.
"Reuben and I were just talking about going to the cinema.
Death in Venice is on. I want to see it again, it's outa sight."

'Reuben spoke up. "Ute might like to come too."

'"Straight after work! She might be tired, eh Ute?" That
intense look flashed again in my direction. I was uncertain
how to reply. "See, Reuben, she's tired." Turning back to
me: "He can be a selfish pig sometimes. Inconsiderate. But
he has redeeming qualities…"

'I felt I had entered a world I did not recognize. Where
everybody else knew more than I did. Where I had no
special place in Reuben' life. Where I was an outsider
among these people who acted so free. Where I was talked
about like a child. I felt confused. Uncomfortable. In the
end I said: "I think, that I need to go and rest," and I set
off up the stairs. When I came down later, the kitchen was
empty. At midnight, when I was already asleep to prepare
for the work ahead of me the next day, Reuben woke me up
putting his head around my door: "Well, now you've met
Franny."

'That was the first time.

'The next time I met her was a while later. I came home
from work and as I came through the hallway I looked into
Reuben's room. He wasn't there, but to my surprise she
was lying on his bed with her eyes closed. She was wearing
a muslin skirt with little bits shiny on; it was kind of pulled
up and spread over the bed and you could see her slim
brown legs curled over the bed and her hair was scattered
all over the pillow. As I came in she opened her eyes and

looked at me without moving: "Oh, it's you!"

'I asked, "You want to see Reuben?"

'"No, no," she said, and she sat up quickly. "In fact, I'd much rather see you." She picked up a lit cigarette from a saucer beside the bed. "I need your help. I think you are the only person who can help me." I sat down on the bed and she looked at me with her brown eyes that were very hard to look away from, and she spoke very quiet and low as if everything she said was a secret so I had to lean forward to hear what she was saying. She told me that she had a problem with a project at her college in Maidstone, something to do with art history, and she was dyslexic and Reuben was the only person who could help her with the writing, but he had told her to ask someone else.

'She told me, "We dyslexics can't spell, you see. Words are cool, but there's other ways of communicating: the language of colour, movement, sound, unspoken vibrations; they're more intuitive, I'm sensitive to those. Spelling is so straight. We dyslexics are specially creative, but when it comes to putting letters in the right order, forget it. Reuben can be very harsh sometimes. He just refused to help me, I don't know why...."

'"But how can I help?" I asked.

'"He'll listen to you," she said. "You're so important to him. He respects what you say. Also..." she leant a bit closer still and I could smell a scent of sandalwood coming from her, "I think he thinks that if he helps me, you'll be upset. His relationship with you comes first. But I said I didn't think you were that kind of person. You wouldn't mind, would you?"

'"No, of course not," I said.

'"You see, I told him so. But he needs to hear it from you. He won't believe me. He won't listen to me. He would rather I failed and got kicked off my course, he really doesn't care."

'I said, "I'm sure he cares, I will speak to him about it."

'She said, "You know, you're an exceptional person, no wonder Reuben thinks so much of you." Then she started hugging me. I wasn't used to that and I felt awkward. Especially because Reuben came in just then, back from his teaching.

'He stopped at the doorway and stared. "You two seem to be getting on like a house on fire."

'But when I told him that Franny had come round because she was worried about her college project, and surely he could help her with it, and of course I didn't mind if he did, he sat down on the car seat and gave me a strange look. "You want me to help Francine?" He always used her full name when he was annoyed with her. "Do you understand what that involves?" he asked. Then he looked at her and said, "I see you've done a good job here. Did you have to drag Ute in on this? Don't you realize that some people in this world act in good faith?"

'When she heard this, Franny got up suddenly from the bed where she was sitting. "What are you saying, you bastard? You hate me, don't you? After all we've been through together. You bastard!" She hurled herself at him on the car seat, beating at him with her fists. He fell off, his face completely disappeared under her breasts and hair and all I could see was her half-naked body on top of him screaming and shouting. "You hate me! You want me to die!" He was trying to protect himself, but he did not retaliate. Then just as suddenly she went quiet, she stopped and she got up. She gave me a look with contempt: "You're welcome to him," she said, and she walked out. As she went through the front door she slammed it so hard that one of the pieces of wood we had nailed on it fell off onto the floor.'

'I remember that patch coming off the door,' said Ren, 'though I wasn't there when it happened. Duncan complained a lot about having to replace it: "Could your guests show a wee bit of respect for other people's housing?"'

There was a pause, then Ren erupted into laughter. 'I'm sorry, Ute, but in retrospect it is quite funny. I appreciate it must have been traumatic for you.'

'Yes,' said Ute, 'I was very impressed with how upset Francine was, and how Reuben didn't seem to take it seriously, and afterwards I asked him several times why he could not help her.

'It was quite soon after that when Reuben went out to post a letter and he did not come back for five days. I did not ask him where he had been, but one time soon afterwards he said to me, "You wanted me to help Francine? Well, I helped Francine. Now, let's hope that's finished. I told her that's that. Please don't get me involved in anything else. Believe me, it's not a good idea."

'But that wasn't the end of it, was it, Ute?' asked Ren. 'Would you like a cup of raspberry tea? To settle the stomach before bedtime? I see Corinne has passed that stage.' Corinne was breathing peacefully in her sleep, leaning on her arms on the table. Her paper hat had fallen off.

Ute pulled a rueful face. 'There was more to come. Franny, she did not do things by the half. You were at work when we were getting down my clothes that she threw into the sycamore tree.'

'What was all that about?' Ren asked.

Corinne stirred and suddenly jerked her head up 'What tree?' She looked around the room as if she did not recognize it, then put her head down again, shut her eyes and went back to sleep.

'I'll put the piece of foam down for her and make up her bed in a minute,' said Ren. 'She's had it.'

'The event with the tree,' said Ute, 'it was more difficult than it seemed at first. My clothes were spread out all over the upper part of the tree. Shaking the trunk – as much as one could – did not shift them. They stirred with the branches like big many-coloured blossoms among the leaves, but nothing fell. Reuben was not enthusiastic to climb up. His frame, you know, was large but not athletic.

'"I'm a city boy," he said. "We didn't have trees where I grew up."

'"Come on, do your bit like a man," said Duncan.

'Reuben stood firm: "I don't bounce".

'Alex was giggling, looking out at us from the kitchen window. I went to borrow a broom from the house next door and made a few things to drop. I was embarrassed that the first object that fell was a pair of my knickers. I was picking up clothes that fell, together with pencils, papers and a ruler that had come from the top of my desk.

'After a while Duncan borrowed a ladder from a house four doors away and he climbed into the branches. With the broom handle he could reach almost everything and down they came like rain, my smart clothes for work and my casual clothes, my blouses, my jacket, more bras and knickers. I tried to gather them up and fold them away as fast as I could. My duvet came down heavy. They always joked about it; only Germans had duvets in those days. Duncan called out from the top of the tree:

"Lucky it wasna raining when your friend Franny came round. They'd all be wet. She had a field day as it is. Did you na try to stop her?"

'I could not explain to Duncan what it was like to be woken in the middle of the night by somebody who pulled the duvet off me as I lay asleep in my room with Reuben beside me. And to see a figure like a shadow moving around the room, picking up pieces of clothing and throwing them with the duvet out of the open window into the summer night. Emptying the drawers. Then clearing the cupboard and throwing the clothes out through the window. For me it was a slowness in waking up, I remember pulling my nightie down to cover myself. In contrast it was like a feverish haste of this dark moving figure. Everything being thrown out. Reuben was even slower to wake, he just rolled towards the wall when the duvet disappeared. He always slept heavy. At last I managed to speak. My mouth was dry and it sounded to me like a frog croaking: "What's happening?"

'"I've had enough," I heard Francine's voice coming from the far corner of the room, "Enough of your intrusion into my life." She came closer to the bed, like a dark shape hanging over me.

'I stumbled in my speech: "Francine, what are you doing here? It is the night time. How did you get in?"

'"Try locking the back door!" it sounded like the hissing of a snake.

'I started to get up off the mattress, but she shrunk away from me as if I was somebody infectious:

'"Stay away from me! Don't touch me!" she backed off across the room. "I've tried to be your friend! It's too late now! I've tried to be fair but you don't seem to get the message." She emphasised her words by pushing everything off the top of my desk out of the window. There was a scattering of pens and pencils falling outside, and papers floated out into the garden.

'By this time at last Reuben was awake. In his naked body, he got up and caught Franny in his arms saying, "Stop it. Calm down." She struggled, but he had a strong hold.

'"Let go of me!" she bit his hand.

'"Oh, fuck!" I heard, but Reuben held strong. "Calm down. Stop. This isn't the time or the place."

'"You bastard! You male pig! Let go of me!"

'"Come on Francine, come downstairs. I'll make you a cup of tea."

'At the end he succeeded to put a towel round his waist

and to take Francine out of the room, he was half pleading and half dragging her. I lay on the mattress and I stared after them. I was still not really awake and the whole scene seemed like it was an unreality. Like a play that has not been properly rehearsed. Reuben always had told me that Francine was melodramatic. But, you know, my body, it had fear and that felt real, and I was cold. I got up and I saw the duvet on the branches of the tree outside the window, with my clothes and my other things on top of it or spread around it or lying on the ground below. I searched around the room and found a pullover that had escaped the attack. I curled up under it and lay awake for a long time. Reuben did not come back to bed. That was when I realized that Francine made her own rules.'

Corinne twitched and snored.

8

Chapter Eight

Tuesday 25th December 1990 11.45pm

It's nearly the end of Christmas Day and I'm worried about Sang. We've had all the festivities here, with all our housemates. And he's been on his own.

'Are you coming to bed, Ant?' Morton is already tucked in.

'I'm just going round to Sang's.'

'At this time of night? Aren't you tired, hon?'

'It's not far. Maybe Freddie'll come with me.'

I knock on Freddie's door but when I go in, he's lying flat out on his bed on his stomach with a joint in his hand. He looks completely out of it. He's staring from his bed across the room at the wall. His floor is covered with a unicycle, two guitars, a skateboard and a violin, and his bedroom walls are covered with posters about 'Make Hemp not War' and 'Beat the Poll Tax' and Jimi Hendrix and Ian Dury and saving whales, but I follow his line of sight and realize he's looking at a small photo which I've noticed before, pinned up there. It's of a woman with long blond hair. She has her head in her hands, with a ring on the little finger of her hand.

'Hi Freddie,' I say quietly. 'Sorry to bother you, you look miles away.'

He registers my presence. 'Perhaps more accurate to say

decades away,' his voice sounds hoarse. 'After all, time and space are a continuum.'

He drags his eyes away from the photo.

'Hi, Ant.'

'Fancy a walk?'

'A midnight ramble, great... But I'm legless. The wine combined with certain substances has left me with no legs... Where are you, legs? Where are you when I need you? Sorry, Ant. Are you going far?'

'No, not far.' He's evidently not in a state to be any help to me as a walking companion.

'Don't go falling off any cliffs!'

Like Hackney's got that many cliffs... But why did he say that?

As I walk down the stairs I'm thinking about my dreams. I haven't mentioned them to Freddie. I haven't mentioned to him how many times in my nightmares I'm falling and falling with nobody to help me.

Wednesday 26th December 1990 00.21am

I have to knock several times before Sang answers his front door. It's late and I don't want to wake him if he's asleep. But I want to make sure he's OK. Christmas on your own can be painful. And his upstairs front window is casting a blaze of light onto his lawn, so I think he might be awake.

Eventually the door opens a crack. When Sang sees me, it opens wider. I'm not sure if he's pleased to be visited, but anyway I'm here now. He is in his Lawrence of Arabia costume which he saves for special occasions. After Greek pottery, T.E. Lawrence is his main preoccupation.

'Happy Boxing Day, Anthea,' he says. 'This is indeed an early visit.' After he lets me in, we stand for a moment in the hall in silence.

'Happy Boxing Day, Anthea,' he says again. Then, after

a pause, 'It is indeed a pleasure to see you. But I am not prepared. If you could bear with me, I would wish to tidy up here a little. Then I shall be ready to entertain visitors.'

I know that he likes everything to be ordered and just so in his life, and he doesn't like surprises, so I tell him I'm happy to wait, and he sets about clearing his kitchen table of a few neat remains of a Christmas meal.

He wraps two Brussels sprouts in a plastic bag, puts it into the rubbish bin and closes the lid. He puts a tub of brandy butter into a plastic bag, sets it on a shelf in the fridge and closes the door. He pours some milk from a big jug into a little jug and puts it into the fridge and closes the door. He washes up the big jug, dries it inside and out, and puts it in a cupboard on the wall. On the cupboard door a slip of paper is attached with sellotape, carrying the typed words: 'All major campaigns call for privations. Think only about the taking of Akkaba.' He dries a fork and puts it into his cutlery drawer. Then he takes it out and puts it in again. He dries a knife and puts it in and out three times. He closes the drawer. He takes a clean J-cloth from under the sink and wipes the table slowly. He puts the J-cloth into the rubbish bin. He washes his brown hands with soap front and back and between the fingers, dries them on a clean white towel and examines them.

He leads me through into his sitting room and glances in turn at the faces looking down from portraits on the walls above the neatly arranged furniture: Sir Arthur Evans, T.E. Lawrence on his motor bike, The Queen, Marlon Brando, Friederich Nietzsche, T.E. Lawrence in Arab costume and his own face in a mirror. I know he admires strong characters. And especially English characters, for some reason. I think he secretly wishes he were English. He turns to some small piles of books and papers set out on his desk. There's a thick handbook of ancient Greek pottery that must be part of his PhD work. I can also see a photocopy of his typed letter to me beginning:

'Dear Anthea,

Thank you for the invitation to Christmas lunch…'

The photocopy is pale round the edges and Sang dusts it as if that might make it look more perfect.

He takes the letter and places it in a folder in a filing cabinet beside the fireplace. He checks the top of the filing cabinet for dust and returns to the table. He turns back and checks that the filing cabinet drawer is closed. He turns back to the table. He adjusts the position of the Greek pottery book. From another pile aligned to a corner of the table, he takes up an A4 writing pad with margin and narrow feint ruled lines filled with neat sloping handwriting. 'May I read you this? It has some relevance.' I nod and he starts:

'T.E. Lawrence's unique qualities coalesced most markedly in the masterpiece of his career: the uniting of Arab forces into a concerted effort to make the move on Akkaba. As he led the Arab army on a route thought to be impassable, to launch a surprise attack on the city, one sees triumph achieved through strategic vision, single-mindedness in pursuit of a goal, secret subtlety in thinking and skill in cloaking genius.'

He picks up a finely sharpened pencil from beside the pad and lengthens the stalk on some of the 'p's. Then he reads on:

'Most of all the English spirit manifested in his ability to cleanse all impure elements of doubt and disorder, to steel his will to achieve the impossible. Privations of hunger and fatigue, mortifications of the flesh, these served only to strengthen his resolve. Only one thing mattered: the taking of Akkaba.'

Sang puts the pad down in the same position on the table and stands in front of the mirror to check his costume. The Arab headgear fastened with a band around above the ears. The capacious cotton robes designed to give protection from the heat of the desert sun. He checks one of the photos of Lawrence of Arabia to make sure he has it right. He bows to the photographs and then he turns and bows to me too. A mixture of Chinese and English courtesy.

I think it means he is ready to talk to me. 'Everything OK?' I ask. 'Did your Christmas go OK?'

'Anthea, I nearly experienced a disaster with my compass, but it was retrieved and all can be recovered.' So this is why he's behaving a little more strangely than usual.

He leads me up to the front room on the first floor. 'Akkaba,' he says, 'Akkaba.'

'Akkaba?' He seems to want my help with something.

He picks up an engineer's compass that is set out on a tabletop with his old gramophone and other collectables and Lawrence memorabilia, and takes me to sit next to him by the window. He draws aside the net curtain, and opens the window on to the city street lying empty below.

'Here, Anthea, I am glad to be able to share this with you. Sitting here can one not picture the burning days of that interminable journey to Akkaba? The endless expanse of desert, the clear cold night sky where a thousand tiny shards of glass shone down to show the way? The soft crunch of padded feet as the camels moved across the sand? T.E. Lawrence on the journey of his lifetime. The journey that made history. A man of letters – did he not translate Homer? A man of action too, moving through the dark air towards the unsuspecting city. There is murmuring, low excited speech in Arabic, the city is in sight.' He reaches a long arm out of the window. 'The Moslem army following the impossible dream. Even the camels hushed. Creeping noiselessly through the desert. Incognito in the night. The British will never believe this feat was done. "Only a genius or a madman...," they will say. But they know genius lurks under cover, behind closed doors, keeps to itself. Now our fortune is in the hands of the stars, the constellations that guide us through the darkness of the desert. To ensure success, we need the constellation of Orion...'

He picks up the engineer's compass from the window-sill, unfolds it and holds it tightly as he stands up and leans out, adjusts, peers, to take a bearing. Finally he says, 'We have it! The impossible dream will be achieved! He sits down and for the first time he looks at me. 'Thank you, Anthea, for being here to share this moment. You notice how tightly I held the compass. No risks can be taken with these things. A previous attempt was made earlier this evening when catastrophe was narrowly averted. The moment came to take the reading and my attention was distracted by a man with two small children coming along the road. My fingers slipped. The pressure of my grasp ejected the compass, sending it flying forward... It landed on the lawn of the front garden.

'Luckily I was able to go down and retrieve it. I do not know why the children screamed and ran away at such a historic moment, but luckily I have been able to repeat the experiment with you. Akkaba is taken. Thank you, Anthea, and may I wish you the very best seasonal greetings.'

Wednesday 26th December 1990 4am

'Help! Help!' I can hear screaming and as I wake up I realize that it's me who's screaming. Again.

'Ant, Ant,' I hear Morton's voice and feel his arms going round me. 'You'll wake the whole house!'

I realize that I'm caught up in the duvet, tugging on it and twisting it around.

I open my eyes without seeing. I gasp, 'You can't save me.'

'What's the matter, hon?'

I wake up and sit up. Now I can see him. 'It was that dream again. The one where I'm falling. It was horrible...'

'Only a dream.'

'It felt so real. You were there. But you couldn't save me.

I think Bert was there too. I fell and fell. My head hurts.'

Morton kisses the hand I put to my head, and kisses the head around it. 'Come on, hon, time to go back to sleep.' He finds my other hand and kisses that too. I realize it's clenched into a fist, and he opens it. There's nothing inside.

'Where is my bone?' I ask, 'Where is my bone?'

'Come on, hon. Forget the bloody bone.'

Wednesday 26th December 1990 11am

Corinne woke up still in her clothes, with her bedding wrapped around her, lying on the foam mattress. It was spread out on the floor alongside the table bearing the remains of Christmas lunch. In front of her eyes was the solid varnished table leg, carved with fluted grooves and with a square bit at the top like the pillar of a Greek temple. Behind it were chair legs and some pieces of wrapping paper that had fallen from the table. She groaned and slowly levered herself onto her feet.

Coming back from the kitchen five minutes later with a cup of coffee, she sat down on one of the chairs at the table and looked around her. The remains of the meal were pretty much as she remembered them when listening to Ute's story. The carbon-copied document written by Alex during the days of the squat was there too. As she drank her coffee, she picked it up and read some more:

'The system failed to fulfill its post-war promises, causing industrial militancy and new demands from the working class during the 1950s. The capitalists tried to recoup the profits lost through wage rises by using inflation and rising prices against the people. The reality of living in the new estates did not live up to expectations. Communities were broken up and people experienced the isolation, cramped conditions and anti-human design of new high-rise developments.'

Corinne rubbed her eyes and wandered into the kitchen

to top up her coffee before returning to the document:

'Women who had played an active role in the war effort found themselves again trapped within four walls facing boredom, loneliness and emotional stagnation in their domestic role. More women needed treatment for depression, stress or nervous breakdown. Their role became even harder as economic pressures pushed women out into low-paid work, so they were in effect doing two jobs, one in the home and one outside it.'

There were footsteps coming down the stairs then a knock on the door, and Ren put her head round. She and Corinne stared at each other as if trying to remember something.

'Hangover?' said Ren. 'You were out like a light. We had to sleepwalk you into bed. Off the chair and onto the mattress just as you were.'

'Hangover,' Corinne nodded. 'Hell of a hangover. Though I didn't drink that much.'

'Good time yesterday?'

Corinne nodded again. 'Thank you. I like your friends. On the wagon again today.'

'Did it help, listening to Ute's story?'

'It did. I felt less isolated,' said Corinne. 'I had put my crisis in 1971 down to my own failure. To hold a relationship together with one person. I saw him mirrored in the cosmos. I didn't realize other people were going through similar stuff. That we were both balanced on a major fault line in the wider world.'

'There was an explosion of questioning at that time,' said Ren. 'It let lots of cats out of lots of bags.'

'I keep wondering, why then?"

Ren shrugged. 'Cuba? Other revolutions in Latin America? The Vietnam War? Then Paris 1968. It all opened up lots that was good. Some that was bad too.'

'Like Pandora opening the jar,' said Corinne.

'Wasn't it a box?' asked Ren. 'Pandora's box?'

'In the earliest versions of the myth it's a jar. Everything came out, good and bad. Only hope was left inside.'

'That's always handy,' said Ren.

Corinne yawned. 'What I don't understand is how all that going on in the outside world could have affected me personally. I was making my own choices – mostly wrong ones.'

'We are not islands,' said Ren. 'We are bound up with one another more than we think.'

'But this stuff,' Corinne waved the document in her hand, 'it's all general. Theory. It didn't have anything to do with my life in the 70s.'

'Yes, she does write in general terms. But we believed that every law, every building, every book, every institution, every idea that's out there will touch an individual human being closely – on their skin, in their purse, in their relationships, in their dreams.'

'Really?' said Corinne.

'The personal is political. And vice versa. Give that thought a chance. We are all joined by an invisible web. A tremour on the edge and every silken thread trembles. Take some more coffee, I'm having a shower.' Her face disappeared.

'There must be a mountain of washing-up. I'll make a start,' said Corinne without moving. She rubbed her eyes and read on:

'Mass education had promised greater opportunities and more job satisfaction to working class and lower middle class kids; and equal opportunity for middle class women. These aspirations were frustrated, and people realized that schools and universities were basically production lines for the labour power required by capitalism. This led to a change of consciousness and a growth in student militancy.

'Other post-war promises fell short: for example, the promise of a better life in Britain for immigrants – who were landed with worse jobs, pay and housing than white workers, and who became

scapegoats for social anger.'

Corinne put the pages down, drained her coffee and started to rummage in her black plastic bag. She undressed and got dressed again in clean clothes, fetched an apron off the back of the kitchen door, and slowly started to clear the table. She brought all the red wooden chairs into the kitchen from the sitting room, and piled up the dirty plates on top of them. She looked out of the window; it was raining again. She tried the sink tap but only a trickle came out. She put her head out of the door and listened to the shower running upstairs. She opened the fridge door and looked at a half-drunk bottle of red wine sitting on a shelf in the door. She shut the fridge again, made herself another cup of coffee, and sat down on the remaining free chair with the typed pages:

'Also, capitalism's need to extend its markets has led to previously private areas of life, such as emotional and sexual relationships, being invaded by commodity relations. The growth of porn movies, sex supermarkets and the constant use of sex in advertising mean that instead of the joy and satisfaction promised by the "permissive society", people experience themselves more and more as objects, usually objects inferior to the models and magazine covers. The emotional and sexual repression inherent in the structure of the family continue to contradict the promise of sexual freedom held out by ads and TV.'

Corinne jumped when the phone rang from a shelf beside her in the kitchen. She stared at it for two rings, then went to the kitchen door and put her head out. It carried on ringing. She stood looking at it while the answer machine picked up: 'This is Ren's phone. Thank you for calling. If you would like to make an appointment for massage treatment or counselling, please leave your name and number clearly. Thank you.' After the pips a woman's voice said, 'About the session you offered me tomorrow: yes please.' Then the phone rang off.

Corinne leafed through to see how much of the document was left, then sat down again to read:

'The result of all this is a change in the nature of the class struggle so that the industrial sector is not the only important area of militancy. As capital tried to recoup in the social sphere what it had lost in the industrial sphere, new sectors of the population have felt the rub and have been drawn into the struggle against capitalism.'

Corinne tried the tap again; the water came through hot, and she filled the basin with soap suds and last night's glasses.

'So what did you think of the manifesto?' asked Ren, glancing at the document on the floor as she carried in the leg structure of the table from the sitting room.

'It's interesting,' said Corinne. 'But a bit kind of... worthy. I haven't finished it. I've read about what was wrong in the post-war years, a bit depressing. I'm just starting the bit about people fighting back. Talking of struggling, do you want a hand with that table?'

'I'm OK,' said Ren, bringing in the table top and starting to re-assemble it. 'Read me some of it. These days I've forgotten what convictions and values sound like.'

Corinne dried her hands on her apron and picked up the pages to read aloud: *'Sometimes the response of the working class has been individual or spontaneous, e.g. vandalism, shoplifting, getting into rent arrears, etc. But in many cases it has been collective and class conscious, e.g. the response to costlier and worse living conditions has been mass squats, rent strikes, road blocks to stop traffic where children need to play, and demonstrations against inadequate public transport. Rising prices have been fought by campaigns against supermarkets, and by food co-ops.'*

Ren groaned. 'Alex always wrote very well, but what dates it is the optimism. I mean, the over-optimism. People did do those things, but only in a few places, not everywhere. If only...'

'Shall I read on?' asked Corinne. 'I'm nearly at the end...?'

'Go for it.'

'People have fought the rundown in welfare benefits through campaigns against closing a local hospital or school, for better childcare facilities and for unemployment benefit through the claimants' unions, while those who are institutionalised, like mental patients and prisoners, have fought for better conditions.'

Corinne put the pages down on the re-assembled table and looked at Ren. 'There's a lot about fighting. It could sound aggressive. Do you think that might put some people off?'

Ren smiled. 'Alex had a poster that said "There comes a time when only anger is love". You're right. It's ironic that the people who make money from human suffering pass judgement, and the people who care about social justice are called aggressive.'

'I don't think I've ever fought for anything,' said Corinne. 'I had no idea any of this was going on in 1971. I was working at a play site on the other side of Hackney. I was on a different wavelength. I remember someone gave me a pamphlet, *The Society of the Spectacle*; I grasped there was something called capitalism, but my sense of how it worked was internal, almost dreamlike. I was immersed in human relationships – well, one relationship – and that blotted out the whole world. My memory of that time is so different. Did everyone else know about these protests going on?'

'Not really,' Ren replied. 'They got erased from public memory too. We were only a small group, but there were lots of groups like ours doing stuff. There was a movement, and it made real gains. Things we take for granted now. For women. Equal opportunities. Much of what we fought for has been incorporated. But it's also true that this document talks it all up. Some people really believed that a bigger revolution might happen.'

'I was trying to visualize someone tapping those pages out on an old typewriter.'

'Alex, she was the brainy one. That kind of language gets lampooned these days in half-baked TV programmes. They try to make out there was never any serious reality in the movement at all. Thatcher moved the agenda so far to the right that some of the ideals seem a joke.'

'Perhaps it's "out of fashion",' said Corinne.

'Convenient for the mainstream media to see it that way, as if human needs like food, shelter and dignity could go out of fashion. Exploitation certainly hasn't.'

'I never heard about any of it.'

'The mainstream press rarely reported it. It wasn't exactly in their interests. But when you were living in east London did you never see a copy of the *Muck-Raker*? Evan would be sorry about that.'

'I don't remember reading any newspapers that year. I had my head in the clouds or in the sand or God knows where.'

'So you'll never have heard about any of these, which we thought were the main hope for people to get better lives...' Ren took the document and read out from the last page herself: *'The years since the late 60s have seen the growth of many movements, by no means all of them self-consciously "political", which have represented a subversive challenge to traditional law, morality, and behaviour in general: alternative films, newspapers and law centres, the women's and students' movements, gay liberation, communal living, collective childcare, self-health centres, free schools, etc. Many of these movements have remained isolated as "exemplary" politics – we can't smash the family simply by building alternatives to it. But we have a lot to learn from them. They show possibilities for better, more equal, more humane, ways of living.'*

'Brave words,' said Corinne.

'Let's face it,' said Ren. 'We were defeated.'

Wednesday 26th December 1990 12.30pm

It was already busy at 'Mon Repas' restaurant when Freddie appeared outside, heavily bandaged, on a skateboard. He zoomed down the wide pavement, turned and zoomed past again, before stopping outside to circle and perform tricks. He braked sharply, he turned the board, he jumped off and on again. On his back was a placard that read 'DON'T BLAME ME, MY BIKE GOT BROKE'. The bandages covered both arms, both legs and the top of his head. The one round his head was stained with what looked like blood.

The customers inside the restaurant noticed and turned to see. In particular Mimi, sitting in the window, saw him and smiled. She glanced over and gave a nod to the restaurant owner, who was standing behind the counter wearing a pressed linen suit and long gold earrings. The waiters inside the restaurant gathered by the window before scattering as the owner strode, earrings swinging, over to the door and out onto the pavement. She went straight over to Freddie, who put up his hands as if in surrender. Without a word she held out a plain white envelope; he took it and watched the back of her immaculate grey coiffure and the swing of her skirt as she marched back inside.

He opened the envelope and counted the £100 in ten-pound notes that was inside. He turned the envelope over; on the front was written 'And now go away.'

Wednesday 26th December 1990 8pm

'I had the weirdest dream last night,' said Brenda, moving her greying hair out of her eyes and putting on a pair of spectacles so that she could see clearly to roll a joint. She was sitting at the table in the kitchen with Ren, Corinne and

Alex and the remains of a reheated turkey supper, which had been served with rice and a spicy mushroom sauce.

'Tell your dream to Ren, she's the expert," said Alex. Her sharp features had softened slightly with age, and dye had reclaimed those bits of her black curly hair that had tried to turn grey.

'Ha ha,' said Ren.

'There was a big old dilapidated house,' said Brenda. 'We were in charge of it. Some kind of community centre. Like the old days. I walked down towards it and there was a group of people walking in. They were all in orange cowls – cloaks and hoods – like monks or something like that. One of them was Clive. Remember Clive from Broadway Market? In the dream I asked him if he wanted something to eat and he told me he was meditating.' Brenda chuckled and it sounded as if a lifetime of unregretted experiences were rolling around in gravel.

'Clive? Meditating? That'd be the day!' said Alex. Her sharp features opened in a kind of snarl.

'More likely medicating,' said Ren.

'Premeditating,' said Alex.

'Deprecating,' said Brenda.

'Hating,' said Alex.

Corinne looked round the table. 'Can I ask who Clive is?'

'He came up from Broadway Market to take part in the occupation of that bit of land,' said Ren.

'A head banger,' said Alex. 'I'll tell you who Clive was, he was the person who made me a feminist.'

'How come? He was hardly sympathetic to women's issues,' said Brenda, lighting up the joint.

'I knew him in Notting Hill before I came to the squat,' said Alex.

Brenda's eyes lit up. 'So what happened in Notting Hill, then, nudge nudge wink wink?'

'Mind your own,' said Alex,

'What?' asked Brenda. 'No nookie?

'With Clive? Credit me with some taste in men.'

'You weren't so retiring when we knew you,' said Brenda.

Alex smiled, showing perfect teeth, 'I was younger when I was in Notting Hill. I hadn't learnt there's something to be said for going along for the ride.'

'That's more like the Alex we knew,' Brenda nodded. 'Remember Reuben?'

Alex sighed. 'Has Ute ever forgiven me?'

Ren said 'I don't know. She was here last night.'

Alex shrugged, 'I did some awful things when I was young.' She paused, then brightened up: 'I guess we all did.' She gave a swift perfunctory smile. 'How's Reuben now? That summer I wasn't sure if he was going to make it. Especially that day we occupied the play space. I thought he might have lost it for good.'

Corinne asked, 'So you went ahead with the occupation of the play space? What happened?'

Alex looked at Ren and Brenda, 'Shall I tell her?'

Brenda filled up their wine glasses. Corinne put her hand over the top of hers.

'You've heard everything up to there, haven't you, Corinne?' said Ren.

'OK,' said Alex. 'Here goes. The squat's finest hour, and – soon after – the beginning of the end.

'It took some planning. When Clive turned up at the meetings, he never acknowledged that he'd met me before. If he was surprised to see me there, he never showed it. He never spoke in my direction and he looked straight through me. The first meeting he sat silent and glowered at everyone as though he could be making the arguments much better himself if he could be bothered to spare the breath. Once it was decided to go ahead, there was a meeting to discuss how and when.

'Several of the mums living in the street were all for it,

but they weren't going to be the first over the fence. Reg suggested doing it very openly, with a procession through the streets first to gather more people, and a plan for entertaining the kids. Others thought the main thing was just to get the fence down by whatever means.'

'That was when Clive took the floor. The meeting was in some musty little room out the back of the church hall, half the chairs were broken. You know, that sort with a grey metal frame and reddy-brown canvas stretched across the seat and the back. Clive stood up and kind of threw his seat aside with a bang so everyone's head turned: "We could go and tear those fences down any time in the night, but they'd be replaced within twenty four hours. Or we can decide to take a direct action with support and agreement from people in the neighbourhood, and we take the waste land in broad daylight in front of the police. If the circumstances aren't right, we're wasting our time, and some of us could end in court, but what's at stake is the safety and happiness of your children. I ask you, is it worth it?"

'Everyone was galvanized, and the vote was to take that chance and go in en masse.

'We'd argued about what to do if it rained, but that Saturday, when it came, was a clear gusty day. We all set off from the house together. When we got down there some kids were pushing each other up and down the pavement in a broken pram, and stray sheets of newspaper were dancing around the streets. Some older kids had climbed into an abandoned car and were hooting the horn. Their mothers shouted at them. The action started with a procession through the nearby streets to collect children and let people know what was happening. Whose idea was it to have the lion and unicorn costumes?'

'I can't remember,' said Brenda.

'I think somebody had one half of a pantomime horse and they thought it would be easy to add the horn,' said

Alex. 'Actually, it took bloody ages. Ute made it out of papier mâché, it was a work of art. Slow and painstaking, just the job for her. The lion costume had been in an amateur play out in Bedfordshire somewhere. The kids were a bit scared of the lion at first but they held the unicorn's tail and nearly managed to pull it in half. We'd collaborated with the residents on the banners. One said "Let Kids in, Weeds out!", and there was "End Property Speculation", and "How many children will die playing on the streets?"

'A busload of policemen had turned up and they followed the procession at a safe distance. When we got to the patch of waste land, we halted next to the fence. Several of us took turns with a loud hailer to hold a dialogue with a growing group of residents. The last speaker was Clive, who was wearing the lion costume. Taking his maned head off, he filled in briefly the history of that patch of land. He explained that a few years before it had been bought up dirt cheap by a property speculator. Now that speculator was hoping to sell it to the Council as a development site for a fat profit, and was holding out for a high price. The Council had been petitioned to buy it by compulsory purchase as a public amenity, with no results. Perhaps they had no intention to buy it. Perhaps the time had come for the people of the area to take the matter into their own hands. Were they prepared to take action for the safety and happiness of their children? There were murmurs from the crowd, but no overwhelming response.

'He raised his voice, "By rights this bit of land belongs to the people of this area. Are you prepared to take what belongs to you?"

'There were shouts of agreement from the crowd, and slowly, in confusion, the whole group began to move towards the fence around the waste land. The police were waiting at the side, and with silent speed moved in front of the fence. They spread themselves out, but there weren't enough to cover the whole area. The crowd moved in close, and gradually – in different places – the fences began to shake. They were tougher than they looked, but rhey swayed backwards and forwards. They were shaken and got looser. The pigs remonstrated but they were outnumbered. A hundred faceless hands tugged at the posts persistently. When a length of fence suddenly fell inwards into the land, a lion was the first to leap over with a shout.

'Soon there were a dozen people inside. Most of them held a child by each hand, and the lion and the unicorn were already dancing in the middle of the high grass. Some of the kids had sticks and were beating down the weeds and nettles. Then the flow of people into the square stopped when a group of policemen blocked the gap. Then some more athletic types went in over the top of the locked gate.

'When I got in, there were lots of kids playing behind the trees. A woman was leaning from an overlooking window and shaking a fist: "Get out of what doesn't belong to you! You'll get our kids in trouble!"

'"It does belong to you! Why should anyone else own it?" Duncan was shouting back.

'Taffy was yelling at her, "Fuck off!"

'Four children had climbed to the top of the tallest tree, and were shouting down for people to look at them. A small black boy had got hold of the loudhailer and was marching up and down reciting "Down with the Fuzz" in a high squeal, amplified several times. A small white girl with long white socks and a pony tail pushed a doll's pushchair in circles. Some larger boys were playing football on an area of flattened grass as if they had always played there.

'I found Duncan standing in the middle looking around. "Going OK?" I said.

'"As long as the fascist pigs don't throw us out now." His voice was a pitch higher than usual. He pointed to a huddle of police down the other end. "Look at them ganged up together like a group of Nazi thugs. In their navy blue and jackboots." To me their tactics seemed quite laid back.

'"I think they're as afraid of us as we are of them," I said.

'"You're no' telling me you're sorry for them! Those fucking middle class attitudes run deep!"

'"They're just ignorant bastards," I said.

'"Thick," he corrected me. He leant down to my ear, "So thick that they don't realize the others are going for the fence down the other end there, while they're standing up this end trying to decide what to do."

'At that moment a sharp crack came from the far end. One bit of fence had fallen outwards and a parked car got scratched. The owner came running out of a front door.

'A police officer came into the square and shouted to the group at large: "I want to speak to your leaders!"

'The lion was holding the loudhailer. He put it to his mouth and shouted, "The police would like to speak to our leaders. We have no leaders, no followers!" Odd shouts of "No police victimization!" from other members of the group.

'The officer went up to the lion which had Clive inside, cornered him against a bush and started speaking to him in a low voice.

"Witnesses! Witnesses!" the lion called out through the loud-hailer, waving a paw. Several of us sprinted in from all sides and crowded in on the policeman. He took a step back, we closed in. He tried to take Clive aside separately, we followed. Reuben arrived with ice creams for the children and in the confusion Clive slipped away.

'After that the blokes took turns in the lion costume, so the police never knew who was in there. The kids lost interest in it after a while. I remember Reuben putting it on later in the afternoon. At one point I noticed him standing slouched under a tree looking disconsolately around him; you couldn't see much from inside that thing. He didn't notice when a mongrel came up and peed on his leg.

'At about 4 o'clock the Brazilians who had squatted the houses next to us turned up with their band. They set up in the middle of the area playing samba. One of the residents started selling cups of tea out of her front garden. One bloke turned up with a crate of beer. Some people were dancing; it was a party atmosphere.

'But then the party went wrong. The action was still a victory for the people on that street, but for us lot personally – disaster struck.'

Brenda said, 'It was daft of Taffy to slip Reuben that acid. Some idea of a joke.'

'The first I knew of it,' said Alex, 'was when Reuben sidled up to me with the lion head under one arm and his eyes open unnaturally wide, and said, "I think we've made a mistake. These people seem to be getting ill now. Their faces are yellow, can you see? Do you think we've all caught something?"

'I looked around. The people all looked well. If anything, more glowing tones of brown or black or pink than usual because they were flushed with the victory of the afternoon. As day slid into evening, people were dancing, chatting, wandering in and out stepping over the felled fences as if they had never been standing vertical. But Reuben was worried. I saw him going from group to group, staring. There was a bunch of policemen still standing on the pavement and Reuben nearly walked into them – one of the coppers turned and put his arm out to stop him. Reuben backed off holding his free hand in front of his face. He definitely wasn't behaving normally, even for Reuben. Some of us went over to see what was the matter.

'"What do these people want?" he said. "I know these people. I've seen them before. It's happening again. History always repeats itself." His usual chubby beam or morose grumpiness was gone. Instead flashes of terror started to zigzag across his face. We relieved him of the lion head. Ute was playing with a group of children; someone went to fetch her and she took him by the hand.

'"Oh, it's you," he said. "Mata Hari. The green-eyed foreign spy who sees into my heart. She sees all my weaknesses. She can read me like a book. But can she heal the illness that is spreading through us all?"

'Taffy arrived. "Look, man, nobody's ill. I just passed you acid instead of speed. Lighten up."

'But Reuben seemed too far gone for it to help. "You bastard. Just goes to show you can't trust anyone. Not even your friends. Friends? Don't make me laugh. The rot has gone too far for that."

'In the end Ute took him to sit down under a tree near the Samba band. She was trying to explain to him: "It's just the drug that makes you feel like this."

'"No, Ute," he stared into her eyes and stroked her mousy hair with a large paw. "You don't understand, this is how things are. It's now that I can see it. Most of the time we get trapped in the externals. We don't see under the skin. I can see. I can see we're all dying."

'I left them to it. The square was taken and I couldn't be bothered with Reuben's personal drama. It started to drizzle. I went back to the house. It was all quiet as I went in and I wasn't expecting to find anyone there. But when I walked into the kitchen I got a shock. Geoff was sitting on one side of the table eating take-away chicken. On the other side of the table facing him was a man I'd never seen before. He was tall and good-looking in a conventional sort of way and his face was as white as a sheet.'

'I remember now!' Brenda put her hand over her mouth. 'It was that German guy. Ute's bloke.'

'Erich,' said Ren.

'Erich,' said Alex, 'Come over unexpectedly from Germany. What a day to pick to turn up. Geoff'd let him in. And with his usual tact and consideration, Geoff'd told Erich about Ute and Reuben getting together. The man looked as if he had seen a ghost. He was sitting there like a frozen mountain watching Geoff's take-away disappear. He was speaking in a slow, deep voice: "So, this, er, childish liaison, it has been started how long?"

'When I came in, they fell silent. I sat down, "Don't take any notice of me!" A long pause. They seemed to have run out of conversation. Erich sat there with his head held high and his neck rigid as if he had been pole-axed.

'Eventually Geoff buggered off and I got talking to Erich. It turned out he had a speech all prepared for Ute. He was having a scene with Ute's best friend Ingrid, and he had come all the way from Frankfurt to make a clean breast of it. He wanted to explain to Ute how what he was doing was politically correct. "The relationship between me and Ute, it was bourgeois, incorrect," he told me. "With exclusive sexual relations we recreate the nuclear family. It is important to understand the links between the economic life and the personal life. We have a duty, yes, to recognize that people's daily experience of capitalism determines their political consciousness and their political actions. The revolution involves a transformation of all social relations. And so with Ingrid together I build a different structure of relationships. Ute should understand this."

'But I couldn't grasp the mental acrobatics through which he refused to apply the same principles to Ute. "She came here to work," he said. "What about the organizing at the Ford Motor Company? What is this about a children's play area? Is she just playing at politics? Did she spend her months in England in bed? Having an adolescent romance, a – what is it – fling?" The last word was ejected from his mouth and hurled across the room like a missile from its launch. His body held tight but with a slight tremour to it, and I could almost picture steam escaping from his ears.

'He was a big healthy figure of a man. Well stacked. If it came to fisticuffs he could have knocked Reuben out flat. Especially Reuben as he was likely to turn up at any moment, on Ute's arm in the grip of a pogrom or the Black Death and ranting about impending disaster and the human condition.

'But Erich calmed down after we got talking about the Car Group. And he seemed even happier when we got into an argument about the role of the revolutionary.

'"We can't set ourselves up as 'political experts'," I said. "We're not above the class struggle, handing down tablets bearing the 'correct political line' to masses who need our guidance."

'"But the common man, you know, he thinks only of beer and football," said Erich. "It is an important task of education to be done."

'"No, we are the ones who have a lot to learn from ordinary people. About what they experience and how. We need to see how working people are finding ways of organizing and fighting back, and help draw out the revolutionary potential in that."

'"But in the working class there are many elements which are reactionary. Even fascist."

'"Our role is to help strengthen those elements which are progressive."

'He disagreed with me: "The important thing is to have the correct analysis. When this is explained to the masses, they will follow."

'I wasn't going to stand for this. "No," I said, "We don't have all the answers. We have to keep learning and changing. There's a tendency among left groups to set our own lives apart. But the revolution isn't a missionary trip, something we need to do for other people. We don't want another set of bosses, authority figures and moralisers who are no better than the capitalist ones. We don't want leaders

– we want everyone to be in charge." He really got me going. I waxed eloquent, if I say so myself.

'He was preparing a reply when the front door burst open and a few seconds later I heard Ute in the hall saying, "We're home now, you'll be safe." Then Ren, Ute and Reuben walked into the kitchen and Reuben saw Erich.'

'What happened?' asked Corinne.

'All hell broke loose,' said Alex.

'At first everything went very quiet,' said Ren. 'Then Reuben looked around the room with wild eyes. "It's a conspiracy, isn't it? You're all in on this, aren't you?" He broke loose from Ute and backed out of the door. Next thing he was running down the street. It had started to rain and it was getting dark. He paid no attention to the traffic.'

'Ren, you were the one who went after him,' said Brenda. 'I never knew what happened.'

'I caught up with him eventually,' said Ren. 'Both totally out of breath. We ended up sitting in a leaky bus shelter. After a while he calmed down and started singing every song he'd ever known. We worked through the 50s and 60s. I remember "Danny" ("It must've been raining the night I was born…"), "Heartbreak Hotel" (he put a lot of feeling into that, he did all the backing vocals too) and "All I have to do is Dream". People stared at us but we must have looked quite strange so they kept clear. Reuben was still wearing the bottom half of the lion, and the tail was hanging in a puddle. He told me he felt like a cross between King Kong and the subject of a scientific experiment. Gradually the songs got more cheerful. We had Lou Reed and Bowie, and moved on to the "Red Flag", "Paniero Rosso Triumphera" and the "Internationale". He's got a wonderful husky baritone, and the songs seemed to make him more solid. We ended up with Smokey Robinson, "The Tracks of my Tears". Remember that one? All about being the life and soul of the party while inside your heart's breaking, Reuben sang his heart out, that seemed to sum it all up for him. When he finished, we just stood up together and walked back to the squat.'

'From what I gathered afterwards,' said Brenda, 'the three of them – Reuben, Ute and Erich – went into Reuben's room, and Erich said that the logical conclusion of their deprivatising relationships was that all three of them should go to bed together immediately. Ute refused and ran up to her room in floods of tears. She'd been talking to Erich in the meanwhile, and she was really upset about him getting off with her best friend Ingrid. That was why neither he nor Ingrid had written to her for months; she'd never known why they hadn't, and had been in a lot of pain about it. After she ran off upstairs, Reuben and Erich were left on their own and they turned it all into a debate about political principles. At some point Reuben started coming down from his trip and rolled a joint for himself and Erich, and they both chilled out and ended up hugging each other with great manly sobs.'

They all giggled. Ren said, 'Even the most wonderful human beings can be ridiculous at times.'

'Alex had gone off to Evan's,' said Brenda. 'So in the end we put Erich to crash in her room.'

'Nobody told me,' said Alex. 'When I got back the next morning I found him in my bed. He was very apologetic and leapt out of it instantly in his pyjamas. He put it to air and then made it with hospital precision.'

'The standard of housework improved while he was staying,' said Ren.

'What happened with Ute?' asked Corinne.

'Reuben disappeared for a while, as he did,' said Ren. 'Erich and Ute went through a lot between them, but it was all behind closed doors.'

'Was it true,' asked Brenda, 'or was it just a rumour, that Erich offered to leave the commune in Frankfurt and marry her?'

'Who knows,' said Ren. 'Anyway, she wouldn't go back with him and he left without her.'

'Taff never meant any harm with the acid,' said Brenda. 'He never did with anything.'

'You could say the same about any of us,' said Alex. 'Is that meant to be some kind of excuse?'

'They were changing times,' said Ren. 'All the goalposts were moving. There were new possibilities. And that meant a greater chance of making mistakes.'

Corinne nodded, 'And what strikes me is the capacity you all had to survive mistakes and carry on. And stay friends. I've never done that: in my life I've felt every wrong turn as terminal.'

Alex said, 'Yes, we were good at mistakes. Guinea-pigs in our own experiment. Idiots. And we still carry on, banging our heads against a brick wall. Except the wall's got bigger.'

Brenda laughed. 'You're a hard woman. We did have a bit of fun along the way.'

Ren said, 'And some things have changed for the better. It wasn't all bad, what people did.'

'Especially not Taffy,' said Brenda.

'If we're getting maudlin,' said Alex, 'I'm off.'

'Give us a song before you go?' asked Ren.

Brenda took her guitar out of its bag and tuned it.

Alex said, 'OK, here's a song that's shit. Sorry, I mean it's about shit. An old favourite from the US of A…' She started singing unaccompanied:

'Oh, put it on the ground, spread it all around

'Dig it with a hoe, it will make your flowers grow.'

'Hang on,' said Brenda, 'Got to find the chords. How does the verse go?'

Alex struck up again with a strong, clear voice:

'Oh, if you want a raise in pay, all you have to do,

'Go and ask the boss for it, and they will give it to you.

'Yes, they will give it to you my friend, they will give it to you,
'A raise in pay without delay, oh, they will give it to you.'

Brenda was trailing with the guitar, but joined in with the chorus as the others started singing too:

'Oh, put it on the ground, spread it all around
'Dig it with a hoe, it will make your flowers grow.'

Alex stopped. 'Corinne, you're out of tune. Anyone for another verse?'

'Yes, go on,' said Brenda, 'I've got the chords now, can you remember the words?'

Alex launched into the next verse:

'The folks who own the industries, they own no bonds and stocks,
'They own no yachts and limousines, or gems the size of rocks.
'They own no big estate with pools, or silken B.V.D.s,
'Because they pay us working folk such fancy salaries. Ohh....'

Everyone except Corinne joined in a rousing rendition of the final chorus,

'Oh, put it on the ground, spread it all around
'Dig it with a hoe, it will make your flowers grow.'

At the end Corinne clapped and said, 'I never could sing...'

'We noticed,' said Alex.

'What's a B.V.D.?' asked Corinne.

'The old tunes are the best ones,' said Brenda.

Alex said, 'Ren's got us crawling up nostalgia alley.'

'Speaking of nostalgia, Taffy's coming here tomorrow,' said Ren.

'The boy wonder himself?' said Alex. 'The only one of us all to make any money.'

'The only one to be a success,' said Brenda, putting down her guitar and starting to roll another joint.

'Since we stopped hoping for victory and started hoping for success instead,' said Alex. 'And to think we all saw him as just another curly-headed nit-ridden hippy who couldn't

229

see further than the end of a spliff.'

'How were we to know he would turn out a computer wizard? After his brush with the law and his alcoholic phase in Spain? I didn't even know he could add up,' said Brenda.

After a moment she added, 'It didn't seem important at the time.'

'Just goes to show that to be a millionaire whizz-kid you don't need to be able to thread two words together.' said Alex.

'He could thread them together,' said Brenda, licking the glue on the assembled cigarette papers, 'he just couldn't write them down. Or put full stops between them. Dyslexic. It was just long strings of words that used to wrap themselves round you like garlands of flowers or Christmas lights. Perhaps they didn't teach punctuation at his school.' She lit the joint and drew on it.

Alex stretched and rubbed her eyes. 'Well, full stops – who needs them? I've evidently wasted my life pursuing literacy. In fact, I'll tell you a true story that proves it. My grandfather,' she took the joint from Brenda, 'My grandfather was a schoolteacher. In east London, early this century, before the slum clearance. I remember him telling me how some kids had no shoes. Poverty, a lot of illiteracy. One boy left school and applied for a job as a toilet attendant, in the public loos. He was turned down because he couldn't read and write. So he started selling vegetables on the street. He did quite well and got himself a barrow, carried on building things up and eventually got a shop. Then another. In the end he had a chain of greengrocers. My grandfather bumped into him one time later in life, heard his story and congratulated him: "You've done all this with no education. Just think what you could have achieved if you'd learnt to read and write."

'"Oh no," says the man, 'If I'd known how to read and

write I'd have been a lavatory attendant."

Corinne smiled. 'That's a lesson for us all.'

There was a moment's silence while they all pondered the lesson.

Then Ren asked, 'Have you seen Taffy at all, Brenda?'

'Last time was a few years ago. He was all broken up because his wife just left him. He said he'd been happy as Larry with her, she was the woman of his dreams. Then one evening he came home from work and found a note from her on the kitchen table, saying: "I've tried everything and I can't stand it any longer. Goodbye." He was still trying to work out what he'd done wrong.'

'That's Taffy for you.' Alex stood up. 'Self-aware and sensitive as ever. At least he's got loads of money to console him.' She gathered her handbag. 'On that note, I do have to go. Would you believe, I have manuscripts to read over the Christmas holiday? Only a ruthless idealistic exploitative non-profit small-time alternative publisher would expect you to come in to work between Christmas and the New Year. For next to nothing. Love you and leave you. Thank you, Ren. Lovely Boxing Day. As usual. Blah Blah.' She blew stylized kisses to Ren and Brenda. 'Nice to meet you, Cora... sorry ... Corinne.'

Corinne looked up. 'What happened to Ute and Reuben in the end? I'd like to know.'

'Must dash,' said Alex. 'Ask Taffy.'

9

Chapter Nine

Thursday 27th December 1990 9.15am

At last a few glimmers of sunshine. I've set out from the house too early for my counselling session with Ren. Typical, Ant. I'm either too late or too early.

I stop to buy some fresh rolls at Lina's bakery at the top of the Kingsland High Street. She greets me and asks after Morton. Lots of women take to Morton, I think they want to mother him. Lina's an exuberant West African woman who's adapted her skills to English tastes: she bakes the best bread in Stoke Newington. But today she's upset. She has no rolls because thieves broke in overnight, through the back of the shop, and stole them all. Is that how bad things are? I know her bread is good, but are people desperate enough to burgle for buns?

I buy some of her currant buns instead, and tuck into one as I stroll through the cemetery. It sticks in my teeth, it sticks on my fingers. The brown layer comes off the top and some of it sticks to my coat. I try to brush it off.

As I walk between the densely-stacked overgrown graves, I wonder whether these phantasmagoric stone creations are just monuments to a fantasy of an after-life? An elaborate con to keep us dying quietly? Does anything really exist beyond the physical world that we see and touch?

Thieves are real. They leave a trail of smashed windows, and you find your bread rolls have gone. Real, material traces of solid people. But what about spiritual beings and the spiritual world? Is that just imaginings? I don't only mean is there a God or not, I'm not even thinking God. I'm thinking about all the other experiences that human beings say they've had. Like prescient dreams? Telepathy? Can people really be reincarnated and recall past lives? Those people who say they've seen ghosts, are they liars? Or deluded? All those phenomena that one set of people dismiss as nonsense – and another set write silly books about and build cults around? What's the truth of it?

Somewhere in there are the strange experiences that have been happening to me. That are wreaking havoc with my understanding of the world. Nothing feels solid or sure any more. Does the world contain deeply irrational elements and events? Or is it just me?

I put my hand into my coat pocket to hold the bone but of course it isn't there.

Deep in the middle of the Abney Cemetery is a small deconsecrated chapel. Why is something deconsecrated always more sinister than something that was never consecrated in the first place? Is it because it has the air of a battlefield where God lost and the dark forces won? Inside this small disused building there are no smashed altars, no broken crucifixes or dented chalices. Just dark earth dimly lit from the small windows that are no longer eyes towards the divine but empty holes in the brickwork with trees outside. An abandonment of hope, a denial of meaning. It was all a con. This is all there is. I often wander in there to savour its bleakness.

But as I approach today I hear voices and I find half-a-dozen people inside. One young man with a strange haircut, short on one side and long on the other, has a camera. The others are heavily made up young women in stylish variations of black clothing. God's cast-off premises are being used for a fashion shoot. Its macabre atmosphere is being exploited as setting for a range of post-punk *noir* clothing. Harsh cuts, spiked heels, ghoulish eyeliner, shaved hair, ripped garments. I stop to watch these young women strut and scowl, sneer and menace in an artificial charade of rage and rebellion. I've seen Che Guevara used to sell underpants, and ads for a 'revolution' in beer, but this takes the biscuit. Is this what's left of our youthful ideals and protest, our lifelong commitment to fighting for a better world: anger as a fashion statement?

In their world of glamour and Thatcherite aspirations, do they have any inkling how much there is to be genuinely angry about?

I'm still wondering about the metaphysics of it all when I come out of the cemetery into Church Street. I'm focusing on the surrealism of reality and the elusiveness of the hereafter and evidently I'm not looking where I'm going because I get a sudden shock when I walk into a lamppost. Ouch! I bang the front of my head with a crack. The front of my body has taken a hit too… That's what comes from pondering imponderables.

I stumble back, stunned.

I'm feeling shaken up and the worse for wear now. That's the second knock to my head in a week. How many more brain cells can I afford to lose?

My mind is buzzing all the rest of the way to Ren's. If there is really nothing there, if life is just a posturing parade in an abandoned building, then I need to forget all about the bones and the dreams and the premonitions, and go to Greece after all.

When I get to Ren's, the jumble in my head spills out, as usual. She listens to it all with her quiet waiting. After I finish talking she sits in silence for a while.

Then she says:

'You know how sometimes bees get stuck in the house? And you open a window for them but they just keep on trying to get out straight through one of the closed window-panes? It's transparent, and they can see out, so they just can't understand why they can't get through? And there's no way to explain to them?

'Sometimes I think we're a bit like that when we're trying to get to understand these metaphysical questions. Perhaps we're just not equipped, and when we keep trying it's like the bee banging its head against the glass. It's beyond us…'

'And do you think there's someone watching us?' I say, 'like us watching the bees? Thinking, "Poor things, they'll never grasp it?"'

'Maybe,' she says. 'Or maybe there's not even anyone watching us. Perhaps we're just there on our own facing the window-pane…'

'Scary,' I say.

She's not offering me any fake comfort, then. Just doubt. I have enough of that already. It's terrifying. On the other hand, because she's sitting facing the doubt with me, side by side, I do feel supported.

Eventually I ask, 'Is that what you believe?'

She replies, 'I make a choice to believe that although there are terrible injustices and things we can't understand, it's worth supporting the best in people and hoping the best for the world.'

'This world or the next?'

She laughs. 'Both, if it comes to it!'

We sit in silence for a while. I can't think of anything to say.

Then I remember something else I don't understand.

'There's something else,' I say. 'It's about Freddie and his bike.'

'Freddie?' asks Ren in a tone of voice that says go for it.

So I go for it.

'I'd better start at the beginning.' The Egyptian mummy fiasco all started with the new bike.

'Freddie'd never had a bike that worked properly before,' I tell her. 'I remember the day the bicycle came. He kept saying he didn't need it, but Steve pressed it on him: "You need something decent to get around on. I'll be away for six months and even when I come back I may not want it. You can't use that heap of junk any more." We were all shocked to see it there in the hall. A brand new racer, handlebars dropped in a sleek silver arc; the crossbar shouted "New! New!" with brilliant stripes of paint in primary colours. The slender curve of the wheels promised flight spinning on air, clouds not tarmac, soaring through the streets of Hackney. I saw him that day carefully propping it upright and opening the front door. Then he turned and stood there, his dreadlocks tufty like a cornfield, his lanky body slumped against the door post, looking back at his tired old bike lent against the hall wall, abandoned. Then he wheeled the new bike out.'

'He'd only gone a mile or so when the crash happened. A woman in a Peugeot 405 overtook him on the Essex Road, and then immediately turned left straight across his path. Without signalling. As if he wasn't there. Was there really no time for him to brake? Could he have braked more sharply? Or was there just a second of bloody-mindedness? After spending most of his life braking and swerving to accommodate other people, not just on the road, did he for a moment think "I'm going to stick to my course, fuck you"? Did he let the bike ride right at her? Or was there really no time for him to brake, anyway? I don't know. Anyway, for whatever reason, he went straight into the car as it turned. The bike just crumpled and he went over the top and down the other side. He was lucky only to get a twisted wrist and a bruised arm and a minor head injury. But the bike was a write-off.

'To add insult to injury, the driver yelled at him. Told him he should have looked where he was going. She was one of those middle-class women who are always certain they're in the right, and as far as she was concerned he'd dented her smart car for no good reason. He was so angry he peeled himself up off the road, went back for the bike and used his good arm to throw it across the pavement. I find it hard to imagine because I've never seen him angry. She took an indecent amount of time to call help. Eventually she accepted he was genuinely hurt and she went into a restaurant a little way down Essex Road to ring for an ambulance. It turned out she owned the restaurant. A pretentious one, "Mon Repas". He was carted off, and the first we knew he came back to the house after a six hour wait in casualty, with his arm in bandages and the cornfield of dreadlocks on his head half-flattened and sticking up at strange angles where he'd cut his scalp.

'Next day he had to go back to "Mon Repas" to pick up what was left of the bike.

'Shall I tell you about what happened then?' I've forgotten why I'm telling this story. I know there was a good reason when I started. What was it? Ren gives me an encouraging nod and I decide to carry on anyway.

'OK. After that he went down to the restaurant a few times out of hours, asking her nicely if she could pay for the bike. He explained it wasn't his and it would cost a hundred pounds to replace. She denied she was liable and sent him packing. So we made a plan. Building on his injured arm, we added a few more bandages and bloodstains and he went to the restaurant and sat at a table near the door looking very ill. A touch of Banquo's ghost.

'We thought that would be enough to jog her conscience, but she was a hard woman. When the waiter asked him to order, he said he couldn't afford it because the owner of the restaurant had smashed his friend's bike and he had a huge debt to repay (which was true). People on the next door tables could hear. It was a posh restaurant, and it was embarrassing for the management. They asked him to leave, which he did looking so pathetic that it caused a bit of a stir. Some customers left because they thought this vulgar altercation lowered the tone of the place. Some took her side, some his. All in all, it wasn't good for trade. A few evenings later he went again. This time they turned him away at the door and threatened to call the police.

'The next night we all went in a group. Even Morton went. He's usually got so many reasons for and against doing things that by the time he's made up his mind it's over. You couldn't see our bandages till we took our coats off, they were fairly subtle and at first sight they could have been genuine. It was disconcerting for the other customers. We went ahead and ordered (some of the cheapest things off the menu) and then after eating we started clutching our wounds and moaning discreetly as if in pain. They asked us to leave but we took our time paying the bill.

'And so it went on. Every few nights a different strategy. We became experts at being turned away at the door in such a way that everyone in the restaurant knew about Freddie's bike accident. The final straw for her was when we turned up in full Egyptian mummy bandages, head to toe, plenty of torn-up old sheets went into that, and when they wouldn't let us in we hovered outside the restaurant explaining the situation to customers as they arrived. We left just before the police got there.

'After that he felt enough momentum to carry on alone. We were all banned from the restaurant, but he took to appearing outside, in bandages or in different costumes. She used to come out to shout at him every time, and call the police; no sign of her relenting.

'Then suddenly yesterday she came marching out of the restaurant as usual but instead of having a go at him she just put an envelope in his hands. Full of notes. £100. The full whack for a new bike. None of us understood what came over her.

'Freddie gave the money to Steve, and he seems determined never again to set his pedal foot on a bicycle that was anything but an old wreck. He seems more comfortable that way.'

There's a silence. Ren is probably wondering why I told her this story. I'm wondering too.

Then I make the connection: 'I think I'm like him,' I say. 'I can't cope with having anything good. I contrive to wreck it like he wrecked that smart new bike. Accidentally on purpose. Deep down I don't think I deserve anything good in life.' At this point something rises in my chest that wants to cry. I crush it; no crying now, keep talking. 'I can't cope with having things go right. Give me problems, failures, injustices and I'm in my element. Give me an expensive Christmas present and I'll break it.' I swallow hard.

'And the question is, how on earth did he get his money back against all the odds? Did the woman have a sudden change of heart? That sounds as likely as the sea running dry. Where did that money come from? Is it just another case of the bee at the window-pane, like you said? Like, the universe works in mysterious ways; don't hope to understand why things happen. Don't ask.' I've run out of steam. I look at Ren: 'What do you think?'

'Maybe,' says Ren, and again she seems as inscrutable as a Buddha. 'Maybe.'

And now I want to laugh: 'But you see, he did get his own back about the bike.'

Thursday 27th December 1990 5pm
'Back in Blighty!' Maureen put her suitcase down on Ren's front doorstep, put her hands on her hips and looked up at

the house. 'Shall I ring the bell?'

Corinne opened the door.

Ren, coming in through the front gate, said, 'Corinne, Maureen, Maureen, Corinne.'

'Hello,' said Corinne holding out her hand in the doorway. 'Did you have a good flight?'

'Hello, Corinne.' As Maureen looked at Corinne's face, a big smile broke out. 'Oh, *Hello!* It's *that* Corinne!' She took Corinne's right hand to shake it, then held it for a moment resting on her own palm and glanced at it. 'Everything OK now?'

Corinne glanced down at the hand. 'Up and down. But I'm still in one piece.'

'Glad to hear it,' said Maureen. She looked back at Ren, 'There's a turn-up for the books!'

'So you know my partner Maureen?' Ren asked Corinne.

'Our paths have crossed in the past – or rather, not crossed but connected,' said Maureen, picking up her suitcases and following Corinne up the stairs to Ren's flat. 'We worked on the same play site in Hackney one summer. Decades ago! How long ago was it?'

Corinne, leading the way up the stairs, stopped and turned to say, '1971. It was 1971.'

Over the remains of turkey curry and nut roast, Maureen sat with her arm around Ren while Corinne washed up and Taffy rolled a joint. Spread across the table were a series of leaflets and pamphlets.

'This bloody Gulf War,' Maureen was saying, 'there's been a lot of opposition to it. Some quite imaginative. They did fake awards – the "Commendation for Replacing Accuracy with Propaganda", the CRAP awards. They invited people to vote for their favourite media lie about what's happening in the Gulf, fun for all the family kind of thing.'

'Reuben would have liked that…' said Ren. 'He was into japes.'

'Loads of protest,' said Maureen. 'Especially on the West Coast and New York. Look at those leaflets. But of course it doesn't get coverage in the straight media.' She disentangled herself from Ren, rolled up her white shirtsleeves and with a large strong hand reached across to cut herself an extra slice of nut roast. 'They've had rallies outside the studios of Fox Network, there's been street theatre, non-violent direct action…'

'There's been a few murmurs here, as usual the Brits are trailing behind our transatlantic cousins…' Taffy said. He swept his mop of brown curly hair out of his eyes; some bright strands suggested grey hairs dyed out. Ash fell off his joint as he leafed through some of the sheets scattered over the kitchen table amongst the food. He picked up one and read aloud: 'BBC = Broadcasting Bias and Complicity. No bombing of Iraq! Stop the War! The truth isn't the only casualty of war…'

Putting that leaflet down, he shuffled through another wadge of papers: 'Hey, this is cool, what's this? One from your archives, Ren?' He held up a dog-eared copy of the *Dandy*. 'Desperate Dan, remember him? Now you're talking!' Taffy read aloud from the front page: '"Shucks! Ma new shirt is even too big for me!"' He did a deep rasping voice for Desperate Dan and gestured to his own expensive silk shirt which hung crumpled on his all-year suntan. '"Ulp! I've got maself a shirt full o'trouble!"' His voice matched the lettering on the page. '"SCRATCH! SNARL! SPIT! SNAP!"' Then, doing a little old lady's voice, '"My poor kitty."' Then, '"They're fighting like cat and dog on the back cover…."'

Turning the comic over, he asked, 'Where's the back cover?' He looked up 'Ren, no back cover! Back cover missing…'

Corinne turned around from the sink. 'So,' she said to Taffy, 'You promised you'd tell me the end of the story. About the commune.'

He put down the *Dandy*. 'You want a happy ending or an unhappy ending?'

'The truth.'

'That depends how you tell it,' said Taffy.

'What happened to Reuben and Ute that summer, 1971?' Corinne asked.

'Reuben, my old mate.' Taffy put his hand inside his shirt and stroked his chest. ''What can I say? I can tell you about the last time I saw him. Before he disappeared. Early 70s. I'm walking by the sea with him. Day trip to Worthing. Tonic for the soul. Broken hearts mended with a touch of sea air. Reuben, where are you now?

'''Wonderful,'' I'm saying, ''Computers. Instant access to so much more information. For the CABs, the answer to everything. Instant advice. People got a problem, hey presto, problem solved.''

'Wide beach, cold wind, one of those grey August days when you forget it's summer.

'''Not so fast,'' says Reuben, ''you're forgetting the people. They need to be heard. We need to find out how they got into a fix and what resources they have for getting out of it themselves. That takes time. Then you need other stuff: money, housing, help, health.''

'''That's where information technology comes in,'' I say. ''It can fix everything. With the right information at your finger-tips.''

'''They want us to think it's all about information,'' says Reuben, ''but really it's about needs and giving people power. Resources, self-belief. Machines can't do that. What solves injustice is human contact, collective action. What's needed is changing ownership of society's resources, redistribution of wealth. Otherwise the only thing information can tell us is how deep in the shit we are."

'"Hey," I say, "Listen to those breakers sucking and spewing with a deep chortling voice like a jazz singer."

'"Rhythmic and remorseless," says Reuben. "Wouldn't want to be drowning in that on a grey day like today."'

Taffy paused.

'Sorry, when was this?' asked Corinne.

'Early 70s,' Taffy replied. 'After the lion and the unicorn, and the world's worst acid trip. Before Reuben went AWOL.'

He carried on with his story: '"Speaking of drowning," I say to Reuben, "That man sitting on the beach over there has wet clothes on. Do you think he fell in?"

'"Does he need information or dry clothing?" asks Reuben. "And what are those objects on the shingle in front of him?"

'Over we go across the beach. Questions to ask, Reuben's right there: "You all right, mate?"

'"Good evening," says the man. His accent sounds like a solicitor, but his hair is standing on end. "Please advise me. This small silver box appeared here since I went into the sea, it's the message I've been waiting for, or rather part of it, I knew they would send it. But some stupid people pulled me out of the water, thought they were helping, wouldn't listen. There will be two more parts to the message, they always send their messages in threes. They watch me constantly. This other object is my left shoe. It came off in the sea. As it parted from my foot I saw a rocket flare into the sky. I'm afraid it may have attracted attention, they're careless sometimes. This other object is an ammonite. Do you know fossils? Not common in Worthing. That rounded pattern like a flattened snail shell, they use them a lot. Spiralling from the past into the future. People don't realize they carry messages. The three things here like this, you see they make a triangle. I stare at the centre and I wait till they make their intentions known. Past, present and future. Are we trapped in one position, or can we move between all three? I can't leave without the message. I know they will not let me down."

'"What was the advice you needed?" asks my friend Reuben.

'"Is the triangle perfect?" asks the man. "So much in life is lost and ruined, only perfection can save us now. That's why they chose me."

'Looking at his clothes and his one shoe, I saw that even before his meeting with the waves they were the worse for wear – full of mixed metaphors and jarring coincidences. A tie and jacket with an old T-shirt, and what a tie, old public school I think. His beard was ragged. What the T-shirt seemed to read was, "All you need is love". And were those ladies' trousers with the flares, and the criss-cross shoe-lace threaded in the flies? And the sock had holes. "You best get dry," I tell him, "Take my coat, you're gonna freeze like that. It's August going on November." I look around the empty beach, the wind is getting up, no help in sight.

'"But first," says Reuben, "This triangle. I think the ammonite should move a little to the side, and the shoe to here, and then it's equilateral. Vibrations resonate around a triangle. Can we wait with you?"

'"You may," the man replies, and then his staring eyes turned glassy and he went quite still. When the shake began it started from his legs and went through his whole body. Was it a supernatural force or just the cold, I wondered in my own pragmatic way. We waited while seagulls yelled in alarm and dark waves reared and pounded on the shore. When he looked up his eyes were clear.

'"At last," he said. "I knew they were only waiting for the perfect disposition. They spoke. I can tell you, because it is for everyone. They said, 'The truth has many sides and some of them are dangerous. Take care.' That's what they said."

'"'Take care'," murmurs Reuben, "That means a dry coat round your shoulders now. Your work's all done."

'We hadn't seen the men in uniform with luminous flap-jackets crunching towards us from the distance. "You're a lucky man," one of them tells him. "Some people raised the alarm. They said they pulled you out and then you wandered off. Last seen at the esplanade. It's good we've found you now, isn't it mate? You need to get dry. Nasty shock falling in the sea. What's your name, mate?"

'"Edwin. I didn't fall. They called me."

'"Not a good time to answer the call, Edwin. Not on a cold day like today. Not in all your clothes."

'They wrapped the blankets round him, he gave me back my coat and turned to speak to them: "The truth has many sides and some of them are dangerous. Take care."

'"Sure, mate," replied one of the ambulance men, "sometimes I feel that way about my job. You need a cup of tea. Paperwork later. Is this your shoe? Come with us, Edwin, we'll get you sorted out. Where do you live?"

'"Live? Can you call it living?" he replied. "We exist. Without guidance from the other side we are like ants busy with our own futility."

'They didn't need their stretcher as they shepherded him away. He limped a bit when his bare foot put his weight onto the shingle.

'"You see," says Reuben, "perhaps what's needed is advice about the purposes of life. Got a computer that could help with that?"'

Taffy stopped and looked at Corinne. 'That's Reuben for you. Practically the last time I saw him for many years. Little by little that Franny sucked him out of the squat and so in the end he lost Ute, he was all broken up. He turned up on Franny's doorstep with his pockets empty, she laughed in his face. When she got him, she didn't want him, that's her type. She stood there in the doorway and laughed in his face, and he whacked her one. Side of the head, she went over like a felled tree. He came back in shock, "What have I done? I never hit anyone in my life…" stares at his hand like there was writing in his palm. Stared at the wall. Forgot to get up in the morning. Forgot he could speak. Next thing Franny's round at crack of dawn with a can of white paint, "THE MAN WHO LIVES HERE BEATS WOMEN," big letters on the pavement outside the front door. Good for neighbourhood relations, that sort of thing.

'Reuben takes one look at it, puts some books in a carrier bag and leaves: walks out the room, walks out the door, walks out of London. Out of our lives. Where'd he go? Story doesn't tell. Someone said the States. Looking for a disaster big enough to drown his own.'

'What about Ute?' asked Corinne.

'Little Ute. The mouse that roared. One of those lonely summer nights when Reuben wasn't there, she falls asleep waiting for him in his bed and wakes up with plod all round the room. The boys in blue. Full uniform. Front door, no problem, kick it in, take the dirty squatters by surprise. Nasty experience when they're the first thing you see through your waking eyelids. But Ute's quick to suss it isn't us they're after. They say, "Got any Brazilians living here?" When they go upstairs, heavy boots crashing on the landing, she nips out back and who knows how she scales that garden wall, brick wall over six foot high, and then gets in next door. How's that for determination? Gets in the basement window, one of the Brazilians in bed in there, she wakes him and he says he's been asleep 100 years and where's his kiss, she tells him not now there are plod on the way and he raises the alarm. Some of them had been round the block, they'd been tortured in Brazil, they didn't mess around. By the time the filth breaks down all the other front doors in the row, the rooms are empty, not a Brazilian in sight. Scattered to the winds. A few days later and they all come back with new Chubb locks for the doors. Thank you, Ute. And he didn't forget his kiss, the Brazilian. He carries her off for a weekend in the country. Sussex, some cottage in the woods. She didn't want to go at first but when she came back she was different. I think a tab of acid helped. Like she spread her wings and flew. Defying gravity.'

'What happened to the Brazilian?' asked Corinne.

'That was Emilio,' said Ren. 'You met him here on Christmas Day, remember? With their kids?'

'A fairy-tale ending,' said Corinne.

'Or a fairy-tale beginning,' said Ren.

Later, back in the sitting room and getting herself ready for an early night while the others still chatted in the kitchen, Corinne opened the wooden chest. She was putting away the typed sheets on 'Autonomy in Everyday Life' when she noticed in another pile a page with three large letters written in green pen: L S D. The letters were decorated with purple and gold stars. Underneath it was a wadge of sheets handwritten in the same green pen. She picked them up and read:

'I have not had the time or space since I came back from Sussex
to write about
the "acid" trip we had together, Emilio and me.
In that small cobweb cottage.
Buried in the woods.

'They call it "acid" but it was
Sugar sweet,
A magic potion to reveal the world

To me.

'I felt things I never felt before
Things that do not fit
in sentences.

'I write in English
The only language
that Emilio and I can share,
apart from love.

'It was a Saturday
The woods were wet, the sky was light grey
Blank and still
We took Ribena with the pill
And then I started cleaning the place, waiting to see
What the effect of the pill would be
I made the bed with the old patchwork bedspread
and tried to put logs into the hearth
To light the fire
And suddenly
I couldn't move.

'Emilio was the expert, "How is your trip? It's started yet?"
Gossiping, making comparison to other trips he had on other
days
as if they were racehorses.
Always so confident.

'I was thrown in to the deep from the start.
It was serious,
I could not look from the outside
or talk about it.
There was not an "it".
Just that I was myself,

inside
more real, more real than at any other time
in my life.
My face fell into bits
My body shook
Emilio said "It starts subito,*"*
"Yes, it does."'

Corinne leafed through to the end. It was signed 'Ute' with a date, July 1971. She put the sheets back in the chest and shut the lid. She went to the door of her room. From the kitchen across the landing came laughter, Taffy's voice and Maureen's. She went to put her nose round the door:

'Ren… You said it was OK to read anything out of the chest, yes?'

Ren's face was unusually rosy, resting on Maureen's shoulder. She nodded across the table. 'I'm not even sure what's in there, but it's all ancient history. Help yourself.'

Maureen said, 'Ren got left with all the papers. That chest has all the rememberings.'

'And the forgettings,' said Taffy, and he turned to watch Corinne leave.

Back in the front room, Corinne opened the chest and again pulled out the pages in green writing. She unrolled the foam mattress on the floor, spread the sheets and blankets, took off her clothes and climbed into bed clutching the papers. She read on:

'Emilio wants to go outside.
It looks far far away.
I can move a bit, but I am shaking
Cold although it is a summer afternoon,
and scared.

'Emilio gives me his woollen jumper

The one his avò *made for him*
back in Brazil
She knits with bigger stitches than my mother.

'To put it on
is such a big effort.
Even to pull over
a pullover
(English joke)
is like a strange journey.
It seems alive like a huge bear.
I put my head inside it and the world goes dark.
Completely.
Then the tunnel opens, I see light ahead
I struggle through
I come back to the world.
I have survived.
Every little thing is an extreme.

'Emilio takes me by the hand.
We go outside.
He is excited, like a child
who wants to show you things.

'The ground is wet from rain the day before
The leaves glow
Everything breathes and dances
"Fantastico" says Emilio.

'We walk through some small young trees.
I think they are called yew trees.
It seems to me
that Emilio is like them
Springy and growing strong
with green leaves that shake like hair

and thick live trunk like human limbs
I want to play with them.

'He leans on one and then he says
"Poor tree!"
But it's as strong as him, I say
...stronger, maybe, I think –
it doesn't suffer the same
problems: exile, loss
and insecurities
like people do
like Emilio does.

'Emilio looks so many different ways
One minute
lovely, colourful, in his Brazilian teeshirt.
The next minute
his hair is spirals of string
His cheek is thin
His brown skin with marks and scars,
looks hunted
his jaunty air is a pretence,
with fear behind his eyes
His lips curled up to get them if they get him,
frail.

'A human being.
So glorious.
So vulnerable.

'I keep falling.
Emilio runs away and hides
Circles, reappears
behind the trees.

'I lie on the ground a lot
It seems the normal place to be
Emilio moves around
It is a big responsibility
to be alone together
in this wood.
Space all around
And just the two of us
One being
Filling everywhere.

'The sun comes out, low just above the trees
The air starts to move
Aeroplanes go over
Roaring close above our heads
The ones that speed with killer bombs
They must be from an air force place.
Emilio doesn't like them
But what can you expect? Erich would say.
Peace? Quiet? Under capitalism?
"They're only practising," I say.
"In Brazil," he says, "they're practising on people."
I know that's why he had to leave
his home.

'Then more aeroplanes come round, and a bird
– a hunter bird –
Emilio knows which kind
but anyway, as he says,
it doesn't matter what is its name, because it is a bird and
beautiful.
Just a huge bird like a black shadow
A bird that preys
A king, a fighter
And that bird goes up and it hangs

Up there, against the heavy sky
as if to argue with the planes
who is master of the air.

'These monsters for a moment
are up there together
and then the planes swoop by
Red eyes glaring
leaving a scar
of sound
Then the bird dives
and the sky is empty

'And we hear other noises.
A distant train?
A sound of something scraping.
It comes from trees in the distance
Emilio says it's like piano strings
A weird sound.
I imagine a man in evening dress
sitting in the English forest
in a glade
with a piano.
"Fantastico," says Emilio
And then he says,
"Everything's fantastico,
I'm using that word so much
I can't remember now
what's normal."'

Corinne heard a crash in the road outside. She got out of bed and went to peer out round the green curtains. Somebody had knocked over some boxes outside the greengrocers over the road. She couldn't see who had done it, the pavements of Casenove Road were strangely empty

except for a figure in a sleeping bag in the greengrocer's
doorway. She crept back into her bed on the foam mattress
on the floor, and carried on reading:

'Why do the English call them the South Downs
when they go up?
We run through hills and ferns and bushes
The leaves we touch are like
musical instruments
Every tree is different
The air is full of sounds
Sometimes we kiss.

'Then Emilio says he is cold
He wants to go back to the cottage
He didn't like the planes.

'Slowly
this idea keeps coming back.
It sinks in
between long gaps in time.
The cottage
He wants to go home
He says it is getting dark
I want to be with him.

'He is cold.
His long thin legs
Big shoulders
Shivering in his teeshirt.
He is so many different people
All at once.
Each time I turn to him
he seems different.
Now he looks exotic

In his shirt of many patterns.
But then he changes – he looks
Like an honest young lad
in his patched jeans.
Then elegant
with his embroidered belt.
Then scruffy and shapeless
where his teeshirt hangs out at the waist.
Kind with his open face
True eyes
Those strong good hands.
Pathetic with his tiny shivering voice
that wants to go home.
And I want to be with him.

'We look around
Where are we?
We start to walk
It seems as if we're rushing
so fast.
At the tree tops
The leaves are moving in the wind
Or is it our imagination?
Or is the air moving
and the leaves still
Or is it us standing still
and the whole world moving?

'We find the right bit of the forest, but we can't see the cottage
Are we lost?
I jump
Emilio hides behind a trunk
I run
He darts
I leap

I fall
I missed him
I fall so lightly
Like in a film
I am not hurt
We laugh
I lie there
No need to move
It's all so easy.

'We see the cottage
We walk
I fall again
into bracken and nettles
looking up at the sky.
That I am free to fall is good
Not feeling scared
I lie there
We keep laughing
My trousers are all over mud.

'Maybe Emilio is annoyed
about me falling in this way
but I'm so tired of being upright
So tired of clean and tidy
Always the good girl
I like to be muddy for a change.

'We find the cottage
It does look cosy
But to me it is
too tiny to go into now
The sun begins to set.
Emilio the master of ceremonies
has another idea

The juice we bought from London
To drink it
 Do I want some?
I don't know
I want everything and nothing
I cannot even imagine what juice tastes like.

'About this time
Emilio does a piss on the grass
"So, I am still human," he says as he zips up his trousers.

'Almost half the sky
is in a huge display of colour
red, pink, blue and mauve.
We sit and watch.
It looks like this sunset is
a show arranged especially for us.
The juice tastes strange and good.
I can lean and fall and drop and bounce
Nothing hurts
Everything's funny.
We watch the show, Emilio and I,
The sunset show
It changes all the time
The canvas is immense
Some bits are roughly shaped, the colours strong
Some bits are delicate, more like the décor
of a 1930s hotel.
And through the gaps between the clouds there are more clouds.
Another show, a window in the heavens,
A sky within a sky.

'Time is all spread out,
every moment is bursting like a waterfall.

'*After an age or so, the sunset turns.*
"*Now it overdoes it,*"
says Emilio.
He wants to go inside,
I don't,
I like the space around me.
Eventually Emilio's theory proves correct
It's getting dark.
Perhaps all theories come out right
If they are given enough time.
He lights a hurricane lamp
and hangs it outside
by the cottage door.
It looks so right hanging there
next to the horseshoe.
It is strange to think of Emilio as a homemaker
I thought of him more
Travelling light
Drifting and shifting
from place to place.
People are always more than you think.

'*The sky is darking.*
About this time I think of Erich.
I hope he is happier than when I saw him last.
I hope he would be happy to see me happy
Laughing like today
High.
I think of my family in Germany.
Reuben who has walked out of my life
So many times.
People I love
They're all around.

'*I go into the forest*

Alone
It's very tall
Straight smooth fir trees
Shooting up
I wish it was bigger
Deeper, thicker
Like in a Märchen *from the Brothers Grimm*
I want to plunge into the heart of it, to the dark centre
And sit there alone.

'Above me, those pine branches and leaves
Make lace against the sky
and move so slightly
Fine green patterns
stroking the air
They could hypnotize you.
Here I feel a bit of space
From Emilio, from Erich,
Reuben, and the people in the squat,
from everyone.

'Sitting alone in the forest
at night
I drink calmness
I need this space
this cocoon of green.
Is it just the LSD, or am I really
Self-sufficient
Just a little bit?

'The forest is quiet
except for the leaves moving
twigs snapping
movements of I don't know what
around the forest.

'I was thinking how
Life takes many different forms,
like music and the way plants grow
Some people are more in tune with some forms
than others.
Emilio is alive to things
that I am not.
He touches the world differently
from what you learn in books.
It is something to do
with not using words a lot
but feeling sounds and shapes and music
& colours and being sensitive
to situations and experiencing
them directly
and playing around with things
trying them different ways.

'I was brought up to move in straight lines
I want to learn to see round corners.

'Emilio comes on a rescue party
with a lantern
A light bobbing through the dark
Can you see me?
Where are you? Are you all right?
It's getting dark & cold.
I go back with him.

'Inside the house the fire is cackling
Emilio is playing the guitar.
His smile – what a smile,
flashing, gleaming, what a
broad set of teeth, what a

glittering gypsy grin
I didn't know that he could smile so big.

'A cup of tea
is an idea
which somehow seems right
A meeting point of cultures for the two of us
But it takes a long time
to do.
Ordinary motions
can be done
But they have to be planned
with big effort
Kettle
Water
Gas
Matches
Each one a major step.

'And there is a problem:
The teapot is disappeared.
Vanished, with no trace.
We had it earlier, green and chipped,
Now it is gone.
We look everywhere
The kitchen table
and underneath it
and in the creaking cupboard where mice have lived.

'Emilio finds this a mystery.
He gives significance to
the disappearance of the teapot.
If that can happen,
who knows what else is going on?
Maybe plots and persecutions

Other, more sinister disappearances
In which the termination of the teapot
is the first clue.
He tunes his guitar,
bending his wandering thoughts
to the wailing string
to make it sing true
He screws his face into a knot.

'Being with him here
is so different from how I usually am –
with daily clutter in my mind,
squeezing out my life
with effort
like toothpaste from a tube.

'In the end we made the tea without a pot
and drink it
with biscuits of a cardboard taste.
Talking to the lantern
We played shadows on the wall

'All this time my legs were
bare
because my trousers got so wet
with all that falling over.
They looked like white, puffy legs to me
I didn't like them
I was afraid Emilio would not like them
But he thought they were OK.
"Anyway, they're your legs,"
he said
"You won't get other legs."
So wise.

'We were still hungry.
The loaf of bread seemed very large
Emilio noticed it too.
He is still troubled
about the teapot.
Sometimes he complains
of tenseness in his stomach,
about how the acid
speeds you up, can't relax.
Where is the teapot?
Straining himself to tuning his guitar
Sudden laughs, imaginings,
Sudden insecurities.

'I am insecure too
Uncertain
Unsure what is happening.
I wonder what he thinks of me
Feels for me
Now I am not good behaviour
any more.

'It is strange to touch him
after all these hours together
as if some part of our senses
has become dead
While others were overflowing.
It is strange to touch him
His eyes brown and narrow, curly-lashed
I want to swim inside them.
Inside him.

'We invent a variation on the kiss,
With eyelashes stroking softly on the skin.
We fuck

Or rather we make love
for it is gentle and dreamlike
on the patched bedspread
in front of the fire.
Then we lie there, exhausted, loving
and tell stories
about dream gardens and high walls and Buddhas and bridges
and rainbow coloured skies.

'I sing the Lorelei song
to lull him to sleep
because we're both speeded up
and exhausted.

'It is three o'clock in the morning.
Living like this is so intense I cannot close my eyes
To live so full, my soul spreads
I am worn out
It will be a relief to be again
normal
Goodnight, my love.

'The next morning we found the teapot
Behind a cereal packet on the shelf.
The LSD shows many things:
That my soul can escape the rules
Can fly and fall and bathe in rainbows
That Emilio's hand is not just the music-player
But can hold me strong
and care for me.
The LSD shows
Who I will love forever
But not how
To find a teapot.'

As she sat reading on her mattress, Corinne stopped and flicked through to find three more pages to go.

At that moment the door opened and a head popped round the door. 'Saw the light, just wanted to say...' When Taffy realized she was sitting up in bed with her naked upper body visible, his face fell and the head disappeared again.

Corinne shook herself out of her shock. 'It's normal to knock,' she said as the door closed.

Immediately there was a knock and the door opened again. She had not had time to move or cover herself.

'Just wanted to say, wicked to meet you and goodnight...' his words faded out at the sight of her still-naked body.

'Goodnight?' Corinne out-stared him over her bare breasts.

'Goodnight.' It sounded final but the head hovered. 'Sorry, I didn't realize... I'm going.' His eyes were fixed on her breasts. She stared back.

'Going?' said Corinne.

'I've run out of alternative ideas.'

Corinne puckered her brow. 'No, there aren't any alternatives to going...' she shook her head, 'except staying...'

'Staying?' Taffy's face broke into a grin. 'Now why didn't I think of that?' He came into the room and shut the door behind him. He looked at the mistletoe above his head, 'Shall I bring some of this over? To bring a traditional touch to my advances?' He broke off a sprig and headed towards her, adding in his Desperate Dan voice: '"Ah've got maself a trouserfull o'trouble."'

With his head between her legs, Taffy opened her lips with his tongue. Corinne caught her breath like someone stepping into freezing water. She opened her mouth as if in pain. Her breath came in gusts. At the last minute she threw her arms and legs out into a star and shook. 'Oh, Jesus,' she cried, 'Oh, Jesus.'

Afterwards as they lay naked side by side on Ren's sheepskin rug, he said, 'I've been called a lot of things in my time, but never that.'

Corinne smiled.

After a while she said, 'I was just reading Ute's account of the acid trip she had with Emilio in 1971. I hope she wouldn't mind. It was left there.'

'Wow!' said Taffy, rolling towards her and wrapping the spare part of the sheepskin rug over them. 'That must be some read! She came back different, that was when she turned. She got the wildness of the forest in her blood, she threw caution to the winds.

'Like with that teapot she forgot to hold just after she got back, crashed on the kitchen floor and broke, hot tea on her legs up to her knees, serious burns, nee-naw nee-naw, hospital. Duncan the hero of the day, took her to A &E, waited four hours with her, did everything. Who knew a romantic heart was beating under that Stalinist exterior? Devotion unlimited expecting nothing in return, the best-kept secret in the squat. She came back from hospital with bandages, went out next day and bought a pair of boots. Oxfam shop. Up to the knee boots, brown leather been dyed white and then pale blue and both were peeling off, looked far out. Not the thing for Mrs. Neat before, but now she walked a new way.'

'Peeling blue and white dye?' said Corinne. 'That's strange.'

'I called them her seven league boots,' said Taffy. 'There was no holding her after that. Next thing she's learning the Portuguese for undying love and Emilio wakes her with a kiss every day for a hundred years. She threw away her return ticket to Germany. Never could understand how it happened. Quiet, cautious little Ute. She made a leap of faith bigger than getting over that wall. Across the language barrier. Into the arms of a refugee with nothing to his name but a guitar. I saw Reuben ten years later and he still hadn't got over it.'

'Poor Reuben,' said Corinne, and yawned.

'Reuben, where are you now?' mumbled Taffy as he rested his head on Corinne's shoulder. She rested her other hand on his curls. Their breaths slowed, their eyelids dropped, and they both dozed.

Half an hour later, Corinne woke with the cold and reached around for the mattress and bedclothes.

Taffy opened his eyes. 'Ah!' he said, 'Hello! There's a little thing I was wanting to ask you: if you're still awake, how about a voyage to the interior?'

10

Chapter Ten

Friday 28th December 1990 8am

I'm woken by Morton kissing my face. 'Good morning, Anthea, Christmas is over.'

Yes. Not quite, but mostly.

It wasn't too bad. The days of festivities are fading. We ate, we slept, we played charades, we washed up. I stalled Bert again about his father, I couldn't face telling him.

I open my eyes and sit up. 'It was OK, wasn't it? Bert kept leaving me notes asking about his dad. Not that I'm going to tell him anything. And Freddie seemed a bit preoccupied.'

'He seemed fine to me.' Morton leaps out of bed and draws the curtain. 'Look, sunshine!'

I say, 'I don't know if it's still about that bike that got smashed, or something else. Maybe he's still pining after the love of his life, and it's worse at Christmas.'

'Now you're worried about Freddie,' says Morton as he climbs back into bed. 'You'll always find somebody or something to worry about. But at least you've stopped going on about that bone.'

It's true. Since I lost that special bone in the forest, the other fragments aren't speaking to me. Radio silence. I feel lost, bereft. But Morton thinks it's a good thing.

'Now are you going to change your mind about going

to Greece? There's no bone now to put you off. And you haven't actually cancelled the tickets yet.'

I know he's trying to be encouraging, but it doesn't help. I'm still afraid of going. That bone was trying to give me a warning. About danger if I went back to Greece. It was a friend, trying to keep me safe. Now I have lost that contact. And I'm still getting nightmares.

'I'm not going,' I say to him. 'I'm not going. I'm not going. I'm not going.'

Friday 28th December 1990 12.30pm

'Bush keeps mouthing off against Iraq,' said Alex from behind her newspaper. 'It's sabre-rattling, but how will he be able to back down? This is not going to end well.' She put the newspaper down on her office desk and started typing furiously.

At the next-door desk, Dora's black-lined eyes looked over the top of her computer out of the window. Absent-mindedly she ran her fingers through her dishevelled and back-combed hair to make it stick out more, and undid the top mother-of-pearl button on her woolly leopard-skin cardigan.

She watched as on the quiet street below a group of young women in smart winter coats crossed the road on a zebra crossing. They walked in a nonchalant and self-possessed way, and took their time. An orange van waiting at the crossing hooted. The last young woman had almost finished crossing when she suddenly stopped, turned and shouted something back to a young man still standing on the pavement behind. The orange van, which had started forward, stopped with a jerk and the Mini behind, which had also started, braked sharply and went into the back of it. The orange van driver leaned on his horn and then jumped out and an altercation started with the driver behind. They both shouted at the young woman, who gave them the finger and strolled off after her companions.

'Weird,' said Dora. 'I look out of the window for a minute and there's an accident. What are the chances of that happening?'

Alex was typing at breakneck speed. 'Best keep your eyes on your screen,' she said, 'if your confusion is that infectious. We don't want you causing any more damage.' She stopped, screwed up her sharp features in thought, and glanced at the posters on the wall beside her desk. One said: 'The trouble with today's super-techno-sophisticated-state-of-the-art electronic society is… people just don't interface anymore.' Next to it was a postcard with the maxim: 'When the going gets tough, the tough go shopping.' She scowled at the postcard and then launched herself back into typing.

'It's no good,' said Dora. 'The letters are leaping around and the digits are dumping themselves in ditches. I need a break.' She rubbed the back of her neck and stretched round to look backwards over each shoulder in turn. 'I think I'm still hungover from Christmas. Alcohol was the only way I could get through. How was yours?'

'I was at my dad's for Christmas lunch. And I had my sister and brother here from Australia.'

'It all comes back at this time of year. You know it was on Christmas Eve that my mum flipped all those years ago. And they took her away.'

'Look,' said Alex, 'I know about that, but tough titties. I don't mean to sound heartless, but at Christmas you just have to get a grip of yourself and get on with it. It's all about consumerism, sentimentality and suffering: it's just capitalism writ especially large, and in this instance there's no point fighting it.' Alex turned away and started typing furiously again.

'I try to blot out the memories…' said Dora. 'But sometimes it helps to talk about it.'

Alex snapped back, 'You think it helps to witter on about things? Then why can't you talk to Giles about it? He's your husband after all. I know he's not the most sensitive of beings, but what do you expect from a man? Why did you marry him in the first place? He must be good for something.'

Dora hung her head.

'Sorry,' said Alex, 'I know I'm not being very positive.'

Dora wiped away a tear before it had fully left the mascara. 'He was good for something, actually. We made love on Christmas Eve right on the button for my ovulation. Who knows? We might have hit it lucky this time.'

'Good for you. Roll on nappies and sleepless nights. Mind you, the Rhythm Method is not exactly foolproof.'

'Thanks for your encouragement.'

'What do you want from me? Bullshit?' Alex shrugged. 'I suppose everyone's entitled to their obsessions. Within reason. Shall we grab an early lunch before the editorial meeting?'

'Mail.' The manicured hands of the office secretary dropped a pile of brown and white envelopes on the corner of the sea of pages which already covered Dora's desk. Then another pile on Alex's tidy desk.

'Cheers,' said Alex. She frowned at her pile. 'What's there to write about two days after Christmas?'

Dora flexed her fingers like claws and started to leaf through hers. One thin white envelope bore the logo 'Good Breaks'. She opened it and examined two tickets for a cut-price flight to Barcelona on June 7th. A large padded envelope held a thick wadge of typed sheets. 'Another unsolicited novel,' she said. 'What are we expected to do with them? If I read them all I wouldn't have time to eat or go home at night.'

Then she picked up a battered brown A4 envelope with spidery handwriting. It had been used many times before, previous addresses incompletely crossed out. From it she pulled out half-a-dozen pages, photocopies of blurred carbon copies, closely typed on an old-fashioned typewriter. 'Don't people ever learn to double space?' She peered at it curiously and started to read aloud:

'The air was thickening along the dusky esplanade. A torn awning flapped over the front of a boarded-up newsagents. Gulls screeched and scratched the sky as the green bus stopped by the pier to drop its last load of passengers before returning to the depot. The engine whirred while passengers clambered off, clutching hats and billowing plastic macs. "Goodnight" muttered the driver. The next day was Sunday, his day off. No one needed a bus on Sunday. No one came or went in the sleepy sea-resort on the Lord's day of rest. It was a place that people retired to, where they sat in small boarding houses spinning out their fragile lives like crochet, waiting to die…'

'Weird what some people write,' said Alex. 'Are you planning to declaim the whole thing, or are you coming to lunch?'

'OK, lunch.' Dora slipped the pages back into the A4 envelope. 'I'll have a look at this later, it's not that long.'

'What for? We're never going to publish that stuff.'

'It's intriguing. Quaint, somehow, childlike.' She took a pencil and wrote on the envelope: '28/12/1990. Read & reply to this ASAP.'

She pulled open the bottom drawer on the right of her desk and took out a fake leopard skin handbag. She checked her make-up and put more black mascara onto her already encrusted eyelashes.

'You're only going to the pub down the road,' said Alex. 'Anyway, you're a married woman, ha ha.'

'I had a husband this morning,' said Dora, 'but by lunchtime I can't believe he exists. By teatime I can't believe he ever loved me and by half past five I can't believe I'm ever going to see him again. The memory of him seems to drain away.' She tried to use both hands to make her hair look more tangled and dropped her handbag onto her desk, scattering papers across the top of it like a stone making ripples in a pond. The battered brown A4 envelope slid off and fell into the open bottom drawer. She finished her hair, picked up her handbag, put on a little black leather jacket off the back of her chair, kicked the bottom drawer shut without looking, and went to lunch.

As they walked along the Clerkenwell Road, they heard a cheery voice: 'Stop here for free kisses! Top up now on seasonal goodwill! Free kisses…' A tall man in a Father Christmas suit was standing on the pavement with a placard saying 'Only 362 days till Christmas'. As they approached he tucked a stray brown dreadlock back into his red fur-trimmed hat. 'Free kisses here!'

The passersby were few and they mostly looked away. Some slowed down to look, read the placard and smile. They saw an elderly lady stop to speak to him and laugh heartily when she received a kiss on the cheek she offered.

Alex looked at Dora: 'Shall I?'

Dora shook her head.

Alex stopped by the man: 'Yes, please!' She held out her cheek.

As he bent to plant a kiss on it, she turned her head at the last minute so that his kiss landed on her lips.

He stepped back. For an instant he looked shocked, then he rallied. 'Another satisfied customer!' he announced. 'Free kisses here! Special offer of festive spirit!'

'You are awful,' said Dora as they walked on. 'You don't know the guy. Aren't you afraid of catching something? HIV?'

'Not from saliva,' said Alex. 'Anyway, he looked like a nice clean-living boy.' She stopped and looked back. 'Rather fanciable, actually.'

'Honestly,' said Dora, and tugged at her arm. 'Don't you ever stop?'

Alex laughed. 'I didn't want to miss a bargain.'

'I'm wondering about blowing it out with Duane,' said Alex. 'It's been a nice few days, but nothing's going to come out of it except disappointment in the long run.'

'Even when you knew from the start that you're a bit on the side?' asked Dora.

They were sitting in a quiet corner of The Hat and Feathers in their lunch hour. Few people had returned to work in Clerkenwell so soon after Christmas, and the pub was empty.

Alex sipped her gin and tonic. 'Even a bit on the side can have feelings and get disappointed. I'm not going to knowingly put my head in the noose. I prefer to get out quick.'

'Cut and run?'

'That's about it.'

'Isn't that what you usually do in your relationships?'

'Thank you, Sigmund Freud. With the men there are around, what else can you do? I suppose you've never had a short relationship, Mrs. Goody Two-Shoes?'

Dora looked into her tomato juice. 'I did have one. My first relationship, actually.'

'How short?'

'One night. I didn't want it to be that short, myself.'

'He buggered off?'

'He did. I was only fifteen.'

'Dora, how did you manage to get yourself laid at the age of fifteen by some bastard who buggered off?'

'It was my own fault, really.'

'No way. You are kidding. What the fuck happened?'

'He was a supply teacher.'

'He was your teacher? That's out of order.'

'OK, I'll tell you what happened. Then you'll believe me. Hear me out. This teacher was rather good-looking. Fair hair, and he used to specialize in Paisley shirts with big lapels. Beautiful even teeth. Little beard. I had a secret crush on him. Or maybe I didn't manage to keep it that secret. He used to say, "Good morning, class." Then, "And good morning, Dora," so everyone laughed and looked at me. I felt embarrassed. Other times he'd say "Good morning, Dora, you're looking very lovely today." I wished he wouldn't do that, but I fancied him more and more. And somehow I got this idea that he fancied me too.

'My mum was in the bin at that point, and my dad was so busy with his job that he didn't really notice what I did. I'd never had a boyfriend, and my friends were always teasing me about that, so when I talked about this teacher one of them dared me to ask him out. So I did.

'One day, I went to school looking what I thought was especially glamorous. We didn't have uniform so I wore my best tartan miniskirt and white sling-back shoes.

'At the end of our lesson he said, "Thank you, class," and then, "Thank you, Dora," and everyone laughed. I hung around in the room after the rest had left, and went up to his desk at the front.

'"Oh, Dora," he said.

'I said, "Could I have a word with you please, sir?"

'He said, "If it's about me teasing you in the lessons, it's only a bit of fun really, livens things up for the others, I didn't think you'd mind."

'"No," I said. "It's not that." Then I kind of gulped and blurted it out: "I wanted to ask you if you would come out with me tonight? For a drink?" He was staring at me, so I added, "I was hoping you might be able to help me with my project on the effects of immigration on football." While he was with us doing supply we were always doing projects on football, in one form or another. It was the only thing the boys in the class were interested in.

'For a moment his face was off guard with surprise, then he smoothed it over, all smiles: "Yes, why not? No harm in that. I'd be happy to give you some extra help."

'So he told me to come back when he'd finished his day's teaching, and we went to the pub.

'All I had was my pocket money, so after the first round it was over to him to do the buying. And he splashed out. I was on Martinis – I thought that drinking them made me look sophisticated – and I'd hardly finished one when he had another on the table. I hadn't eaten all day so it went to my head. If we ever discussed immigration or football I couldn't remember it afterwards. After a couple of hours I said I ought to go home, but when I stood up my head was spinning.

'"What you need, adorable Dora, is a coffee," he said. "That'll set you to rights." He said I could have one at his place which was close by, so we got on a bus and travelled quite a while and got off somewhere I didn't recognize, I was pretty far gone by then and my vision was a bit smudged.

'From the bus, he took me on his arm to steady me, and he kept saying, "Not much further. Concentrate, Dora, we need to get you back to my place."

'When we got near his house he told me to shut my eyes so he could give me a surprise, and he led me up some steps to the front door, then up some more steps inside. When he told me to open my eyes we were in a big room with a long desk along the window. It all looked very stylish and sophisticated to me. Shiny empty surfaces like an office.

'He said, "You'd better lie down for a minute until you feel better." He pulled the blinds down. Once I was resting on the double bed, I shut my eyes and then I felt really giddy, like a boat being washed this way and that, miles from land.

'"I'll put the kettle on," he said. He must have had an electric kettle there in his room, I remember him pouring water into something.

'I never did get that cup of coffee.

'While the kettle was boiling, he came to sit on the bed next to me.

'"Dora?" he said, "Dora? Are you all right? You don't look too good. May I feel your forehead?" That was the only part he did ask permission to touch, as for the rest he just helped himself.

'I could feel his hand on my forehead, and then he said, "Dora, you're a very attractive girl. I don't think you know what you're doing to me, lying there on my bed. I know I'm your teacher, but I'm only human."

'Somewhere through a sensation of fuzziness I felt his hands on my breasts and then he was lifting up my jumper. I could feel him clasping my breasts with both hands, and then he pulled my bra off and he was sucking them. It wasn't like anything that ever happened to me before, I wanted to gag.

'I remember him saying, "Dora, Dora, what are you doing to me?" Then his hands were under my mini-skirt, I could feel them tugging at my tights. There was more fumbling with underclothes, I can't remember.

'Somewhere during it all he must have undone his trousers because the next thing I felt was something between my legs.

'And then something inside me that didn't feel right.

'It felt rude, unexpected. Guilty, all wrong. He was poking inside me with little jabs. It hurt a bit.

'There were drafts round my hips like I was exposed on a mountainside. Sensations oozed through my body. If I opened my eyes I got a close-up view of the hairs in my teacher's beard. He was on top of me grunting and pushing, he grabbed hold of me and squashed me. I was terrified. Parts of my body I didn't know I had were screaming things I couldn't hear. I was like an electrical system out of control with parts exploding, short-circuiting, sizzling, blowing out. His smell invaded my nostrils with alcohol breath and men's perfume.

'He shoved and shoved and then suddenly it stopped hurting and started to feel nice. Hot, cold, very hot. It felt like it belonged in there. I started to push back. I woke up. Hot, hot… it was like a fire that burnt up the alcohol and I realized that this was what it was all about. Life couldn't be writ any larger than this.

'At the end, when I came, I forgot all about him. I felt my crutch pulsating and I think I started yelling too because he told me to hush it, and then some cosmic broom swept through my body and blotted everything out.

'After a bit I heard his voice saying something about going to have a shower, and I opened my eyes. The thing was gone from inside my body and I realized I didn't have any knickers or tights on. My skirt was round my neck. I lay there in a stupour like someone who's been run over by a train, too shocked to move and I wondered if my dad would notice I was out late. Then I think I passed out.'

Dora paused.

Alex said, 'He raped you.'

Dora said, 'I don't see it quite like that.

'I remember waking some time in the night and there he was in pyjamas, over the other side of the bed. I was still lying spread-eagled with my clothes undone and the inside of my thighs wet. The main thing I felt was that I wanted to do it again.'

Alex leant forward and screwed up her face. 'You what?' she said. 'You cannot be serious.'

Dora bowed her head. 'I suppose I thought I'd got

through the worst: in for a penny, in for a pound, might as well be done for a sheep as a lamb. I wanted to get the hang of it properly. I remembered the bits of it that felt great. Perhaps we would have a relationship. It could be the start of something. But he never touched me again.

'In the morning when I woke up he was by the window holding a round mirror and trimming his beard. He was very formal and said, "I'm sorry about what happened last night, but I think you must take your share of responsibility for it. I hope we can keep this between ourselves. You'd better go home now before you get us both into trouble.' I felt like I'd been told off.

'I went to the bathroom to try to tidy myself up. There was peeling paint and dirty towels. The whole house outside his room was pretty much a ruin. I had a hangover hammering at my head. It was like a dream turned into a nightmare. I got out of there as fast as I could and set off down the street to find my way home.'

'You poor idiot,' said Alex.

'I felt wretched,' Dora replied.

'I'm not surprised.'

'It wasn't what you think. I felt wretched not because of what happened but because it didn't happen again. He obviously wasn't interested any more. It would have been all right if he'd become my boyfriend; it could have turned into something good that just had a dodgy start. We could have gone to football matches together. But by ending it there, he made it something not nice.'

'I think sordid is the word you're looking for,' said Alex.

'After that, he never once registered my existence. He even stopped saying "Good morning, Dora," in the classroom. The others noticed it too. He just blanked me.'

Alex drained her glass and put it down on the table with a bang. 'Honestly, Dora, I can't believe you would have gone on seeing him after what he did to you.'

'I was only fifteen, remember. A lecturer in his twenties would have been quite a catch. I didn't know any better those days about what went on between men and women.'

Alex asked: 'What happened to your anger about what he did?'

'I don't know. But the week after that happened I started wearing black. I went to Camden Lock and bought myself a necklace made of bent nails.'

'When I first met you in the early seventies,' Alex said, 'you were already back-combing your hair to stick up at ferocious angles and painting black lines round your eyes that would scare a burglar.'

'I must have thought it was the right look for a fallen woman. A rejected fallen woman.'

'A furious fallen woman, I should bloody hope. He raped you.'

Dora shrugged. 'In my teens I took it for granted that all men were pushy and were after what they could get. And it was down to you to protect yourself or more fool you. It was a long time before I realized you could expect anything different.'

'He sounds a really nasty piece of work. You remind me of the story about the gorilla.'

'What story?'

Alex raised her eyebrows, 'You haven't heard it? OK.' She turned to Dora with a sarcastic smile. 'Woman goes to the zoo. Leans too far over the wire and a male gorilla pulls her into the cage. Jumps on her, has his way with her till she passes out.

'When she comes round in hospital, the people standing round hear some vague words coming from her lips as she regains consciousness. They lean closer and they hear her murmuring: "He hasn't called… He hasn't rung…"

Dora joined Alex in gales of laughter gusting out from the corner of the pub, until tears smudged her mascara.

Friday 28th December 1990 11.30pm

Alex and Duane were wrapped in towels after taking a shower and were climbing into her bed. From the flat above they could hear the monotonous drone of one word being repeated.

'What's going on upstairs?' said Alex. 'Since last week there's been weird noises coming from there.'

Duane shut his eyes to listen. 'Somebody's chanting "Hallelulya,"' he said, and pulled the duvet over him.

'Who is?'

'Some geezer. Some white geezer, by the sound of it.' The voice was getting louder.

'They *are* white upstairs. That must have been what I heard yesterday too.'

'It's very romantic, right?' Duane stroked Alex's naked white body under the duvet.

From upstairs came 'Hallelulya, Hallelulya, Hallelulya, Hallelulya' in a continuous stream.

'You got some kind of religious nutter living up there?' Duane smiled.

'Not usually. But they're a big family. People come and go.' She pulled him onto his side and towards her.

From upstairs came, 'Hallelulya, Hallelulya, Hallelulya, Hallelulya, Hallelulya.'

'Some people need to get a life,' said Alex as they started to take deep breaths in time.

'They can be crazy, you know what I'm saying?' Duane's movements were smooth, his face composed. Only his lips parted a little in pleasure.

'Hallelulya, Hallelulya, Hallelulya, Hallelulya, Hallelulya,' the voice droned on.

'Aaaaah, aaaah,' Alex's moans rose as they built towards orgasm.

'Hallelulya, Hallelulya, Hallelulya, Hallelulya, Hallelulya,' the voice from upstairs got louder.

'Hallelulya!!' Alex yelled suddenly as her body shook at the final moment, 'Hallelulya!! Hallelulya!! Hallelulya!! Hallelulya!!' she yelled, and then she fell loose back onto the bed as her limbs spread and trembled with physical relief and laughter.

Then a calm of closeness fell on both their bodies as they sank into the mattress side by side.

Duane smiled. 'For a moment there I thought you'd gone crazy,' he said. 'Bet the geezer upstairs did too.'

'Listen!' in a second Alex was sitting up, 'Listen! He's stopped!'

They both strained their ears. No sound came from upstairs.

'Well, at least now I know how to shut him up,' she said.

'Any time I can help you with that, you tell me, know what I mean?' said Duane, rubbing his hand absent-mindedly across her nipples, and they laughed as they lay back again and, after a few minutes of silence, sank together into a doze.

Half an hour later Alex looked up at the ceiling on her way to the toilet. 'The religious hysteria seems to have exhausted itself.'

Duane said, 'I do believe in God, myself. But not the one other people go on about. To me, he's like a friend. I can talk to him. Especially if I'm painting a window high up, and I'm on the scaffolding, right, I can say to him, "This is a tricky one, I will maybe need some help in this situation."'

'So he keeps an eye on you?' asked Alex, standing in the bathroom doorway, her skinny body naked as she cleaned her teeth.

Duane closed his eyes and opened them again. 'Yes, but I think he turn away sometimes. What people do is too much. He says, "Man, I do not wish to see this. I am not going to look." Otherwise you might say, how come certain things take place that would be better not to?

'My mum, she says God sees everything, but I am not so sure. She used to keep everything so clean at home in case he was overlooking things.'

'Cleanliness next to godliness,' said Alex, getting back into bed.

Duane nodded. 'Our front room was like a palace. We had a three-piece suite in purple sateen stuff, and all the best plates in cupboards with glass fronts. My mum dusted the plastic flowers and kept the curtains closed. They were thick red ones. There was a clock in a glass case, from the kitchen we could hear it ring each hour with a particular tuneful chime. There was photos of me and my cousin when we were very little, all smiling, in silver frames. But we never went in there and I don't imagine God did for all it was so clean. There was always sheets over the sofa, right, it was not what you would call comfortable. She said it was for best occasions but there never seemed to be any.

'I found there were other places God did not go. When I was a kid I thought maybe he like it so much in the Church that he stay there with his feet up and not bother to go out, especially if it was cold or raining. And then things went on that he did not see.'

'Like disasters and wars?' Alex asked.

'And little things that happen to people. It could be something that happens to just one person. But it is not nice for that person. I'll give you an example. It is a true story, actually. When I was a child one particular thing happened that I was sure he must have missed. Or why did he not do something?'

'What was it?'

Duane stretched and then looked at Alex. 'I'll tell you straight, this is not something I would talk about to anyone. But since you ask me, I'll tell you. You have got me started. You are a woman of intelligence. Maybe you will understand.

'That morning my mother took us to church as usual. I must have been about six, my cousin Leon is two years younger. Him and his family lived with us, right? My mum always put on a white straw hat in summer and she made me get scrubbed and clean. She had a loud voice: 'Duane! Time to go. I don't mean in five minutes, I mean now!' Me and Leon was always spotless. We sat there quiet as mice although the service was boring. The only piece I liked was when my mum sang along with the others, it was the only time I saw her smile. My mum told me to listen carefully and I would hear God talking.

'I used to do a deal with God, right. I'd say inside myself, "Sorry, God, don't take it personal, but I can't follow all this," and he'd tip me a nod as if to say, "That's OK, boy." Sometimes he used to tell me, "I'm your friend. When you walk out of the church service, you walk straight and true and I'll be holding your hand." I could hear him in the church. But other places when I needed help, he seemed to forget me sometimes.

'That day after church my father took us to see my uncle, that's his brother. So my mother could have some peace and quiet to make the house clean and get the lunch. That uncle he lived in Queen's Park. His wife was a nice fat lady. She cooked the best salt fish and ackee in the world apart from my mum.

'It was a hot day. When we got there my aunt was out, 'cause her grown-up daughter was ill. My uncle was wearing a vest and drinking beer. "Now you behave nice," my dad said. "I'll be back in an hour or so." He didn't say where he was going. So me and my cousin we kick a ball about in the back yard for a while. It was not very big and the Sunday clothes got in the way. Then we came into the house, and my uncle called us up into the sitting room, it looked down onto the street. He had the window open, one of those big sash windows. We leaned out to have a look, with our elbows on the window sill, know what I mean? We were watching some guys talking to some chicks, an old man was cleaning his car, and an ice-cream van stopped outside. Playing some Elvis tune in ping pong music, "Love me Tender".

'Then just like that without no warning my uncle bring down the sash window onto us so we were stuck, front half outside, bottom half inside. "Now don't try and move," he says. I didn't understand what he was doing. I couldn't see, but I could feel him pulling down my Sunday trousers and my underpants. My back hurt with the window jammed down onto it. My uncle whispered to me to keep quiet and keep smiling to the people in the street. The ice cream van kept on playing "Love me Tender," the same bit over and over again. I watched a bit of newspaper flapping outside in the gutter. I'm not going to tell you what he did, I leave that to your imagination. I'll just say, it was not nice and for a little kid it was scary in a strange kind of a way and it was painful, right. Then he stopped and he started doing stuff to my cousin. I couldn't see, but I could see Leon's face out the front looking like it was smiling when it wanted to cry.

'Afterwards my uncle whispered to me and my cousin that if we told anyone about what he'd done we would be in a lot of trouble and he would do it again and really hurt us. Then he pulled the window up a bit and told us to "Get dressed – ain't you ashamed of yourselves?" Soon after that my dad came back.'

Alex was sitting up with her eyes sparking. 'The bastard! The rotten bastard! To do that to two little boys! And he got away with it?'

'We never told no-one. Me and Leon didn't like to go back to the uncle's after that. My Sunday clothes never felt clean no matter how much my mum scrubbed them. And God, he did nothing. I was thinking, if he saw it, why didn't he tell my mum? In the end I decided God was outside on the street, so he just saw me smiling. He didn't realize what was going on behind. I wasn't sure how to tell him. I was afraid he might not think so much of me if he knew. I was ashamed. I thought he would be disappointed in me.'

Alex stroked his cheek. 'I would put it the other way round. God must have been quite a disappointment to you.'

She got out of bed and went to the window to close the blind. At the windowsill she paused and looked up at the night sky over the city. 'Hello?' she called. 'Hello? Anybody there? If you are up there, pay a bit more attention to what these poor sods down here are going through. You asleep on the job?' She paused for a minute, her skinny body silhouetted against the blackness behind the glass. Then she pulled the blind down.

'No answer,' she said as she climbed back into bed. 'Being religious must be like playing Bridge with a dummy as a partner. You have to make all the responses and play all the cards yourself.'

'Bridge?'

'A card game my dad likes playing. A bit like Whist.'

'You like to play cards, right?'

'Not really. In Bridge you have to really concentrate to remember what cards have been played, and I can't be arsed. There's too much else to think about in life.'

'A game for clever people, right?'

'Everybody's clever,' said Alex. 'Everybody has gifts. It's just that some people don't get the chance to use them.'

'Some people do things wrong. Like me. I was a disappointment. All my life. To my mum. She hoped I would become somebody, and I never did.

'I was her pride and joy. At school I was a star at athletics, they used to put me in for competitions. I kept winning and they called my mum into school and told her they wanted to test me to stand for London in the All-England Sports.'

'Sports?' said Alex. 'Sporty? You don't seem the type.'

'I could have been. My mum did extra work to pay for coaching. She worked as a cleaner. She used to get up at 5 o'clock in the morning and get the bus to work. Then evenings she would go out again, she used to leave our tea out on the table and come back late. "That's for you that I'm doing this, Duane," she used to say. "You go to your coaching lessons, make me feel proud."

'She could see my name in lights. She thought it was a way I could get out of the Grove, buy a car, do all the things my dad couldn't do.

'But I never did. The day came for the selecting, right. We had to do a long journey on the bus to get to the sports arena. South London. All the other contestants were there, in their flash track suits, warming up. Mostly white. "Just do your best, son," said my mum, and she went to sit up in a box at the side.

'But I didn't. The first test was running, and when the pistol fired my legs went heavy. It was like my top half was trying to run and my bottom half was cut off. It was like paralysed, it moved slow. It let me down. I could not say exactly what happened, but I couldn't try to do anything. Inside I knew it was useless. I felt ashamed of myself. Then I more or less walked through the rest, just to show I couldn't do it. Better that way. She would have been disappointed later. That way, I was out of it. She didn't have to do the extra cleaning. I never touched athletics after that. She didn't say nothing afterwards, she went very quiet all the way home on the bus.'

'I'm sorry,' said Alex. She hummed a tune to herself then said, '"There must be some way out of/ Going through all these things twice."'

'What "things" is that?' said Duane.

'Feeling ashamed. Disappointing people. We all get caught in traps.'

'What you mean, a trap?'

'It's just a song,' said Alex. 'I'm just wondering if we can ever get out of the loop. Free ourselves from our memories, our patterns. From that lethal merry-go-round of self-repetition. Do something different instead.'

11

Chapter Eleven

Friday 1st February 1991 4pm
'Good afternoon, Anthea. Morton is ready to give his lecture?' Dr. Lefteris Chrysostomos's tall figure hovers and then sits down next to me at a low table in the archaeological library's Common Room.

'Yes, thank you, he's well prepared,' I reply. 'He does everything ahead of time. Unlike me. He made the last edits yesterday. The bit about the origins of the Greek novel had to come out.'

'The origins of the Greek novel? Interesting,' he says, running his hand through his thick greying hair.

'It was in danger of running over length.' I take the cellophane off my cheese and chutney sandwich.

'Perhaps another time.'

'Is producing fiction, like a novel, so different from producing myths?' I take a bite from the corner of my sandwich.

'Myths too are creative fiction,' he says. 'But their consolidation through transmission in an oral culture gives them a special status. Like something intrinsic to the air we breathe.'

I finish my mouthful and add, 'You mean that it's because they're not originally written down, that they are given the status of eternal truths?'

'Perhaps the lack of a named author makes them seem god-given.' Lefteris shrugs slowly and sips his coffee. 'So people use them as universal god-given metaphors for living. Incidentally making them mean what they want, to suit their own needs. Especially Greek myths.'

'Why do you think that happens?' I ask. I take another mouthful of sandwich and look at my watch. It's not long till time for Morton's lecture.

Lefteris strokes the scar on his left cheek. 'Myths are seen as offering a key to the Western psyche and experience. Anyone returning from hell, struggling against insuperable odds, falling to their death, aiming too high, dying for a principle, wrestling with revenge, returning from hell, suffering the loss of a child, or fairly much any other human dilemma, they can find characters and stories in the ancient Greek tradition which give a picture of that situation. Rather gory, some of them. Antigone was walled up alive for trying to give her rebel brother a decent burial. Her lover who tried to free her, he died too. Orestes had to kill his mother to revenge the murder of his father…'

'But why Greek myths?' I put the rest of the sandwich into my mouth and lick my fingers.

Lefteris shrugs. 'Because Greece is seen as the birthplace of Western civilization, so our earliest stories are privileged.'

'Does that make you proud to be Greek?' I ask him.

Lefteris puts his coffee down then leans back. His mouth falls into a big smile that crinkles up his whole face. 'I am proud to be Greek, of course. But not because of that. We had our moment. Like most of the so-called "great" times, it had the basis in imperialism. Your culture, the British, you had your moment, the Empire. And that is finished too. Now the Americans are the roosters crowing all over the world. Those moments always pass.'

OK, I'm going to ask him the question that's bugging me. 'Do you think the myths tell us anything about the rituals they used at the *nekromanteia*, the oracles of the dead?'

'I know that is your interest. It is possible. Ritual actions are perhaps reflected in the passage of Aeschylus' *The Persians* where Darius calls up the dead. But we can't know for sure.'

'I believe they spoke to the dead. And perhaps the dead spoke back.'

'Perhaps on your next field trip you will find the evidence you need. You are going in two weeks, yes?'

'No. I'm afraid not. The trip is cancelled.' I stand and pick up my bags to leave. 'It's a shame, but we can't go.' How can I explain to him why not? I look back at him and say, 'It was very nice to talk to you. Will I see you at the lecture?'

'Of course,' says Lefteris, twisting his head in the Greek version of a nod.

Friday 1st February 1991 6.30pm
Corinne and Ren filed into the lecture theatre, carrying coats and scarves. The auditorium sloped steeply down to the platform where a slight man in his forties stood testing the microphone. 'One, two, three… One, two, three… How now brown cow…' The seats rose in banks of old varnished wood, with the curved continuous line of a wooden desk top running round in front of each row. The audience entered at the lower levels near the stage.

'Are you sure this is the right place?' asked Corinne in an undertone.

'It must be.'

'And why did you want to come?'

'A client asked me to. I can't say more. Confidentiality.'

Corinne looked around uncertainly.

'I want to go to the back,' whispered Ren. 'Inconspicuous.'

There were shuffling sounds of footsteps on wood, rustlings of paper and polite mutterings as the rest of the audience made their way to their seats, squeezed past each other, closed umbrellas, settled their bags, located their spectacles and got ready to take notes.

As they sat down, Ren whispered to Corinne: 'I'm afraid I need to leave as soon as it's over. I got an urgent message from Reuben, he wants to come and stay tonight.'

'Reuben?'

'The same Reuben. His father's died. So he's in London unexpectedly and he needs somewhere to crash.'

A plump woman with red hair went up to the podium and said something in the speaker's ear. He smiled. She sat down again at the end of the front row. A Chinese man sitting next to her looked anxiously from her to the speaker. Then an elderly man with bristling grey eyebrows stood up to set the proceedings in motion.

With a benign expression he looked up at the rows of faces turned towards him, then spoke slowly and with a little effort. After welcoming those attending and thanking them for turning out on such an inclement evening, he announced that 'Morton Donahue needs no introduction, so I shall give none.' He mentioned how his department had been galvanized by the arrival of Donahue. He referred to the College's proud longstanding association with the Folklore Society. In conclusion he admitted with a raise of the bushy eyebrows that he had no clear idea of what Dr. Donahue would be presenting, but he could promise the audience a 'Magical Mystery Tour' (spoken with a self-deprecating professorial chuckle) of storytelling through the ages: 'I understand we shall be hearing not only about Homer but about narrative traditions of our own time, including a number of examples from the silver screen. Ladies and Gentlemen, it is with great pleasure that I call on Dr. Morton Donahue to present his thoughts on…' (he peered at a sheet of paper in his hand) '…"Homer, Post-modernism and the Many Dreams".'

The small, slim man took a sip from a glass of water on his lectern, and began to read his script with a barely detectable American accent:

'Every society tells stories about its realities and its fantasies. The purpose may be to entertain; to escape; to transmit history, values and skills; to buttress religious beliefs; to endorse community; to give an emotional or spiritual experience; to teach people how to live; or to fulfil a number of other purposes.'

He looked up from the pages, let his eyes wander over the audience, and continued in a more conversational tone, 'It has been said that there are only seven stories in the world, and these are forever retold with subtle variations.' He smiled, checked himself and looked back at his text.

'There are those among the scholars studying stories who have tried to find recurrent or indeed "universal" themes. Carl Gustav Jung set a mould by identifying "archetypal" characters like the wise old man and the earth mother, and singling out recurrent themes such as journeying, the quest and transformation. Lévi-Strauss suggested that all stories break down into opposing pairs: cooked/raw, male/female, wild/tame and so on: he identified such binary modalities as a key to the structure and symbols of traditional stories and myths world wide.

'As early as the 1970s, such approaches were critiqued as reductionist, prescriptive and tendentious. In relation to Jung, feminists asked why there should eternally be wise old men and no wise old women. Mary Douglas, who worked in this very institution, pointed out that Lévi-Strauss, and I quote, "...cannot come up with anything interesting about cultural variations (which are local and limited) since his sights are set on what is universal and unlimited to any one place or time."

'Or as Pasolini put it more briefly at the start of his 1974 film of The Arabian Nights, *the truth lies not in one but in many dreams.'*

Ren was looking at the red-haired woman in the front row. Her frizzy hair did not entirely conceal her face, which was turned towards the speaker. Even from the back row it was possible to see her parted mouth, her tipped nose and the lean of her shoulders upwards and forwards as she followed every syllable.

Corinne was using her pencil and paper to start a sketch. She drew a front view of a country pub. Her sketch included one side of the building, trees beside it, a road in front. The last part of the lettering across the front of the building read: '...way House'. The style of the drawing was impressionistic, but she devoted care to the pub sign which hung from a wrought iron bracket sticking out from the side of the building. Across the top of the sign was the name of the pub 'Halfway House'. Underneath, the sign showed a picture of the pub itself, the same picture that she had drawn but on a smaller scale.

The speaker was bringing his thoughts on Homer to a conclusion. '...*Suddenly Homer is looking rather up-to-date. Multi-authored, multi-charactered, temporally displaced, set in metaphysically heterogeneous arenas, the Homeric poems weave their yarn in a way strangely fitting to contemporary tastes. Thus these texts, which could in the past be seen as stylized or primitive, now seem curiously resonant with our* zeitgeist.'

Ren turned to Corinne with her bare eyebrows raised into a question. On the corner of her sheet of paper, Corinne wrote 'zeitgeist = spirit of the times.' Ren nodded.

Corinne returned to her drawing. When she next looked up, the speaker was moving on from Homer.

'*From my discussion of early Greek epic, I now turn to some examples of 20th century film – a medium which has crept up alongside written text as a site of narrative discourse. Specifically I will note how some portmanteau texts have been transferred to feature film, and let my gaze rest on the implications of the multiple structure and metaphysical backdrop so curiously adumbrated by Homer.*'

Corinne leant over her drawing, the pencil tip poised

over the vanishing point. Ren took the pencil from her fingers and on the edge of the paper wrote 'adumbrated?' Corinne took it back and wrote beneath it '= foreshadowed.' Ren smiled and looked back at the speaker.

'*From* TV *soap operas we are familiar with multiple storylines and the episodic structure, already well developed over a hundred years ago in the part-work publication of Dickens' novels. However, to find these elements driven not by chronological sequence nor by human character development and motivation, we need to turn to modern cinema. The vitality of the portmanteau story format is testified by that weirdest of weird works,* The Saragossa Manuscript. *The book, written by the eccentric Polish scholar Count Jan Potocki who died in 1815, was made into a movie by Wojciech Has in 1965. This film version of* The Saragossa Manuscript *is an intriguing Chinese box of stories within stories, held together by a force that is neither human nor divine, but based in a metaphysics which is contested within the work itself.*'

The speaker took a sip of water and looked over the top of the lectern at the audience. With a distracted half smile, he explained in a more relaxed tone of voice: '*A Captain of the Walloon Guards, Alphonse van Worden, is trying to cross the Sierra Morena to get to Madrid. At an abandoned inn he meets two beautiful young Moorish ladies, but after a night of pleasure wakes up beneath the nearby gallows where the corpses of two bandit brothers are hanging. As his journey continues, all the characters he meets tell intertwining stories. However hard he tries to get to Madrid, the stories – and his path – repeatedly lead back to the abandoned inn where adventures – which may be real or envisioned – inevitably end up beneath the gallows.*

'*Several of the stories are about disillusioning the credulous. But the whole structure of the piece – blurring dream, reality, poetry and the mystical – challenges our understanding of what is (fictitious) narrative reality and what is imagined. We are freed from a limited engagement with human character. That the universe goes to infinity in each direction, from the multiplication of stars to the sub-division of atoms, is mooted in the text and embodied in the structure of the work. The adventures begin simply and the listener thinks they will soon come to an end, but – as one of the characters, Don Velasquez, puts it – "one story creates another and a third is woven from the second. Something like quotients which can be divided infinitely." The strivings, pleasures and mishaps of the characters are set against a backdrop of mystery. As the character Velasquez puts it: "Only an ignorant man who sees a thing every day thinks he understands it. A true researcher moves amongst enigmas."'*

With her eyes down, Corinne was completing her work on the pub sign sticking out from the side of the pub. Within the frame of the hanging sign she had repeated on a smaller scale an identical drawing of the pub itself: the last part of the name across the front, the trees, the road, and then another, even smaller, version of the pub sign attached to that pub pictured within the sign.

Meanwhile the speaker had shifted ground.

'Between 1972 and 1975 Pier Paolo Pasolini produced his trilogy of "portmanteau" films: The Decameron, The Canterbury Tales *and* The Arabian Nights. *Here again, human character and linear narrative do not dominate. The films are more about texture – bodies, landscape, battered faces, light, eroticism, atmosphere, irony – and the erratic and mysterious forces that bind all our human stories together.*

'I shall close by saying a few words about Luis Buñuel's film Le Fantôme de la Liberté, *made in 1975. This is usually translated as* The Phantom of Liberty, *although Buñuel stated that he took the title from Marx's famous comment that there was a spectre haunting Europe, "the spectre of liberty," so perhaps that would be a more accurate translation. A phantom is an imagining, a spectre suggests a vision with power to scare. Such a pedigree for the title suggests that it in some way represents a radical political discourse. Let us investigate.*

'The structure of the film – which Buñuel identified as his favourite among those he made – certainly represents a radical departure from linear narrative. We have a collection of tales sewn together, a series of strange situations which one way or another subvert bourgeois society. A man wakes in the night to see an ostrich in his bedroom. He goes to his doctor for a check up. The camera leaves the doctor's surgery in the company of the doctor's nurse, who drives to stay at an auberge which is accommodating a number of bizarre guests, including some card-gambling monks and a sado-masochistic businessman.'

The speaker stared at the audience blankly for a second, then glanced at his watch, sharply brought his eyes down onto his script and started reading again, at high speed:

'On her onward journey the nurse gives a lift to a senior policeman who is heading for a police academy to give a lecture to a class. The film now hitches a ride with his story and we enter the academy with him. His lecture focuses on the relativity of social mores, and he narrates an example which the camera represents cinematically. We enter a bourgeois household where guests are invited to sit politely round a large table on toilet seats while occasionally someone excuses themselves with embarassment to lock themselves into a cubicle to gulp down some food.

'This is just one strand of the chains of circumstance which characterize this work. With the same metaphysical breadth that we find in the world of Homer's poems, the camera during the course of events witnesses the characters' night visions, reminiscences and communication with the dead. The film ends with the sound track of a concerted street demonstration set against shots of the heads of large birds in the zoo.'

Corinne pushed her piece of paper towards Ren. On the edge she had written: 'Reuben – i.e. tin-opener Reuben???!!!' Ren nodded.

Corinne wrote, 'I thought he disappeared?'

Ren took the pencil and wrote, 'No. He works in Paris!' and focused again on the speaker, who was continuing:

'It is a number of years since Susan Sontag challenged the distinction between form and content. The idea that a traditional form can carry an innovative or radical "message" has given way in many quarters to the recognition that form and content, like space and time, are two qualities of the same point of creation.

'Thus in The Phantom of Liberty, we are deprived of that comfortable companion, a main character. We are deprived of that pleasurable pouring of ourselves into identification with one human being, and that fictional recreation of the ongoing narcissistic illusion, fostered by our society, that only one person matters, i.e. "me". Brecht starved audiences of the possibility of identifying with his characters by constantly cutting away at their suspension of disbelief – addressing the audience directly, reminding them that they are watching a play not real life. "Don't get lost in this, go and do something out there instead."

'Buñuel, in his own way, also gives and takes away his characters. We cannot merge too closely with any one character without being aware of the rest. We are used to one important central character who resonates with each viewer's obsession with their own ego or "I". But in this work of Buñuel's, the sympathies of the spectator are dispersed. More than one person matters, and each person has their own story. Different characters become protagonists in turns. The narrative is robust and tolerant enough to encompass a diversity of people, all of whom matter in relation to each other.

'What "message" does this "form" carry about the individual and his/her relationship to other people in the collective venture that is humanity? Characters take up the narrative baton from each other as if involved in some overriding cooperative effort. The issue of human relationship is raised even within the structure of the work. There are no islands: we all impinge inexorably on one another.

'And what are the laws governing that impingement, that chain of unexpected happenings which constitutes the Buñuelian world view? Certainly, these processes are not driven by character

298

and society, as in conventional narrative. Faced with the dilemma of contingency, Buñuel himself speaks of chance as the overriding factor in the bizarre procession of events which he shows. To quote him: "Chance is purer than necessity, which comes later."

'The explicit articulation of the director's preferred meanings should serve to contain the film's polysemy and to establish the boundaries of its reception, but it does not constitute an absolute restraint. I venture to add some observations of my own. While not baulking at allowing inequality and injustice to show themselves in its frame of view, the film's structure offers a vision of equality. As with Pasolini's "portmanteau" trilogy, the many characters are equal in the eye of the camera. And on some level they are all equally powerless to dictate the narrative. People are not in charge. Nor is society. In Buñuel's emphasis on chance and on the fundamental mystery of life, I take the liberty of finding a willingness to accept the unknown forces which influence our lives: if not gods, as in Homer, then perhaps a broader and freer spirit. Moreover, I see in his humour a saving grace which makes life bearable and death imaginable.'

Corinne was concentrating on drawing a miniature version of the pub on the pub sign within the pub sign. It was almost impossibly small. She frowned, put her pencil down and rested her head in her hands.

The speaker, like a marathon runner with the finishing line in sight, launched into his last page with renewed vigour. *'In a world such as Buñuel creates in this film, there is no plot. This is another comfort which we are denied as we watch* The Phantom of Liberty. *There is no clear development of character or narrative from beginning through middle to end. No handrail to reassure us that our journey along this path has a purpose and will lead us somewhere. No movement or evolution towards illumination. The film stops, more or less as it starts, at an apparently arbitrary point without preparation or resolution, challenging the notion of purpose which has attended works of art from Aristotle to Hollywood. There is no linear progression, rather an engagement with circuitous loops of space/time.*

'Curiously, here again we find a resonance with Homer. The opening paragraph of the Odyssey, asking inspiration from the Muse to tell the story of the many wanderings of Odysseus on his return from Troy, declares at line 15: "Begin it, goddess, at whatever point you will." The text – which follows a circuitous route of flashback and flashforward rather than a direct progression – tells a story that is known to its audience; like a circle it can be joined at any point. In selecting for any particular performance various passages from the total known story repertoire, the bard or rhapsode was in a sense performing pars pro toto, alluding to the entire compass of the known cycle. Odysseus is eternally setting off from Troy, eternally wandering, eternally reaching his home. Just as in The Saragossa Manuscript, Captain van Worden is forever returning to the delights of the flesh at the abandoned inn, and – as in the last shot of the film – forever riding up the green slope to the skull-strewn gibbets at the top. Just as we all ride continually and inexorably on the cycle of life and death. A life as a linear narrative has a beginning and an end; the circular journey takes us beyond one life to a different perception of human existence.*

'The opening passage of the Odyssey tells us that its stories could be told in any order. The Phantom of Liberty's linked stories, too, lead us around on a merry dance and end as inconsequentially as they began – as it were, in mid air. Thus both works resonate with the post-modernist revolt against the linear, and against time itself.'*

Corinne let out a quiet snore.

'We are left with few reference points to anchor us in the world of reason. In The Phantom of Liberty, as one story turns into another within it, the ground gives way beneath our feet so that we are no longer sure of our starting point. The collapsing of certainty is sustained over multiple viewings where it remains impossible to hold the thread of "reality", just as in the Odyssey it is impossible to hold the boundary between the "reality" story* *line and characters' inventions, dreams, visions, the divine, magic, the fabulous. "I've lost where reality ends and fantasy takes over," says Alphonse van Worden in* The Saragossa Manuscript. *Don Velasquez comments "We are like blind men lost in the streets of a big city. The streets lead to the goal but we often return to the same places to get where we are going."*

'*It has seemed important to me to come to terms with this complex discourse, and I apologize if my paper has itself followed a labyrinthine route in drawing an unlikely analogy between the earliest European poems and some examples of late 20th century European cinema. It hardly needs be said that the differences between the two sets of* oeuvres *are huge, but I have tried to suggest that both offer freedoms from certain established requirements of narrative convention.*

'*For those of my audience who are more familiar with the cultural products of the first millennium* BC *than of the second millennium* AD, *I hope you may feel that such cross-cultural comparisons bear witness to the enduringly vibrant contribution that study of the Classics can make to the modern, or perhaps I should say post-modern, world. And that such comparisons suggest challenging possibilities for revitalizing the study of the ancient world through a dialogue with the scholarship of current literary and cinematic theory. Thank you for your attention.*'

There was a moment of silence, as if the audience were in shock, then some tentative clapping which swelled, as more of the audience joined in, to fill the auditorium. Under cover of the noise, Ren tapped the shoulder of Corinne, who woke with a start and looked around. Following Ren's lead, she stood up, supporting herself on the desk, and gathered her things.

As the applause died away, the elderly professor stepped forward again, hands clasped together intently as if to express the extent of his appreciation. 'I am sure you will all join me in thanking Dr. Donahue for this most…er… stimulating and thought-provoking lecture. I think one could say that his paper reached parts of Homer which other papers haven't reached... ' his eyebrows worked up and down as a polite murmur of laughter trickled around the audience. 'I am sure we have all learned a lot from Dr. Donahue's dazzling array of analogies and indeed I would venture to say that I think Homer himself (if I may be given licence to use that name in the singular as a figure of speech) would have done so too...' The eyebrows moved again. Ren and Corinne were tiptoeing round the back of the seats.

'Next door,' the professor went on, 'liquid refreshment awaits us and there will be the opportunity to engage Dr. Donahue in person over sherry, but before we repair to the Senior Common Room, I wonder if there are any questions?' he spread his arms out wide towards the audience as if to embrace the whole room, and then lowered them slightly so that the gesture almost became a shrug. There were muted rustles and bangs as some more of the audience stood up, collected their papers, dropped umbrellas and tried to slide out from their seats. Ren and Corinne were treading quietly down the wooden steps at the side of the lecture theatre towards the exit door as the speaker stepped forward from his lectern towards the audience, his eyes fixed trancelike on a place in the middle distance.

Some hands went up and as Ren opened the door a thin voice from the back was responding: 'We must thank Dr. Donahue for such a stimulating – if somewhat vertiginous – tour of storytellers past and present, but I would like to ask him whether...' Ren and Corinne slipped out and closed the door behind them.

'So we're missing the sherry?' whispered Corinne.

'I only wanted to hear the lecture,' said Ren. They put their coats on and set off down the stairs. 'My client wanted me to hear it. She thought it would help me to understand.'

'And did you?' asked Corinne. At the bottom of the stairs, the lift landed beside them with a chirrup and opened to disgorge other members of the audience who had also left early.

'Understand?' said Ren. 'I don't know.'

Outside, sleet was cutting across Gower Street, but it had not settled. Corinne pulled her coat collar up around her throat as they set out along a side street towards Warren Street station. 'Understand what?' Ren wondered. 'About Homer? About cinema? About the universe?'

'About anything,' said Corinne.

'I know what I saw,' said Ren. As the sleet came down harder, they squeezed into a crowded bus shelter outside the Tube station. 'I saw her energy pouring out of her and surrounding him. I didn't hear much of what he said. It was a kind of peachy colour. Her energy. Moving from her chest area. That's often the circulation for a woman in relationship with a man. Out from the chest and in at the pelvis. For the man it's the other way round.'

The 73 bus arrived. They climbed up the stairs of the Routemaster and sat on the seat at the back. 'You can see things like that...?' said Corinne. It was half a question and half a statement, as if she were trying to absorb the information.

'Sometimes,' said Ren. 'I don't often talk about it. People tend to think you're nuts.'

The window was steamed up and from the outside there was now the sharp sound of the sleet throwing itself at the side of the bus in squalls. Corinne cleared a patch in the window with her fingers and wiped her hand dry on her coat. She peered out.

A man sitting near the front of the bus raised his voice loudly. 'Does this bus go to Mare Street Mare Street Mare Street?' The half-dozen other passengers who were spread over the top deck of the bus all froze, looking studiously straight in front of them. 'Mare Street Mare Street Mare Street?' Silence. The man turned around. His face was smooth and anonymous; he could have been a stockbroker but the collar of his puffa jacket was dirty. 'Don't nobody know where this fucking bus is going?' Every passenger avoided his gaze.

Then a young black man sitting with his arm round the girl next to him called out from the middle of the bus: 'You want the 38, mate. Get off at the Angel. Get the 38.'

'Get the 38. Don't talk to me about angels. Hackney, load of tossers. Trying to get to Mare Street Mare Street Mare Street. My girlfriend, she used to see angels.' He turned round a bit more and leant on the back of the seat in front as if settling in to harangue his captive audience. 'Angels. She used to see them. Now she's with them. Abney Road. You know Abney Road? It's a cemetery. Anybody been there? Abney Abney Abney. I'm not scared of death. I seen it all. You think I haven't seen it? You don't believe me about angels? You think you know it all. They say dead men don't talk. You believe that?' His face scanned his audience. 'Well, go on then! You scared to say something? You look half dead yourselves.'

The other passengers stared away from him in stony silence.

'I'm interested in photography,' he continued. 'Must get my Olympus out. Take some photos in the cemetery. I'm interested in those who have passed away. It's nothing to do with religion. I'm not political, I'm not religious, I'm scientific.' He turned back to face the dark window at the front of the bus.

After the conductor had taken their fares, Corinne asked Ren quietly 'What about gay couples?'

'What about them?'

'That circulation you described. How does it work if partners are the same sex?'

'It still works, one way or the other. There are all kinds of hidden exchanges between people who are close to each other. They can be very healing. And between total strangers. As I see it, as I see energy moving around, we are all involved in a huge collaborative venture. Collaborative in ways we're not even aware of. Giving and taking energy. We help each other.'

'Kings Cross! Anyone for Kings Cross!' the conductor called from the bottom of the stairs. The lights of the station splashed like melting stars on the glass of the bus window. Below, umbrellas scurried across the pavement between the bus stop and the entrance to the Tube.

'Help each other get to Mare Street Mare Street Mare Street?' Corinne whispered.

Ren peered at the big clock on the front of King's Cross Station. 'I hope we get home in time for Reuben.'

The man at the front turned round again, looked at his audience and shook his head. 'They talk,' he said. 'Any of you tossers spend the night in Abney Cemetery and tell me they don't talk. There's wise ones. Yeah. They'll listen to your problems. Then there's the unwise. You heard of the unwise dead?'

'Leave it out, mate,' chimed in a silver-haired white man from near the back. 'We got ladies on board here.'

The man at the front ignored him, as if he were an unauthorised heckler at a public lecture, and carried on. 'Abney Abney Abney. Abney Abney Abney. You seen them statues there? Them winged creatures and ancient carved stones? I can tell you. The dead don't look like that. My girlfriend told me. There's the kind ones, they want to help you. Then there's the other sort.'

The silver-haired white man lit a cigarette.

After a few moments the man at the front turned around again. 'People are so unhealthy. It's all that junk food they eat. Do you know there are 2,000 poisonous chemicals in a cigarette apart from the tar and resins? As soon as I get off this bus I'm going to have a cigarette. I can't stop myself.'

Everyone else on the top of the bus continued to sit frozen.

Ren spoke in a low voice to Corinne. 'Can you feel it? Nobody's speaking, but everyone is reacting to him. Some are scared, they're pushing him away. Others don't know it but they're reaching out to support him. There's always an exchange between performer and audience. You break the connection with the clapping at the end.'

'Then there's the angels,' the man went on. 'People in this world, they just laugh. I don't take any notice. They're not worth bothering with. I let it wash off me.'

'Angel,' came the voice of the conductor from below.

'Angel angel angel. Angel angel angel.' The man leapt to his feet and grabbed hold of his bulging Marks and Spencer's plastic bag. 'Excuse me, got to leave you. Don't let anyone tell you they don't exist. Sorry and all that.' He rushed down the centre gangway and as he clattered down the stairs muttered, 'All you got to do is reach out to them.'

Friday 1st February 1991 9.30pm

When they got back, Reuben was waiting on Ren's front door step. His thick black hair hung in damp swathes, and his smart navy coat, a size too small, hung open so that the suit he wore underneath was also wet down the front. His eyes were red with tears, his huge shoulders hunched and he was carrying a holdall. When he saw them, he nodded at Corinne and gave Ren a bear hug.

She led him up to the kitchen, sat him down and gave him an Irish whiskey. 'I'm sorry about your dad,' she said.

'The fumes got him in the end,' said Reuben. 'But not the ones he was worried about. He got lung cancer. He did smoke like a chimney.'

'I'll put the kettle on,' said Corinne.

Ren asked, 'Was he in a lot of pain before he died?'

'His life had been hard for a long time. He lived through real horrors. And they were echoed by unreal horrors that he couldn't shake off.' Reuben shrugged. 'In comparison, the illness was short. In a way it's a relief not to see him suffering any more.'

'How's your mother taking it?'

'Like someone who's been knocked down by a falling beam and picks themselves up and carries on walking. Her back is rigid and she looks like she's sleepwalking. She's gone to stay with my Aunty Hetty.'

'I didn't know you had an Aunty Hetty,' said Ren.

'I have a lot of little aunties,' said Reuben. 'I've got an Aunty Golda too; she never made it out of the East End like the others did. Hetty got out like my mum and dad. But my mum didn't want to stay the night in her own house tonight. I can't say I blame her, I don't want to stay there either after what happened this morning before the funeral.' He looked round as if for a place to escape.

'Here's tea if anyone wants it,' said Corinne.

'Thank you,' said Ren, and asked Reuben: 'What happened this morning?'

Reuben ran a big hand through his wet hair. 'It's weird. Look, you know I've always believed the supernatural is a myth created by the rich to intimidate and pacify the poor. So maybe it was stress. Or lack of sleep. Maybe that's why it happened.'

'What happened?'

'OK, I was in the house. My parents' house. I was in the sitting room looking through some drawers. Old photographs, mementoes... For some reason I looked up. And I saw him standing in the doorway... My dad. In the old jumper and trousers that he liked to wear. Just standing there staring. All the breath fell out of me. My body went into lock-down. I don't know how long I sat there. The next thing I know, I'm shaking, I'm really cold and when I look he's not there any more. I couldn't get out of the house fast enough. Went upstairs, grabbed my old suit for the funeral and got the hell out of there.'

Ren poured three cups of tea. 'Remind me if you take sugar, Reuben? Sounds like you need treatment for shock as well as grief.'

'Two please. So what was that? What happened? I'm not the kind of person who sees ghosts. Are the hallucinogenic substances of my misspent youth finally catching up with me? Was I day-dreaming or am I falling apart?' Reuben pulled out a packet of tobacco and some Rizlas and started to roll up.

'I thought you gave up smoking,' said Ren.

'I did. For years. But since Dad went into hospital I got back into my bad old ways.'

Ren laughed. 'All of them?'

'No, no.' Reuben finished rolling his cigarette and lit up. 'I'm reformed, revised, reconstituted. All therapied out. Mr. Understanding, me! Reichian therapist. People come to me, they remember their past and scream, shout and weep. Then they go away feeling better. I help them.' He rubbed his hands together, his mouth opened in an extreme smile and his eyes stared wide, miming a Harpo Marx face of maniacal glee. Then his face fell, heavy with features and folds. 'That's the idea, anyway.'

'You're a therapist?' asked Corinne. 'May I ask what is "Reichian"?'

'Wilhelm Reich,' said Reuben. 'Successor of Freud. Disagreed with him. Believed the work of healing has to take place through the body. Instead of stewing in your feelings till you transmute them, like you do in psychoanalysis, instead you express them. You physically release the muscle blocks holding in the original feelings that were suppressed in you as a child.'

'Sounds painful,' said Corinne.

'Can be,' said Reuben. 'But not as painful as living with them for the rest of your life.' He paused and drew on his cigarette. 'That's the theory, anyway.'

There was a silence.

Ren said, 'OK. This evening. What do you need? There's a bed made up for you upstairs. What else can I do to help you? Food?'

'No food, thanks,' he patted his thickening girth. 'Fatso, me. No, you having me to stay is great. After what happened I couldn't face sleeping at the house. I thought my dad might come back again to pick up a few things. Or to check my mum had left the windows shut. I didn't want to pass him on the stairs. Or find him in his armchair in the sitting room having one last fag.'

'Anything else that would help?' asked Ren.

'I need to talk. Mourn. Get out of this monkey suit. Don't know why I'm wearing it, my dad wouldn't have minded, he never put on airs and graces. I need to relax... My stress level is through the roof. I'm stretched tight like a piece of hide on a drum. I feel I might snap...' He rubbed his neck and then looked up at Ren: 'Do you still do massage?'

Corinne waited for an hour in the kitchen until Ren came out of the sitting room.

'How is he?' Corinne asked. 'The kettle's just boiled.'

'He's a bit better now,' Ren said. 'He's relaxed a bit. He's dozing.' She washed the massage oil off her hands.

'Do you want more tea?' Corinne filled the pot.

'Thanks. It's great to see him again. I haven't set eyes on him for years.'

'I thought no-one knew where he was,' said Corinne, getting the milk out.

'He says he tried to break ties with past. That hardly ever seems to work. Apparently he has been over from France a few times, kept in touch with his parents, but didn't contact anyone from the squat.'

'Has he changed?'

'Like a river changes: different and the same.' Ren poured two cups of tea, took one and stood up. 'That's for you. I'm taking this to bed with me, I need to turn in. He might like one if there's enough left in the pot.'

'It's not a good time to ask him for the rest of the tin-opener story?'

'He's a big boy,' said Ren. 'You could ask him, he can always say no. It might take his mind off things.'

Friday 1st February 1991 11.30pm

Three-quarters of an hour later Reuben was sitting on Ren's sitting-room carpet in his underpants. His best suit was in a damp pile in a corner of the room; he had a large blanket wrapped around him and a chest of thick black curly hair was visible at the neck. Some of the hairs were greying. Two empty teacups sat on the carpet between him and Corinne.

'Remember, Alex wasn't usually so friendly, that threw me a bit,' he was saying. 'One minute I'm coming back to the squat from the corner shop, got the tin-opener in my pocket, with my donkey jacket stinking of rotting vegetables; the next I'm sitting there at the kitchen table with a full plate in front of me. Bacon, toast, tomatoes…'

'You're sure you don't mind talking about this?' said Corinne. 'You've got more important things on your mind now.'

'The past can always feed us. And there's always a place for distraction.'

'Even for a therapist?'

'Especially for a therapist,' said Reuben. 'We don't

always follow our own advice, you know.'

'I've only just met you.' said Corinne. 'I'm not usually so upfront.'

'You be as upfront as you like. You're a welcome surprise. So there I was in the kitchen at the squat. Alex had opened the tin of baked beans herself. She'd bought a brand new tin-opener, a deluxe model. I'd gone through all that at the corner shop for nothing. Clever woman, that one. Smart Alex, we used to call her.' He glanced at Corinne. 'You've heard about the squat?'

She nodded. 'Read about you all too.'

'Is that an accusation?' said Reuben. 'What did you read, the bailiffs' form or the local paper or the Special Branch report?'

'No need to be paranoid. Have you seen the stuff in that chest?' Corinne pointed. 'It's full of ephemera from that time. Newscuttings and diaries and political statements and diatribes against capitalism... I was living in east London myself in 1971. A few miles away. You do look vaguely familiar to me.'

He glanced at her sideways. 'You must have been frying other fish.'

'I was. Having my own disasters. Go on with yours. If you're really sure you don't mind talking about such things on a day like this.'

Reuben thought for a moment and then looked Corinne full in the face. 'At a time like this, it feels good to remember. Who I was. Who I am. And stories are healing, whether you listen to them or tell them. So, where was I...? In the kitchen with Alex.

'I'd never spent much time alone with her. She offered me tomato ketchup and told me about how she'd just been to the pictures.

'The rashers of forbidden pig were a delight to my tongue, but somehow the baked beans fell short of the build up in my imagination. That's sometimes the way with fantasies. The tomatoes that the guy at the shop had given me were slightly off. I felt I owed Alex some conversation, so I asked whether it was a good film.

'"Unadulterated shit." She didn't mince her words, our Alex.

'I asked her what it was.

'She sliced the rind off her bacon very neatly as if she'd like to do the same to the film's director. "*Women in Love,*" she says. "Ken Russell doing his usual pretentious film director ego trip. Based on D.H. Lawrence's crappy novel: male chauvinist fantasies of a skinny nerd."

'"Lots of sex in it?" I asked.

'Alex waved her fork. "Masturbation fantasies. If he felt inadequate he didn't have to inflict the rest of us with all this verbiage to make himself feel better. I walked out."

'It wasn't any fondness for the book really, but rather a vague sense of male loyalty which prompted me to try a half-hearted defence of D.H. Lawrence: "It's well written, some of it," I said.

'"Little men need big fantasies," she retorted.

'Forget male loyalty. I couldn't afford it. "Who did you go with?" I asked.

'"Went on my own."

'As I wiped the last bits of baked bean juice off my plate with a bit of Mother's Pride toast, and put down my knife and fork on the empty plate, I was wondering where to go from here. I felt wrong-footed; perhaps I should offer to wash up. "I thought you'd be with Evan," I said. That was Alex's boyfriend.

'"Evan's gone to see his mates in Stratford," she replied, and scrunched a handful of her curly black hair as if she would like to do the same to Evan.

'"What about the others?" I asked.

'"Taff and Brenda went to a party."

312

'I put my plate in the washing-up bowl and filled the kettle with water but I think I forgot to light the ring. I was a dozy kid. Eventually I put the question I most wanted answering. "And where's Ute?"

'Alex said, "Ute's gone to a meeting about the Right to Work campaign, with Duncan. He told her it would be educational. They're probably in the pub now." She took an apple from a paper bag on the table and crunched into it before adding, "Though I don't expect Miss Goody Two-Shoes will be drinking anything except orange juice. She's probably already writing the report for her German comrades."

'That was when I started to feel uncomfortable. Was it the damp shirt still sticking to my shoulders or was it the way she was talking about Ute?

'Alex laughed at me outright: "Face it, she's dumped you for the cause on a Saturday night."

'I tried to take stock of the situation. I looked around the kitchen strewn with dirty pans and plates. So it was just me and Alex at home that evening. I was facing a depressive evening with a good book. Or chat to Alex. At least somebody seemed to want to know me. So I invited her to share a joint; I had a bit of Thai grass stashed in my room.

'I tried to make the best of a bad job. I took my wet donkey jacket off and dropped it on the floor beside the mattress while I fumbled underneath for the dope I'd hidden. Anything that was left visible in my room always got smoked by someone else. I sat on the bed piecing together the Rizla papers over my open tobacco pouch. Alex made herself comfortable on the car seat, and looked around.

'I remember she asked me whether I was ever going to do anything with my room.

'I said, "Maybe. I've got a lot of teaching to prepare at the moment."

'She said, "Any excuse is better than none." That was her style. Sharp and stroppy.

'But I noticed that as we smoked together she got more mellow. Each time we passed it across, I had to reach up from the mattress on the floor, and she had to reach across from the chair. Eventually, when I was rolling the second joint, she moved over and sat on the bed next to me. As we passed it to and fro, our arms and hands sometimes touched. The next thing I knew, she seemed to be leaning against me. It was a bit awkward, but not unpleasant. I'd never really taken much notice of her before, in fact I'd tended to steer clear of her.

'She seemed to be thinking the same thing: "You've never really noticed I exist, have you? All wrapped up with the German au pair."

'Something didn't seem right about the way she talked about Ute, but I let it go. I didn't have the heart. Everything was at cross purposes that day, and it was too late to try to set things right. Anyway, I was annoyed with Ute myself. Going out to a meeting instead of being there when I got back from football. I had typical boy attitudes at that time.

'Alex was looking at me. I noticed her eyes for the first time. They were penetrating. She asked me, "Do you only like mousy women?"

'What could I say? I just shrugged and told her the truth, "I'm broadminded."

'That did it.

'I'll leave the rest to your imagination. All I will say is that naughty things went on. They went on for quite a long time. She was a very thorough lady once she got going, quite a tease with her bony body, I seem to remember positions I'd never even thought about, but let's not go into that. I'm a good-natured guy. Always ready to oblige, especially in the area of nookie. When Ute got back with Duncan, we heard him singing "We demand the right to work" in the hall and we hid under the covers. Alex got the giggles. I felt like a heel, but what could I do? Ute thought I was asleep and went off to her own room. But I don't remember sleeping much that night.'

'You were a rotten sod to do that to Ute,' said Corinne.

'To tell the truth,' said Reuben, 'I did go over it many times afterwards with regret. I cannot defend myself. What can I say? The selfishness of youth.'

'What were you thinking of?'

'Probably something along the lines of "Any port in a storm". I admit, the first kiss was nothing special. Women smell different, you know, that was a bit strange at first. And they are different shapes, it takes getting used to. But then it was the excitement of the new. Remember, it was the early 70s and we were meant to be "free". The culture was "Do it! Do it now!". To be honest, during the night I reached the point where I was past caring and I really didn't remember who I was in bed with. Shocking, isn't it? We carried on until the early hours. Then we reached the point where we both dropped into sleep like rocks into deep sea. I guess we were pretty numb from our exertions and we kind of fell apart.'

'And that was when the tin opener came in,' said Corinne.

'You got it.'

'The nudge of conscience, I call it.'

'More than a nudge. More like a fierce prod. As I rolled off the narrow mattress, the thing drove itself into me. Anyway, I paid a heavy price for that night of fun, so perhaps I got my just deserts.'

'Ute?'

Reuben nodded. His head sank lower and his body seemed to crumple again. 'Ute. All these losses seem to be hitting me at once.'

'I'm sorry,' said Corinne, 'I didn't mean to bring up difficult things at a time like this.'

'It's OK,' he said. 'Things need to be brought up. Need to be felt. It's my job, it's what I do. Give me a moment.'

'Is that your champagne in the fireplace?' Corinne asked.

'Help yourself. It's open. I found it at my parents' house.'

Corinne raised her eyebrows. 'The high life?'

'My dad could never afford it. So when I started earning a decent income, I brought it over for them. But they never opened it. Poverty's like iron in the soul. After a certain point it's relentless: it can't bend, it can't let plenty in. So they never drank it. I opened it today to drink a toast to my dad.' Reuben looked up at Corinne with red eyes. 'He was past the point where he could let in anything happy.'

'I'm sorry,' said Corinne. 'I suppose I'm lucky that I still can.' She picked up a glass of water she'd had by her bedside, emptied it onto the roots of the bay tree, filled it with champagne and drank. 'So what happened to you after the squat?'

'I wandered,' said Reuben. 'America, back to Europe.'

'Did you keep your ideals?'

'Ideals? That's a dangerous word.'

'OK,' Corinne corrected herself: 'Did you carry on being a troublemaker?'

'Well, I kept trying. You never know how much difference you manage to make. I did stuff in the States in the late 70s. In the early 80s I was in Holland, in a mass squat in Nijmegen.'

'Nijmegen? That's weird. I knew some people from there once.'

'In the 80s? From Piersonstraat?'

'No. In the early 70s.'

'The squat ended traumatically. In February '81 the Dutch army and police raided it. They were 2,000 strong with over a hundred riot vans and a helicopter. They smoked us out with CS gas and demolished the block. They wanted to build a parking garage there. Local people wanted affordable housing.'

'I never heard about that squat.'

Reuben shrugged. 'Like with all left history, they tried to disappear it. They didn't want it giving other people ideas.'

'What did you do after that?'

'I couldn't face coming back to Thatcher. I was depressed about whether direct action could work. Depressed about the passivity of the masses as they rolled over to let their rights and services get steadily eroded. I decided the problem was in people's minds, their attitudes, their conditioning: that's what stopped them fighting back. That was where Reich came in.'

'Was he a troublemaker?'

'In his own way, yes. He said people are socialized into conformity. That once the blocks from their childhood conditioning are released, they're freed to act appropriately in the present and fight for a better world.'

'And does it work?'

'Sort of. But it needs to be widely available to make any real difference. Without charge. It should be on the National Health. There's a huge weight of external and internal repression militating against people being freed in that way.'

Corinne drained her glass and poured herself some more champagne. 'Don't you want any of this?'

Reuben clasped the glass she held out to him, and took several large gulps. 'Drink and be merry!' he said. 'What else can we do? It's the human condition.'

He gave the glass back to her, put his hands over his face and started to shake convulsively. He looked as if he could be laughing, but tears dripped through his fingers and ran down the backs of his hands. He was making an intermittent growling sound that came from his chest, quietly at first, then louder as he let his hands drop and his body moved with the grief, curling and uncurling with each sob like a sea creature in the ripples of the ocean.

Corinne moved closer and put her hand on his, 'Are you OK?'

'Don't worry about me,' he managed to say between gasps. 'I'm just letting it out. Like I was saying: release, integrate. I'll pull round in a few minutes.'

The words caught in his throat and he started coughing, his chest catching in spasms. He sounded as if he was choking. With her other hand Corinne gave him a couple of hard pats on the back.

He nodded. 'Again, please.'

She gave three more whacks and let her hand rest on his massive back like a tree trunk.

The coughing slowly subsided.

Then he started to cry again.

Corinne moved her hand in uncertain wandering circles over his back, smoothing and soothing the unknown contours. Raucous groans again started to heave through his frame, but now quieter, more moderate. His rubbery, swarthy face trembled with sorrow. The blanket around his chest was wet with tears by the time the sobs slowed.

She brought her hand back to the point at the centre of his shoulders where she had started and was about to move away.

'Don't stop,' he said.

She knelt up again and moved her hand with more confidence. Over his shoulder she saw quieter tears falling slowly onto the beige carpet.

'Thank you,' he said. 'Thank you.'

His breaths were heavy and his sounds more like low moans, caught by the occasional hiccup of a sob.

A last few shakes and sighs, and then there was silence and Reuben said, 'That's very nice what you're doing stroking my back.'

'Good.'

He added, 'But I'm afraid it's given me an erection.'

'Oh,' Corinne bit her lip. 'What happened? A moment ago you were crying like there was no tomorrow.'

Her hand stopped, then she carried on.

'Oh dear. This is embarrassing,' he said.

'You came round quick,' she said.

'I know,' said Reuben. He started to dry his eyes with the heels of his hands, and shuddered. 'Bio-energetic theory…' he started, but his voice failed him. He cleared his throat and shook his head and tried again: 'Bio-energetic theory does say that loosening up character armour through expressing emotion unlocks sexual energy. According to the books. Sounds more polite than talking about lust. This isn't the time or the place. Down, boy.'

Corinne continued stroking his shoulders and back, as if he hadn't spoken.

After a while Reuben said, 'That feels so good. I'm wondering, how far exactly are you prepared to go with this consolation business?'

'I don't know,' said Corinne. 'I don't know anything any more. I'm a lost person. Gales are blowing through me like an empty doorframe.'

There was a silence. Reuben took some deep breaths, and took her other hand in both of his. 'I must confess, I keep imagining you with no clothes on.'

Corinne hesitated, then said: 'Feel free.'

The blanket wrapped around Reuben slipped down, showing grizzled hairy shoulders. She stroked them along the top and between the shoulder blades.

Eventually he spoke: 'Did you by any chance have plans to go any further with this?'

Corinne replied, 'The way things are at the moment, I don't make plans. Plans happen to me.'

He turned towards her, studied her face, hesitated and then kissed her on the lips. He paused. 'Well, this is a surprise,' he said.

She looked at his face and then kissed him back.

He put his hands round her head, stroked her faded blond hair, looked her in the eye and kissed her again. 'You taste nice,' he said.

'Your father wouldn't mind…?'

'Me being with a *shicksa* on the night of his funeral? His life was taken from him, long before he died, by the cruelty and hatred of the world. What better way to redeem his death? Than by creating joy? What he'd say would be, "Is she a nice girl?".'

Corinne took her hand away. 'I was nice girl once.'

Reuben reclaimed the hand, pulled it towards him and kissed it. 'You *are* a nice girl, How can you doubt it?'

Corinne shrugged. 'I seem to be available.'

'Is that an invitation?'

'No invitation, but the door is open.'

'I don't want to trespass.'

'Oh, for goodness sake,' said Corinne. She took the blanket away from the rest of his body. Then she lifted off her jumper and undid her bra.

He reached out to touch her small breasts and then withdrew. 'Your body's very cold,' he said.

She moved closer and wrapped herself round him so that her breasts disappeared into the curly black hair on his chest.

'Wow,' he said, 'What are we doing? This is serious consolation.'

He paused, then spoke in a soft musical voice:

'"*Let us roll all our strength and all our sweetness up into one ball*

And tear our pleasures with rough strife thorough the iron gates of life".'

She asked, 'I get wooed with poetry?'

'You do. Andrew Marvell could tell it like it is. ' He

reached one arm across to delve in his hold-all and produced a condom.

'Oh,' said Corinne, 'I see you came to England prepared.'

'I too am available,' he said. 'At all times.'

'Some things don't change,' she said.

They kissed again while they tried to get the clothes off their lower bodies.

After a while he asked: 'Permission to come aboard?'

Corinne was lying on her back on the foam mattress as he climbed on top.

Then he stopped. 'Am I squashing you?' he asked, 'You seem so fragile I'm afraid you might break. Or evaporate in my hands.'

Corinne's face was blank, as if thinking about the answer to another question.

'I tell you what,' Reuben said. 'You on top of me?'

He lay on his back and Corinne climbed over. As their eyes linked again, he grinned: 'Consolation should always be like this.'

As Corinne lowered her thin body onto his broad hairy one, he made a guttural sound. His mobile features mimed shock, yearning, abandon, lust. The emptiness drained out of Corinne's face; it filled with suppressed laughter as his face played and his hands prowled and he kept reaching inside her to find a response. Their gasps melded into a duet as they found their pace and moved in unison like two experienced dancers mounting a neon-lit staircase step by step, their eyes never leaving each other's. At the top of the staircase, they grasped each other as they fell, weightless.

12

Chapter Twelve

Saturday 2nd February 1991 1am

Afterwards Corinne nestled into Reuben's arm.

He said, 'Are you all right? Sorry it was a bit short and sweet.'

'It was long enough,' she said. 'And it was very sweet.' Her tears were dropping onto the thick hairs of his chest.

'Crying?' he realized.

'Yes. Good tears. It's a relief.'

'Better out than in, as they say.'

'I've been frozen inside. You're like the Gulf Stream Drift, melting the glaciers.' She paused and wiped her eyes. 'Well, as you said yourself, any port in a storm.'

He said, 'Any port? More like a magic harbour decorated with fairy lights leading up to an enchanted castle with a maiden sat at the window waiting for something, I don't know what.' He paused. 'I'm not sure she knows either.'

Corinne said, 'It's a long time since I've been called a maiden.'

'Once a maiden, always a maiden,' Reuben replied. 'Has anyone ever managed to warm you?'

'You ask difficult questions.'

'That's my job, I'm a psychotherapist. We read people's feelings and bodies.'

'You're not at work now.'

'You can say that again. My work is never this pleasurable.' He kissed the top of her head. 'I would call these extra-curricular duties... It's tough,' he added with an exaggerated sigh, 'but someone's got to do it.'

They were stretched out on their backs on the narrow foam mattress on Ren's sitting room floor, looking up at the leaves moulded in plaster around the central light fitting above. Outside on Casenove Road there was no sound of traffic. He put a big hand on her naked stomach. She smiled and shut her eyes.

'It would be great if you could bottle happiness,' she said. 'You could rub it on yourself like fake suntan oil. I wonder if people would notice the difference.'

'Of course they would,' said Reuben. 'Screw that. Happiness comes from inside.'

'Does it?' she looked under her armpits and in her belly button. 'I never noticed any bursting out of me. When I'm alone and I look inside all I see is a long empty cold staircase leading down inside without light or colour. Harsh metallic walls and not a glimmer of comfort all the way down. Give me a fake suntan any day.'

Reuben raised his eyebrows. 'Ever gone down the staircase to see what's at the bottom?'

'I spend most of my time trying not to.'

'You don't want to know yourself better? Fair enough. It's not everyone's cup of tea.'

'I know you don't mean it that way, but I feel criticized,' said Corinne.

'No, I don't mean it that way. How about the comfort that comes from people around you? Good people who want you and care about you?'

'Like who?'

'Ren's a great person. She's having you to stay, evidently wants to look after you. I'm not a bad person. I have just shown you that I want you.'

'When I'm with other people I feel caught in a grey web, like a spider's web. With emptiness at the centre. It's not that I'm not grateful. It's just that nothing feeds my happiness. Things are still grey and cold.'

'She's wanted and she can't feel it. Tut tut.' He squeezed her close to him. 'What am I to do with you?'

'OK, you say you read bodies. So how do you read my body?'

He started to stroke it slowly. 'You really want to know?'

She smiled and rested her hand on his to keep it still. 'Go on, then.'

'If I'm right, I won't be telling you anything you don't know already.'

'Are you prevaricating?'

'I have to re-adjust. We just made love. To me right now your body is a wrap-around experience: a sensation, a delicious presence that blends into mine and I'm not sure where the edge is. You're asking me to step back and scan your body, respond to it, as something separate from me.' He sat up and looked down at her lying on the mattress. 'To me it just looks beautiful...' He stopped and smacked his head: 'Start again!'

He shut his eyes and waited. When he opened them he said, 'OK, you did ask. As I look at it now, to me, your body has a lonely feel to it. Your shoulders, the way you draw them in, it's like you're permanently cold and there's nobody to warm you. As a man who has just got to know you in the biblical sense, I want to put both my hairy arms round you and draw you in to me. As a therapist, of course, I would leave you cold and encourage you to feel the feelings.'

'Why?'

'Because one hug doesn't heal anything. It's a temporary solution. Like Elastoplast. That coldness comes from your past. As long as the childhood feelings stay locked away, they'll keep sending that chill through your body. Feeling them again, that's the only way you can ever work through them and free yourself. That's the theory. Regression, re-enactment or re-living of childhood pain; then re-assimilation, resolution and healing. That's the underlying principle of most therapies. Revisiting past difficulty in a situation where you have awareness, support and a compassionate presence in the now. A compassionate presence...' his face lit up in an expression of exaggerated glee. 'That's me!'

'Regression. Re-enactment. Sounds scary. What else do you read in my body, Mr. Therapist?'

'You want to go on with this?'

She nodded.

'Your arms, see how thin they are. You hold them close to your sides. To me they look underused. Like they've given up. How would it feel to reach for something? And believe you might get it?'

Tears sprang back into Corinne's eyes. 'I may as well tell you. My lover rejected me.'

'He's a foolish man. But those arms grew into that posture when you were a child.' Reuben paused. 'This is all a bit personal. You OK with this?'

Corinne sighed. 'I have no edges any more. Anyone can step inside.'

'Anyone?'

'Well, not quite anyone, but you can. Say what you like. I'm past caring.'

Reuben hesitated, then said: 'Like I said, my sense is that you are wanted now; how could you not be? You're a lovely woman. You are wanted, but you can't feel it. As if being rejected was a way of life. Maybe some ongoing lack or loss early on in life... Not daring to reach out...'

'Not daring to reach out?' Corinne frowned. 'What would I reach out for? I'll just be disappointed.'

'You don't know till you try,' said Reuben,

'Believe me, I've tried.'

'Have you? I know it's scary.'

'What, just doing this?' Corinne took a deep breath and lifted her arms out in front of her as she lay.

'Hold on!' said Reuben, 'You want to try it now?'

'No time like the present,' said Corinne. 'It can't make me feel worse than I already do.'

Reuben put on a pretend professorial voice. 'This is very irregular, madam. Not consistent with clinical practice.'

'I thought your lot were all: "Do it, Do it now!" Have you renounced your past?'

Reuben pretended to stroke a non-existent professorial beard, then let his hand drop. 'Oh, well, break a few rules…'

Corinne held up her arms and her breath speeded up.

'Take it gently,' said Reuben. 'Long out breath. You don't want to hyperventilate. Hold the position and let your body do the rest.'

As she breathed slowly and regularly, more tears started to spill from Corinne's eyes down the sides of her face onto the pillow.

'All very unprofessional,' he said. 'But I see you're going for it and it doesn't look like anything can stop you…' He scratched his head and spoke quietly: 'Do you have a picture in your mind?'

'Yes, sort of… I'm lying waiting for something. I can't move. I'm listening, there's something I want to hear but I can't hear it. My ears are straining. I'm waiting.' She made a stifled sound.

'You can make a noise if you want to,' said Reuben, 'On the out breath. You could call for the thing you're waiting for.'

'I can't,' said Corinne.

'You could if you wanted.'

'It won't help.'

'It might.'

'How do you know?'

'You could try.'

'It would make things worse,' she said.

'You don't know that.'

'I can't do it,' said Corinne.

Down on the pavement outside Ren's sitting room window, two male voices passed by, laughing and discussing football.

'If you did make a sound,' said Reuben, 'What would the sound be like?'

Corinne made a quiet broken cry. Then a half-choked moan. Than a strangled shout.

'Is that it?' said Reuben.

Corinne took some more deep breaths with a long out breath. Then her jaw dropped and she let out a wail. It was a piercing wail that galvanized her body like an electric shock. It drew itself out, on and on like elastic stretching beyond its limits. It stopped, she took a breath, and it started again louder than ever, the howl of a wounded animal without hope or consolation. On and on. She took another breath and the wail ran on again, like a river that has burst its banks flooding free. Eventually she fell silent, her limbs went limp and she curled on her side, coughing and crying.

Reuben put a hand on her back. After a while he said, 'That was some wail.'

'Was it?' whispered Corinne.

'Yes,' said Reuben. 'I think it searched every room in the house, ruffled the surface of the water in the sink, shook the kitchen cups on their hooks and made the pile on the stair carpet stand on end before it soared up the stairs and set the window panes rattling as it escaped at the top. It was some wail. You've probably got a few more of those in there.' He stroked her back. 'Did you have a picture of the time when you needed to wail like that? Who you were? Where you were?'

She nodded. 'You want me to tell you?'

'Only if you want to.'

'In the picture in my mind I was very little. Lying in some kind of cot.'

'Yes.' He brought his hand to rest on her upper back. 'Rest now.'

She wept for a while, then pulled herself to sitting and put her hand on his chest. 'Would you like to make love again? It may sound strange but it would give me some comfort.' Her hand strayed down the front of his body as tears still trailed down her cheeks.

He moved her hand back and put both arms around her. 'Not now,' he said. 'You need to stay with what's going on. There's nothing I'd rather do than share another moment of passion with you. I'm not rejecting you, far from it, but it wouldn't be fair. Your body's too open and vulnerable now. It needs time to process what's been happening. Let it find its own comfort. I don't want to interfere with that.' He paused. 'Much as I'd like to.'

Corinne dropped from him face down onto the floor and sobbed. Reuben wrapped the blanket around her and put his hand on the place behind her heart. 'Let it out,' he said. 'Muggins is here.'

Saturday 2nd February 1991 12.15pm

We're lining up along the Embankment getting ready to march. It's a fine clear day, but there's an icy wind straight from Siberia. I think we're going to get more snow this winter.

It's a familiar ritual: the huge crowds gathering along the Embankment with a hum of excitement that builds until it's echoing up into the trees like a giant cathedral. More people than you can count. More people than you can imagine.

Everyone from our house is here. Even Morton, though he's knackered after his lecture yesterday and he was debating the effectiveness of large demonstrations all the way down on the bus. Even Freddie, who's all for peace but doesn't like to shout about it.

The big organizations are at the front. CND, the Green Party, and the few Labour MPs who have the courage to speak out against the war in the Gulf. There's the National Union of Students, the miners of course – the NUM – and the Fire Brigades Union, and then you get all the little local groups and branches. Then there are banners you'd never expect. Pensioners for Peace, some of them don't look as if they'll make it to Hyde Park. Wetherby Co-operative Society. The Anglican Pacifist Fellowship. Truro Anarchists. We walk down from the front, looking for a space where we can slot into the procession as it waits to begin. We slip in behind a branch of the National Union of Teachers from Leeds. They've given up their Saturday after a hard week and must have got up at 5am for a long coach journey to get here on time. It's a massive display of the human ability to connect. Everyone here cares that people they don't know at the other end of Europe – innocent people in Iraq – are being bombed in their homes.

I'm used to being in crowds. Like anyone who lives in London. But this is different from most crowds. Shoppers on a busy pavement squeeze past each other. Travellers at a big railway station dodge each other, race and circle. Morton's always telling me what a collective project life is, like when you see footage of cars at a roundabout, speeded up on film. They weave through each other with such grace and care. Miraculously avoiding crashes. He's right, it's a huge feat of cooperation. But in all those situations, each is pursuing their own individual path and negotiating around the others. Each car driver wants to go where *they* want to go. Each passenger's thinking about *their* luggage, and getting in time to *their* train.

This is different. Everyone here has a common purpose. All these people. It's so powerful it's overwhelming.

I'm starting to feel a migraine coming on. My eyes are hollowed out. Somewhere under the skin of my face there are tears.

As we stand there in line waiting to move off, sometimes people come up and speak to us.

A woman gives me a leaflet headed 'Angry women say STOP the killing'. I read that they're doing a women's peace vigil outside the Foreign Office twenty-four hours a day. If I was more organized I'd get myself down there. I show it to Morton.

'Angry women for peace,' he says. 'Now there's a contradiction.'

I'm indignant. 'Where d'you get that idea? You can be angry about injustice and want to stop it! You can be angry about war and demonstrate against it in the hopes of getting peace!'

He gives me one of his 'whatever-you-say-dear-I'm not going-to argue-with-you' looks, and a big smile. He can be infuriating sometimes.

A small dark man carrying a placard 'Revolutionary Left (Devrimci Sol) in Turkey' comes up to me with a wadge of leaflets.

'This is a brutal massacre,' he tells me. 'One of the worst we've seen in the Middle East. And that says something! They're drowning the area in blood and fire, and turning Iraq into a hell.' He hands me an A4 sheet with close lines of typewritten text on it and says, 'The press are under the control of the powers that be. They're using lies and distorted news to try to hide the horror and savagery of what takes place…'

The language sounds OTT. This man could be labelled

an extremist, that's how the media make us think. I have to remind myself it's the powers that be, who are ordering the killing, that are the extremists. And anyone who points this out is seen as deranged. The truth is so far-fetched that people don't want to hear it; they want to shoot the messenger.

A frisson passes down the long chain of humanity, like wind across a cornfield. We're going to move.

I take the leaflet from the man. It's produced by Turkish Moslems in solidarity with Iraqi Moslems who are getting hammered by the West. I wonder how many of the Turkish restaurants in Stoke Newington are closed today. I read some of the leaflet:

'The war is being waged in the name of the imperialist monopolies and oil sheiks. Their assault is led by the USA and actively supported by Britain, France and Saudi Arabia, while...'

Then a roar of excitement stops me. The march is starting to go forward. I fold the leaflet and put it in my pocket.

We move forward a few yards, and stop again.

I hear somebody calling 'Freddie!' I look up and see it's a small woman about my age with wispy blond hair. She's in a group walking in the opposite direction down the other side of the road, they must be looking for a space further back down the march. One of them's carrying a placard saying 'BUSH IS A MURDERER', and another has a placard 'NO WAR FOR OIL!'.

They too will be labelled 'extremists' in the newspapers. If the demo gets mentioned at all. I still can't get over the injustice of that. It's what western governments are doing that's beyond the pale. Thousands of civilians being killed in their beds.

Freddie's next to me. He hasn't heard the woman calling his name, and she's carried on by her group. She turns back and calls again. He hears too late, turns and sees her waving, goes white as a sheet and stops in his tracks. The march starts going forward again, and people behind us get held up in a jam. By the time he unfreezes, she's gone, lost in the crowd. Then everyone starts moving forward faster and he just about keeps up though he keeps looking backwards. Very uncool for Freddie.

Now that we're moving steadily, the singing and chanting starts to build. It rebounds between the buildings on either side. 'STOP THE SLAUGHTER!' It's a kind of sing-song, down on 'the', up on 'slaught' and back to the first note on 'er'. So many voices that the first ones are starting again before the ones behind have finished on the 'er'. Like there are so many of us that the front banners will have arrived at Hyde Park before the last marchers have left the Embankment.

Now we're turning into Whitehall. The Ministry of Defence building is on our right. There's a statue of Field Marshal Montgomery, and someone's put a pink tutu on it. Off on the other side is the unhearing door of 10 Downing Street behind those new iron gates.

There are people wandering up and down with buckets; they're on a drive to collect for victims of the bombing. Morton won't donate: 'Makeshift solutions,' he says. 'Stopping the war in the first place, that's the challenge.'

The buildings at the side of the road slide by in a haze. I lose a sense of which part of London we're in. The demo creates its own geography, a complex internal dynamic of groups and strands and friendships with different chants and banners, drumming and songs. Solid blocks with linked arms, pile-ups, gaps, people running to catch up. Every so often I catch the strain of a brass band playing nearer to the head of the march.

Bert is carrying a placard that he made himself, it says 'WAR KILLS PEOPLE'. Good slogan: simple and direct. We persuaded him to leave Dusty at home, this would be too much for her. I hope it isn't too much for him. It could feel threatening if you don't understand why people are here. I look up and see a window full of watching faces. I wave. I hope we look friendly. Not like a hostile mob. I'd like to shout up to them: We're on your side! We're on the side of human beings, and against bombs and corporations and suffering. But they can't hear me, stuck on the other side of the glass pane. Inside there they may be reading the *Telegraph* or the *Mail* and watching the TV spectacle of the war being played out like a video game; they may think we're extremists too. They may enjoy the vicarious violence of the Gulf War, thinking our country has God on its side. And that we who are against the war are the baddies.

As the sounds of the march lift and soar, I feel myself dissolving into them. I am part of one giant creature, a creature of compassion. I can feel my heart stretching sideways to include all these people. My eyes are aching. My head is exploding. The first real warning I get of the migraine is a zig-zag lightning flash on the left of my vision. I realize the light is too bright. The sound is too loud. That fierce caring voice of 10,000 people is racing through my veins. I think of that quote about how the just man rages in the wild… It's a fallacy that a just person has to be quiet and peaceful… No. If you want justice you have to yell and rage against the injustices committed in our name. These people are raging at the world's cruelty.

Apart from us, the streets are deserted. We're singing to no audience, but we are the show and the audience in one, filling the theatre of central London. All you see is faces, faces, and feet on the tarmac. We have come out of the earth, crawled out of the woodwork, swarmed into the streets. I am part of one huge body with thousands of legs, a monstrous millipede singing as it goes, serenading the empty auditorium of central London. The shouting is so vast that it seems to come from the air itself and bounce off the clouds. I am melting into our common soul.

It is lucky that Freddie, still ashen-faced, is there to catch me when I fall.

Friday 8th February 1991 11am

I sink heavily into Ren's wicker chair. 'Hello.' I'm dreading telling Ren what I did on Monday night. Why did I do it? Maybe I was still disoriented after that heavy migraine and fainting last Saturday on the demo. Or maybe I'm just trying to think of excuses.

Ren smiles. 'I'll start the tape. I guess you're used to it by now?'

'Sort of.'

'How are things?' she asks.

'In the daytime, fine. In the hours of darkness, nightmares… And a lot's been going on. Lectures, demonstrations… And since I last saw you I did something really drastic. And stupid. About Dr. Scheiner. I'd like to get it off my chest. The truth is that I feel ashamed…'

'Do you want to talk about it now?'

I stand up and walk up and down. I stop to touch the potted plant by the door. I take a tissue from the low table and wipe my nose. I'm stalling. Then I make a tentative start.

'All I can say in my defense is that I was convinced Dr. Scheiner had tried to save my life in some previous world. The dream I told you – where I'm trapped, walled in, and him with his bare hands trying to move the stones – that dream kept recurring. As you know, I did try talking to him face to face in his office. It didn't work. I needed to know if I was imagining things or if there really was a connection between us. Something old. Something that still existed perhaps at a dream level. Then I had an idea: incubation.'

'Incubation?'

I sit down to explain. 'Do you remember me talking about it? How in the ancient world people would go and sleep in a special place – at a sanctuary or in someone's tomb – to communicate with the dead person. Could be an ancestor or another person, or could be a healer who has been deified. They thought that in your sleep, in a dream state, you could have special access to non-physical beings – spirits, I suppose you'd call them, of the dead. So I decided to try it.' I wonder how this is sounding to her. 'I know Dr. Scheiner isn't dead,' I add, 'but I thought if it was a time he was asleep it might work the same way.'

Ren raises her smooth hairless brows. 'You decided to try incubation – where?'

'I decided on his office. Dr. Scheiner's office. If he couldn't acknowledge the connection via his conscious self, then maybe he could unconsciously. And the best way to reach his unconscious was through a special place that was permeated with his being. He's an academic – so that would be his office.'

'I see…'

I look at Ren and try to work out what she's thinking. 'I told you there was a reason for people to say I'm going crazy. Can you bear to hear this?'

Ren smiles. 'I am happy to hear anything you want to tell me. It is not my role to judge in any way.'

'Thank you. Obviously it had to be at night. I won't go into the logistics: how I went in to the archaeology library and worked there till it closed, then I went to the toilets closest to his office and hid. I waited until all the lights were off everywhere and I was sure everyone had gone home and all the offices were empty.

'Then I crept out of the toilets and let myself in to his office. They don't lock the individual studies at night.

'Inside it was quite overpowering in the dark. The high bookcases lining the walls up to the ceiling. The whole

place absolutely dripping with books, they were like a
dark enveloping presence watching me from all around the
room. I flashed my tiny torch around. That, my front door
key, my membership card for getting into the library, and
the money for my fare home, they were all I had with me.
Normally I carry loads of bags, you've probably noticed,
but it felt important to go with nothing. I felt naked alone
in the dark in this stronghold of learning with the books
looming over me.

'His desk was neat and tidy. There was a little old
portable typewriter sitting in its case. What looked like an
'in' file and an 'out' file in metal trays. A pad of paper and a
sharpened pencil. A phone. A paperweight in the shape of
a replica of a prehistoric figurine, a 'fat lady' squatting – I
could identify with her. No photographs on the desktop. I
realized how little I knew about his personal life. Academics
tend to keep that separate from their jobs.

'There was a large window which looked out on to an
internal courtyard of the university. Some decades ago the
authorities decided they needed to use the space in that
courtyard, so it was filled with ugly ramshackle buildings
and Nissen huts. The paths leading around them were
empty, only a little light spilling onto them from the street
lights on the other side of the administration block.

'I sat on the floor and waited till it was late enough
to sleep. I didn't want to sit in his chair at his desk, that
would be intrusive. It had been a cold day, and at some
point the heating switched itself off. The floor was hard. I
shut my eyes and tried to blend into the atmosphere of the
room, but I was so anxious that my pulse was racing and I
couldn't relax.

'It seemed like hours passed before my watch said 11 pm.
I was wearing a warm fleece and I spread it on the floor to
curl up on in one corner. I took the hard-edged things out of
my pockets – the money, the key, the library card, the torch

– and tried to make myself comfortable.

'I lay and waited.

'It took me ages to get to sleep. The place was so quiet. You could hardly hear the traffic on the road. Parts of central London are fairly abandoned at night. Around me all the empty portals of learning of the university were holding their breath in the dark. At one point I thought I heard tiptoeing footsteps in the corridor, but then I put it down to imagination. I thought about Dr. Scheiner and wondered if some part of him knew I was there or would somehow contact me.

'When I finally dropped off it was a cold, hard-edged sleep where part of me was always a bit awake and protesting at the discomfort. I think those incubation rooms at places like Epidaurus were not luxurious either – they were basically underground chambers with earth or stone floors and no mod cons. And the ancient Greeks put up with it, hoping that a vision of the dead hero Asclepius would appear in their sleep and give them medical advice. So I had to put up with it too.

'I don't know how late it was when it happened.

'I can't remember how long I'd been asleep when I opened my eyes and saw the thing. I don't know how to describe it. It wasn't making any noise apart from a kind of shimmering sound like a whoosh of electricity or the hum of light. It was huge and it was shaped like a human figure, a man, and its outline was picked out in a kind of pulsating glow and there were lines of light all over it like a net, or like arteries carrying not blood but light. It was quite close, it towered over me as I lay there, I felt it was looking at me and it kind of shone or radiated stuff at me. It felt threatening. Maybe because I was so terrified to see such a thing, or maybe because it didn't want me in there.

'I went rigid. I don't know how long I stared at it and it stared at me but at a certain point the terror was so great that I passed out.

'I woke up in the most bitter early morning hours, shivering and wishing Morton was there. I'd told him I was staying with a friend.

'I felt convinced of one thing: that I shouldn't be there. That this was all a terrible mistake. That if the conscious Dr. Scheiner didn't want to speak to me in the day world, then his unconscious sure as hell did not want me in his office in the night world. I felt devastated at what I'd done and been through.'

'What then?' asks Ren.

'I heard cleaners further down the corridor. I had to get out fast. I crept out into the corridor in the first glimmers of early morning light. I went to hide in the toilet until I could merge with the general traffic of people along the corridors later in the morning. I went home and ate half of what was in the fridge then went to bed with a migraine. I couldn't talk to Morton about it.'

'You couldn't?'

'He and I are very different, maybe that's why we get on. He's calm and impassive. It's not that he isn't spiritual, though he would find some clever argument to reject that word. But his idea of spirituality is sitting back and watching. It makes me feel as if he's acting superior.'

'Is that a problem for you?'

'It makes me feel like a blundering idiot crashing around. Over the top. I didn't dare tell anyone what I'd done. I never wanted to go back to the library or anywhere near that place again.

'But in the event, I was found out anyway by the last person I wanted to know about it: Dr. Scheiner himself.'

'That must have been difficult,' says Ren.

I bury my head in my hands remembering how terrible it was. 'It was Monday night I stayed there. Last Monday. That must have been the 4th. Then on Wednesday I got a phone call at home from the departmental secretary saying could I come in to see Dr. Scheiner at his office as soon as possible. I feared the worst, though I never imagined what had actually happened: I'd left my library card on the floor in there.

'When I picked up the other little things, for some reason I had forgotten the card. The cleaners found it and handed it in to the departmental secretary, and when I plucked up courage to go in there yesterday, it was in Dr. Scheiner's hand as he stood there in the door of his office staring at me. His gingery hair stood on end as usual. His glasses rested on the bottom of his nose. His face looked alarmed. Over his shoulder I could see the towering shelves of books inside. He did not invite me in, as if I needed somehow to be kept at bay.

'"This seems rather strange," he said. "I find it hard to understand how this card made its way into my office. You have not had any reason to be in my office in the last few days?" He handed it over and after a pause he added, "Without my being here?"

'I didn't know what to say. I just looked at him. And the strange thing was, he stood there and just looked at me too. For much longer than would happen in a normal conversation. He stood there, looking at me, and I stood there looking back. As if there were a conversation going on that neither of us were aware of. As if the situation enchained us in a dialogue I couldn't hear. At some level I felt sure that he knew what I'd done. It felt like we were chess pieces in a game being played by someone else, and some over-riding intelligence held us both in place.

'His face worked and changed. Then in the end he spoke:

'"Connections cannot be forced. You need to remember this."

'Then he turned round and went into his office and shut the door.

I look into Ren's face. 'What did he mean by that? Was he talking about my research and me trying to make links between divination and bones? Was it him coming out with a general comment about my work? Or was it about the connection between the two of us that I was experiencing? How did he get to that comment from the appearance of my library card in his office? I couldn't understand any of it. Can you?'

Ren thinks for some time. 'You had a strange experience, Anthea, that much is clear.'

I ask, 'Can you explain it? Was it just a silly imagining?'

She replies, 'I'm not here to judge your experience, that's not my role. I'm here to witness it and to help you process it. To make what sense of it is right for you.'

I can't let go of the question that's preoccupying me: 'How can I find out if what I'm experiencing is real?'

She says, 'Intellectual assertions can be tested and contested. But that's not true in the area of religion. Or the world of the spirit more generally. Millions of people the world over believe that Moses saw a burning bush and that an angel appeared to shepherds when Jesus was born. How can we question such beliefs? Just because we haven't seen such visions ourselves? For centuries people have reported similarly strange experiences, waking and sleeping visions. Some think they are proof of the existence of supernatural beings. Some think they are the products of an overheated imagination. Was what you saw the result of your fear, tension and loneliness sleeping in that office? Or was it the presence of some entity in that room responding to your presence? Or even some manifestation of Dr. Scheiner himself? Did you imagine the whole thing? We can't know the answer to that. But there are some things we can know.'

'What are they?' I ask Ren. I am trying not to sound pathetic. But I feel pathetic. 'I feel so lost with this.'

'You know that you felt uncomfortable in that office.

That means it was not a good place for you to be. That is not a matter of blame, and it has nothing to do with breaking university rules. The issue is self-protection, to keep you safe from others' ill-will, situations you'll regret, and your own self-criticism.

'It's also a question of awareness of others. You know that Dr. Scheiner can't respond to you in the way you want him to. You've said this yourself. He has told you that himself in several ways, as best he can. Even if what you believe about your link with him were true, he can't hear it. Respect him for who he is: a kind academic who finds your ideas and behaviour plunge him way out of his depth. You don't need to unleash every genie from every bottle. Some things need to stay contained.'

'But is it true? I don't know what kind of place the world is any more.'

'Nobody knows. None of us can know. The art of living is about learning to survive as best we can with that uncertainty.'

Sunday 10th February 1991 11am
Inside the café the windows are wet with the breath of walkers and tobogganers trying to get warm after playing on the Heath. I'm sitting at a table sipping a hot chocolate with our sledge leaning on the back of my chair. I speak my thoughts. 'I shouldn't be drinking this. I am going to get a migraine.'

'You need to get warmed up, Ant,' says Morton, 'Gives me a chance to read the news.' He settles into his chair and opens up the *The Guardian*.

I gulp my chocolate down. I want to get out. 'Let's go back and do more tobogganing.'

'More?'

'More!'

Morton looks at me with that half-amused look he specializes in. '"More! More! is the cry of a mistaken soul…"'

'Don't tell me, that's Blake.'

'"…Less than all cannot satisfy man."'

A wave of annoyance sweeps over me. 'I'm not even sure what it means. I bet Blake liked tobogganing and came back for more.'

'He didn't want to settle for less than all.'

This is the disadvantage of living with a clever clogs university lecturer. You can't argue with them. I say, 'What is "all" except more and more and more?'

Morton wipes the steam off the window pane with a maroon paper napkin and looks out. 'It's the space around the more.'

I try again. 'All I know is, when we're racing down Kite Hill I can feel the speed skimming past my ears. The shouts coming over the frozen air like a symphony in stereo. It's glorious. And I want more.'

Morton gestures towards the hill, 'Look at the heavy birdless sky. The rooks' nests in the trees. You can fly there without moving.'

So he's turning romantic. Two can play at that.

'No, no,' I say, 'it's the rope in my hands. The wind from Siberia making my eyes water. The shine on the runway. The rust on the toboggan blade scraping on the snow. The staring, wide-eyed whiteness. The cold burning my lungs. I want to drink in more. Forget the newspapers.' I slide back my chair to make more room for a big gesture of dismissing newspapers and, as I do, the sledge slips and falls on the café floor with a crash. People at the nearby tables turn to stare. Morton sighs, puts *The Guardian* away, and picks up the sled off the floor. I win. Enjoy it, Ant. It doesn't happen that often.

As we're walking back up the snowy hill, with the toboggan following us on its lead, Morton rests his arm on my shoulder and starts whispering in my ear: 'Look at the bundled-up figures dotted over the hillside like dice in a marathon game of chance. Hear the hush of the blanket of whiteness. Feel the waiting that envelops us all, like time stood still. You don't have to do anything, just witness.'

I sometimes think he has secret ambitions to be a poet. Perhaps all academics are mourning a side of their nature that is not meant to enter the process of scholarly research. That's why they end up writing children's stories about elves and lions. Maybe that's why Morton's in full metaphorical vein today. Or maybe he's feeling a release as the relief sinks in of having finally done his big public lecture the other week.

At the top of the hill I sit myself down on the toboggan. He pulls my red hat down over my hair, kisses my nose and whispers, 'Sense the rhythm of the sledges scooping down, the insistent pull of gravity making idiots of us all. You get the wider picture?' His breath in my ear tickles.

'You're watching instead of living,' I say.

'You're omnivorous,' he says, 'But you can't eat the snow. I'm breathing it in. That way I have it all.'

'All or nothing,' I say.

'That's it,' he says. He gets on behind me and pushes us off down the slope.

Sunday 10th February 1991 11am

'How're you feeling?' Ren asked Corinne as they got off the North London Line train at Gospel Oak.

Corinne shrugged. 'A little bit better. Enjoyed that demonstration last week. Your friends made me feel very welcome. I'd never been on one before.'

'I'm sorry I missed it. And was it sexual healing the other night with Reuben?'

'Afraid so. Do you mind?'

'Should I?'

'It was your friend and your sitting room floor.'

'No problem. If you're treating both well and enjoying them. If it helps,' said Ren. They came down the steps and out of the station and turned to walk towards Hampstead Heath. 'But I don't know how you do it. There was Taffy too.'

'Everything pours into a void,' said Corinne. 'It passes through me and leaves no trace. Nothing sticks. I can't hold anything.'

Snow that had fallen in the past few days lay in dirty piles along the side of the pavement, and the cold air pinched their flesh.

'Is it always like that with you?' asked Ren.

'When I'm in crisis. When I'm in meltdown. Like now. Like in 1971. Everything inside me has been washed away. There's an abyss that needs filling. At least I'm not filling it with alcohol any more.'

'And Reuben helped?'

Corinne nodded. 'And I've remembered where I saw him before. In 1971, when you were all at the squat, I was working on a play site not far away. He came round one night and talked to us about collaborating doing activities with kids on the patch of land you'd occupied, though we never did. He left a copy of *The Society of the Spectacle* which I read from cover to cover. That was twenty years ago. I wonder what happened to it.'

'It was his favourite book', said Ren.

They walked on in silence. On the slopes of Hampstead Heath there was still an uneven carpet of white, in some places worn threadbare so that the grass showed through, in other places crispy white corrugations showing traces of human activity: footprints, furrows, sledge marks, the remains of snowmen.

'Honest,' said Corinne. 'I haven't been doing a survey of

the talent from your squat. Honest.' She laughed.

'Some talent,' said Ren. 'We're all getting on a bit... Anyway, it's good to see you laughing.'

'They're both nice guys,' said Corinne.

'But only for a one-night stand?'

'It's like billiard balls brushing past each other. Or stars passing in outer space. Dazzling, but we're each on our own trajectories. No way to team up. I'm in no state to start a relationship. I'm still bleeding from the last one.' Corinne dragged her feet through the snow at the side of the path. 'I've learnt so much from your squat. In different ways.'

'You have?' said Ren. 'Like what? That gang of ne'er-do-wells, railing against the system and causing each other grief?'

Corinne thought for a few minutes, then said, 'I've never felt part of anything. Never felt I belonged. Your lot – despite the problems and personal failings, which you're all honest about – you worked together. And for the good. You believed you could work things through and go for something together.'

'With varying degrees of success.' Ren smiled. 'Who can tell what is achieved in terms of making a better world... And forgiveness is always hard...'

'Forgiveness?'

'Hanging in calls for big doses of forgiveness on a daily basis. Forgiving the imperfections of oneself, of other people, of the world...'

'I never thought it was possible to make a difference to anything. Or even to try.' Corinne pulled her coat collar up round her neck. 'I wonder if people will still be tobogganning on Kite Hill? Shall we go and have a look? Perhaps I should take advantage of my last day of freedom.'

Ren asked, 'How many months do you think they'll give you? Or rather, take away from you?'

'The solicitor said maybe three months. But I might get

let off with community service.'

Ren glanced sideways at her. 'Are you nervous?'

'Since I got dry, there is constant fear. Like steel in my bones holding me rigid.' She stared at the ground. In a pair of too-large wellingtons borrowed from Ren, and padded inside with Ren's socks, her feet were moving slowly one in front of the other up the tarmac path towards Kite Hill. She avoided the icy bits. 'I am just going through the motions,' she said.

'I'm sorry I can't be in court with you,' said Ren. 'The insurer's assessor wouldn't come any other day, and we all have to be there.'

'Was a lot taken?'

'What's to interest a burglar in rooms used by alternative therapists? Half-used scented candles, mandalas and orthopaedic couches… ? But I had all kinds of small bits of equipment and clutter taken, important to me but worthless to anyone else. The taperecorder, confidential tapes of sessions, a nice vase which might have looked valuable. Some of the others had cash on the premises. Do you have anyone else to turn up in court, to support you?'

Corinne shook her head. 'I haven't told anyone. Terry doesn't know anything about what's going on.'

'Terry?' Ren turned her head.

'My bloke. Or rather, my ex-bloke.'

'Oh. You never mentioned his name before.'

'Terry. Tel,' said Corinne. 'We've been together about ten years. But he feels so far away now, it jars to say his name.'

'Tel,' Ren repeated the name. 'Does he know where you are?'

'No. He said he never wanted to see me again.'

'And you believed him?'

'I'm not expecting to see him.'

'After ten years?' Ren screwed up her face. 'You've given up on him just like that?'

'Guess so.'

They were passing the café and looked up towards the hill where muffled figures moved like dots on the white backdrop. Distant whoops bounced around the sky while the sledges disappeared down the snowy slopes. Corinne turned to Ren: 'Could watching them cheer us up?'

As they approached Kite Hill, Ren sneezed. She took off her gloves finger by finger to reach into her pocket for a tissue. Corinne watched two people on a old wooden toboggan speeding down towards them. Their faces were wrapped up, but she could see that the woman in front, wearing a red hat, had a smile of triumph on her face.

At the same moment Corinne saw a youth ambling out from behind a bush into their path. He was looking behind him, talking to a friend. He had an improvised sled, a yellow cement bag, tucked under his arm, and he was laughing. Round his neck he had a knitted woollen scarf, a patchwork of bright colours, hippy style. Corinne took it all in like the click of a camera: the couple sledding down at breakneck speed, the young man looking backwards, the scarf, the collision about to happen.

The woman on the toboggan was closer now; she saw the danger too. Her face changed but she couldn't change course. Corinne and Ren were nearly at the bush. The youth in the scarf was taking a last step backwards onto the sled's path. Ren had turned away, blowing her nose. Corinne stepped out. She grabbed one end of the scarf and yanked it hard. It pulled tight round his throat. He stopped in his tracks and put his hand to his throat.

'What the fuck…?'

The toboggan skimmed past him and Corinne turned to watch it slow at the bottom of the slope, veer off course, and eventually empty its two riders gently in a tangle of arms and legs cushioned in the snow.

She looked back at the young man with the scarf, who

was pulling on it and staring at her.

She let go of the end. 'Sorry,' she said. 'Nice scarf.'

We're half way down, going at rip-roaring speed, when I see a boy ahead stepping out into our path. He's not looking where he's going. How do you steer these things? Pulling on the rope does nothing. I tug on it, it's useless, we could kill him at the speed we're going. Or kill ourselves. Nightmare comes quickly. I shut my eyes, bracing myself for the collision.

Then nothing happens. When I open them, we're past that place. I lurch to one side as I try to look, we swerve and lose balance where it levels out near the bottom of the hill. We end up capsized, rolling over in the snow with the sledge behind us. I roll into Morton's arms and we kiss.

'See what I mean?' Morton says laughing, and he gets onto his knees and shakes the snow out of his coat sleeves. 'That guy! Nearly a nasty accident. I thought we were gonners. Or was it part of a grand plan? Our pathways on the ice crossing with other people, our stories intersecting. Steering a course between hazard and choice. Do we choose to touch each other or not, as we pass?'

'You saw him too? I couldn't avoid him,' I say. 'I tried. Then I just shut my eyes. I don't know why I didn't crash into him.'

'"Trying". Ineffectual.' Morton is still smiling as he sits beside me. 'For some reason that young man changed direction. So maybe without doing anything one can dodge fate. With a bit of luck.'

I throw myself back flat onto the snow. 'OK, OK, we'll go. I give in. I won't cancel the field trip. I'll stop being stupid about it.' I think about the thing I saw in Dr. Scheiner's office: no good comes from messing with that superstitious nonsense. None of it makes sense.

'OK!' I say to Morton. 'Maybe I can dodge fate. We'll go to Greece.' I drum my heels on the ground, fling my arms out to either side and gaze up at the sky. The size of it takes my breath away. 'We'll go!'

'That's my girl,' says Morton, 'Off we go!' He grabs my two feet and starts to pull me along through the snow. I'm surprised he's strong enough to shift me.

'Leggo!' I grab him round the legs and fell him, and we roll together in a ball, half cuddling and half fighting.

When eventually we stand up, I take my hat off and shake the snow out of my hair and he dusts himself down. 'As I was saying...' he says, 'before I was so rudely interrupted, the singular can be exquisite. But it's one-sided. Why should we take what is individual as the essence of life rather than multiformity?'

We set off up the hill round the other side, pulling the sledge behind.

'Great creative works are produced by individuals,' I say. 'Take Aeschylus with his craggy, monumental tragedies, towering over the start of western literature.'

'But before him, there are Homer's epics. Homer is many. Many singing voices over the centuries, many hands on the lyre, many imaginations weaving the ancient stories together. And what about the *Thousand and One Nights*, a labyrinthine multiplicity of tales? Remember Pasolini's quote at the start of his film of it: "The truth lies not in one but in many dreams..."'

The speed he's walking and talking, I'm getting out of breath. 'I know,' I say. 'I've heard your lecture. But it takes one person to write a novel.'

'And think how many people's experience that can encompass. Anyway, the novel is a local obsession, historically. Much older is the folk tale. Rediscovered by scholars in the 19th century. Not the grand narrative of a single hero or heroine but a patchwork of stories reflecting ordinary lives over the centuries: people's daily work, their hopes and fantasies. Each person perfect and different like snowflakes or a million daisies in a field, linked by the hidden beauty of their collaboration in the dance of life.'

At the top of the hill I turn to face him: 'You're smug, opinionated, and you could talk the hind leg off a donkey. I can't argue with you. All I know is, I'm sure that's not what Blake meant about experiencing things. It's not either/or. What he meant was both. Hearing the scrape of the toboggan blade on the ice and knowing it's the creak of the planets turning. Sitting on a monument of snow and waiting till all the sadness of the world melts. "When the doors of perception are cleansed, we see everything as it really is, infinite" – or something like that. That's him again. I've read him too.'

'I thought you only read archaeology.'

I pretend to cuff him, he ducks and I fall over. From the ground I say, 'What I don't understand is how Blake got into all that stuff without the help of Freddie's illegal substances.'

'The secret is time,' says Morton, pulling me up. 'Blake gave it time. He waited till the universe opened itself out before him and he could see all the things that are hidden in its crevices.'

'That's all very well, but I don't have time. For me time always seems to be running out.' I sit myself on the sledge. 'Are you getting on or not?'

'For the crack.'

'And – yes! – I'm going to Crete. I'm going, I'm going, I'm going...!'

He climbs on behind me, leans over my shoulder and wraps his arms around my breasts so tight that our breath mingles as we weave our way down the snow run, swaying from side to side like one large sheepskin-clad creature dodging an invisible pursuer.

13

Chapter Thirteen

Monday 11th February 1991 11.45am
In the cell, three women were huddled in the corner beyond the furthest bed, sitting on the floor. When the keys rattled in the lock they turned their heads sharply like conspirators surprised, peering over the top of the bed towards the door.

'Hey, Karina,' called Debs, reaching up a skinny hand with chipped silver nail varnish. 'What you doing back in here?'

Corinne paused at the doorway, and looked across the room. 'I was in court today.'

'What d'ya get?'

'Three months.'

The prison officers directed her to a bed and she put her things down on it. They left and locked the door behind them.

Debs beckoned urgently, 'Psst! Over here. You know Michelle from when you was in before Christmas,' she pointed to a woman with long brown hair. 'And this here's Billy Jean. Come on. You'll get off on this.'

The room was a dormitory for four, with bedside tables. One of the beds had a pink furry cushion on it, another had a teddy. Beside one of them, a photograph of two children was sellotaped to the thickly painted cream wall, and there was a book on the pillow.

As Corinne walked over and sat down on the end bed, Michelle eyed her up and down.

'She's all right,' said Debs, 'she was in with me and Mandy before. Told us all about her past. Blokes on the beach in Greece. Been round the block a few times. She's all right.'

'I like a woman with experience,' said Michelle. She had a silvery charm on a chain round her neck. With a hand marked with eczma, she put the charm in her mouth and sucked it as she stared at Corinne. 'I remember you. You were in one of them touchy-feely sessions in Detox. Before Christmas. You got three months? That's six weeks you'll do, with good behaviour.'

'Six weeks too long,' said Corinne.

Michelle let the charm drop out of her mouth and it fell, a shiny four-leaved clover, to nestle on the soft pink skin above her breasts. 'That's assuming you do good behaviour,' she said. One of her eyelids almost winked.

'Back off,' said Debs. 'She's straight.'

'What you on about?' said Michelle. 'I didn't say nothing.' Stretching like a lazy cat, she pulled her hair up into a twist above her head and then tossed it loose again. 'Are we going to listen more or what?'

Between the women on the floor was a small ghetto blaster, plugged into a socket in the wall.

'Where did you get that?' asked Corinne.

'We ain't in Detox no more,' said Debs, 'we're allowed. But the tapes we got, they're knocked off. We just got them in. Some of them are weird music with bells and chanting. But there's a load with a woman talking. Got sex in it, n'all. Pouring it all out, she is. Go on, find that bit, Billy Jean, rewind.'

Billy Jean, in a track suit with wet hair, put the machine on her lap.

Michelle was still staring at Corinne. 'You...' she said,

'you've got a weird vibe. I'm getting a picture of water. You got problems.'

'What d'you think she's in here for if she ain't got problems?' said Debs. 'Some psychic you are.'

Billy Jean pressed 'Play' with a delicate clean-scrubbed finger, and a voice came from the ghetto blaster.: '...she just put an envelope in his hands. Full of notes. £100. The full whack for a new bike. None of us understood what came over her.'

There was a pause, then the voice continued:

'He gave the money to Steve, and he seems determined never again to set his pedal foot on a bicycle that was anything but an old wreck. He seems more comfortable that way.'

Billy Jean stopped the tape. 'That wasn't the bit. That's the end of the bit about the bloke's bike. The one who got dressed up in bandages and stuff to get his money back.'

'Weird, things some people do,' said Michelle. 'All that, for a fucking push bike.'

'Some people can't get hold of money like you, 'Chelle,' said Debs, 'Some people are glad to have a push bike.'

'Sad,' said Michelle.

Billy Jean said, 'Some people prefer a push bike. It's healthy, enit.'

'Don't talk to her about healthy,' said Debs. 'It'd give her a heart attack. She don't know the meaning of fresh air.'

'Even if I had a bike,' said Michelle, 'I can't see going to all that trouble over it, dressing up and that.'

'So what'you do?' asked Debs, 'You'd let someone just total the bike and do nothing? "Go ahead, walk all over me"?'

'Sod that,' said Michelle. 'I'd send my brothers round to do their windows.'

'Yeah, but you wouldn't get the bike back,' said Debs.

'Neither did this guy.'

'He got the money to buy a new bike and he got his own back, enit?' She turned to Billy Jean. 'Go on, babes, find that sexy bit. About doing it on the train.'

Billy Jean puckered her petite features into a frown and pressed rewind again. Michelle lay back on the floor and kicked her legs up. Her Gap jeans slid up her legs and showed a pattern of small scars on her skin. 'I can bicycle, look!' She pedalled in the air, then kicked sideways. 'I used to be able to do the splits. Athletic, me.'

'I was a gymnast once,' said Billy Jean. 'Used to do competitions and stuff. Look at me now.'

'Try and find that bit,' said Debs. 'And while we're waiting,' she turned to Corinne, 'you never finished that story you was telling. Greece. Travelling back, that journey. You had a few sexy adventures n'all.'

'I told you everything. You don't want to hear any more.'

'Yeah, we do,' said Debs. 'After you left that island where you was camping with those blokes. What about travelling back to England with that American with the notebook?'

Debs looked at the others, 'She tells it good.'

Michelle turned to Corinne. 'What happened to you in Greece, then?'

'It's a long story,' said Corinne, 'and I was near the end of it.'

'Travelling back, hitch-hiking,' said Debs. 'With an American guy with big ears. I got a good memory.'

'You don't want to hear the rest,' said Corinne.

With a rattle of keys the door opened. 'Here's your lunch, ladies,' said a young officer with a smile. From the trolley she took paper plates each holding a lump of scrambled egg, some overcooked carrots, and chips. Billy Jean switched off the tape player. The women took the plates without enthusiasm, and went to sit on their beds.

'Go on, then,' said Debs to Corinne, examining the egg with disgust.

Corinne shrugged. 'I just hitched back with this American guy Walt. There's nothing to tell. Nothing, really. I told you all the exciting bits already. He was just a gangly guy with big ears who kept writing in his diary with tiny handwriting.'

'We like to hear you talking,' said Michelle, munching on her chips.

'You said that American made a move on you,' said Debs.

Corinne looked at her. 'With a memory like yours, you should be a lawyer,' she said.

'Yeah, well, I got stuck on the other side of the fence,' said Debs. 'Go on, you'll feel better when you've finished the story. You know, get yourself back to London after all that pissing around abroad.'

'There's nothing to tell,' said Corinne, sitting on her bed, looking at the expectant faces around her. 'We hitched up Italy together. In 1972. Nights we stayed at little boarding houses, mostly in separate rooms…'

'Except…' Debs prompted.

Corinne shrugged. 'OK, here goes. After that time camping on the beach on the island, we got off the boat at Piraeus and it was from the sublime to the ridiculous. Or something. I should have realized from the first day in Athens what it was going to be like travelling with the American guy. He had an enormous rucksack with tin cups and things hanging off it. They rattled. His ears stuck out. Everything stuck out. He caused a public commotion every time he stopped to ask the way or try to get on the bus. On the bus he stood so close I could smell his breath. In Omonia Square he insisted on taking over the business of changing some money of mine and his, and he made a mistake and lost about £10 of mine. And all the time he was making a mess of things, he kept telling me how to do things as if my life depended on it.

'We stopped for a coffee in the centre of Athens. People

sat at tables on the street with crowds walking by in the evening sunlight: street sellers and businessmen and students and peasants up from the countryside and shady-looking characters and blind beggars selling lottery tickets, while behind them the cars surged and squealed their brakes and drivers hooted and yelled and made hand gestures giving each other the evil eye, and he didn't look at any of it. He just got out his notebook and put his head down and wrote pages of his tiny cramped sentences. He seemed to be too busy writing about his experience to have any.

'We were low on funds, especially me, so next day we went to sell blood at the hospital. It was a modern building that already looked old, cheaply built and tatty. Where we queued up there was a graffiti saying "The Americans out!". In Athens the heat was almost stifling. Walt standing too close made it feel even hotter. At the hospital the system was that the people who wanted your blood paid you directly for it. They came and chose you out of the queue like cattle, for the right blood group. Then they followed you in and waited while the blood was taken. A middle-aged woman in black wanted mine, for her sick nephew; she pressed the money into my hand with tears in her eyes and many Greek "thank you"s.

'When it came to Walt's turn, he couldn't stomach it: when this skinny man with a big moustache took the phial of blood and gave him the wadge of notes, Walt gave him the money back. The man argued, he got angry, but Walt insisted. It was a noble gesture but it apparently insulted the man's honour, and made me feel a complete heel for keeping my money. I needed every penny to get back to England. He had a way of being good that made me feel bad. He had a way of being sincere that made me feel sticky. He said the kind of things they say in second-rate American films, like "Sometimes you know what you've gotta do".

I should have seen it was going to be a problem getting across Europe with him before we got on the long-distance bus to Patras. By that time it was too late.'

'Yeah, yeah,' said Debs. 'So do us all a favour and get on with the story. What happened with this Walt Disney guy?'

'Nothing much till we got to Italy. We took the bus across Greece to Patras on the west coast. Then a boat to Italy. To Brindisi. It was a very rough crossing. I remember being sick as a dog, hanging over the side of the boat.'

'What about the American?' asked Debs.

'He disappeared into the toilet for the duration of the boat journey. When we got to Brindisi we went to the train station, but I didn't have enough money for the fare through Italy, so I persuaded him to hitchhike. On the way we stayed in separate rooms at *pensiones.*'

'What's a *"pensione"*?' asked Debs.

'A kind of small inexpensive family hotel. For some reason my mother was on my mind. I kept feeling I had to get back to her as soon as possible.'

'Separate rooms?' asked Debs. 'So he didn't try to make a move on you?'

'Not straight away. The first lift we got was up along the coast, it was beautiful. The day had been stormy and the sea was swelling in dark brown surges and lashing against the harbour walls with a strong smell of fish. There were lots of old grey ships lying derelict – perhaps they were from the war? – and the setting sun made everything look carved. The driver wanted to chat but Walt didn't seem interested in talking to him, so he tried to keep up a conversation with me in Italian, using gestures to explain and turning round to look at me in the back seat. It was a fast car and I could see what was coming towards us on the road and it made me nervous. But we got as far as his home town and he kindly dropped us at a *pensione* on the main road outside town so that we'd be in a good place to start hitching in the morning. The Italians were all very friendly.'

'Get on with it,' said Debs.

'Things went OK till one night we arrived late at a *pensione* in a little town south of Florence which only had one room free. My Italian isn't very good, I mimed two separate beds and they nodded but when we got up there it was just one big bed. While Walt was systematically unpacking his huge rucksack to get to his pyjamas, I tried to make light of the bed situation. "There should be plenty of room in there for both of us to sleep undisturbed," I said, with emphasis on the "undisturbed." He didn't say anything. He spent about ten minutes cleaning his teeth very rigorously over the room's tiny basin, and disappeared to the bathroom down the passage for a good half hour. By the time he came to bed I was practically asleep. I said "Goodnight" with an air of finality, and he switched off the light. I had put a big pillow down the middle of the bed, in case there was any doubt left in his mind about my intentions. I turned away from him and curled up and pretty soon I was asleep.

'What woke me more than anything else was the bed shaking. It was an old one, rickety on its legs, and it was making a rhythmic knocking against the wall. I realized that there was the sound of loud breathing too. Then I realized that the breathing was in my ear, the pillow in the middle of the bed had somehow gone and instead there was Walt thrusting around behind me with his hands on my nightie.'

'So what happened?' asked Debs. 'Give us the details.'

'Nothing happened,' said Corinne. 'That's what I'm saying. There's nothing to tell. I pulled away in time, he made a speech about how much he respected and cared about me, I managed to disentangle myself and put the pillow back between us and told him I needed to sleep.'

'I'd have whacked him one,' said Michelle. 'Did you never learn to stick up for yourself?'

'I'm learning,' said Corinne.

'Bit bloody late if you ask me.'

'Anyway,' said Corinne, 'the next day I was woken by the sound of him shaving very thoroughly and officiously, looking through the window at the brick wall outside as if it urgently needed his attention. When he spoke he was a little more formal than usual, as if he were trying to recover some injured pride. He didn't say "Sorry."'

'They never do,' said Billy Jean.

'He told me that he was going to catch the train to Florence and leave me to hitch on my own. He said he would meet me there at the Youth Hostel. He packed up his things and left.'

'So you went on and met him after he did that?' said Billy Jean.

'What could I do? I think he was sincere. Just misguided.'

'You let people walk all over you. Mind you, I seen worse.'

'I had a good wash,' said Corinne, 'and got dressed. I didn't put on my blue dress that I'd worn all summer, but a high-necked T-shirt and sturdy shorts so as to feel chaste and reinforced. When I got down to the reception, they said he had paid the bill. We usually split all the expenses on the journey, and him paying made me feel like...'

'Like one of us,' said Debs.

'Speak for yourself,' said Billy Jean. 'I ain't never turned tricks.'

'You ain't never done heroin,' said Debs.

'Anyway,' Corinne went on, 'I guessed that somewhere inside him there was guilt. Or shame. And most men seem to think they can buy their way out of that.'

'So that's the end of the whole story? What a fucking let down,' said Debs.

'It wasn't quite the end.'

'Tell,' said Debs.

'Just a couple of little twists in the tail,' said Corinne.

'That would be tragic if they weren't farcical. Hitching on my own that day I was picked up by a man called Mario. He was in his thirties, good looking in a heavy fleshy Mediterranean way, broad built, the kind of person you know would come through in a crisis. He had a bit of English, we got chatting, we liked each other. He was driving a tiny Fiat, travelling from his home town of Naples back to Germany where he was working. He liked animals, and we'd been talking about cats and dogs and donkeys and horses and – for some reason – llamas while hurtling along the motorway for about an hour when he turned to smile at me, and put his hand on my knee.

'My insides felt like when you go down several floors fast in a lift. The conversation faded away. I didn't put his hand back on the steering wheel. So it stroked my knee and started to venture further. Everywhere, in fact, that a hand can venture when the owner of the hand is hitting the speed limit down an Italian motorway. Then of course the owner of the hand starts to have problems keeping in lane while breathing deeply and seriously distracted from the road ahead. And he has a struggle to open the zip of his passenger's shorts which he can't see. And the passenger feels that her body is being swept along and caressed at 100 kilometres an hour and soaring through space like a mythological creature with glossy wings, and she starts to feel weightless and invulnerable and she just wants to go with the thrill of what's happening, whatever it is.

'And as her body soars through Italy, the hand continues to venture until there isn't any more venturing that can be done while driving, and then suddenly the other hand steers the Fiat off the motorway onto a service road and then onto a side road and into a small track leading into a forest where the Fiat stops. All very bouncy and bumpy because only one hand is driving, and when the car brakes you get thrown into the windscreen. Then the driver and the passenger look at each other in surprise and fall onto each other.

'I think things would have turned out differently if it hadn't been for the shorts. And the fact that he was such a generously built man in a small car with so little room to manoeuvre. Getting sturdy well-fastened shorts off in these circumstances is difficult, especially while kissing passionately with huge mouth-open kisses and lavish sharing of saliva, pretending that you are not trying to get the shorts off at the same time. You kiss and fumble, you kiss and fumble, then eventually you realize you are going to have to stop the kissing and concentrate on the fumbling if you are going to get anywhere. So we stopped kissing and looked at my zip, which was stuck. Then we looked at each other, and saw a stranger.

'I noticed that I was in an Italian wood a few hundred metres off the motorway about to embark in broad daylight on an ambitious exchange of fluids and feelings with a charming and large unknown Italian man in a small car. He remembered that he had a girlfriend in Germany who was waiting for him and whom he wanted to marry. We looked warmly into each other's faces and thought better of it. He gave me a few more of those large moist kisses, reminded himself was it was like to fondle my body all over, with both hands this time, then gradually ran out of steam. He smiled, patted my head, and restored my clothing as best he could. I put my legs together. He reversed out of the wood and drove back onto the motorway. When we got to Florence, we parted affectionately as if we had known each other for years. I went off to see the Uffizi Gallery and Michelangelo's David. They were amazing, but twenty years later my memories of Mario are the more vivid.'

'So that was it?' said Debs. 'What a cock-up.'

'Or rather, a cock not up,' said Michelle.

'We both felt the better for that,' said Corinne. 'The

reasons to be naked are not always good ones.'

'Everyone's into spoiling my fun,' said Debs. 'There's me, just wanted to hear about a bit of sex. I can't get it in here so at least I could listen and get turned on, and everyone's missing the place and missing the point and crashing their push bikes and putting their clothes back on again. It's pissing me off. Let's find that bit on the train again. At least she did it with him.'

As Billy Jean and Debs pressed buttons on the tape machine, Corinne asked Michelle: 'Have you heard any news about Mandy? When I was in before Christmas, the last we heard was that her bloke had been killed.'

'Yeah,' said Michelle. 'A mate come to visit me from Peckham. She seen Mandy's mum. You know Mandy got pulled out of here. To identify Dave's body. Then they interviewed her as possible witness. Wanted to know who had it in for him. Seems it was murder, they knocked him out cold and then they torched the car. Payback for some dodgy deal, I'd say. She was home over Christmas, got bail. She saw her little Cheryl and that. Then they took her off to another prison out of London. Safety, I suppose. Dunno. My mate said her mum was in a right state and her little Cheryl can't hardly get to visit her now she's so far off.'

'Mandy's life,' said Corinne. 'Between a rock and a hard place.'

Billy Jean called from the ghetto blaster, 'I think I've found something.' The others gathered round her.

'I feel strange about listening to this woman talking,' said Corinne. 'What she's saying is personal.'

'We was listening to you with all that stuff you were saying,' said Debs.

'But I agreed to tell you. For whatever reason. This woman here doesn't know we're listening.'

'And she won't never know,' said Debs, 'So what's the harm? Play, Billy Jean.'

The tape turned, and the same voice started again, speaking faster this time.

'Morton and I first went to Knossos together nearly a year ago. What happened there tipped me over the edge…'

'Stop it, mate. We heard that bit,' said Debs. 'She eats some heavy hash cake and goes into one, thinking she's in ancient times somewhere and people are going to kill her. And she throws up all over the floor. Then she picks up some bones at some weird place and brings them back wrapped in her smalls. And she thinks they start talking to her. And she thinks maybe she's reincarnated from ancient times. And she thinks she's going mad. And I agree. Driving me mad n'all. Where's that fruity bit got to?'

Debs pressed 'Stop'.

Michelle said 'You don't understand what that woman was going through, do you?'

'Bad gear. We all done that,' said Debs.

'Yeah, but what it opened up,' said Michelle. 'Like she said somewhere in all that, a gash. Between now and history. That's what you call a past life experience.'

Debs rolled her eyes to the ceiling. 'And we think we've got problems. At least we haven't lost our marbles.'

'She ain't neither,' said Michelle. 'Them past life bleed throughs, they're no fucking picnic. I was a witch in a past life. I get dreams where people are throwing stones at me. It hurts, n'all.' She put her locket into her mouth and rolled it on her tongue. 'I'm psychic, right. I'm into all that.' She looked at Corinne. 'Bet you know about that stuff, too.'

'You don't believe in bleeding bleed throughs?' Debs looked from Michelle to Corinne.

'I don't believe in listening to personal stuff without asking,' said Corinne.

'Spoil sport,' said Debs. 'There's always one.'

Billy Jean was leaning over the machine, swapping tapes and speeding backwards and forwards. Suddenly she looked up, 'I found that other bit again,' she said, 'You know, the sexy bit on the train.' She pressed 'Play' and the voice started again:

'It was one day in 1981 we met again. By chance. Thanks to British Rail Inter-City. I can't remember why I was travelling back from York. I was still single then. It was long before I met Morton. I was sitting on the train and suddenly I realized he was sitting opposite me. Brown leather jacket, nice jumper…'

There was a rattle of keys and the door swung open. 'Jenkins,' said a blue-uniformed nurse consulting a clipboard. 'Medical. Doctor's waiting.'

Corinne picked up her shoes. As the door closed behind her, the tape was playing on:

'At first I didn't recognize him but he recognized me.

'"Ant?"

'I closed my archaeology book and stared at him. "Terry!"'

Monday 11th February 1991 3pm

Dr. Scheiner was sitting at his desk when his secretary brought in his post. He thumbed through some memos from university administration and a letter from an archaeologist in Italy asking permission to use one of his illustrations in a forthcoming book on the Greek Dark Age. Then he opened a small white envelope and unfolded a handwritten letter. He read:

'Dear Dr. Scheiner,

I am so sorry if I have caused you any inconvenience or embarrassment over recent weeks. I have been uncertain about a number of things which created confusion. Most of all I really wanted to thank you deeply from the bottom of my heart, indeed from the bottom of my socks; you have helped me more than I think you know. Perhaps you do know.

I am leaving for Greece on a fieldwork trip shortly. I wish you a pleasant spring and send you all best wishes,

Yours sincerely,

Anthea'

Ten minutes later his secretary came into his office: 'Dr. Taylor rang asking why you're not there at the meeting.'

When Dr. Scheiner turned to reply, his eyes were red with tears.

Tuesday 12th February 1991 1am

The cell was tucked into a corner of the prison building away from the traffic, and it was quiet at night. Billy Jean's breathing was regular. Debs clutched her screwed up bedclothes as if someone was trying to tug them away. Only a few strands of Corinne's hair were visible on her pillow when Michelle tiptoed over and pulled at them gently.

'Oi, here y'are, put them under your pillow.' She posted six cassette tapes into Corinne's bed. Corinne stirred, half sat up and peered blindly from side to side. With eyes half shut she llifted the bedclothes and looked at the tapes as if she wasn't sure what they were.

'Then they won't be able to listen no more. They don't understand that stuff anyway. Pearls before swine. Hide them in your bag.'

With difficulty Corinne gathered the tapes in her hands. 'Thanks,' she breathed. She opened her regulation bedside cupboard and put the tapes in. 'Thanks.'

'You and me,' whispered Michelle, 'We know. You and me.'

'Yes?' mouthed Corinne.

'Yes,' Michelle nodded. 'And now I'm here, fancy a cuddle?'

Tuesday 12th February 1991 10am

It was a grey morning and the strong winds outside made dull thuds against the window panes. Inside the cell the heating made the air muggy. The remains of rejected breakfasts were scattered around on paper plates. Billy Jean sat up holding her teddy. Corinne got out of bed, walked across and opened one of the windows. They were narrow, like arrow slots in a medieval castle, but a gust of cold air immediately invaded the room.

'Fuck off,' mumbled Debs, pulling the bedclothes around her as she sat up.

The body-shaped lump in Michelle's bed did not move, and a faint snoring came from underneath. Corinne reached out through the window with her hand, held her palm to the sky where rain was spitting down, and breathed deeply. 'I once danced in the rain,' she said.

'We ain't heard that bit,' said Debs.

'You haven't heard the half of it,' said Corinne.

'We ain't even heard the end of that travelling,' said Debs. 'I thought you was trying to get back to see your mum.'

'I was,' said Corinne. 'All roads lead to Mum. I did see her. I clapped eyes on her. But that was all. End of story.'

'You trying to wind us up?' said Debs. 'That ain't telling it properly. What happened, after all that? And you can shut that fucking draught.'

Corinne turned round so she was standing with her back to the window. The wind made her blouse tremble in the dull light. 'O.K.' She stretched her hands to the ceiling and started dancing. 'I travelled back across Europe…' she made two hitch-hiking thumbs and spun round making circles with her arms.

Debs looked at Billy Jean, 'She's gone nuts, n'all.'

'And I got to England,' Corinne punctuated her words by holding the palms of her hands in front of her as if pushing something away. 'And London,' she kicked.

'Can see you didn't want to go there,' said Debs.

'It was 2nd August 1972.'

'Blimey, you don't look that old,' said Billy Jean.

'And to the BBC.'

'What ya go there for?' asked Debs.

'That was where my mother worked,' Corinne kicked to the side, she turned around and kicked to the front.

'BBC? Get you!' said Debs, rolling her eyes.

Corinne kicked again. 'I went to this place in the basement of the building where she worked, called the BBC Club,' she shook her body like a rag doll as if she was trying to rid it of an infection. Suddenly she froze. 'But I didn't go in. I walked around outside,' miming tiptoeing, 'and climbed down a bank at the side, where I could look in. I knew she'd be there.' Corinne crouched and peered.

'You should of been a dance teacher,' said Billy Jean.

Michelle's brown eyes peered over her bedclothes.

Corinne took up an artificial pose and mimicked polite people drinking with a little finger out. 'The BBC Club. Glamour and cocktails, my mother could never resist. I looked in through the window.' Corinne clapped her hand over he mouth, and rolled her eyes as if in horror. 'There she was, standing in a group. I hadn't seen her for a year, but she hadn't changed. Cosmetics see to that. There was a man, looked like a typical BBC Producer, holding forth with a drink in hand. Expensive jacket, bow tie,' Corinne twiddled an imaginary tie at her throat, 'and slightly balding. I watched his lips move and wondered what he was talking about. What story he was telling in that bubble of complacency beyond the glass? There she was, my mother, hanging on his every word.' Corinne's body twisted and contorted. 'And there, with her back to me, was a bright young thing. Young woman. Dark curly hair. Smart mini skirt. High heels. Tights with no ladders. Head poised intelligently on one side to listen and respond. Lapping it up, G and T in the hand. Just the kind of daughter she always wanted to have. Instead of the misfit she got when I was born.

'I saw her face for a moment when she flashed a glance over her shoulder.

'And I saw my mother give this young woman a look.' Sweeping, thwarted gestures. 'That look. Approval. Affection. Respect. Trust. Never in my life had she given me a look like that. That's when I knew it was over. That she would never look at me like that. All we would ever find was mutual anguish. There was no point. She had what she needed. And I had to look for what I needed. That would be the next part of my story.'

Corinne paused, standing at the window. 'I turned and walked away.' Slow, heavy movements like someone wading through deep mud. 'I was free,' she came to a halt in front of the window again with peaceful circular movements, and ended with her arms stretched in the air. 'Free, in a prison of my own.'

Michelle gave a slow handclap.

'Now shut the fucking window,' said Debs.

Corinne held her pose for a moment and then looked out of the window to see an aeroplane from Heathrow crossing London towards Europe. It was trailed by a distant, dislocated roar, and as she closed the window it disappeared overhead.

Tuesday 12th February 1991 9.30am

There's a roaring in my ears. Fasten your seat belts, the sign says. If I could only fasten my mind...

It's waiting for me, it's ahead of me, in the Cretan mountains. Those towering, crushing mountains. Iron grey crags stabbing the blue sky. Anything can happen. Out of the blue.

I'm not sure whether I'm travelling into the future or the past.

No Smoking, the sign says. I'm not smoking. I'm choking. It's clutching at my entrails, it's filling my throat with brambles. Stop the plane. I don't want to die. A woman in a spotted cardigan on the other side of the aisle is looking at me strangely. Is it so obvious that I'm freaking out inside?

Morton is beside me. He's reading a book already, his face serene. His eyelids lowered as his gaze glides along the lines of type. His elbow has staked his claim to the arm rest between us. As usual. He'll probably doze off like that and I won't have the heart to shove his arm off, in case it wakes him.

The old dread is back and I am on the plane and it is too late. I'm not going to get any sleep. I've been awake for hours already. If I can't sleep under my own duvet, how can I expect to sleep here with the engines revving for take-off and the universe vibrating? I have one of the other bone fragments with me. It's in the handbag between my feet. But it's not the same.

'You're taking a risk', Morton said when I packed it. 'What if they search your bag in customs? I can see the headlines: "Archaeologist shamed in antiquities theft", "Archaeologist smuggled human remains".' I took no notice of him and put it in a zipped pouch along with my scissors, sellotape, pencil sharpener and tape measure. An archaeologist's tools of the trade. They won't find the little bone there, I thought. That was when I was still euphoric, when I thought I could dodge collisions and fly and swim and run and jump, when I thought I could sweep through the clouds and escape my fate.

What mischievous intervention of destiny was that on Kite Hill, that temporarily made me believe things could be OK?

I get my notepad out and toy with my pen in a fickle

way. For the umpteenth time, I list the sites I need to visit, and again fret about the order, the best way to get from A to B, which sites are most important, which will be hardest to find. I don't have my maps to hand. They're with my notes in the carry-on bag which is already tucked away in the overhead compartment.

A few more decisive clips of the lockers, and stewardesses sweep past checking what is at our feet. I look around. Rows of human beings strapped into their seats in a large machine that thinks it can fly. The engines roar. A sense of melancholy comes over me. In this artificial world I have no connection with the ground.

And then the panic begins. My teeth are clamped together. The plane is crawling forward and the engines are building up power to hurl the giant machine into the sky in defiance of gravity. In defiance of common sense. Everyone knows that heavy things fall. But apparently not this pilot, not these passengers. Everything is preparing to rush me towards the end.